SMITTEN

USA Today and International Bestselling Author

Lauren Rowe

BOOKS BY LAUREN ROWE

Standalone Novels

Smitten

The Reed Rivers Trilogy (to be read in order)

Bad Liar

Beautiful Liar

Beloved Liar

The Club Trilogy (to be read in order)

The Club: Obsession

The Club: Reclamation

The Club: Redemption

The Club: Culmination (A Full-Length Epilogue Book)

The Josh and Kat Trilogy (to be read in order)

Infatuation

Revelation

Consummation

The Morgan Brothers (a series of related standalones):

Hero

Captain

Ball Peen Hammer

Mister Bodyguard

ROCKSTAR

The Misadventures Series (a series of unrelated standalones):

Misadventures on the Night Shift

Misadventures of a College Girl

Misadventures on the Rebound

Standalone Psychological Thriller/Dark Comedy

Countdown to Killing Kurtis

Short Stories

The Secret Note

PLAYLIST

"Buddy Holly"—Weezer
"All Day and All of the Night"—The Kinks
"You and Me Song"—The Wannadies
"Only Love"—Ben Howard
"I Don't Want to Change You"—Damien Rice
"Grow Old With Me"—Tom Odell
"Baby I'm Yours"—Arctic Monkeys

ONE

FISH

"I know what you're probably thinking . . ." our business manager, Clive, says to Dax, Colin, and me—the three dudes of 22 Goats. It's a sunny Saturday afternoon in downtown LA and my band is sitting across from our business manager at his desk. We don't normally meet with Clive on Saturdays. But due to our recent tour, and the fact that Clive's wife just had a baby, we decided to hold our regular meeting today, on a Saturday afternoon, before we three Goats head over to the home of Reed Rivers, the owner of our label, for a pre-party at his pool.

Clive holds up his hand, halting any responses from the three of us. "Before you give me an answer, you should know Pepsi is offering *ten million* bucks, guys—and that's for only *one* commercial! After taxes and my commission, you'd each clear almost *two million*."

"Damn," Colin murmurs next to me, succinctly expressing my exact thoughts. Our band has turned down a lot of lucrative endorsement offers, ever since our debut single blasted to number one around the world four years ago. But we've never turned down anything with a payout *that* big before.

I look at Dax—my lifelong best friend—and, instantly, know what he's thinking: *I'm not going to hawk soda, no matter the pay day.*

And I'm not surprised.

Dax isn't thinking that because he's selfish, by the way. It's never a "my way or the highway!" kind of thing with that dude. It's just that he genuinely doesn't give a shit about money or fame. He's a true artist. A guy who lives to make and perform music. To share his soul. Sure, Dax appreciates fame in the sense that it expands the sphere of people coming to our shows. Also, he's not a saint. He likes the large house he shares with his wife and kid in Malibu. He also likes that fame gives him a platform that allows him to raise funds for his favorite causes—chief among them the cancer charity founded by his wife, Violet. But the other stuff tied to fame? The way people *literally* worship him? The dehumanization of it? The lack of personal freedoms? He can't stand any of that stuff.

It's true our fans sometimes get pretty amped about Colin and me, too. Mostly, Colin. But the way they treat Dax, our lead singer/guitarist, is on a whole other level than the way they react to Colin and me—our drummer and bass player, respectively. It's like fans think Dax is a *literal* god among men. Which, if you know Dax at all, is the last thing in the world he'd ever want anyone to think.

When Dax, Colin, and I remain silent, Clive sighs and says, "This is a lot of money, guys. I could help you invest it to ensure you've always got a big safety net, no matter what might happen in the future."

Aw, poor Clive. All he wants, even more than his fat

commission, is to make sure we three Goats are squared away for life. Like Clive always says, he doesn't want us blowing through our millions at age twenty-five, only to wind up penniless by thirty, or whenever the world inevitably moves on from its current obsession with our band.

But money isn't everything. That's something I've learned these past few years. A guy's got to be able to look himself in the mirror and like what he sees. And I know Dax would never, ever be happy to look in the mirror and see the face of Pepsi. Neither would I, to be honest. But I could stomach it, if necessary. But Dax? I think selling out like that would decimate a large piece of that boy's soul.

I look at my best friend, and not surprisingly, he looks a bit out of sorts, to put it mildly. But when Dax shifts his gaze to Colin, and he sees Colin's hopeful expression, his features noticeably change. Suddenly, I'm reminded of something that happened when Dax and I were in fifth grade when this popular kid, Keegan, came over to Dax and me at our lunch table and invited Dax, but not *me*, to his elaborate birthday party. I remember Dax initially looking excited about Keegan's invitation. Because, come on, Keegan Harris was the height of cool in those days. But when Dax looked at me, and saw something on my face that made him realize I hadn't been invited along with him, his features instantly transformed. Kind of like they did, just now, looking at Colin.

Without missing a beat, Dax replied to Keegan, "Sorry, I'm busy with Fish that day. Happy birthday." And that was that. No matter what I said afterwards about not minding if Dax went to the party without me, Dax wouldn't budge. I'm pretty sure the day of Keegan's cool birthday party, Daxy and I skateboarded and sat on his couch playing video games. Nothing special. But Dax never mentioned the cool party he was missing or made me feel bad I'd held him back from hanging out with our school's most popular kids.

Dax looks away from Colin, his featuring broadcasting the tug of war that's surely going on inside his head. "Wow, man. That's a lot of money . . ."

"Yeah, it is," Clive agrees.

"Especially for one day of work," Colin interjects.

Dax runs his hand through his long, blonde hair and sighs. "We'd be fools to turn down that kind of money, wouldn't we?"

"I think so," Colin says.

I look at our drummer, as if to say, *Really*? And Colin shrugs.

I shake my head. How many sports cars does Colin Beretta need? I admit I was a greedy bastard in the beginning, too. But now, I've got everything a man could possibly want. A nice car. A bungalow on the beach, right on the sand, that I own debt free. Every musical instrument I could ever desire in my home studio. Plus, last year, I was able to gift my mom a house in Seattle—a cool two-story with a view of Puget Sound. And Colin's got everything he could possibly want, too! So, at this point, there's no amount of money that's worth making *any* of us feel like we're selling our souls—especially to a goddamned soda company. Colin knows how Daxy's soul is wired! Also, that Dax's mom, Louise, is a health nut who banned soda in her house for her five kids, and all their friends, growing up.

I look at Dax again, and it's clear he's feeling absolutely tortured about his decision. So, fuck it. I decide, this time, I'll be the one who's got *Dax's* back. Leaning back in my chair, I say, "Sorry, guys. I know it's a lot of money, but I'm just not feeling it. My vote is no."

Now it's *Colin* who flashes *me* a look that says, *Really?* But I don't care what Colin thinks this time, to be honest, because the grateful smile Dax is flashing me in this moment is *everything.*

"*Fish,*" Colin says, looking annoyed. "*Come on.*"

I look at Dax pointedly. "Do you want to do this commercial, brother?"

Dax subtly shakes his head. But he says, "I will, though, if that's what you both want to do." His face brightens with an idea. He looks at Clive. "Hey, would Pepsi do the deal without me—with just Colin and Fish?"

It's a ridiculous question with an obvious answer. But somehow Clive manages to keep a straight face while saying "No. Sorry. It has to be all three of you." In truth, I'd bet anything Pepsi would do the deal with Dax alone. So, technically, it doesn't have to be "all three of us." But for purposes of this conversation, I don't blame Clive for tweaking the truth a bit to spare Colin and me a bit of humiliation.

I shrug. "Then our answer will have to be no. I personally can't stand the idea of shilling for Pepsi." I look at Colin to find him glaring at me. "Aw, come on, man." I swat his shoulder. "You know I've always been a Mountain Dew man."

Colin rolls his eyes. "Mountain Dew *is* Pepsi, ya dumbass."

"*No.* Mountain Dew is Coke."

"Nope," Colin says. "Pepsi owns Mountain Dew."

I look at Dax. He nods and says, "Pepsi."

"Oh. Well, whatever. Either way, no amount of money is worth getting my ass kicked by Momma Lou again. No, thanks."

Colin can't help himself. Despite his irritation with me, he chuckles at my inside joke. And that's how I know my brother from another mother is going to be able to let this one go, without too big a fuss.

The inside joke I've just now invoked was a reference to the time Dax's mom, Louise—Momma Lou—got pissed at me for smuggling Mountain Dew into her soda-free home. We three Goats were thirteen at the time. It was a few months after we'd first formed our band—known back then as "Dax Attack." One night, we'd just finished rehearsing our first ever original banger in Dax's garage. And at the end of our song, I was so pumped about how amazing we'd sounded on it, and how bright our musical futures surely were—we were going to become rock stars, yo!—I pulled out three cans of the bubbly green stuff from my backpack to celebrate. You know, like how an actual rock star might pull out a bag of blow or a bottle of Jack. Well, Dax turned down my illicit offering, since his momma's soda ban had been clearly stated by then, given that Dax was the fifth child in his family. But Colin took my contraband offering, clinked my can with his, and proceeded to chugalug, right along with me . . . just as Momma Lou popped her head through the garage door to tell her darling son it was time for bed.

Well, shit.

When Louise Morgan's sapphire eyes fixated on the can in Colin's hand, he immediately pointed at me and shouted, "It was Fish!" Which, sidenote, birthed yet *another* lifelong joke. To this day, whenever anything goes wrong, Dax or Colin will point at me and shout that same refrain, even when I'm obviously an innocent bystander. But anyway, in that moment, Colin shouted, "It was Fish!", causing Mrs. Morgan to beeline to me. "Matthew Fishberger," she said on a fierce whisper. "That's like putting carbonated battery acid into your growing body. Drink what you want at your own house, honey. But at mine, you need to respect my rules."

Louise wasn't the kind of mom who constantly nagged her kids and their friends. In fact, it was the first time I'd ever seen her looking anything but relaxed and happy. And so, as she stood there in front of me, looking disappointed in me, I remember being super bummed. I *adored* that gorgeous woman—and not as a maternal figure, to be clear. No, I *desired* her in a highly carnal way. Plus, I genuinely *liked* her, too—and, therefore, hated the sensation of disappointing her.

I distinctly remember thinking in that moment, "Well, shit, Mrs. Morgan, drinking Mountain Dew can't be any worse for my 'growing body' than the big fat blunt I smoked with your son today after school." But, of course, I didn't say that to the woman I wanted to impress. I loved her son dearly and would have died before ratting him out. So, all things considered, I responded by going *mea culpa* on that gorgeous woman's ass. I apologized profusely, without dragging Colin into the muck with me, and even went so far as to swear I'd "never" disappoint her again.

"Colin?" I say. He's been looking out the window of Clive's office. "Ready to move on?"

Colin returns his attention to the group. And by the look on his face, it's clear he's now worked through his irritation and is ready to move on—to turn the page on whatever stupid purchases he was hoping to make with that easy two mill.

"It's fine," Colin says on an exhale. "As much as I'd enjoy watching Momma Lou kick *Fish's* ass again, I'm sure she'd *also* kick *my* ass this time. And I like her thinking I'm Dax's 'good influence' friend while *Fish* is the bad one."

We all chuckle at that bit of ass-backwards ridiculousness.

Also, at Colin's implicit confirmation that any sort of genuine schism between the three of us has, once again, been averted.

"Okie doke," Clive says. "I'll tell Pepsi the answer is no." If Clive is disappointed to miss out on his commission, he's not showing it. He returns to his laptop, his face businesslike and neutral, and says, "Two more quick items, guys, before you head to Reed's. First, the Seattle Tourism Bureau. They want you guys to shoot a commercial. The money would be nominal. You'd probably want to donate it to a local food bank or whatever. But you'd be in great company. Dave Grohl did a similar spot for them a few years ago."

Ding, ding. He's said the magic words. *Dave Grohl.* He's one of our idols. A musical god, as far as we're concerned.

All three of us quickly say we're in, and Clive runs through the details. Dax mentions he and his wife, Violet, are coincidentally flying home next weekend for his niece's birthday party, so Clive says he'll try to arrange the shoot in Seattle for the end of this coming week for ease of logistics.

"That's great timing for me," I say. "It's my mom's birthday on Saturday. I wasn't planning to fly up to see her for it, but if we're going to be in Seattle for that spot, anyway, I'll stay the whole weekend and take Mom out to dinner on her big day." I look at Dax. "Can I come to Baby Claire's birthday barbecue on Sunday?"

"Of course," Dax says. "My whole family will be there. They'll be stoked to see you." He turns to Colin. "You should come, too, man. It's been forever since all three of us have hung out with my entire family."

Colin asks, "Is the entire 'LA Branch' of the family flying up to Seattle for the weekend?" It's a reference to Dax and Violet, of course, plus, Dax's older brother, Keane, and his wife, and Keane's lifelong best friend, Zander, who's an honorary Morgan, every bit as much as Colin and me.

"I'm not sure about everyone's plans," Dax admits. "But when they find out all three of us will be at the party, I'm sure they'll get their asses up to Seattle, too."

"Okay, last thing, guys," Clive interjects, leaning his forearms onto his large desk. "I've received an interesting individual offer for *Colin*—something I wanted to tell him about when all three of you were present."

Dax, Colin, and I look at each other, intrigued. Clive always has individual offers for Daxy, almost all of which he declines. But Clive never has anything specifically for Colin or me. Plus, he rarely tells Daxy about his individual offers when Colin and I are present.

Clive steeples his fingers. "Remember that interview you guys did on German TV at the end of the last tour?" He looks at Dax and me. "The one where you two told that funny story about Colin's latest nickname?"

Of course, we remember. Yes, we were stoned during that interview, admittedly, but it wasn't all that long ago, and it was highly memorable. A particularly funny interview, like Clive mentioned.

Basically, the story Dax and I told that day on German TV, in tag-team fashion, was this: Before 22 Goats left on tour, I threw a Halloween party at my small beach bungalow. I dressed as Shaggy from *Scooby Doo*—a nod to one of my lifelong nicknames. Dax and Violet dressed as Napoleon Dynamite and Pedro. And Colin, our resident gym rat, came dressed as Tom Cruise in *Risky Business*, wearing nothing but a button-down shirt, tighty-whities, and tube socks. But, of course, Colin being Colin, he wound up ditching his shirt after a few shots of tequila, and thereafter spent the remainder of the party showing off his ripped abs in nothing but his under-wear and socks . . . Which quickly gave rise to a new nick-name for our chiseled drummer—*Underwear Model*—a nickname that followed him around throughout the entirety of our tour.

Clive chuckles. "It seems someone at Calvin Klein saw that German interview, Colin. And now . . . " He smiles. "They want to make you an *actual* underwear model."

"*No*," Colin says on a breath, his dark eyes wide.

Clive laughs and nods. "They're offering you a major ad campaign! Print, digital, and a huge billboard in Times Square!"

"Holy shit."

"And you want to know the pay?" Clive pauses for effect, his dark eyes sparkling, before saying, "*A half-million bucks.*"

Well, that's it. We all lose it. We're pounding on Clive's desk. Grabbing Colin's arm and shaking him. Losing our minds, basically. Because, as much as we razz Colin for this or that, we know this is a huge thing for him, personally. Colin has worked harder than anyone I know to transform his body over the past several years—to tighten and sculpt his middle school pudge into a goddamned work of art.

"*We* did this," I shout at Dax. "You and me! We cast some sort of 'Underwear Model Spell' on our boy on German TV!"

Dax is dying of laughter. "We're warlocks, dude! We're *magical* beings, Fish Taco!"

"Quick!" I reply. "Let's go back to Berlin for another interview and, this time, say Colin's new nickname is 'Smart Guy.' God knows he could use some help in the brains department!"

Colin quips, "Yeah, and while you're at it, you should

probably say *your* new nickname is 'Big Dick.' God knows *you* could use help in *that* department."

I laugh with glee, along with everyone else. It's a reference to yet *another* inside joke among the three of us. I'm not small, I don't think. But I'm not packing a donkey dick like Colin, either. I'm just an average dude with an average dick. And, through a series of events one night in our teens—events involving tequila, a hot tub, and Colin's brilliant idea to throw my briefs and shorts over a fence—Dax, Colin, and about eight other people—are well acquainted with the precise size of my package.

"So, I take it that's a yes on this offer?" Clive asks Colin.

To my surprise, Colin doesn't shout "Yes!" Instead, he addresses Dax and me, his dark eyes looking earnest. "I'm only going to do this if you're both one hundred percent cool with it."

"*Of course, we are!*" Dax shouts.

I add, "Are you kidding? We *insist* you take this gig, if only to prove we're warlocks."

Dax pats Colin's stomach. "Show off these washboard abs in Times Square, son! Get yourself paid!"

Colin exhales with relief. "I just don't want you guys thinking I'm selling out or tarnishing the band's brand."

Dax scoffs. "We don't have a *brand*. We just have the truth." He nudges my arm. "The same goes for you, Fish Kebab. Don't let your washboard abs go to waste because you're worried about our 'brand.' If you want to make some ducats on the side, then do it."

I roll my eyes. First off, my brain is literally incapable of worrying about our *brand*. That's way above my pay-grade, dude. Also, nobody's going to be hiring me in this lifetime to model underwear. I'm a fit dude, thanks to all the skateboarding I did with Dax in my formative years—and, these days, thanks to our grueling touring schedule and daily surfing sessions whenever I'm home. But I'm no dark and smoldering Casanova, like Colin—a guy everyone says looks like a tattooed version of that cartoon smolderfest from *Tangled*. And I'm certainly not a perfectly symmetrical golden god, like Dax, either. I'm just a normal-looking dude. The one who provides the everyman comic relief in our music videos and interviews, while Dax and Colin turn up the heat.

"Why are you rolling your eyes?" Dax says. "Who knows what offers you'd get, if Clive puts feelers out for you. Seriously, Clive. See what you can get for Fish Head, would you? Ever since Colin put him on protein shakes a while back, he's turned into quite the heartthrob."

"It's true," Colin says, pinching my cheek. "Thanks to me, you're a babe magnet now, Matty-boy. You're welcome."

I scoff. "Nobody needs to see me smoldering at a camera in my underwear." I look at Clive. "Unless, of course, Calvin Klein suddenly comes to their senses and realizes they made their offer to the wrong Goat." I flash Clive my best male-model smolder. "When CK comes calling, tell them my answer is *yes*."

Everyone chuckles. Which, of course, was my desired result. But still, I can't help feeling a tiny bit salty at the laughter I've provoked. It was a funny joke, yes, but not *that* funny.

"So, are we done?" I ask. "We need to get Daxy to his beautiful wife—and I need a fucking drink."

"All done for now."

We say our goodbyes to Clive and make our way through his expansive lobby.

"Oh, I told Kiera we'd swing by to pick her up on our way

to Reed's," Colin says. "She's only five minutes out of the way from here."

"Not a problem," I say as I push the call button for the elevator. But in truth, Colin's comment kind of annoys me. Not because picking up his on-again, off-again girlfriend, Kiera, will be an inconvenience. As he rightly said, she's hardly out of our way. But because . . . frankly, I'm sick of being a third wheel. Sick of going stag to every party. Every school dance when we were teens. Sick of always feeling like the "sidekick" in the movie of our lives, whereas Dax and Colin are so obviously the "leading men."

I'm not begrudging my two best friends their success with women over the years. And I'm certainly not begrudging Dax his blissful happiness with his wife and young kid these days, or Colin's ability to get literally any woman he wants, whether it's Kiera when they're "on," or some other hot woman when they're "off." Honestly, I'm not wishing Dax and Colin didn't have everything they do . . . I guess I'm just wishing I had it, too.

The doors to the elevator open, and we step inside.

"You okay?" Dax asks, scrutinizing me.

"I'm great."

"You look upset."

I shrug. "Fuck it, shit happens." It's what I always say at times like this—when stupid shit gets me down. It's the catchphrase I coined in middle school that cleverly turned my life-long nickname—Fish—into an acronym.

"You're sure?" Dax says. He's always been able to read me, better than anyone. The same way I've always been able to read him.

"I'm just ready to drink."

The elevator reaches the ground floor, the doors open, and

I stride out with my head held high. As I walk, I toss out, "Come on, Goats! It's time to celebrate. We're home. We get to hang out with the people we love the most." I pause, waiting for Colin to catch up to me, and then slide my arm around his broad shoulders. "And, best of all, this hot and smoldering Underwear Model *hunk* is going to get *paid* a half-million bucks to become the next Marky Mark!"

TWO
ALESSANDRA

Is this real life?

Thanks to my amazing stepsister, Georgina, I'm sitting on a pool ledge in a location I never thought I'd be. At the sprawling, hilltop home of Reed Rivers. A guy well known in the music industry, not to mention to every music student at my school, as "The Man with the Midas Touch." For the past week or so, Georgina has been having a torrid romance—or is it a passionate fling?—with Reed. Which is why I'm sitting here now in my purple bikini on his pool ledge, like this is a totally normal thing.

I let my gaze drift from the sparkling pool water to the spectacular hilltop view to the small group of glamorous people lounging around the sunny patio. I watch a sophisticated brunette and her strawberry blonde bestie lounging on chaises for a long moment, enamored with how relaxed and comfortable in their own skins they both seem.

From there, I take in Reed's four closest friends—two couples—as they chat and laugh easily with my stepsister. When I was briefly introduced to all six of these people earlier today, I somehow managed to squeak out the polite hellos required of normal people. In fact, I even managed to answer a few brief questions. But as soon as the group focused on Georgie—as all groups eventually do, given how magnetic and personable she is—I crept over here to this pool ledge to sit by myself and people-watch.

I'm almost positive the sophisticated brunette over there on that lounger is the wife of Dax Morgan, the lead singer of 22 Goats. She was introduced to me as "Violet, Reed's little sister," however. With no last name provided and no mention of Dax Morgan. So I'm not positive she's the same Violet who inspired 22 Goats' iconic *The Violet Album*. And, unfortunately, I left my phone in the guest room upstairs, so I can't google to find out. If my hunch is right, though, and she *is* the wife of Dax Morgan, then I can't help thinking Dax might show up to this pre-party at some point. And, if he does, that he might come with his two bandmates—Colin Beretta and Matthew Fishberger. Which would then mean I could very well be sitting here, out of nowhere, breathing the same air as all three members of my favorite band! I clutch my stomach at the thought. Crap. The very notion makes me want to puke into the sparkling pool.

Speaking of wanting to puke, I sure hope I don't lose my lunch—which was delicious, by the way—when Reed Rivers finally appears at this pre-party. I glimpsed him earlier today, from afar in his expansive living room, while Georgina was giving me a tour of his mansion—the place she's been staying for the past week—and I legit almost had a freaking heart attack at the mere sight of the dude. At my school in Boston, every music student would give their right arm, leg, kidney, soul to get signed by River Records. Me included. In fact, I once joked to Georgina I'd give Reed my V-card to get signed to River Records. It's a bit of a disgusting thought now that I'm actually here in real life. Not to mention the fact that my beloved stepsister is *actually* sleeping with the guy. So, yeah, I guess joking about giving Reed my V-card is no longer an option for a whole lot of reasons now.

I'm actually relieved Georgie didn't introduce me to Reed earlier when we glimpsed him. In that moment, Reed was in the midst of chewing out a worker who'd made some error while setting up a huge stage for tonight's big bash. As Reed fumed, Georgina grabbed my arm and said, "How about I introduce you to Reed later? I'll show you his car collection now." It was a great suggestion, as far as I was concerned. I'm terrible at making small talk with normal people under the best of circumstances, so trying to do it with a freaking music mogul, in his mansion, *after* watching him rip some poor dude a new butthole wasn't my idea of a good time.

"Let's get this party started!" a male voice yells playfully, eliciting a cheer from the small group. And when I turn my head, the proverbial puke attack I've been staving off for the past few hours rises sharply in my throat. *It's 22 Goats.* All three members, walking onto the patio, along with a beautiful young woman.

Based on his body language, it appears it was Matthew Fishberger—Fish—the bass player in the band, who shouted that boisterous greeting. Or maybe I'm assuming that because in every interview I've seen of 22 Goats, and in every one of their music videos, Fish is the one who makes me smile and laugh the most.

I know this is a minority opinion, but I think Fish, not Dax, is the heart and soul of that band. Simply because I get the feeling Dax is only free to let loose the way he does, because he's got his trusted best friend holding down the fort next to him—singing those incredible backing harmonies and playing his bass so brilliantly. Or maybe I'm just projecting that dynamic onto the band, since, my whole life, Georgina's been the Dax of our sisterhood, while I've been the Fish.

As the three rock stars waltz onto the patio, the crowd enthusiastically greets them. Violet, the sophisticated brunette who was sitting on a lounger earlier, beelines to Dax and throws herself at him, and he kisses her like a drowning man gasps for oxygen. So, I guess that answers that question. Reed's little sister, Violet, is definitely Dax's wife, Violet. The woman who inspired 22 Goats' masterpiece of a second album.

As I continue staring at the happy crowd greeting the Goats, the young woman who arrived with the band slides her arms around the drummer's waist in a way that suggests she's his date. Hmm. Does that mean Fish doesn't have a date today? Or will she, or he, be coming later?

Gah.

Fish is *so* cute.

Obviously, I'm excited to see all three members of the band in person. Even if they weren't famous, they're three young, incredibly attractive dudes, so I'd surely be peeping at them, regardless. But . . . *Fish.*

There's just something extra special about him. I love that he's got boy-next-door charm mixed with a touch of rock star swagger. I think it's that juxtaposition—his innate humility and normalcy mixed with the unmistakable glow of his stratospheric success—that makes him so damned mesmerizing to me. He seems attainable and relatable, and yet, also like a rock star, all at once.

In person, Fish is a bit taller than I'd expected. More fit, too, although his muscles are lean, and not bulky. Which means he's exactly my type. I mean, if a girl who's never had a boyfriend can be said to have a type.

Fish is dressed in a T-shirt and swim trunks. His light brown hair is tousled and a little shaggy, while his facial hair is well trimmed. As he hugs a pregnant blonde—a woman named Kat whom Georgie and I met earlier—I catch a glimpse of Fish's iconic fish tattoo going down his left fore-arm. And for some reason, seeing that well-known tattoo in person gives me goose bumps.

"Are you totally freaking out?"

I look down at the pool to find my stepsister, Georgina, standing in the shallow end below me, her hazel eyes twin-kling with amusement.

"You knew they were coming today, didn't you?" I whis-per-shout. "You didn't tell me because you didn't want me to puke in the pool?"

Georgina chuckles. "No, I swear. If I'd known, I would have warned you. I know how much you love that band."

"I don't *love* them. I'm *obsessed* with them." I slide into the water, up to my waist, and grab Georgina's hand. "Georgie. Please. Hold my hand while I regain my equilib-rium, or I might pass out and sink to the bottom of the pool, never to rise again."

"Oh, God. We don't want that." She squeezes my hand. "I've got you, baby. Take deep breaths."

I take several deep breaths before murmuring, "Although, I must admit, there are worse ways to go than 'Death by 22 Goats.'"

"Well, if you're going to die today, then you should at least say hello to your favorite band. Come on."

"Oh, no." I rip my hand from hers.

"*Ally.*"

Georgina tries to retake my hand, but I hide it behind my back.

"Life is short, honey," she says. "Let's say a quick little hello."

"I can't. Please, Georgie. Maybe at the party tonight I'll be able to work up the courage. But I need time to process this miracle. It's just too much for my little brain to comprehend that the faces I've watched a million times in the 'People Like Us' video are standing right there, in real life."

"It's crazy for me, too, and I'm not even obsessed with them."

I let my gaze return to Fish. He's laughing with his friends. Looking adorable and sweet, yet oh so cool.

"Oh boy," Georgina says, chuckling.

I peel my eyes off Fish. "What?"

"You're thirsting hard, sister."

I frown. "I'm not *thirsting*. I'm simply starstruck."

Georgina smirks. "You're thirsting." She clucks her tongue. "Which one is making you drool like that?"

I roll my eyes. Damn. Georgina knows me *too* well. "The tall one with the shaggy hair. Fish. He's their bassist." I swoon. "I think I'm in love."

Georgina giggles and peeks at Fish. "I should have known he'd be your choice. He's totally your type."

"Can a girl who's never had a boyfriend truly be said to have a type?"

"Of course. Every boy you've ever crushed on, whether in real life or a celebrity, has always been the same type as that guy."

"The same *how*? My crushes are all over the map. Every race and physical type. The only thing they have in common is they don't know I'm alive. Well, or they're gay or they 'only want to be friends.' Either way, they're not interested in me. Is *that* my type—'Guys Not Interested in Alessandra Tennison?'"

"I meant they've all got the same *vibe*. They're all emo artist hipster boy-next-door types. Usually, with a very strong overlay of 'wouldn't hurt a fly.' Just like Fish."

I make a face that concedes Georgina's point. "Add 'great sense of humor' to your laundry list, and I think you've perfectly described my ideal man."

Movement at the entrance to the patio diverts my attention. And when I behold the celebrity walking into the patio area, I gasp loudly. It's Aloha Carmichael. The Disney-star-turned-pop-star I grew up watching on TV. She's entering the patio with a beautiful, muscular Black man, who's holding her hand, and a fit blond guy who's holding hands with an adorable brunette.

"Georgie!" I whisper, indicating the incoming foursome. "Look!"

Georgina looks where I'm pointing and gasps the same way I did a moment ago.

"Do you recognize the people she's with?" I ask.

"Yeah, I researched tonight's guest list, so I'd know everyone on sight." Georgina gestures to the handsome man holding Aloha's hand. "That's her husband, Zander Shaw. Her bodyguard." She gestures to the fit blond guy. "And that's Keane Morgan—the brother of Dax Morgan."

"Oh, *wow*." I look from the fit blond dude to the lead singer of 22 Goats. "Yeah, I can see the resemblance."

Georgina tells me Keane Morgan is an actor on some popular Netflix show I've never watched. And that his wife, Madelyn, is a documentary filmmaker who was nominated for an Academy Award last year. We babble about how beautiful and talented Aloha is. How striking she is in person. We talk about how much we both adored her Disney show—*It's Aloha!*—as kids. But, finally, we're interrupted by Kat, the pregnant blonde in a string bikini, who's standing over us on the pool ledge.

"Georgina?" Kat calls out. "You're planning to interview the Goats for the magazine, right? Would you like an introduction now?"

"I'd love one! Thank you, Kat."

Wordlessly, Georgina grabs my arm and begins pulling me through the shallow end of the pool with her, straight toward the steps. And I'm too excited—also, too shocked—to pull away or say a word in protest. Apparently, whether I'm ready or not, I'm going to meet 22 Goats now. All three members. Including the cute-as-hell bass player who's been making my pulse race since the minute he walked into the party.

THREE

FISH

"Let's get this party started!" I shout as Dax, Colin, Kiera, and I enter the patio area, and everyone cheers and hoots in reply. Predictably, we're greeted by Violet first who throws herself into her husband's waiting arms. Kat arrives next with her husband, Josh, followed by their good friends, Henn and Hannah.

In short order, our small group is engaged in animated conversation. But as everyone talks around me, I can't help noticing Dax kissing and whispering to Violet nearby, the same way he always does with her—like she's the only person in the entire world. And, as I so often do when glimpsing Dax and Violet canoodling, I can't help thinking: *I want that.*

Not Violet herself, of course. I don't covet my best friend's wife, though she's stunning to look at and cool as hell. No, I want their *connection.* I want a woman to run to *me* when I enter a party. I want a woman to look at *me* the way Violet looks at Dax. Like he's some kind of god. And, when a woman does all that to *me*, I want to know, without a doubt, she's not gaming me. Not trying to further her career or other-

23

wise use me for backstage passes or whatever. I want to know, the way Dax does, that I've got a woman who loves me. The real me. Matthew Fishberger. Not "Fish from 22 Goats."

Dax is lucky. When he first met Violet, our band hadn't blown up yet. In fact, she thought Dax played in a struggling bar band. But she fell in love with him anyway, because she didn't—and still doesn't—give a shit about fame or money. We all know Violet loves *Dax Morgan*. Not "Dax from 22 Goats." And I can't deny I want the same thing for myself.

I'm sure that's the gist of why Colin keeps getting back together with Kiera, despite their ups and downs. Because, no matter how much they might struggle, Colin knows Kiera's with him for all the right reasons, thanks to the fact that they, too, met before our band blew up. Whether Kiera hates or loves Colin on any given day, he knows she's telling the truth about what's in her heart. Man, that must be nice.

Unfortunately, though, there's nobody who fell in love with me *before* our astronomical success. Actually, there's nobody who's *ever* fallen in love with me, period. So, if it's going to happen for me now, it's going to be with someone who knows my band, and therefore knows my bank account is a fat one. Given that, I can't help wondering how I'll know, for sure, if a girl really likes me for *me*? I'm notoriously gullible when it comes to women. Always have been. And it turns out that's not a great thing for me to be, especially now that I'm "Fish from 22 Goats." I'm an easy target for women with ulterior motives, and I know it.

Plus, the logistics of my life make it hard for me to find true love. With all the travel we do, I don't have time to get to know anybody beyond surface shit. Sometimes I wonder, if my version of Violet came along, would I even recognize her? Or would I be so jaded, so guarded, so careful, I'd assume she's a clout chaser and not give her the time of day? Or, worse, would I be so gullible, I'd fall head over heels for a clout chaser, convinced she really loved me, only to find out later I was duped?

My gaze drifts to Violet and Dax again, just in time to see them lean in for another passionate kiss. And, just like that, I feel another pang of envy.

Damn.

I didn't always want what Dax has. At the beginning of this crazy ride, I was stoked to live out my rock star fantasies, especially after all the rejection I'd endured from girls in high school. At first, I was elated there were women willing to fool around with me after shows—and especially that I didn't have to do anything to make it happen. I just had to be "Fish from 22 Goats." The guy who'd just played a concert in a packed arena. That was enough to attract them, despite my obvious shyness and lack of game.

But by the time we headed off on our third tour, I was done with fame vampires and groupies. Ready for something real. As it's turned out, though, feeling ready for something and getting it are two different things.

Kat walking toward me pulls me from my wandering thoughts. She's got two women with her—a stunning brunette with olive skin and curves for days, plus an adorable young woman in a modest purple bikini.

Kat and her friends stop in front of Dax and Violet, a few feet away from me, before Kat beckons for Colin and me to come over, which we do. As Colin and I come to a halt in front of Kat and her friends, Kat says, "Guys, this is Georgina." She motions to the curvy brunette. "She's a writer for *Rock 'n' Roll* who's going to be interviewing you."

The three of us Goats say hello to the reporter, and she

returns the greeting. But I can't deny it's the cutie in the purple bikini who's got my full attention. I like the way her long dark hair glimmers with auburn highlights in the sun. Also, the way she keeps blinking her big blue eyes, like she can't decide if she's hallucinating. Not gonna lie, I also like the small, perky breasts peeking out of her bikini top.

When I force my eyes up, off the cutie's bikini-clad body and back to her face, I'm surprised to catch her peeking at me. When our eyes meet, she quickly looks away, blushing. And that's how I know I'm not the only one feeling an attraction.

"Do you work for *Rock 'n' Roll*, too?" I ask the cutie.

"Oh, excuse me. This is Alessandra," the reporter says, putting her arm around the cutie. "She's my sister. My stepsister. Reed kindly said she could be my plus-one for the party tonight."

We greet Alessandra, and she waves shyly at us in reply, her face turning a deep shade of crimson and those big blue eyes blinking a mile a minute.

"Alessandra just finished her second year at Berklee," the reporter continues. "The music school in Boston?"

"That's cool," Dax says, just as I'm mumbling something similar. We know several musicians who graduated from that school, and they're all badasses to the extreme. In fact, now that I know this cutie is studying there, I'm feeling kind of intimidated. I'm not classically trained on any of the instruments I play. I'm totally self-taught on all of them. If this girl is studying at a conservatory like that, the kind with auditions to get in, she must be more than damned good at whatever she does. She must be amazing.

"Do you play an instrument?" I ask.

Alessandra's blue eyes widen. "Uhhh."

Georgina jumps right in. "Ally plays guitar and piano.

Ukulele, too. But, mostly, she writes on her guitar. She sings and writes the most incredible songs!"

I look at Georgina like, *I get that you're proud of your sister, dude. But how about you let her speak for herself.*

"Alessandra is really shy," Georgina explains, reading my mind. And, instantly, I feel like a dick for the scornful look I just flashed Georgina. Obviously, she's Alessandra's proverbial emotional support animal. Nothing wrong with that.

"No problem," I say quickly. I smile at both Georgina and Alessandra. "I know all about being shy. I'm actually pretty shy, too, by nature."

Alessandra shoots me a lovely smile before gazing down at her polished toenails. And just like that, with that one bright smile from Alessandra, I feel like a hooked Fish. Bound and determined to draw this shy girl out, until she's showing me whatever personality lies beneath.

The group starts chatting with the extroverted reporter, Georgina, so I move closer to the introverted cutie. "Hey there."

She looks up at me and smiles shyly. "Hi."

"Do you *love* going to Berklee? Everyone says it's amazing."

She nods. And as she does, I can practically see her heart thumping in her chest.

"Did you know Davey from Watch Party graduated from there?"

She nods again.

"Yeah. I bet you know all your famous alums."

She smiles and shrugs, like, *Yeah, I do.* But that's it. She doesn't speak.

"So, Georgina said you write songs?"

"Mm-hmm."

Okay. Well. It wasn't much. But she did use her vocal cords. Minimally. So, it's progress.

"I write songs, too," I say. "My main instrument these days is bass guitar, but I love pulling out the ol' acoustic guitar and writing a little song, now and again. Guitar was my first instrument, actually. But we didn't have anyone to play bass when we formed our band, so I volunteered as tribute and learned it."

"And now, here you are, a *master* at it."

Bam. Under the circumstances, that felt like a veritable TED Talk from her. At least, it was enough words to spur me on to keep fishing for more.

"Thanks so much," I say. "That means a lot, coming from someone like you. So, you know my band, then?"

She flashes me a snarky look like my question is a ridiculous one. "Yes, I know your band. I *love* your band."

There's so much goodness here, I can't believe it. First off, her shoulders have softened considerably since we first laid eyes on each other. Her crimson blush has faded. And, hey, we're having an actual conversation now! That's pretty cool. But best of all, I'm relieved Alessandra has copped to loving my band, right off the bat. I don't care if a girl loves 22 Goats or hates us, or anything in between. I just want her to be honest about her opinions, whatever they are. There's nothing worse than a girl who knows my band but pretends she's never heard of us because she thinks that's her best strategy to hook me. And on the flip side, I can't stand a girl who falsely overstates her opinion of my band, simply because she thinks I'll be offended if she doesn't believe we're the second coming of the Beatles. Bottom line, I guess I just want authenticity from a woman. That's all I want. And, glory be, I can already tell this cutie doesn't have an inauthentic bone in her lithe, little body.

Out of nowhere, Alessandra says, "What did you mean 'someone like me?'"

"Huh?"

"When I complimented your bass playing, you said 'that means a lot coming from someone like you.'"

"Oh. Just that everyone I know who went to Berklee is a badass—wildly talented and smart in a way I could only dream of being. So, I'm assuming you're like that. A badass who's wildly talented and smart."

She scoffs. "Fish, you're a wildly talented badass. One of the best in the business."

Damn. That was unexpected. "Thank you," I say, my heart racing. "But I'm not educated or trained or whatever. That's what I meant. It's not easy to get into a school like Berklee, right? You have to *audition*."

She shrugs like that's an obvious—but highly irrelevant—statement.

"My point is that I didn't have to audition to do what I'm doing. I've known Dax since second grade and Colin since middle school. I got into the band because I was lucky enough to have the right two friends."

Alessandra shrugs again. "I'd say they were pretty lucky to have you as a friend, too. Either way, however you got here, I think it's pretty clear you've done it based on your extraordinary talent and musicianship. Not to mention your extreme charisma."

Aw, fuck. This is wild. Is she gaming me? I've been complimented before by girls. Lots of times. But never like this. Never with so much apparent sincerity. And certainly, I've never been complimented on my "charisma" before. In fact, funny story that's not actually funny at all. When Reed Rivers signed my band five years ago, he initially only wanted Dax. As far as he was concerned, Colin and I were necessary evils. Especially me, thanks to my "tepid" skills on bass and my "complete lack of charisma," according to him. And now this pretty girl who attends Berklee in Boston is complimenting me on both of those *precise* things? I can't believe it. Seriously, she must be gaming me.

Keane and Zander jump into the swimming pool nearby, diverting our attention for a moment. And I'm glad for the distraction, so I can pull myself together. These past few years, I've gotten better at conversing with pretty girls than I was in high school. Thankfully. But not by much. And Alessandra is so pretty and seemingly sincere, she's making me feel intimidated like I used to feel when I tried to talk to a crush back in the day.

I clear my throat. "So . . . Are you always really shy, or just at first with new people? Or are you feeling especially shy around me, because of my band?"

She twists her mouth adorably. "All of the above? Although, to be fair, I'd be just as shy around you if you weren't in one of my favorite bands—if you were just some random cute boy I'd met in one of my classes or at the café where I work. Assuming, of course, I knew how talented you are. I always get extra shy around really talented, cute boys."

She called me cute. She thinks I'm cute. Out of everything Alessandra said, that's the comment that's sticking the most and making my body feel like a riot of pure excitement. I clear my throat and say, "I get pretty shy around cute, talented girls, too." I smile . . . and then add lamely, just in case my comment wasn't clear enough, "By that I mean to say *you're*

cute and talented, specifically. That's what I meant by that."
Shit. I'm terrible at this.

Alessandra bites her lip, like she's trying not to laugh.
"Thank you. But you really can't pronounce me talented,
since you've never heard me play."

I roll my eyes dramatically. "We've been through this
already, dude. *You go to Berklee.* They don't let untalented
wankers into your school."

This time, she can't keep herself from giggling. And, I
swear, at the sound of her adorable laughter, I feel like
fucking King Arthur after pulling the sword from the stone.

"Lemme guess," I say, my smile stretching from ear to ear.
"You're the kind of person who's shy and quiet, at first, but
then, after you get comfortable, everyone goes, 'Who the hell
is this talkative girl?'"

"Yes! If I'm comfortable with you, and passionate about a
topic, I'll talk your ear clean off!"

Hot damn. Something amazing is happening between this
girl and me. Something different. Something *real*. I can feel it
in my bones. On my skin. In my quickening pulse.

"Challenge accepted," I say. I gesture to two vacant
loungers in a far corner of the patio. "How about we move our
conversation over there? Frick and Frack are getting pretty
rowdy in the pool. It's getting harder to talk over their
splashing."

Alessandra looks at Keane and Zander in the pool, who
are splashing and roughhousing like crazy, before returning to
me with a lovely smile. "I'd love that."

"Great," I say calmly. Even though I want to shout, "Hal-
lelujah!" And as we begin to walk together to the corner, I
add, "By the way, I've got two ears, but I only need one. So,
please, feel free to talk one of 'em clean off."

FOUR

FISH

As soon as Alessandra and I reach the loungers in the far corner of the patio, a roving waiter appears like a genie to take our drink orders. We make our requests—a craft beer for me and bottle of water for Alessandra—and get situated.

There's another splash in the pool and we both glance over. This time, it appears Keane and Zander are competing in some sort of belly flop contest.

"They've been friends forever," I explain. "They're total goofballs."

"They're funny."

And you're cute, I think. But what I say is, "Yeah, they're really funny."

We're quiet for a moment.

Smiling at each other.

Fidgeting.

I can't believe she's not immediately launching into asking me a thousand questions about my band. About Dax, maybe. The making of the video for "People Like Us." How we got our name. How and when we formed the band. All the usual topics that always flow with every pretty girl I've met around the world—especially the ones who cop to loving my band.

But, nope. Apparently, even though Alessandra has already admitted she loves 22 Goats, she's apparently not going to gush about us. Nor is she going to flirt with me or otherwise blow smoke up my ass. Which, I freely admit, is something I've come to count on in situations like this. I've got no game, after all. Or, at least, very little, when it comes down to it. So, of course, I'm relieved when a woman I'm talking to takes the reins and starts brazenly flirting.

I fidget again, at a loss for what to say. I kind of feel like I should stop asking her about school, but it's the only thing popping into my head. I ask, "What year are you at Berklee?"

"I just finished my second year."

"So, that makes you . . . nineteen . . . twenty?"

"Nineteen. I'll be twenty at the beginning of August."

"Cool."

There's a beat. Another awkward silence. Another series of shy smiles exchanged.

Alessandra chews on the inside of her cheek while I twiddle my fingers and race through possible discussion topics again. World news? God, no. My band? No. If we're going to talk about that, she should be the one to bring it up, or else I'll come off like a narcissist.

The waiter comes with our drinks, saving me from myself, and we thank him. When he leaves, I sip my beer and try to act relaxed and casual, even though my heart is racing and my skin is alive with an intense attraction to her.

"Where are you from?" I ask. That seems safe.

"Antelope Valley. About an hour from here."

"I've never been there."

"There's no reason to go. It's in the boondocks. Known for poppy fields and not much else. My mother is a florist, so it's a good place for her to live."

"Ah. That's cool. My mother is a teacher. Third grade."

"That's cool. Where are you from?"

"Seattle."

"I've never been there."

"It's awesome. You should go."

"I'd like to. From what I've seen in movies and stuff, it looks amazing."

I nod. "Dax, Colin, and I grew up there."

"That's so cool you grew up together, and now you're traveling the world together, living your dreams."

"Yeah. It's the best."

Kat's laughter rises up, and we turn to look at her. She's throwing her head back while conversing with her husband and their two best friends.

"That's Dax's big sister. Kat."

"I met her. She seems nice. I don't think I realized she's Dax's sister, though."

"Keane's, too. She's evil, by the way. Pure evil."

Alessandra's eyebrows ride up.

"I meant that as a compliment. She's the best. Very good at getting what she wants."

Alessandra grins. "My stepsister Georgina is evil in that same way. She's insanely smart and always figures out a way to get what she wants, without anyone realizing that's what she's doing."

"*Exactly.* That's an impressive skill, isn't it?"

"Very impressive. Unfortunately, I'm not evil like that. *At all.*"

"Me, either," I say, chuckling. "Not at all."

We share another smile and then sip our drinks again.

There's another long moment of silence. Clearly, she's still nervous around me. And, frankly, I'm still nervous around her. Clout chasers and fame vampires are easy. They do all the talking and flirting, while I sit back and do absolutely nothing but answer the same questions, time after time. But with Alessandra, I feel like I've got to keep the conversation going. And that's not my strong suit when it comes to pretty girls.

Oh, I've got it! *Astrology.* I know nothing about it, but Kat *loves* talking about that shit. I can't even count the number of times she's gone on and on about it. Specifically, about me being a Taurus meaning such and such. "I just turned twenty-five at the end of May," I say, out of nowhere. "That makes me a Taurus."

"Oh. Cool."

"You?"

"I'm a Leo. You're into astrology?"

My cheeks blaze. Maybe this wasn't such a brilliant conversation starter. "No. Not at all. You?"

"No. I only know the basics about my sign."

"Same. All I know is I'm supposedly stubborn. That's supposed to be my defining characteristic, actually. But I'm not stubborn at all."

"Taurus is the Bull, right?"

I nod. "But if I were an animal, I'd say I'm more like a dog. A really happy dog who likes chasing tennis balls and taking naps."

She giggles. And as she does, a swarm of butterflies releases into my belly. Damn, she's got a cute laugh.

"I'd have thought you'd say your animal is the *fish*," she says.

"Clever."

"See what I did there?"

"I do. I think the fish is for Pisces, though."

"I thought you said you don't know anything about astrology," she says.

"I don't. But, come on. Pisces is the fish. That much, I know. Probably, I should have been a Pisces. I generally like going with the flow. That's what Pisces do, right? Given their animal."

She shrugs. "I'd assume so. Either way, can you imagine the perfection of being a dude called Fish who's a *Pisces*?" She does a chef's kiss with her fingers, making me laugh.

"Sadly, though, life isn't always perfect like that. It turns out I'm a Goat called Fish who's supposed to be stubborn as a bull, but isn't."

She giggles again. This time, even more heartily. "Wow, Fish. Who's the doctor who delivered you? *Doctor Dolittle*?" She laughs uproariously at her own silly joke, and, of course, I laugh with her. Not so much at the joke itself, but at the way *she's* laughing at it. And, damn, that swarm of butterflies in my belly is turning into an entire flock of seagulls as we laugh together.

I sip my beer. "So, what's Leo's animal? Lion, right?"

"Correct."

"That makes you a lion-*ess* named Al-*ess*-andra. That'd be a sick lyric."

She nods. "Yeah, it's got a nice little internal rhyme to it."

"It does."

"I'm imagining a song kind of like 'Buddy Holly' by Weezer. Do you know that one?"

"Do I know it?" I slap my thigh energetically. "Dude! *I love Weezer!*"

"*So do I!* They can do no wrong in my book!"

"Same!"

And that's it. We're off to the races, finally, babbling nonstop, without another awkward silence, about our favorite Weezer songs. From there, we talk enthusiastically about how much we both love internal rhymes in lyrics, which leads us to a discussion of the rap and hip-hop artists we revere the most for their amazing word play and internal rhymes. And, through it all, it becomes starkly clear to me *this* is the way to lure this shy girl out of her shell on a rocket. *Get her to talk about music, dummy!* How did I not realize that, right away?

I motion to the waiter for another round of drinks, and then return to Alessandra with a relaxed smile. "So, what kinds of songs do you write? Who are your biggest musical influences?"

She leans back onto her lounger with ease and confidence, before rattling off an eclectic, impressive list of bands and artists. "But I think my biggest influence is Laila Fitzgerald," she says. "People often say I remind them of her."

"That's a huge compliment."

"I agree. Laila is my idol. My songs have that same sort of jazz-infused quality to them, even though they're foundationally 'indie singer-songwriter.'"

"I'd be happy to introduce you to Laila tonight at the party, if you'd like."

Alessandra's bright blue eyes bug out. "Really?"

"Sure."

"*No.*"

"Yes."

She gasps. "Thank you!" And then opens and closes her mouth in rapid succession, like she's been rendered speechless. She reaches for my arm, like she's going to grip it excitedly, but then jerks back suddenly. She palms her forehead. Puffs out her cheeks. And, finally, fans her bright-red face. "You know I wasn't angling for an introduction to Laila when I mentioned her, right? I'd honestly forgotten who you are for a minute there. I'd hate for you to think—"

"I don't." I chuckle. "It's all good. I swear. I only offered because Laila is a friend, and I know she'd love to meet you." *And also because I want any excuse to hang out with you at the party tonight.*

"Thank you *so* much, Fish."

"It's nothing. I'm happy to do it."

Alessandra physically shudders with excitement—a move that causes arousal to rocket into my dick. She takes a deep breath and visibly collects herself. "So, what about you?" she says. "Who are *your* biggest musical influences?"

I cover my growing hard-on with my forearm. "Uh. Musical influences for me, personally, or for my band?"

"Oh! I love that those are different things. For you, personally."

I name several bands and artists, and Alessandra listens intently. She comments enthusiastically and asks multiple questions, never seeming shy or reserved in the slightest. And, again, it's obvious: *music* is the key to this pretty girl's kingdom.

"I know this is going to sound like I'm sucking up to you," Alessandra says. She pauses for dramatic effect, leans in, and whispers, "One of my all-time favorite bands, *ever*, is 22 Goats."

I scowl playfully. "*One* of your favorites? Not your top favorite, *ever*?" I point toward the far end of the patio. "Get the fuck outta here. For shame."

She laughs heartily with me.

"Seriously, that's a huge compliment," I say. "Especially coming from you."

"There you go again. Fish, I'm a student. You're a world-famous musician."

"You're a *music* student at one of the most prestigious music conservatories in the world, and you've got seriously awesome taste in music. The fact that my band is even in your top twenty is a *huge* honor."

"Top twenty? Try top four. And it's a tie for first, by the way. 22 Goats isn't fourth."

"Seriously?"

She nods. "I love all your songs. Every album is a masterpiece."

"Which 22 Goats album is your favorite?"

She waves at the air. "I couldn't pick. You've evolved so much with each album. Each one is a whole new experience. The perfect soundtrack of whatever I was going through at the time. That's what I love about your band the most. That you guys aren't afraid to grow and take risks. As an aspiring artist, I find that incredibly inspirational. After the huge success of your debut album, you could have 'stuck with what got ya there,' forevermore. But you decided to stretch yourselves. Also, I love that every song on every album is top quality. Innovative. Heartfelt. Interesting. Even the simple love songs are produced with simplicity for impact, not because you were cutting corners or because the song was some kind of throw-away or filler."

Damn. That was a lot of words from her, all at once. Not to mention, a lot of fucking awesome words. "Wow," I say. "You really *are* a fan."

Alessandra cringes. "Did I fangirl too hard?"

"Not at all."

"I told you I'd talk your ear off if I got comfortable and felt passionately about a topic."

"And I told you I've got two ears and only need one. I'm loving this conversation."

Her blue eyes widen adorably. "Really?"

"Really."

She picks at the label on her water bottle. "I'm sure everyone you meet says all these same things about your music, though. You're probably sick to death of hearing it."

"Uh, no. *Nobody* says what you just did. Honestly, I never get to have conversations like this with anyone. Ever."

She flashes me a look of complete incredulity.

"It's true," I insist. "Yes, I admit fans tell me they love my band. But they never articulate what they love the way you just did. I never get the chance to talk to someone who's so knowledgeable about music, in general, and also about our catalog. We never want to rip ourselves off or become a caricature of ourselves, you know? But that approach is risky in terms of marketability. And you obviously understand that. You get our need to grow and evolve."

"Of course, I do. The songs on your first album were written when you guys were, what, eighteen?"

I nod. "Eighteen and nineteen."

She shrugs. "Anyone would grow and evolve in their early twenties. But you guys, especially. Since writing that first album, you've toured the world. Become superstars. Not to mention, you're different musicians now, after playing so many shows. You're no longer the boys, the *aspiring* musicians, you were at age eighteen. You're men now. Professionals. Masters of your craft."

I'm totally blown away. Too overwhelmed to speak. Too intoxicated by her words. Her big blue eyes and auburn hair.

The scent of her shampoo and sunscreen. Not to mention, her undeniable sincerity. If I wondered about her genuineness before, I'm not wondering now.

"Take your bass playing," Alessandra continues. And it's the first time *she's* filled a silence between us. "When I put your albums in chronological order and binge-listen to them, I can plainly hear how much you've all grown as musicians. But especially you. You've gained so much confidence and skill over the years—especially the last two albums. Which isn't to say you were anything less than stellar on your first two. But you were so raw and green back then, compared to now. I love being able to hear the difference. The confidence you've gained."

"Holy shit," I whisper, my heart thumping. "You're seriously able to hear all of that in my bass playing?"

She nods. "And in your backup vocals, too. Sometimes, when I listen to my favorite albums, I close my eyes and concentrate on what each musician is doing. I hone in on the voices, specifically. Then, the bass. The guitars. I listen to the production. All the various choices that were made in creating the songs. And, when I do that, from album to album, I feel like I get to appreciate the musicians' journeys so much. As musicians—and as people."

I can barely breathe. But before I've figured out what to say in response to that amazingness, the waiter appears with our second round of drinks. We thank him, and when he leaves, I clink Alessandra's water bottle with my beer.

"Cheers, Al-*ess*-andra the lion-*ess*. I'm damned glad to meet you."

"Cheers, Fish. I'm damned glad to meet you, too. Or should I call you The Goat Called Fish who's supposed to be a bull, but isn't?"

"I dig it. Cool. Although . . . on second thought, if someone were to overhear that nickname, they might get the wrong idea about me. Maybe call me The Goat Called Fish Who's Hung Like a Bull, instead?" I blush, thinking maybe I've made a misstep, and quickly add, "I'm not, actually. Hung like a bull. Not at all. But I think the nickname sounds way better like that, don't you? You know, for branding purposes."

She laughs uproariously, thank God. "Yeah, that's so much more 'rock 'n' roll' that way."

"Right?"

"Duly noted. The nickname has been hereby officially amended—you know, for branding purposes."

"Thank you. Much appreciated."

She giggles again. "Seriously, though, do you prefer I call you Fish or Matthew?"

I shrug. "It's all the same to me. Maybe call me Matthew when it's something particularly important, to make sure you get my full attention when it matters."

She nods and blushes. "Okay."

Butterflies. Seagulls. There's flapping around inside me in full-force again. I say, "So, the chron order binge-listen thing. I'm intrigued. Tell me more."

"Oh, man, you need to do it! You put your favorite artists' catalog in chronological order and listen from beginning to end in one long marathon. It's the best way to truly under-stand and appreciate their musical journey. Their *human* journey."

I'm in awe of her brain, her passion, her beauty—and I'm sure my face shows it. "Did you learn to do that in school?"

"Oh, no. I started doing that as a kid. But I've certainly learned all kinds of other cool things at school. And not just in classes. From other students and from talking to professors. It's amazing to be at a school where *everyone* shares the same passion."

"I bet. I'm on the road so much, my interactions with other musicians aren't nearly as frequent as you'd think. I mean, yeah, I know amazing people in the industry. And I love going to parties or hanging out with them. But it's not like what you're doing."

"Well, I think every student at Berklee would kill to trade places with you. What you're doing is the dream."

She's right, of course, and I know it. But I also know the realities of this "dream" can be a bit more challenging than anyone on the outside understands. But there's no need to tell her about that, when she's looking at me like I walk on water. "So, humor me," I say. "Do you have a favorite 22 Goats song? I know it's the height of narcissism to ask that question, but I can't resist. I'm putty in your hands, Alessandra the Lioness. Dying to hear whatever nugget of brilliance is going to come out of your mouth next."

"*My* mouth? Are you crazy? I'm hanging on your every word!"

We share a huge smile. And, suddenly, I'm feeling fucking helicopters. But not only that, a weird kind of tightness in my chest, too. Tingles on my skin. She's so damned pretty. *And now I find out she's got an awesome personality, too?*

"I really couldn't pick my favorite 22 Goats song," she declares. "That'd be like a mother picking her favorite child."

"My mother has no problem doing that."

"Are you an only child?"

"I am."

Alessandra laughs. "Me, too. My mother calls me her 'favorite daughter' all the time." She shrugs. "Seriously, the best I could do, *maybe*, would be naming a 'favorite' off each of your four albums. But even that would be pure torture for me and come with the disclaimer that my 'favorite' could change at any minute."

"The small print shall clearly state you can change your mind at any time."

"No small print. Big, huge font."

"Deal."

"All right, then. I'll torture myself." She flashes me a smile that sends arousal straight into my cock, forcing me to cover my swim trunks with my forearm again. "I'll have you know, though," she says, batting her eyelashes. "I'd never, ever pick a favorite 22 Goats song—let alone one off each freaking album—for anyone in the whole, wide world but you, Fish." She pauses. "*Matthew*."

FIVE

FISH

Alessandra twists her mouth, considering which song to pick as her favorite off my band's self-titled first album. And as she does, I can't help staring at her plush lips. Wondering what it would be like to kiss them. They're stained with the faintest hint of cherry red. It's not a pinup girl red. More like she's wearing cherry lip balm. If I kissed those full lips right now, would they taste sweet, like cherries?

"Okay," Alessandra finally says, drawing my gaze from her lips to her blinking blue eyes. "I hate myself for being obvious, but I think I have to go with 'People Like Us.' But only because that was the first 22 Goats song I ever heard, and it hit me like a ton of bricks." She sighs dreamily. "There's nothing like a girl's first love." Her breathing halts. "In music. First love in *music*."

I smile. "I know what you meant."

She shifts position on her lounger. "I'm not a stalker, Fish. I swear."

"Yeah, I've gathered that. If you are, you're doing a shitty job of it. You're far too sane."

She exhales with relief.

"Out of curiosity, did 'People Like Us' 'hit you like a ton of bricks' before or after you saw the music video?"

She palms her forehead. "Oh, God, that video! I'm sure half those billion views were mine!"

Okay, I've definitely had *this* particular conversation before. Many times. Also, I've seen the look on Alessandra's face, too, on every girl who's been talking about that music video. And it's no wonder. Our debut video went batshit viral, thanks not only to the dope song, but also to Dax's golden-god, naked perfection. Colin and I appeared in that video, too, of course, in the performance scenes and a B-line subplot meant for comedic effect. But, undoubtedly, the reason that video launched 22 Goats into the stratosphere was Dax Morgan and those glimpses of his naked ass as he rolled around on a white-sand beach with a stunning supermodel.

"Dax actually *hates* that music video," I confess.

"*No.*"

"Yep. He appreciates that it launched us into the stratosphere, as designed. The entire goal of that thing was rocketing our song to number one."

"Which it did."

"Thankfully. But, as Dax quickly found out, having an endgame, and then living with the consequences of that endgame actually succeeding, are two different things."

"What consequences? You mean fame?"

"Yeah, Dax struggles with that aspect of things sometimes. More specifically, he can't stand the whole 'heartthrob' box he's always put into, especially because he knows it's a box partly of his own making. Dax is all about the music, so the fact that his face and ass are still such cornerstones of our band's identity, thanks to that video, is a genuine struggle for him."

Alessandra looks sympathetic. "Well, at least you're all in it together. The 'heartthrob box,' I mean. Have you found that to be a struggle for you, too?"

I stare into her blinking blue eyes for a long moment, trying to gauge if she's being sarcastic, and quickly determine she's asking her question sincerely. *This girl actually thinks I'm a heartthrob?* "Uhhh . . . The heartthrob thing has been okay for me. Dax and Colin take the brunt of that sort of thing, to be honest. I'm pretty much the funny one. The comic relief."

Alessandra frowns like she's not buying that explanation but says nothing. And I can't help feeling pretty awesome about that.

"Okay, second album?" I say. "What's your song selection off that one?"

This time, she doesn't hesitate. "'Fireflies.' Just because it was a bit of a departure for you guys, which I really respected. That song, more than any other, felt like you were refusing to be put into a musical box after the success of your first album. Plus, it's so damned catchy."

"That's my favorite off that album, too."

"Really?"

"Yeah. I think it's so romantic. So honest. Dax wrote it for his wife, Violet, right after they met." Reflexively, I glance across the patio at Dax and Violet, and, not surprisingly, they're tangled up in the hot tub, like they're the only two people in the world.

Alessandra asks, "Did Dax personally write every song on *The Violet Album* for her? I've always assumed he did, based on the album's title. But your band's writing credits are always listed as '22 Goats,' with no individual contributions noted. So, it's impossible to know who wrote what."

"Yeah, Dax wrote virtually everything on both our first and second albums. Colin and I contributed our parts of the instrumentation and maybe a bridge or lyric here or there. For the third and fourth albums, though, we both started contributing a lot more to the writing process. Me, especially. By then, I figured out I'm actually a pretty competent song-writer. I also bumped our old producer out of his chair on the third album and started co-producing everything with Dax."

"Wow! How cool!" She holds up her arm. "Look! I just got goose bumps!"

I laugh. "We're just about to start writing our fifth album this coming week. I can't wait."

She squeals. "Oh, to be a fly on the wall when 22 Goats writes their amazing songs! I can't even imagine how cool that must be, to be a part of that, especially now that you're co-producing. With no middleman 'translating' your ideas for you, your songs can now come out into the world *exactly* as intended."

"Exactly! Yes!" My heart is thundering. Talking to this girl is fucking amazing. She just *gets* it.

Alessandra asks me some questions about my producing philosophy, and I answer her with enthusiasm. But, after a bit, I prompt her to return to our prior topic. "Back to your favorite songs," I say. "What's your pick off our third album?"

"Ugh. That's a toughie," she says. She twists her mouth in contemplation for a long moment, before saying, "Okay, I think I'll go with another obvious choice this time and pick 'Three.'"

I chuckle. "That's not an obvious choice, Alessandra."

"It was a huge hit."

I shake my head. "The obvious choices would be 'Sweet Craving' or 'Don't Count Me Out.'"

"Also great ones. But 'Three' is so heartfelt and lovely. I just love singing that one."

"You know how to play 'Three?'"

She nods. "I know a bunch of your songs."

"Holy shit!" I stand excitedly and extend my hand. "Come on, Little Lioness. I'm positive Reed's got an acoustic guitar somewhere in his house. Let's find it so you can play me 'Three'!"

Alessandra looks shocked. She stares at my extended hand without moving for a moment. And then, "No, I . . . Thank you. But, no."

I drop my hand, in shock. "What?"

"I'd die of stage fright."

"*Stage fright?*" I blurt. "But going to Berklee, you must play in front of audiences all the time."

"But I don't play a 22 Goats song in front of a member of 22 Goats."

"Fair enough." I extend my hand again. "Okay, so, let's go find a guitar so you can play me one of your originals."

She's a pale shade of green. Again, she doesn't take my hand. She shakes her head. "I'd love to hear *you* sing a song to me, though. If anyone is going to play a song to anyone right now, it should be the professional playing one for the student."

I sit back down, sighing. "I don't do that."

"You don't do what?"

"Sing lead vocals on songs. That's not my thing. I sing backups. Write songs, now and again, that I hand off to Dax to sing."

"But you've got an amazing voice, Fish."

"Thanks. I'm a good backup singer. I know my lane."

She flashes me a look of incredulity, as if to say, *If you say so.*

She sips her water. "Well, if you're not going to sing for me, then I'm perfectly happy to continue sitting here, talking to you."

I can't believe my ears. Doesn't she realize, if she were to march inside that house and play for me—and maybe impress me enough—I could possibly, maybe, help her career? Granted, I haven't helped anyone's career *yet*. But in theory, I *could*. For instance, I might lobby Reed to give her music a listen, not that Reed would listen to me. To put it mildly, that guy doesn't consider me a towering figure in his empire. But Alessandra doesn't know that! For all she knows, Reed and I are tight as ticks, like Reed and Dax. For all she knows, I could be her ticket to making her dreams come true! Or, at least, a means of getting her one step closer. *And she's turning down the chance to try to impress me?* It's unthinkable.

"Okay, fourth album," she says, filling our first awkward silence in a while. She taps her chin. "That's another toughie. I guess, if you're *forcing* me to pick, I'd have to go with . . . 'Delightful Damage.'"

My heart stops.

I can't believe it.

That song is the only one ever released by 22 Goats that was written *entirely* by me, with no input from Dax or Colin. Prior to that one, I'd always added my two cents to whatever songs Dax had created. Or, if I'd written something, Dax wound up changing parts of it for the better. *But not with "Delightful Damage."* That one was all me, baby. Every word and note was written by me in one furious late-night session in a hotel room in Prague.

When I brought the song, fully written, to Dax and Colin the next day, they both blew me away by saying they loved the song, *as is*, and wanted to record it for our next album. And when Dax ultimately sang my words and haunting melody in the studio, and I heard my lyrics and emotions expressed by a true artist like him, I felt like weeping. I didn't lend my voice to the song on the record—and rightly so—but I still felt in that moment, and still do, whenever I hear the recording, like that song marked *my* coming of age. *And that's the song Alessandra has chosen as her favorite off our fourth album?*

"I can't believe you picked that song as a favorite," I manage to eke out.

She furrows her brow. "Why? It's a masterpiece."

"It wasn't a big hit."

Alessandra shifts onto her side on her lounger. "Yeah, well, it should have been. I love that it's so different from your other songs, both melodically and lyrically. I love how honest and raw it is. It always hits me right here." She touches her chest. "I love Dax's voice on that one. It's so full of angst. And I love the way your voice blends with his on those harmonies in the chorus. It's definitely my all-time favorite 22 Goats song to sing. I love singing that one even more than 'Three.' It's just so *mesmerizing.*"

Okay, I'm officially losing my shit here. I take a sip of beer to calm myself down before saying, "You're not going to believe this, but 'Delightful Damage' is the *only* song in our entire catalog written completely by *me*, without any contribution from Dax or Colin."

Her jaw drops. She sits up and whispers, "Oh my God,

Fish. *Matthew*." She reaches out and grabs my forearm. "You're a *genius*." Her blue eyes widen and her cheeks flash with color before she pulls her hand away, leaving my skin tingling where she touched me. She asks, "Is that song autobiographical? Did someone break your heart?" She grimaces when I say nothing. "Sorry. Is that too personal?"

My mind is reeling. My heart crashing. "No, no. I'm only speechless because nobody has ever asked me about this song before. I didn't sing it on the record, as you know. And we don't perform it in concerts. So, it's not a typical topic of conversation. I only paused so long because I want to be sure to answer you with complete honesty."

Alessandra's chest rises sharply and remains expanded, like she's literally waiting with bated breath for whatever I'm going to say next.

I take another long swig of my beer while gathering my thoughts. Finally, I say, "Yes, the song *is* autobiographical. But not in the way it comes across when Dax sings it. It's not about that *one* girl who broke my heart. It's not actually a breakup song, at all, in a traditional sense." I take another sip. And then, another deep breath. "To be honest, the song is about my experience with women in general. The fact that they've always rejected me, for one reason or another. The ones I've wanted, anyway. It's about the fact that, once my band hit it big, women sometimes flirt with me, but it's not real. I guess, the song is a confessional about how I've come to realize . . . it's far worse feeling used and lonely than simply being alone."

"Wow," she whispers. She touches my arm again. "I'm so sorry you've felt like that, Matthew."

My eyes locked with hers, I nod. "I've actually never had a serious girlfriend, though I'd like to have one. That's the 'heartbreak' I was writing about. That feeling where you start wondering 'what's wrong with me?' And 'why doesn't anybody want me?'"

She nods slowly, keeping her fingertips pressed against my arm. "I've never had a boyfriend, serious or otherwise. So, I guess it's no wonder that song connects with me so deeply." She slides her hand away, and my arm physically tingles with yearning at the loss. She sighs. "To be honest, I've shed a lot of tears listening to that song. Also, while playing it." She looks down. "I've also wondered those same things you said. Many times."

Suddenly, all I want to do is kiss this beautiful girl. In fact, my lips feel like they're physically aching to press against hers. But I don't have the courage to do it. Not yet, anyway. If she's never had a boyfriend, then I'm assuming she'd want to take things extra slow.

"Alessandra!" It's Georgina, tangled up with Reed in the swimming pool. When Alessandra turns her head, Georgina beckons enthusiastically to her. "Reed's here, honey! Come meet him!"

"Aw, fuck," Alessandra murmurs. She rubs her forehead. "I hope I don't barf on him."

"I'd honestly pay good money to see that."

She doesn't laugh. She's too nervous.

"Aw, it's okay, Little Lioness. You've got this. Hey, you want me to come with you? His bark is worse than his bite."

She waves at the air. "No, no. Hang out with your friends and relax. I've monopolized you long enough." She stands, displaying the small, tight curves of her lithe body in her purple bikini. "I've loved talking to you, Matthew. Thank you for hanging out with me for so long."

"I've loved talking to you. Come back and chat with me

again after you meet Reed. Or, if that doesn't work out, then let's make sure we connect at the party."

"Okay. Yeah. I'm sure I'll be done talking to Reed in two seconds. My plan is to say hi to him as quickly as possible and then run away with my arms flailing."

I chuckle at the visual. "Don't do that, dude. Don't you know Reed's the guy who can make all your dreams come true?"

Alessandra rolls her eyes like that's a ridiculous notion. "I've got two more years of school before I need to think about that. I just want to escape the conversation with him without barfing."

"Good luck."

She holds up crossed fingers and makes a cute face. "Well, I guess I'll see ya later, Matthew Fishberger."

"You sure will, Alessandra . . . What's your last name?"

"Tennison."

"See ya later, Alessandra Tennison."

"Bye."

With a cute little smile, she turns and walks away. As she does, I watch her backside, enjoying her tight little ass. And all I can think, on a running loop, as I watch her is: *Holy shit.*

SIX
ALESSANDRA

"Fish is here," Georgina whisper-shouts to me, squeezing my forearm. She juts her chin across Reed's expansive living room, past the packed crowd toward the front door, and my heart physically palpitates at the sight of him. Fish just walked into the massive party with his friends—the Goats and their dates, Keane and Maddy, Aloha and Zander. And, hot damn, he looks yummy. Even hotter than he did at the pool earlier today, now that he's dressed for a night out. Once again, Fish has that *thing* about him I can't resist—boy-next-door charm mixed with a touch of rock star swagger.

Just inside the front door, Fish and his group are greeted by another group. I don't recognize the people hugging and high-fiving Fish's group, but they all look like musician types to me—which is a logical deduction in this crowd, given that this is Reed Rivers' party, and he's throwing it to celebrate a special issue of *Rock 'n' Roll* magazine.

I peel my eyes off Fish as he continues interacting enthusiastically with his friends and pivot toward Georgina next to me. "Hey, Georgie. I know you're going to need to mingle for work soon. And, please, don't worry about me tonight. I'll be happy as can be, people-watching in a corner. But will you please not leave me until Fish has seen us together? He's got so many friends at this party, and I know he's going to be hanging out with them for a long while before he even thinks of coming over here, so I don't want him feeling obligated to—"

"Hey, Alessandra!"

My heart stops. It can't be. I turn around and, yep, it's Fish standing before me!

At the sight of his wide, beaming smile and the faint scent of his delicious cologne, I physically wobble into Georgina, who quickly puts her arm around my shoulders and gives me an excited squeeze.

"Hey there!" I chirp, far more loudly than intended. "You look beautiful!" I cringe at my word choice. "You *smell* beautiful." Crap. *Stop talking, Alessandra.*

But Fish's smile has only widened and brightened at my dorky words. He leans in and pointedly inhales, before saying, "You look and *smell* beautiful, too."

I wobble again as he pulls back and looks me up and down pointedly.

"I *love* that dress," he says. "It looks amazing on you."

I'm wearing a simple dress. Nothing particularly amazing, I don't think. But I've got no doubt he's being sincere. "Thank you," I choke out. "You look amazing in those . . . jeans."

Georgina stifles a chuckle. "So, hey, kids . . ."

"Oh, hey, Georgina," Fish says quickly. "You look beautiful tonight, too."

"Thank you. I'm sorry to say hi and run, but tonight is a work thing for me, so . . ."

"Oh, no, yeah, feel free," Fish stammers, just as I babble basically the exact same thing.

Georgina smiles at Fish. "If I don't talk to you again tonight, let me say now I can't wait to interview you and the other Goats in Seattle. Kat's helping me nail down a date."

"Awesome. We're looking forward to it."

"Me, too." Georgina turns her hazel gaze on me. "I've got my phone in my pocket. Just text me if you need me for any reason."

Fish surprises me by sliding his arm around my shoulders, mimicking Georgina's hold on me a moment ago. "Don't worry," he says. "I'll make sure our girl is well taken care of the entire night."

Our girl?

Well taken care of?

Entire night?

Every damned thing about that sentence has made me feel giddy.

Georgina bites back a massive smile. "Awesome. Have fun, you two. See ya around." With that, she winks at me and disappears into the party.

Fish releases my shoulders and opens his mouth like he's going to speak, but a voice calling his name prompts him to turn his head.

It's a guy I recognize vaguely. I think he's a member of the rock band Danger Doctor Jones? Whoever he is, he hugs Fish enthusiastically.

"I thought you guys were on tour!" the guy says.

"We got back six weeks ago. You?"

"About to head out."

Fish motions to me. "This is my date, Alessandra. Alessandra, this is my buddy, Cash."

I'm his date? "Hi," I manage to say.

Cash says hello to me and quickly returns to Fish. The two guys chat for a moment about this and that. Until, finally, Cash looks at me and says, "Well, I'll let you two kids get back to your date."

"Bye, brother," Fish says.

And off the dude goes, into the packed crowd.

"He seems nice," I say.

"He's a good guy. Damned fine guitarist. He plays with Danger Doctor Jones."

"I thought so."

"Let's get out of this main area," Fish says. "It's too crowded for me. You want a drink?"

"I hope you know you don't have to hang out with me all night, like you said to Georgina. I know you have lots of friends here. I'm sure you're excited to hang out with them, especially since you just got back from touring."

Fish flashes me a smile I'd caption, *Silly girl.* And warmth pools in my chest. He says, "Alessandra, you're literally the *only* reason I came to this party tonight. If not for you, I'd have gone home after the pool party and crashed there for the rest of the night."

"*Oh.*" I'm too excited to say anything else.

Fish smiles shyly, his cheeks blooming. "So, are you down to get a drink?"

"I'd love it."

We reach one of the bars in a far corner and take our place at the back of the line, just as a group of musicians starts playing on a large nearby stage.

"Sorry it took me so long to get here tonight," Fish shouts above the music. "I would have been here an hour ago, but I was at Aloha and Zander's having drinks, and Aloha demanded we play Cards Against Humanity before heading over."

"I love that game."

"I would have preferred to be here with you. Have you been here long?"

My heart is bursting. Fish isn't being subtle about his attraction to me tonight, is he? And I couldn't be more elated about it. I say, "Georgina and I were the first to 'arrive' tonight, so to speak. But only because we're staying the night in one of Reed's guest rooms upstairs."

"Oh, that's convenient."

"Yeah, with me flying back to Boston on Monday morning, we wanted to squeeze in some one-on-one time before then."

In a heartbeat, Fish's smile fades. In fact, he looks crestfallen. "I didn't realize you're heading back to Boston so soon," he says. "I assumed, with school out for the summer, you were going to be staying in LA until the fall."

My heart squeezes at the look of disappointment on his face. In this moment, I can perfectly imagine what he must have looked like at age five, the day his mother first dropped him off at kindergarten. I shake my head. "I only came home for a week—for Georgina's graduation from UCLA. I'm staying the summer in Boston to work and take a class. I didn't want to lose my apartment near campus for this coming school year, and they wouldn't let my roommate and me sublet."

"Oh."

I suddenly feel the need to babble. "The good news is I'm taking a really cool summer class that's impossible to get during the normal school year. And my boss at the café is letting me work twice as many shifts as usual, so I can put away lots of money for tuition and expenses."

"What's the class you're taking?"

I tell him about it—and how excited I am to get to take it from one of the most popular professors in the school. Someone who's impossible to get during fall and spring semesters. And Fish agrees the class sounds amazing. Something he'd love to take himself, even now.

"It's the best class I've ever taken," I say. "And that's saying a lot. Between taking the class and working extra shifts, I should be pretty busy this summer."

"What's your work?"

"I wait tables at a popular vegan café near campus."

"Are you a vegan?"

"No. Pescatarian. The only 'meat' I'll eat is fish."

Fish smiles, like I've made a dirty joke—and I suddenly realize . . . *I did.* Albeit unwittingly.

"I didn't mean that like it sounded," I quickly add. "I meant I *literally* only eat fish. Lower case 'f'. As in actual food. I wasn't trying to say something titillating or naughty . . ." *Oh, God.* I clamp my mouth shut. *Gah.* I'm terrible at this.

But Fish looks nothing but amused. "I know you weren't trying to be 'titillating.'" He chuckles. "That's what made your comment so damned cute—because you looked so sweet and clueless when you said it."

Even as I'm blushing, I can't help returning his broad smile. Who knew being called clueless could feel like such a supreme compliment?

We reach the front of the bar line and place our orders. A vodka soda for Fish and a water for me.

"You don't drink?" he asks. "Not that it matters."

"Sometimes, I do. I'll drink a White Claw at a party. A

beer, now and again. But I'm a total lightweight. So, I don't want to risk me saying who knows what at a party filled with some of my favorite musicians. This is a work thing for Georgina, and I'm her plus-one, so—"

"Fish!"

It's another friend of his. Another round of hugs ensues. Another round of introductions, during which Fish, yet again, introduces me to his friend as his *date*.

But, quickly—far more quickly than I would have expected—Fish says to his friend, "I'll see you later, dude. Have fun tonight." Which unmistakably signals his buddy to take a hike.

Fish smiles at me. "Hey, how about a game of ping-pong out back? It's too crowded in here for my taste."

"Awesome. Fair warning, though. I suck at ping-pong."

"So do I. We'll fight to the death to see who sucks slightly less." With that, he puts out his hand and I take it. Like it's a totally normal thing to do. Like I'm his date, as he's now declared *twice*. Like he's just some cute guy at a party near campus, and we're not at the home of Reed Rivers, surrounded by literal rock stars. And off we go, hand in hand, toward some large French doors leading onto the patio.

SEVEN

ALESSANDRA

"**W**hy don't I play with my left hand?" Fish suggests, midway through our game, after it's become obvious I'm hopeless.

"I told you I suck at ping-pong. Sorry."

"No, no. This is fun. It's the journey, dude—not the destination. So, let's even the playing field for the journey." He flips his paddle into his left hand and holds up the ball with his right. "It's a brand-new game, okay?"

"This time, don't go easy on me."

"Of course not," he says, like I've offended him. But, come on. He so obviously went easy on me before, and still wiped the floor with me.

Fish holds up his paddle, murmurs "zeroes" under his breath, and ever so gently serves the ball to me like he's playing against a freaking toddler.

I catch his incoming ball in my hand. "Matthew Fishberger. Don't patronize me." I glare at him sternly, making him laugh, and then bounce the ball over the net back to him. "Try again. And this time, do your best."

Fish flashes me an adorable smile. "Sorry, Little Lioness. I'll bring it this time."

"You'd better."

He serves it again. And this time, true to his word, with far more velocity. But since he's using his left hand, I'm able to return his serve pretty well. And, shockingly, the next volley and the next one, too. Ultimately, Fish wins the point. But it doesn't matter. It's now clear, thanks to Fish's voluntarily assumed disadvantage, we're now well-matched opponents.

I hunch over slightly and rock back and forth, like I'm gearing up for a wrestling match, and say, "You're going down, Fish Taco." That's the nickname I heard his friends call him earlier. And, to my surprise, it slipped out of my mouth like I've been saying it my whole life.

Fish doesn't miss a beat. He hunches down, matching my physicality, and says, "Ha! I've never lost a left-handed match before, and I don't intend to do it now, *sucker.*"

I giggle. "Have you ever played a left-handed match before?"

"*No,*" he responds indignantly, as if he's saying, "A thousand times!"

And, of course, we both laugh uproariously.

As our game proceeds, we engage in an uproariously fun back-and-forth fight to the death that confirms we're both literally the same person with the same sense of humor. Also, that Fish isn't *actually* playing his hardest, no matter what he says.

But in the end, our actual ping-pong playing isn't the point. It's our smack talk and joking around, all of which gets sillier and crazier and looser. Until soon, I can't help noticing I already feel as comfortable with Fish as any of my good friends at school, including my roommate, McKenna. Which is a crazy thing, considering how short a time I've known him. Also, considering how attracted I am to him. Oh yeah, and that he's a famous dude in one of my favorite bands. Not to mention, we're playing this game of ping-pong at the freaking mansion of Reed Rivers, while surrounded by some of the most successful and famous musicians and celebrities in the entire world. And yet, here we are. Acting like two nobody kids playing ping-pong on a date in one of our garages.

As our match reaches its climax, a few of Fish's friends—Keane and Maddy, and Aloha and her husband, Zander—wander over to the table to watch. And, suddenly, with my childhood idol, Aloha, watching me, I can't return a ball to save my life.

When Fish's victory is swiftly secured, I lay down my paddle, eager to sprint away from the famous people in our audience.

"Good game," I murmur, fidgeting like crazy. I turn to the waiting foursome and motion to the table. "It's all yours. I hope you have better luck than me."

Fish laughs. "I'll give you a rematch later." He turns to his friends. "Guys, you remember my date, Alessandra, from the pool?"

And there it is again. *My date.* The boy is most definitely making himself clear.

The group makes small talk for a moment as the foursome picks up their paddles. And then, Fish and I, with our hands firmly clasped, stand to the side to watch their game.

Fish leans down to me. "You okay? You seem a little stressed."

"I grew up watching Aloha's show. It's just kind of mind blowing to me to be here with her."

"She's a sweetheart. No need to stress."

"I'm not trying to stress. It just . . . happens. It's outside my control."

He squeezes my hand. "I've got you." His phone buzzes and he pulls it out. "Oh, hey, guys. Dax is summoning us to the basketball court for a game of HORSE. You guys in?"

The foursome playing ping-pong confirms they'll head over to the court after their current game.

Fish looks at me. "Are you down to play a friendly game of HORSE with my friends?"

His friends. I can't believe this is my life. But, somehow, looking into his earnest green eyes, I forget about the collective fame and glamour of his friend group, and manage to reply, "Only if you don't mind me kicking your ass, *sucker.*"

He hoots with laughter. "God, I love it when you talk smack."

I blush. "Just so you know, I can't back it up *at all*. I'm even worse at basketball than ping-pong."

He winks. "Who knows? Maybe today will be your lucky day."

My heart skips a beat. *It already is,* I think.

Hand in hand, we head to the basketball court, where we find not only Dax and Colin and their beautiful dates . . . but the one and only Laila Fitzgerald, too.

I freeze at the edge of the court, incapable of commanding my limbs. "Oh, God," I whisper. "*Fish.*"

"You'll be fine," he says. He grips my hand and pulls me forward. "She's super chill. She's gonna love you."

I stand my ground. Refusing to move. "Please, Fish, don't let me embarrass myself. Be my wingman."

"Dude, I told you. *I've got you.*"

He pulls on me again, and, this time, I let him lead me

onto the court. When we reach the group, he reminds his bandmates of my name, since we met only briefly earlier at the pool. And then, Fish turns to Laila. "This is my date, Alessandra," he says. "She's a student at Berklee in Boston. A kickass singer-songwriter."

"Oh, wow. Impressive." Laila extends her hand. "Hi, Alessandra. Nice to meet you."

My heart is clanging wildly. But I manage to take her hand in perfect mimicry of what a sane human would do. "Hi, Laila. I'm a huge fan."

"Thank you so much."

"I . . . I'm so happy to meet you," I babble. "*I love you.*"

Fuck.

Fish chuckles. "She's a big fan." He slides his hand in mine again. "Don't get a false sense of security around her, though. I promise, this one's about to wipe the floor with you in HORSE."

"Is that so?" Laila says playfully.

"No," I say. "Not at all. I'm terrible at basketball. And I'm sure I'll be especially useless around you."

"Aw, no need to feel nervous around me," Laila says. "We're all friends here."

"Speak for yourself," Fish taunts. "You're *all* my mortal enemies until this game is over." He squeezes my hand again. "Come on. Let's show 'em how it's done, Little Lioness."

As Fish is speaking the foursome from the ping-pong table arrives, and, quickly, our game begins. Unfortunately, for the first few rounds, I'm too starstruck to throw the ball anywhere near the basket. Like, seriously, I'm flailing so badly, you'd think I was making a joke. But, after a bit, I calm down, thanks to Fish's smiles and little whispers, until, soon, I'm able to sink a few shots. At which point, I slowly begin laughing and smack-talking with Fish and his friends, the same way I did when it was just Fish and me at the ping-pong table.

After Keane wins, we start again. But before our second game is over, Dax holds up his phone and says he's been advised it's now his turn to assume the large stage in Reed's living room, along with his choice of musicians.

The three Goats powwow to figure out which friends they want to invite onstage with them as part of their "supergroup." When they're done, our large group meanders toward the house—with Fish and me, yet again, holding hands.

"Don't judge this performance too harshly," Fish says. "This is just gonna be a sloppy jam session with no prior rehearsals."

I look at him and pointedly roll my eyes. "Your sloppiest jam session will undoubtedly be the best thing I've ever witnessed in my life."

We make it into Reed's large living room, and Fish pointedly leads me to the front of the stage. "Watch the show from here, okay? I want to be able to look down while I'm playing and see you."

"I'll be here."

As he strides away he shouts, "See you on the flip side, cutie!"

And I reply with an enthusiastic, "Break a leg, Matthew!" That's what I've yelled at his retreating form in a weird, high-pitched, giddy voice. But what I'm thinking as I watch his cute butt and perfect shaggy hair gliding away is: *Holy shit.*

It's official. Matthew Fishberger is a swoon factory. A smoke show. A stone-cold fox.

Or, I suppose . . . a rock star.

As I watch Fish performing with his band and an array of guest musicians and vocalists—including Aloha and 2Real!—I feel the need to change my panties. Even among the megawatt stars surrounding Fish on that stage, he's a star. Mesmerizing. Drool inducing. Panty melting. Glorious.

I love every subtle nod of Fish's head and shake of his sexy hips as he masterfully plays his instrument. I love the way he sings the most tasteful, perfect harmonies. The way his tattooed forearms flex as he manipulates the strings of his bass. I love the way his lips rub against that mic, making me imagine what it'd be like to kiss him. And last but not least, I'm losing my mind over those beaming, heated smiles he keeps sending me throughout his performance.

I'm standing at the foot of the stage, as directed, immediately underneath Fish, dancing and singing with Georgina and her new gaggle of friends—Kat, Violet, and a few more—and, through it all, I feel like I've been transported to another dimension. A dream world. A perfect fantasy.

Unfortunately, though, all good things must come to an end. Much too soon for my taste, the group ends their short set, making the crowd cheer like crazy and then converge on the band as they descend from the stage. I'm expecting Fish to stop and take a moment to chat with the partygoers who've crowded him and his friends—to revel in the praise he so rightly deserves. But, no. The minute Fish steps off the stage, he bolts from his adoring friends and beelines straight to me.

As he closes in on me, he opens his arms, inviting me to hug him, and, without hesitation, I do. Indeed, I fling myself into his waiting arms like a missile, and he wraps me in a warm embrace. As I crumple into his chest, I babble stupidly about how amazing that performance was. How talented and charismatic he is. How good he smells. I blurt, "This is the best day of my life."

"What?" Fish says, not catching my words in the noisy room.

I look up from his chest and realize what I just said. "I . . . said I'm having a blast."

He smiles. "Me, too."

We stare at each other for a moment, heat coursing between us. Attraction. Electricity. His eyes drift to my lips, and I can't help thinking, "He's finally going to kiss me!" It's what I've been dying for him to do since we walked away from the ping-pong table earlier.

But, no.

Despite the fact that I'm nonverbally *screaming* at him to kiss my lips, Fish leans down and softly kisses my cheek. Which isn't a terrible thing, for sure. In fact, when his lips meet my skin, every nerve ending between my legs jolts with extreme arousal. But I can't deny I want *more.*

Fish presses his lips against my ear, in order to be heard above the dance music that's suddenly piping through over-head speakers, and my body jolts at the intimacy of his voice in my ear. "I can't tell you how amazing it felt to see you down there, dancing and singing at the foot of the stage," he says. "Watching you down there was the most beautiful thing I've ever seen in my life."

My heart lurches and begins pounding, along with the nerve endings between my legs. Swallowing hard, I pull back and stare into his green eyes. *Kiss me,* I think. *Do it now.*

Once again, his eyes drift to my mouth. But he doesn't

kiss me. No. He takes a deep breath and clears his throat. "I could use some fresh air."

I say something incoherent. Whatever I said, it certainly wasn't English, though I don't speak any other languages.

"Cool," Fish says, as if the incoherent sounds that escaped my mouth actually made any kind of sense. He grabs my hand, the same way he's been doing all night. Like it's the most natural thing in the world. And off we go, toward the double doors leading to the patio.

EIGHT

ALESSANDRA

Fish and I find a quiet, dark corner in a remote part of the large patio—a perfect little haven behind a low retaining wall with a lovely view of the twinkling, hilltop view. We step over the wall and get ourselves situated against it, sitting shoulder to shoulder on the ground. As we take in the view, Fish points out various landmarks to me.

I ask, "Where do you live from here?"

"Venice Beach." He points southwest, toward the ocean in the far distance. "I've got a cute little bungalow, right on the sand. My house was the first big thing I bought when the ducats started rolling in. I always wanted a place where I could walk out my door and feel sand under my feet. I like being able to wake up and surf, even before my first cup of coffee."

"I think that's what I'd buy, too, if I were in your shoes. Or, rather, your bare feet. A cute little place on the beach. What more could a person want?"

He smiles, but says nothing, so I part my lips, inviting him to kiss me.

"Are you cold?" he whispers.

I shake my head. *Kiss me.*

"You're shivering," he says.

Because I want you to kiss me so badly, I think. *If I'm shaking, it's only because I'm dying to feel your gorgeous lips on mine.* That's what I'm thinking, of course. But what I say is a calm and measured, "No, I'm fine."

Shit.

As soon as those stupid words escape me, I regret them. What if Fish asked if I'm cold because he was looking for an excuse to put his arms around me? If I'd said yes, I'm freezing, would Fish have cuddled me . . . and then, finally, *kissed* me when I was in his arms?

The faint din of the party drifts through the air. Dance music is blaring. People are laughing and talking energetically in the distance. But Fish and I have grown quiet and still as we stare into each other's eyes.

Fish swirls his thumb across the top of my hand, sending arousal into that pulsing spot between my legs. "So . . ." He takes a deep breath. "Tell me about you, Alessandra."

I want you to kiss me. "What do you want to know?"

"Everything."

I consider my answer. "Well, I'm an only child, as I mentioned." *Besides being a girl who wants to be kissed.* "For about a year, when I was nine and Georgina was eleven, we lived together, as sisters, after my mother married Georgie's father. But our parents divorced after only a year. It was a blip for our parents, but Georgie and I have remained sisters ever since."

"Best of both worlds. You're an only child with a sibling. That's like me, too. I'm an only child with a whole bunch of siblings. Dax and Colin, Dax's brothers and sister. Dax's whole family is my adopted family. I shudder to think who I'd be without them."

"That's like Georgie and me. She saved me."

"From what?"

Damn. Why'd I say that? I didn't mean to steer the conversation that way. All I want to do is kiss this cute boy— not talk about my life's greatest tragedy. *How the hell do I get him to kiss me?*

"If you don't want to talk about it . . ." Fish begins.

"Oh, no. It's fine." I take a deep breath. "My father passed away when I was eight."

He frowns. "I'm sorry."

"Thank you. My mother was too heartbroken after that— and then too distracted by her whirlwind romance with Georgie's dad, Marco—to pay all that much attention to me and my grief. So, for a while there, Georgie became a much-needed lifeline. My guardian angel. My best friend, protector, and cheerleader. She was the one who encouraged me to get into music, actually, to help me deal with my grief. She's the one who listened to my very first songs and told me I was destined for greatness." I chuckle, remembering Georgina's passionate exuberance about me, even back then, before adding, "To this day, Georgina is the first one to hear any new song of mine, no matter what."

"How'd your dad die, if you don't mind me asking?"

"He was killed by a hit-and-run driver while out for a morning jog."

Fish looks deeply pained. "I'm sorry."

I nod. "It's a terrible thing to lose the person who 'gets' you the most. My mom loves me, of course. But she doesn't get me. My dad always did. He was a musician and so sweet and gentle. So accepting and kind." I sigh. "Sometimes, I wish he were here, and then I think how cruel it is that, if he were still here, I wouldn't even know Georgina. And, of course, I can't imagine my life without her. Life is crazy like that sometimes, huh? The way it forces a person to choose between two amazing things as an either-or proposition?"

Fish nods. "I'm really sorry for your loss, Ally. But I'm so glad you have Georgina."

I lean my cheek on Fish's shoulder and inhale his delicious scent. "Who's the person who gets you the most?"

"Dax. He can read me better than anyone. I don't even have to tell him what's on my mind. He just knows."

I feel flushed, all of a sudden, being cuddled up with him like this. Telling him about the deepest parts of myself. I feel tingles and flashes of heat in my body I've never felt with anyone before. But I can't help wondering, despite all the times Fish has called me his date tonight . . . Is he not feeling the same kind of physical attraction I'm feeling to him? I've never been kissed before, so, obviously, I'm not an expert about how first kisses finally happen. But I feel like I've been nonverbally shouting at this boy to lay one on me for at least the past two hours. Am I *that* bad at flirting? Or has Fish decided to friend-zone me, like so many others have done in the past?

I swallow hard, and keep my eyes trained on the view. "Hey, Fish?" I whisper. Suddenly, I feel determined to ask him, once and for all, if he's interested in kissing me tonight. If he says no, I'll be crushed. But, at least, I won't have to wonder. But when I raise my head from his shoulder and look into his green eyes, I immediately lose my nerve.

He raises his eyebrows, waiting to hear whatever's on my mind.

I clear my throat. "Do you . . . have any . . . advice on . . . overcoming stage fright?"

Fish chuckles. "I still don't get how it's possible you get stage fright. Don't you play in front of people at school?"

"Yes, but not nearly as much as I should. Not as much as other people, because I don't put myself out there as much as I should. I've recently decided to perform a lot more, though. This summer, I'm going to audition a ton. I've already signed up for a huge one on Tuesday, right after I get back to Boston."

"What's the audition?"

"Well, I probably shouldn't have called it 'huge,' considering who I'm talking to. It's just a weekly solo gig at a popular coffeehouse near campus. And I won't get the gig. It's highly competitive. But getting the job isn't the point. It's learning how to push myself outside of my comfort zone."

"That's exactly what you should be doing. Putting yourself out there, until your discomfort turns to comfort. And then do it again. That, and have faith in yourself." He rubs his thumb over the back of my hand again. "At every audition, show them the Alessandra I've been hanging out with tonight. If you do that, I promise they won't be able to resist you. Any more than I have."

Oh, for the love of fuck. Really? He hasn't been able to resist me, huh? It sure doesn't feel that way, when my lips are literally aching to be kissed.

But even as I'm thinking my salty thoughts, I suddenly realize Fish is leaning into me. Leaning forward and parting his lips, like he's going to kiss me!

Yes!

He's finally doing it!

I lean in to meet him halfway, my heart exploding with

excitement . . . But the instant before our mouths actually meet, jarring noises immediately behind us, on the other side of the low retaining wall—footfalls and male voices, right above our heads!—invade our quiet bubble.

We both jerk back.

And the moment is lost.

Fish exhales and looks immediately above us. "Well, hello there, fellas," he says.

I look up . . . and then lean back against the wall and cover my face with my hands. Of all people, it's Reed Rivers, along with Keane and Zander, standing above us. Fucking hell!

And, just like that, the kiss I've been waiting for all night —no, for my entire fucking life!—slips from my lips' proverbial pucker.

NINE

FISH

"Well, hello there, fellas," I say on an exhale. And at the sound of my voice below them in the dirt, Reed, Zander, and Keane simultaneously look down and grimace.

"Sorry, brother," Zander says in his low baritone. "Carry on. We came out here to smoke a joint, but we can certainly find another spot."

Fuck.

I want to reply, "Please do." More than I want to breathe. But I also know this could be a hugely serendipitous moment for Alessandra. She's got dreams of making it in music, after all, and Reed is one of a handful of people in the world who could instantly make her dreams a reality. Maybe now that Alessandra has loosened up so much with me, she'll be able to engage Reed in substantive conversation, unlike what happened earlier today at the pool.

"No need to find another spot to smoke," I say, rising to standing. I pull Alessandra up with me and say, "Did everybody meet Alessandra?" But, of course, I'm looking straight at Reed.

Everyone says yes, they've met her, while Keane lights the joint. After the three men take hits off the thing, Reed hands the joint to me, so I suck on it and offer it to Alessandra. I'm not expecting her to take it, considering she's been drinking water all night. But you never know. Reed's here, getting stoned. I certainly wouldn't blame her if she decided to bro-down with him. Plus, not offering it to her, when everyone else is partaking, would be downright rude.

Not surprisingly, though, Alessandra declines my offer. And I must admit, I'm kind of impressed. I can't imagine too many aspiring singer-songwriters would turn down the chance to get stoned with Reed Rivers. The Man with the Midas Touch. To kiss his golden ass, in any way possible. But not Alessandra Tennison, apparently. From what I've seen of her, I don't think she's even capable of kissing ass, even when doing it would be in her best interests. Yes, she's effusive with her praise, at times. But even then, there's never a doubt she's being sincere.

"Give her share to Reed," Keane says. "Murder can really fuck up a guy's life."

"Not if they don't catch ya," Reed replies with a wink.

I don't know what any of that means. But I don't care. All I care about is getting Reed to focus his full attention on Alessandra, so she can convince him to listen to some of her original music. Granted, I haven't heard any of Alessandra's music myself. So, there's no guarantee she's as good as I'm guessing. But my gut tells me she's a little diamond in the rough. A little lioness. How could she not be, when she's so adorable? Even her speaking voice is mesmerizing to me.

Kind of soft and breathy and soothing. So I've got to figure her singing voice is pretty incredible, too.

"If you're worried about breaking the law, don't be," Reed says to Alessandra. And it's impossible to miss his snark. His dismissal of her. "Weed," he clarifies when she looks at him blankly. "It's legal in California."

Dick, I think. *What are you—the bully in an after-school special?*

"Oh," Alessandra says meekly. "But only if you're twenty-one, right? I'm nineteen."

Reed chuckles, along with Zander and Keane—all of them apparently thinking Alessandra is kidding. But I know her well enough now to know she's being serious. Every bit as much as she was when she told me the only "meat" she "eats" is *fish.* I swear, if any of the groupies I've met on tour had made that same comment, I'd have known, without a doubt, they were lowkey offering me a blowjob. But when Alessandra said it with wide, innocent eyes, her total lack of awareness of the double entendre was undeniable. Not to mention, adorable.

"You want another bottle of water?" I ask Alessandra, simply because she looks on the verge of freaking out. "Something to eat?"

"Uh, yeah, I could use a water," she says, her blue eyes bugging out. "I'll come with you."

Fuck. Doesn't Alessandra understand the potential opportunity here? She can't come with me for water! She needs to stay here and charm Reed! But before I can reply, Reed swoops in and saves the day.

"Why don't you stay here and chat with me for a minute, Alessandra?" Reed says. "Just for a couple minutes."

"Uh-oh," Keane says. "What'd you do to get called to the

principal's office, Ally Cat? You done fucked up, sis. *Godspeed.*"

"She didn't fuck up anything," Reed says soothingly, smiling at Alessandra. "I just want to chat with her for a minute about music. Georgina mentioned you're studying music at Berklee. I know a lot of people who graduated from there. It's a great music school." He looks at Keane, Zander, and me. "Will you boys excuse us for a few minutes?" He returns to Alessandra. "That is, if you've got a couple minutes to spare?"

Alessandra looks at me and I nod enthusiastically. This is the best-case scenario, after all. A perfect chance for her to dazzle Reed with her sweet sincerity—hopefully, enough to persuade him to check out her music.

"I'll come back in a bit," I say excitedly. "If you're not here when I get back for some reason, I'll find you." With that, I flash Alessandra a reassuring smile and head toward the house with Keane and Zander.

"Cockblockers," I spit out when we're out of earshot of Reed and Alessandra.

Zander chuckles. "I figured we interrupted something good."

"I was just about to *finally* kiss her when you three dumb-asses barged in on us."

"You were 'just about' to '*finally*' kiss her?" Keane booms. "You haven't *kissed* that girl yet?"

I look behind us, even though I know Reed and Alessandra couldn't possibly hear Keane's outburst. "No, I've been taking it slow. Waiting for the perfect moment. Which, by the way, *finally* came right before you three fuckers walked up and ruined everything."

"Oh, no," Zander says. "You can't blame us for your total

lack of game, Fish Head. That girl has been nonverbally begging you to kiss her all night."

"Amen," Keane says. "From all the flirting I've seen going on between you two, I would have thought you'd have kissed her lips off by now."

My stomach clenches. Damn. They're both right. This whole time, I thought I was being a gentleman. I thought I was waiting for the right moment. But, now, I'm thinking I done fucked up. "She said she's never had a boyfriend before," I say defensively. "Not even a casual one. I wanted to take it slow and do it right."

"You did it so 'right,' you did it *dead wrong*, son," Keane declares.

I speak on an exhale, "The truth is, she's so damned pretty and awesome, it's taken me all night to muster my courage to finally make my move."

"Your *courage?*" Keane and Zander yell at the same time, both of them coming to a stop outside a pair of French doors.

I stop with my friends and hang my head in shame. "I know. I'm so bad at this."

"News flash, Matthew!" Keane booms. He raps on my head, like he's knocking on a door. "You're a fucking *rock star* now, you dumbshit! The days of you needing to 'muster your courage' are over! Especially with a woman who's been sending you *obvious* green-light signals all night long!"

I grunt in frustration and embarrassment, and then run my hand through my hair. "I don't feel like a 'rock star' with Alessandra. I just feel like *me*. And the real me—Matthew Fishberger—has *zero* game!"

"No shit!" they both shout at the same time.

Zander looks at Keane. "I think our Fish Taco has body- and coolness-factor-dysmorphia, Peenie Weenie."

"It sure seems like it." Keane looks at me. "Don't you realize you're not the same dude you were back in high school? The past couple years, especially, you've really come into your own."

"It's the classic 'glow-up,'" Zander declares.

"Indeed. Even my mom has noticed."

"*What?*" I shout, astonished.

"Yup," Keane says. "Momma Lou said so last year at your show in Seattle. She said 'Fish is so handsome these days, isn't he?'" Laughing, he ruffles my hair. "Listen, baby doll. Alessandra's *not* going to reject you. Fuck all those girls who used to be mean to you, back in the day. Every one of them would give their right ovary to get with you now."

"But I don't want someone who only wants me *now*! That's the point."

Zander pats my shoulder. "Aw, buck up, little rock star. The night isn't over. You've still got plenty of time to swoop in and give Alessandra the kiss of a lifetime. Pull yourself together and give that girl an amazing memory, Fish Filet."

I take a deep breath and nod. "Thanks. I needed that." I take another breath. "I'll give Alessandra a few more minutes to charm the hell out of Reed, and then, I'll pull her into another quiet corner and give her the kiss of a lifetime."

"Attaboy," Zander says.

"Make her swoon with those sexy fish lips of yours, baby!" Keane shouts, making all of us laugh.

We head into the house and discover Dax, Violet, Maddy, and Aloha near one of the bars. So, of course, Keane and Zander launch into telling everyone the story of how they just intruded upon Alessandra and me. Which, in the end, only results in *me* being universally chastised for dragging my feet, rather than Keane and Zander being called out for cock-blocking me.

"Yeah, yeah," I say. "Bonnie and Clyde already ripped me a new one for my total lack of game. No need to pile on." I flap my lips together. "Maybe, in addition to everything else, I've been holding back because I'm subconsciously protecting my heart from going all in. Alessandra is heading back to Boston on Monday. So, really, what would be the point of me kissing her tonight, and then falling hard? I'll never see her again after tonight."

Violet rolls her eyes. "If you've only got one night with her, then isn't that all the more reason to make it a memorable one?"

"Plus, you never know," Maddy says. "A lot can happen on video chat."

Keane hands me a double tequila shot, and I throw it back.

"You know what?" I say. "You're right. I'm gonna go back out there and give that girl a night to remember . . ." I look at my watch. "In approximately three minutes. I want to give her enough time to charm Reed. Hopefully, he's listening to one of her songs, even as we speak."

"Are her songs any good?" Aloha asks.

"I haven't heard any of them yet. But Berklee doesn't let in hacks. If her music reflects half the sweetness and under-stated star quality I've seen from her tonight, then it's pure gold."

Maddy pulls out her phone. "Let's give her a listen. What's her last name?"

"Tennison."

Maddy taps on her phone for a brief moment. "Found her on Instagram. She's got several videos where she's holding a guitar." She looks at the group. "Does anyone have some earbuds?"

Dax shoves a pair at me. And, two seconds later, I'm listening to the musical stylings of one Alessandra Tennison. Not surprisingly, she's every bit as talented as I knew she'd be.

"Her voice is *exactly* how I imagined it'd be—only better," I gush. "Sweet and breathy with kind of jazzy inflections. *Wow.*" I pause to listen again, butterflies ravaging my belly at the sound of her loveliness. "She sounds a lot like Laila, only sweeter. Without the edge. She's *really* good, guys."

I pass the phone and earbuds to Dax, who listens and passes them along. Until, finally, our entire group has listened and agreed that Alessandra is fantastically talented and uniquely adorable.

"I knew she'd be crazy talented," I say excitedly. "She said she struggles with stage fright, so, I figured, if Berklee let her in with that going against her, she must have blown them away in terms of raw talent."

"Yup," Dax agrees. "A person can improve their performance skills, but you can't teach raw talent."

"You either have it, or you don't," Aloha agrees.

I nod. "And Alessandra's got it in spades." My heart racing, I look at my watch and jolt with excitement when I realize enough time has passed. "Okay, guys. I'm going back in. Wish me luck."

"Wait!" Keane says.

He hands me another double shot, which I throw back with gusto.

"Thanks, man."

"Go get your girl," Keane says, patting my back like a coach sending in his star quarterback.

"Roger," I say.

"Rabbit," Keane replies.

And then, as my friends cheer me on, I grab two bottles of water and lope toward the double doors, determined to sweep the talented and adorable Alessandra Tennison off her gorgeous feet.

TEN

FISH

As I approach the dark corner where I left Alessandra with Reed, I find the big boss sitting alone on a bench with Alessandra nowhere to be found.

"Where's Alessandra?" I ask, coming to a stop in front of Reed. "Did she go inside?"

Reed looks down at an empty tumbler in his hand. "Yeah, I think so. I'm not sure."

I furrow my brow. "She didn't say where she was going?"

"No. But I can tell you where she hopes *I'm* going. To hell."

Anticipatory dread streaks through me. "What happened? What does that mean?"

Reed looks at me flatly. "It means I said something that upset her, apparently. She ran off, on the verge of tears."

My heart drops into my toes. How could I have been so stupid to have left Alessandra alone with Reed, when I knew full well about his total lack of a filter? I know Reed has said some seriously thoughtless and fucked-up shit to *me* over the years, but I figured his relationship with Georgina would prevent him from doing the same to Alessandra. Not to mention, Alessandra is *literally* the sweetest person who ever lived!

"What'd you say to her?" I choke out.

Reed shrugs. "I told her the truth, without sugarcoating it. I told her I listened to her demo and, basically, that she's got to get past the *bullshit* if she wants any shot—"

"Goddammit, Reed!" I shout, rage and regret exploding inside me. "Why are you always such a *prick*, man?"

Reed leans back into the bench and sighs. And, for some reason, the smug look on his face sets me off even more. Why can't this asshole ever show the slightest bit of empathy? Why can't he realize it's not always about *him* and his big swinging dick?

I shout, "Before you came out here, Alessandra and I were having the most amazing conversation! She was telling me how she got into music after her dad died when she was a kid. She was telling me about her stage fright. Asking me for tricks to overcome it. And then you had to come out here and tell her she *sucks*, and her music is *bullshit*? Goddammit, Reed! Fuck you, you fucking prick."

Reed's eyebrows shoot up in surprise. But he says nothing. Which is fine with me, because I don't want to hear a word out of his stupid fucking mouth, anyway.

With an angry wave of my hand, I turn on my heel and sprint away, determined to find Alessandra and make things right with her. To let her know whatever Reed said to her was stupid and wrong. That he's not God, after all, although he obviously thinks he is. And, most of all, to let her know I've blown it tonight—that I think she's beautiful and talented and the coolest girl I've ever met—and that I've wanted to kiss her for hours now.

Inside the house, I look high and low for Alessandra, but she's nowhere to be found. As I'm standing in a corner, surveying the packed room, Aloha approaches, riding piggy-back on her former bodyguard, Barry.

"What are you doing here all by yourself?" Aloha says. "Aren't you supposed to be outside, giving Alessandra the 'kiss of a lifetime'?"

I'm physically shaking. "Have you seen her?"

"Who? Alessandra?"

"Yes! *Obviously.* Apparently, she ran inside the house after talking to Reed."

"I haven't seen her."

Aloha says something to me as I run away, but I don't hear it. I do another lap of the party. And, again, Alessandra is nowhere to be found. But when I run into Kat and Josh partying with their best friends, Henn and Hannah, I get lucky. Kat says, yes, she recently noticed Alessandra racing up Reed's staircase, looking upset. So, off I go.

My pulse pounding, I make my way through the dense crowd to Reed's staircase and ascend the steps as fast as my fish-legs will carry me. At the top, I turn left and barrel down the hallway, simply because I had to make a random choice between left and right. But, quickly, when I hear the faint sound of female crying coming from behind a closed door, it's clear I chose the correct direction to run.

I stop in front of the closed door and rap my knuckles on it. "Alessandra? Is that you in there?" There's no reply, but the crying stops. I rap again. "It's Fish, sweetheart. Is that you in there?"

"It's me," her tiny voice says from inside the room.

"Can I come in?"

There's a pause. A sniffle. And then, "I'm a snotty mess. Could I have a few minutes to pull myself together? I texted Georgina, but she hasn't replied yet."

I press my palms on the wooden door, feeling like my heart is physically ripping in two. "Do you want me to try to find Georgina and tell her to come?"

"Yes, please. Thank you."

"You bet, sweetheart. I'm going now."

"Thank you, Fish. Matthew. I'm sorry."

"Don't apologize. Just, please, don't listen to Reed. He's a prick."

"Could you find Georgie for me?" she squeaks out.

"Yeah. I'm going now."

My heart crashing, I race downstairs and do a lap of the packed party, frantically looking for Georgina, chastising myself all the while for leaving Alessandra alone with a megalomaniac who thinks he's an expert on anything and everything having to do with music. Well, Reed was wrong about me, wasn't he? He told me to dip out of my own fucking band! And look at me now!

Finally, after what feels like forever, I notice an angry-looking Georgina bursting through a set of distant French doors, followed closely by a desperate-looking Reed. Oh, man. Reed looks absolutely wrecked. *Vulnerable*, I'd even say. Which is a new look for him. So much so, I barely recognize him. What the hell just happened between him and Georgina? Did Georgina get Alessandra's text and instantly break up with Reed on the spot? It sure looks that way. Now, that's a fucking badass!

I bound through the crowded party toward Georgina,

where she's now breathlessly talking to Kat and Kat's friend, Hannah.

"Alessandra needs you," I announce, even before I've come to a full stop before Georgina. As I say the words, I glare at Reed, letting him know whatever tongue-lashing Georgina has given him was rightly deserved. That, if I were forty pounds heavier, I'd beat his ass for shattering Alessandra's hopes and dreams. I look at Georgina again. "Reed told Alessandra she sucks, and that her music is bullshit, so she ran upstairs to your room to cry." I'm sure she already knows all that, but I want to be sure she's not buying whatever bullshit version of events Reed has been trying to sell her.

"That's not how it went down at all!" Reed shouts, throwing up his arms.

But I ignore him. "I tried to comfort her, but she said she preferred being alone, until you could come."

"I was trying to *help* Alessandra!" Reed shouts, his dark eyes filled with panic. "I was *encouraging* her." He looks pleadingly at Georgina, but she doesn't give him a moment's consideration. Instead, she wordlessly turns and marches toward the staircase, prompting Reed to follow her, shouting her name as he goes.

"Holy crap," Kat murmurs, looking at Georgina's and Reed's departing frames. "What the hell did he do?"

I run my hand through my hair. "He listened to Alessandra's demo and told her she sucks. I found Alessandra upstairs, bawling her eyes out in a guest room. She begged me to find Georgina." I scoff. "Arrogant prick."

"But why was *Georgina* crying, then?" Kat replies. "Didn't you see her face? She's obviously been crying —*hard*."

"Yeah," Hannah, Kat's friend, says. "Would Georgina sob because Reed was a bit harsh about her stepsister's demo?"

"Absolutely," I reply. "Georgie and Alessandra are really close, and he steamrolled her confidence. Alessandra struggles with stage fright and anxiety, guys. Reed's assholery was the last thing she needed." I take a deep breath, trying to get a grip on my racing thoughts. "Honestly, I don't know exactly what's going on. All I know is Reed was a dick to Alessandra, and when I tried to comfort her, she didn't want me. She only wanted her sister."

"Aw, Fish," Kat says, placing her hand on my forearm. "Don't feel bad about that. I'm sure, when she calms down, she'll find you, and you can comfort her then."

I scrub my stubble with my palm. "You don't understand, Kat. Alessandra is leaving for Boston on Monday morning. If this is going to be our only night together, I wanted to make it special. Memorable."

"It will be," Kat says. "The memories have just been delayed slightly. That's all." But when she sees the look of despair on my face, she juts her lower lip with sympathy. "Aw, poor little Fish Taco. You really like her, huh?"

I swallow hard. "It doesn't matter. Realistically, nothing serious could come out of tonight, anyway. Not with my crazy schedule and her being a full-time student in Boston for the next two years." I let out a long, audible sigh. "Fuck it, shit happens. The thing I hate most is knowing Reed smashed her confidence. God, I hate him. He's such a prick."

Kat and Hannah exchange a look, clearly telegraphing their unease. Their husbands are Reed's two best friends, after all. So, obviously, these women have spent quite a bit of time with Reed, as his friend, unlike me. So, they've probably seen a much softer side to the guy than me. But fuck it. And fuck him. I'm only speaking the truth, as I know it. And what I know, for a fact, is that Reed Rivers can be a first-class *prick*.

"Whatever stupid things Reed might have said tonight," Hannah says, "I'm sure he meant well, somewhere in there. He always does."

"Absolutely," Kat says.

I open my mouth to say who-knows-what, but before I've said a word, a new supergroup kicks off loudly onstage, filling the expansive room with blaring music.

Kat and Hannah, along with everyone else at the party, immediately turn toward the source of the music and start rocking out with the band. And just like that, our conversation about Reed is over. Which is fine by me.

I work my way through the packed crowd, to a relatively quiet corner, where I can stalk the base of the staircase to await Reed's appearance. The minute that prick comes down those steps, I'm going to drag him outside and make him listen to the song I heard on Alessandra's Instagram. I don't know what song he heard before calling Alessandra's music "bullshit." But I can't imagine he heard the same song I did. Because that song was brilliant! Alessandra sounded *exactly* like Laila Fitzgerald on the track, for fuck's sake! And Laila is one of the most talented and successful singers in the world— one of Reed's top-selling artists! What the fuck is wrong with Reed, that he can't appreciate that amazing similarity?

Out of nowhere, Georgina appears, yanking me from my thoughts. She's barreling down the staircase, dragging a blue rolling suitcase behind her. And, unfortunately, Alessandra is trailing right behind her, with a backpack strapped to her back and a cardboard box in her arms. Clearly, Alessandra and

Georgina are headed out, for good. No longer staying the night in Reed's guest room upstairs. Which is probably why Reed himself is trailing behind the women, looking distraught.

As I behold Alessandra, every atom in my body ignites with the urge to race to her, pull her aside, and tell her everything I've been thinking all night. Besides telling her she's beautiful and amazing, I want to say, "Maybe tonight doesn't have to be the end for us!" I mean, obviously, I have no idea how to do something like that. But I'm thinking maybe we could, at least, keep in touch.

But despite the chaos swirling inside me, I don't move a muscle—and, this time, not because I'm a loser with no game. But because, clearly, this is a massively emotional moment for Georgina and Reed. A moment of passion and turmoil that shouldn't be intruded upon by an outsider. I don't give a fuck about Reed's privacy in this moment, obviously. He can go to hell, as far as I'm concerned. But I do care about Georgina, and preserving her privacy, no matter how much I'm aching to say what needs to be said to Alessandra.

Shifting my weight and breathing hard, my heart pounding like crazy in my ears, I watch Georgina, Alessandra, and Reed march along the back wall of the party, unbeknownst to the party guests, all of whom are now turned toward the stage on the opposite wall. I watch Georgina swing open Reed's large, wooden front door and fling herself through the opening like a cannonball, angrily dragging her rolling suitcase behind her.

I watch Alessandra reach the open doorway . . . and then stop and turn around. Her eyes wide, she scans the party, ever so briefly, and I wave my arm above my head in reply, hoping to attract her attention. I shout her name, loudly. But the band is even louder, and my location in the room too obscure, for Alessandra to notice me.

After a brief moment, as Reed approaches her on a bullet train, Alessandra turns and races through the door to avoid a collision. And that's it. She's gone. Heading to wherever with Georgie tonight, and to Boston on Monday morning—which is now only about thirty hours away.

For a long moment, I stare at the closed door, irrationally hoping Alessandra will reappear. I imagine her eyes finding mine this time. I imagine her dropping that box she was carrying and rushing to me, while I rush to her. I imagine us crashing into each other in the middle of the crowded room . . . and kissing. *Finally.* And, of course, in this scenario, our kiss is perfect. Deep. Passionate. *Magic.*

Damn! Why didn't I kiss Alessandra when I had the chance? Why did I second-guess myself, over and over again? When I got offstage tonight I had the impulse to kiss her right then! So, why did I second-guess it? Why did I think it would be better to take her outside to kiss her in private, without so many people around? *Why, why, why?*

I let out a loud, tortured scream into the packed room that's instantly swallowed by the blaring music and dancing bodies around me, and then drag my sorry ass toward one of the bars in a far corner.

I know *why, why, why* I fucked up tonight. Because Alessandra was the first girl I've genuinely liked in a *really* long time. And the thought of moving too fast and making things awkward, or less than perfect, or, worse, getting flat-out rejected, the same way all those girls used to reject me in high school, felt like too big a risk to take.

I reach the bar and order a double shot of tequila, which I quickly throw back.

Well, lesson learned, eh? It's now blatantly obvious to me it's far better to take your shot with your dream girl and mess it up, or get stiff-armed, than to not take your shot, at all . . . and then have to watch her walk away, knowing you're going to be asking yourself "What if?" forevermore.

ELEVEN
ALESSANDRA

Strumming my guitar, I sing the second verse of the song I've been writing for the past several hours, and then scratch and scribble on my notepad. I'm sitting on my bed at my mom's apartment, in the exact spot I've been in since I got home from Georgina's dad's condo this morning. And I must say, this new song of mine, "Blindsided," about last night's horrible run-in with Reed, is the best song I've ever written.

To say I was blindsided by Reed's unexpected speech on that bench last night is an understatement. But, still, I wish so badly I'd pulled myself together and actually reacted in some way. You know, actually said something to him in reply. Anything at all, rather than merely sitting there, like a deer in headlights, and then running away so he wouldn't see me cry.

"I've listened to your demo, Alessandra," Reed told me, even though Georgina had *sworn* Reed hadn't listened. "And you've got a lot of work to do." As I sat there in shock, Reed told me I'm a "Laila Fitzgerald knockoff." He said I've been "hiding behind" my music, rather than "revealing myself" through it. He said some other stuff, too. Maybe even some encouraging stuff. I don't know. My brain is currently fixated on a few specific things. "Laila knockoff" being chief among them. When Reed said those words, I'm surprised I didn't burst into tears right then. I guess I was just in too much shock.

But then, as Georgina and I sat in the back seat of that Uber last night, heading to Georgina's dad's place in the Valley, the shock I'd felt on that bench morphed into acute mortification. Suddenly, I felt embarrassed about every song I've ever written. Every song I've stupidly posted on Instagram because I thought they were pretty damned good. So, I quickly deleted all of them from my account. Gone, gone, gone! Never to be heard by anyone again.

At Georgina's dad's place, I crawled into bed with Georgie and hugged her to me. As she cried about her breakup with Reed, I bawled, too. By then, not so much about what Reed had said, but my *reaction* to it. At that point, I realized I'd missed a huge opportunity to impress Reed. To show him that I'm open to criticism and have a genuine willingness to learn.

In that moment in the dark with Georgina, my brain started remembering *everything* Reed had said to me. The bad *and* the good. And I realized he'd been right about all of it. I realized he'd only been trying to help me. And that, if only I'd had a stronger backbone—a thicker skin—I might have received his advice without shutting down. I might have asked him questions. Learned from him. I might have seized a golden opportunity that had nothing to do with getting signed to his stupid label. Regardless of my big dreams for the future, I might have used the opportunity to get *better* in the present. Which, in the end, is all I really want to do.

And, of course, I'd be remiss if I didn't admit I was also crying last night about the way things ended with Fish. I looked for him at the last minute, just before following Georgie out the door, but I couldn't find him. I realize I'm leaving for Boston tomorrow morning, so nothing could have come of our little one-night "romance," regardless. But not getting to at least say goodbye to him . . . not getting to hug him and tell him how much the night had meant to me . . . And, of course, not getting to share my very first kiss with *him* of all people . . . Sigh. Talk about a tragedy. But even more than wanting Fish to be my first kiss, I simply wanted to thank him for being so sweet to me. So attentive and kind. For giving me *literally* the best night of my life.

And then, against all odds, this morning happened. I opened my eyes next to Georgie, who was still fast asleep, and I realized I'd been dreaming a *song*. A crystal clear one that was still there!

Immediately, I grabbed my phone and sang everything from my dream into my audio recorder. Some lyrics. A catchy melody! And when I got to my mom's place this morning, I raced into my bedroom, sat on my bed with my guitar, and got to work. And that's what I've been doing ever since.

There's a knock on my door. "Ally?" Mom pokes her head into my bedroom. "Are you still alive in here?"

"Just finishing that same song."

She clucks her tongue. "You've been working on that for a while." She leans against the doorjamb. "Come on, sweetie. Put your guitar down. It's your last night at home. You can write a song any time. But you can't spend quality time with your mother on your last night home until Thanksgiving."

She's wrong. I can't write a song like *this* any time. In fact, I've got a hunch this song is a once-in-a-lifetime sort of thing. But I've long since accepted my mother doesn't fully understand my creative process. Plus, she's right that I'm leaving tomorrow and not coming back until Thanksgiving. And I did spend last night with Georgie, so I should probably focus on her tonight.

"Okay, let's have ourselves a 'date' night," I say, and my mother cheers. "Just give me an hour to wrap up, and then I *promise* you'll have my undivided attention for the rest of the night."

Mom squeals and claps, making me laugh. "I'll make dinner now! You want to help me design some wedding arrangements after dinner?"

"I'd love it!"

Mom's a florist, and our favorite thing to do together has always been designing floral arrangements for Mom's wedding clients. I love helping Mom pick just the right blooms and colors to tell each couple's love story.

When Mom closes my door, I return to my guitar. But after only a few minutes of work, my phone buzzes with a notification. Apparently, I've got a direct message on Instagram from someone named "Channing_Tate-Yumm." Which, of course, I recognize as a reference to one of my all-time favorite movies—the apocalyptic stoner comedy, *This Is the End.*

The message reads:

Hey, cutie! It's Fish from my finsta. Just wanted to say hi and see if you're feeling better today. If you want me to beat up Reed for ya, lemme know. He's got muscles. But I'm quick like a bunny. A bunny called Fish. I bet I could take him.

I laugh out loud with glee. I never thought I'd hear from Fish again! Not after the way I melted down in front of him!

Well, in front of him from behind a closed door. Not to mention, we didn't even exchange numbers last night and I wasn't sure how to go about reaching a rock star like him. Not that I'd have contacted him, anyway, even if I'd figured out how to do it. And, now, he's found *me*? Breathing hard, I tap out my reply:

Me: Thanks so much for checking in. I'm good today. I wanted to say goodbye to you last night, but Georgina had to leave suddenly.

Fish: I saw you leave and totally understood. Sisters before misters! I just want you to know that, whatever Reed said to you, he was dead wrong. I listened to a song of yours on IG last night and it was amazing.

Shit. Fish listened to a song of mine before I'd thought to scrub my account? I'm mortified.

Me: Please don't judge me by what you heard. That's the same stuff Reed said wasn't good enough. And he was right.

Fish: No, he wasn't! Reed's word isn't gospel. Before he signed my band, he told me the best thing I could do was to bow out of 22 Goats and let Dax become a solo artist. Was he right about that?

Me: He did not say that!

Fish: He did. I didn't tell Dax about it at the time. But I told Colin and he goes, "Prove him wrong!" So that's what I did. And that's what you'll do, too, Little Lioness. Prove. Him. WRONG.

I feel electrified. Like everything I've been feeling all day, writing this new song, is dovetailing with what Fish is telling me. Like Fish, contacting me now, is a sign from the universe that I'm on the right track.

Me: Don't worry about me. I know I seemed like a total wreck last night, but this morning I've been writing the best song, ever. I'm just putting the finishing touches on it now. From the ashes rises the phoenix, right?

Fish: YASSSS! Record the song and send it to me RIGHT NOWWWWW!

Me: Uh . . . no.

Fish: YES!

Me: No. I always play every new song for Georgina first, remember?

Fish: Rules are made to be broken!

Me: In concept, yes. But you intimidate the hell out of me! You're the guy who wrote "Delightful Damage"!

Fish: All the more reason to send it to me. I already loved what I heard on your IG, didn't I? So, I'll love this, too!

Hmm. He's got a point. And I admit I'd *love* to get his feedback on the song . . .

Me: I need a few days to polish it up, and then, MAYBE, I'll gather the courage to send it to the genius who wrote one of my all-time favorite songs.

Fish: You've got a couple days. And then I'm going to start nagging you mercilessly.

I smile broadly to myself. He's assuming we're going to keep in touch after this conversation?

Me: Deal. But only if you sing me "Delightful Damage."

Fish: Uhhhh. The thing is . . . I've never sung that song for anyone but Dax and Colin.

Me: Cool. I can't wait to be your first.

I wait. And wait. And, finally, Fish sends me a thumbs-up emoji, followed by this message:

Fish: So, heeeyyyyy, girl. Before you bounce to Boston tomorrow, you want to come to my place for dinner tonight?

No bull will be on the menu. Only fish. (Note the lowercase spelling.)

"Oh my God!" I whisper-shout to the ceiling of my bedroom. I can't believe I just got asked out on a date by someone I actually *like* for the first time in my life—*and I have to turn him down.*

Me: Thanks SO MUCH for the invitation. I'd loooooove to come to dinner tonight. But, unfortunately, I promised my mom I'd hang out with her on my last night here, since I'm not coming back until Thanksgiving.

As I press send, I literally whimper with distress, even though a piece of my brain knows it's probably for the best. If I were to go to Fish's place tonight, and *finally* kiss him, I'd surely fall *hard* for him. Even harder than I already have. And what good would that do me, with me in Boston and Fish traipsing around the world, playing arenas?

Fish: No worries. Family first. Have a good time with yo momma. Hopefully, I'll get to make you that fish dinner when you're back in LA for Thanksgiving. Although I usually go to Seattle for T-Day, so . . .

He adds a frownie-face to the end of his message—which accurately reflects my actual facial expression in this moment. The good news, though? It seems Fish is willing to stay in touch with me for months!

Me: If you're in LA when I'm back, then I'd LOVE to see you again. Even if it's only five minutes! And, of course, if you're ever in Boston, or anywhere on the East Coast, let me know and I'll come see you, if that'd be okay.

Fish: I'd LOVE it! Hey, would you want to FaceTime with me tonight after you're done hanging out with your mom? I'm a night owl, so you could call me any time. I'd love to say a proper goodbye to you.

Me: YES!

He sends me a dancing-man emoji with his phone number, so I reply with a dancing-woman emoji and my number, along with the following message:

Me: If you're a night owl, maybe we could watch This Is the End together on Zoom tonight? It's one of my all-time favorites.

Fish: OMFG! Calling you now.

Even as I'm reading his message, my phone rings with an incoming call from an unknown number—and when I quickly compare the number to the one Fish just gave me, it's a match.

"Alessandra's Pizzeria," I say in greeting.

"Hello, yes, I'll take twenty large cheese pizzas. Hold the cheese. Hold the sauce. Extra crust."

I laugh. "So, you want a Frisbee, then?"

"No, I want twenty."

We both laugh.

"I know you have to go, but I had to call real quick," Fish says. "I had to tell you I love *This Is the End* more than I love taking air into my lungs!"

I giggle. "Me, too!"

"Dude! That movie, more than any other, is a litmus test for me. If people hate that one, then I hate *them*."

"Amen. My other litmus test movie is *The Incredible Burt Wonderstone*."

"I love that one, too!"

"Oh, thank God. What a pity if I had to hate you. Isn't that movie the best?"

"The best. Second only to *This Is the End*."

And we're off. Talking about our favorite scenes from both movies in a rapid-fire back and forth that makes me feel like we're right back at the party last night. Like our hands are clasped and all's right with the world.

But, crap, mid-sentence about Rihanna slapping the shit out of Michael Cera in *This Is the End*, I'm interrupted by a knock on my door.

"Ally?" Mom says. She pokes her head into my room. "Are you coming? Dinner is ready."

I point at the phone against my ear and raise my index finger, and, thankfully, she quietly dips out of the room.

"That was my mom," I say as the door closes. "I promised her we'd have dinner and design floral arrangements tonight."

"Oh, yeah. You said your mom's a florist."

"I'm surprised you remember that."

"I remember everything you said."

My heart skips a beat. "One of our favorite things to do together has always been designing flowers for her wedding clients."

"That sounds fun."

"It is. Besides the obvious considerations—color and shape and scent, et cetera—there's a whole language of flowers, dating back to Victorian times, that's super fun to decode and send secret messages with."

"Huh?"

"Yeah. Back when people couldn't say what was on their minds, they'd send flowers to say it for them."

"Give me an example."

"Well, a really obvious one is roses. If you give someone a bouquet of *yellow* roses, for instance, that means friendship. But if you send *red* ones, you're making it clear you're interested in a red-hot romance."

"Hubba-hubba."

I laugh. "There are lots more examples than that, but that's a little taste."

"Very cool. Huh. You learn something new every day."

"When I was a kid, I was obsessed with flowers and their meanings. I used to pretend I was a lady in Victorian times, fending off my suitors, all of whom were romancing me with an endless barrage of flower bouquets."

He chuckles. "What are your favorite flowers?"

"It depends on my mood. I do love roses. They smell so good. Lilies, too. Peonies. Like I said, it depends on my mood. The occasion. The season."

"Ally!" Mom calls from the kitchen.

"Shoot, I have to go. My mom goes to bed around ten. I'll call you as soon as I can."

"Go. The sooner we hang up, the sooner we can start our second date."

I feel like I'm going to pass out from excitement. *Our second date?* "Okay, well, bye, Fish. *Matthew.*"

"Bye, Little Lioness. Can't wait to see you later."

We disconnect the call and, even though I know my mother is waiting for me, I nonetheless sit for a long moment on my bed, replaying the highlights of our conversation, over and over again, in my head. Finally, though, when the smell of Mom's dinner lures me, I get up and jeté across my room like I used to do as a kid in ballet class, feeling like last night's heartache is already a distant memory.

TWELVE

FISH

I yawn and force my eyelids open. I know I should have let Alessandra hang up from our video chat two hours ago, right after our movie ended, to let her get some sleep before her early morning flight. But I've been having too much fun with her to do the selfless thing.

I turn on my side in my bed, taking my laptop with me. "How are you getting to the airport in the morning?"

"You mean in four hours?" She smiles. "Georgina. My mom has to work, so Georgina said she'd take me."

"I'll take you."

"Oh, Fish. You're the sweetest. But I live in the boon-docks, remember? Georgina has tomorrow off from work and said she really wants to take me, so we can say our goodbyes in person."

I'm feeling irrationally crestfallen. *I want to say my good-byes to you in person, too,* I think. But, of course, I don't say it. I'm tempted to ask which airline, which terminal, just so I can drive there to say goodbye in person, even if I'm not the one driving her . . . But I refrain. An early morning first kiss on the curb at LAX, when we're both sleep deprived and rushed, isn't the magical moment I've been fantasizing about. And certainly not the one she deserves.

Alessandra yawns and rubs her droopy eyes. "Do you know if 22 Goats has any upcoming tour dates in Boston?"

"The next tour dates aren't set yet. They're planning everything now. For the next couple months, we're going to be hunkered down in LA, working on our next album. Otherwise, I'd already have booked a flight to visit you in Boston in the next couple weeks."

Her droopy eyes suddenly shoot open. "Really?"

"If I could."

"Wow. I'd *love* to see you, whenever you're able to visit. Any time."

My heart rate is quickening. "It might be a couple months. Just because of my schedule. But, I promise, I'll come."

"That's so exciting," she says, but she's yawning even as she says the words.

I chuckle. "You'd better get some sleep, cutie. I've been selfish to keep you up this long."

"I've been having fun."

"Me, too. But it's time for you to get some sleep."

She yawns again. "Okay."

"Let me know when you've landed safely, okay? So I don't worry."

She bats her eyelashes. "Okay."

"And let me know how your audition at the coffeehouse on Tuesday goes."

She lifts her head from her pillow, her mouth in the shape of an "O." "I can't believe you remembered about that!"

"Dude, I already told you. *I remember everything you've said.*"

She sinks back onto her pillow and swoons. "Oh, Fish. *Matthew.*"

"Are you going to perform that new song you wrote at your audition?"

"No, I was thinking I'd perform a cover. Maybe even my version of 'Delightful Damage.'"

"I really think you should sing your new song at the audition. That's what's going to impress them the most. Although I'd absolutely *love* to hear your version of 'Delightful Damage' some time."

"After you sing it to me, maybe. When are you going to sing to me, dude?"

"After you sing me 'Blindsided.' We've got a deal, remember?"

"Oh, yeah."

"How about we sing for each other during our next date?"

Alessandra's expression turns decidedly flirtatious. "Ooooh, we're gonna have *another* date?"

"*Duh.*"

She's beaming. "When?"

"I gotta figure out my schedule. The Goats and I are gonna be working hard this week in long writing sessions. That's how we do it. Marathon sessions. It's the only way we ever get anything accomplished."

She nods. "Creativity doesn't happen during 'normal business hours.'"

"Exactly. You've got to make hay while the sun shines. So, let's text each other our schedules in the next few days."

"We've also got to deal with the pesky problem that Boston is three hours ahead," she says. "Plus, I'll be starting that class and working extra shifts." She looks worried.

"Aw, don't stress, Little Lioness," I say. "We'll make it work."

"I can't wait to . . ." She yawns and rubs her eyes. "I can't wait to hang out with you again."

I chuckle. "Time to close your eyes, cutie."

"Okay." She blows me a kiss. "Good night, Matthew."

"Good night, Alessandra. Travel safe. Sweet dreams."

"They will be, if I dream of you." With a cute little wink, she ends the call.

And that's it. The coolest, prettiest girl I've ever met is heading back to Boston in mere hours. And I'm not going to see her again for weeks, if not months.

"Fuck it, shit happens," I whisper into the silence of my bedroom.

For a long moment, I lie on my bed, listening to the waves crashing on the beach outside my bedroom window. Man, I'm aching in all the best and worst ways. How is it possible I've *finally* met a girl who makes me feel like *this*, and she lives three thousand miles away?

With a deep sigh, I close my laptop, reach underneath my blanket, and jerk off, imagining myself licking Alessandra's pussy the whole time. After I get off, I take a long, hot shower, come back to bed, and send a quick text to Kat— asking her to get Alessandra's address in Boston from Georgina—and, finally, close my eyes, focus on the nearby sounds of the waves, and drift off to sleep.

THIRTEEN

FISH

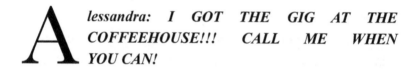

lessandra: *I GOT THE GIG AT THE COFFEEHOUSE!!! CALL ME WHEN YOU CAN!*

When my phone buzzes on the small stool next to me, I abruptly stop playing my bass and jerk to standing. "I'll be back in fifteen!" I shout to Colin and Dax.

Without waiting for their reply, I put my bass down and bound out of Dax's home studio, gripping my phone with white knuckles. I pass Violet in her kitchen. She's sitting at a table with her and Dax's towheaded toddler, Jackson. And then make my way into a nearby game room. Once in the large room, I close the door behind me, settle into an armchair, and place a call to Alessandra.

"Can you believe it?" she shrieks in greeting. "I did it, Fish!"

"I'm not surprised at all."

"They hired me on the spot! I'm just leaving the coffee-house now, and I feel like I'm floating six inches off the ground!"

"Congrats!"

"I wish you could have seen me! I *nailed* that audition! Your Little Lioness made that audition her bitch! Her *prey*!"

Your Little Lioness. The words make my very atoms vibrate. Laughing, I shout, "Gimme a little roar, Little Lioness!" And to my surprise, Alessandra complies, gifting me with a roar at full volume that sends my heart jolting and my dick tingling.

Alessandra squeals with laughter. "I'll have you know I just *roared* at the top of my lungs while walking along the sidewalk back to my apartment. An old lady across the street just looked at me like I'm crazy . . . Which. I. *Am. Because I got the gig, sucker!*"

I laugh and laugh. "Did you play your new song? Tell me *everything*, woman."

Alessandra tells me the whole amazing story, from begin-ning to end. How she walked into the coffeehouse and initially felt like she was "going to barf." She says several ballers from her school were already there when she arrived, set to audition before her—all of them renowned performers who intimidate the hell out of her. "I almost turned around and walked out, right then!" she says. "But then, I heard your sweet voice, telling me I'm talented. I heard Reed's voice, telling me I've been hiding behind my music, rather than revealing myself through it. I heard Reed saying I'm a 'Laila knockoff.'"

"Prick."

"And I thought, 'Fuck you, Reed. You want to see me

reveal myself, motherfucker? Well, watch *this*!'" She laughs gleefully. "*And I did it!* I got up there and sang 'Blindsided' like I've never sung anything before! I didn't even recognize my own voice! *And they said they were blown away!*"

"I could cry, I'm so happy for you right now. I could literally *weep* with joy, Ally."

"Aw, Fish. Matthew. You're the sweetest."

"It's the truth." And it is. Before this call, I knew this girl made my heart beat in a new way. I knew she makes me laugh and smile so big, my cheeks hurt. But now, hearing this elation in her voice, I'm feeling physically overwhelmed with affection and attraction, like nothing I've felt before. I say, "Honestly, I couldn't be happier if my own band had just won a Grammy."

She hoots with laughter. "Well, let's not get *too* crazy now. They gave me Monday and Wednesday nights—the bargain basement time slots. And it's not even a paid gig. Did I mention that yet? Ha! All this excitement for an *unpaid* gig!" She giggles uproariously. "The only money I'll get paid is whatever customers generously stuff into my tip jar. But I don't even care about making money. I'd pay *them* to get to do this gig. If needed, I'll pick up some more shifts at the café. Or get another student loan. All that matters is this *amazing* chance for me to become a better performer, right?"

"Abso-fucking-lutely."

She sighs happily. "Oh, Fish. I couldn't have done this without you. The things you said to me—" She abruptly stops talking and gasps.

"Ally?"

She says something offline in a muffled voice. And then gasps again. "Matthew Fishberger!" she shouts at me. "*I got your flowers!*"

My heart bursts with excitement. "I was hoping they'd make it on time."

"I just walked into my apartment and my roommate handed me the biggest, most spectacular bouquet I've ever seen in my entire life!"

"Red roses, I hope?"

"Yes! They're the deepest, most romantic and *passionate* red the world has ever seen!" There's a pause. "Oh, they smell incredible! Thank you!"

My phone pings and I look down to find a photo of Alessandra holding a large bouquet of red roses.

"Wow. Beautiful," I say, my heart bursting. "And the flowers are pretty, too."

"Aw, Matthew. How'd you get my address?"

"Kat got it from Georgina."

"Georgie didn't say a word!"

"Yeah, it's this crazy thing called a surprise."

She squeals. "Thank you!"

I chuckle. "The only expression of gratitude I want from you, besides this beautiful photo, is to finally hear you play 'Blindsided' for me. Now that you've played it at an audition, your 'Georgina First' rule no longer applies."

"Good point."

"Call me back on video chat. You can play it for me now."

"I can't. I've got to change my clothes real quick and race to work."

"A likely story."

She giggles. "It's true. How about I play it for you later tonight?"

"Shoot. I'm going to be in a writing sesh with the Goats until late. We've all agreed to turn off our phones and power it out. I was just waiting to turn off my phone until I'd heard from you."

"How about tomorrow night?"

"I'm flying to Seattle tomorrow. We're filming a tourism spot on Thursday, then doing dinner at the Morgans' that same night. I might have time after dinner on Thursday, but with you three hours ahead, I don't have high hopes."

"I'm free Friday during the day," she says, "but I know you're doing your interview with Georgina in Seattle that day."

"Yeah, we're going to give Georgina a tour of 'our Seattle.'"

Alessandra says, "Georgina is really excited about it. Oh, when you see her, don't ask her about Reed. They're still broken up, and she's heartbroken about it."

"I won't say a word. What'd Georgie say about your new gig at the coffeehouse? I can only imagine how loudly she shrieked when you told her."

"I haven't told Georgie yet. I called you first."

My heart stops. "I'm honored."

I can hear her smiling across the phone line. "*Of course.* I got the gig, thanks to you. Well, you and Reed. But, obviously, I can't call him."

"Prick."

"No. He was right."

"Nope. So, did we figure out a time for our next date, and I missed it?"

"No, we got off track. How about Friday night, after your interview with Georgie in Seattle? I'm free that night."

"It's a date!"

"Woo-hoo! Our *third*," she says coyly. "How exciting."

"No, our fourth, by my count."

"Our *fourth*? How do you figure?"

"Well, we met at Reed's pre-party. So, that's ground zero. Our 'meet-cute,' if you will. When we saw each other *again* at Reed's party, after *specifically* agreeing at the pre-party to hang out again later, that was our first official date. Our second happened on Sunday night, when we video chatted and watched *This Is the End*. But—loophole alert!—after the movie that night, as you'll recall, we hung up to change into our pajamas, before reconvening. Which means, my dear, the clock reset at that point."

"It did?"

"Yes. When we talked again, in our pajamas, and wound up talking for almost two more hours, that qualified, under a little known loophole, as a totally new and different date than our movie date earlier. Which means this Friday night will be our *fourth* date."

"I like that loophole," she says, her voice intimate and sexy. "I've never been on a *fourth* date before. That feels kind of . . . *serious*."

My cock is tingling at the flirtatious tone in her voice. "Oh, it is. Very, very serious."

"Although, I should confess I've never been on a first, second, or *third* date, either. Much less a fourth. So I really don't know what the hell I'm doing."

I laugh with her. "Believe me, I'm as clueless as you are. I've never been on a date, either."

"*What?*"

"Not like, you know, an actual *date, date*."

"Liar."

"No. I've never been on a date. I've hung out. I've been in groups. I've, you know, messed around and had one-night stands. But a *date*? Like where I say, 'I will see you at such and such time, pretty lady, and I can't wait!'" I chuckle. "No."

"*Wow.*" She sounds flabbergasted. "So, we're each other's firsts. That's pretty cool."

"There's nothing like a girl's first, right? That's what a really pretty girl at a party told me recently."

"Whoever she is, she's a freaking genius."

"Yes, she is."

Oh, God, I feel high when I talk to this adorable girl. She's better than the finest weed. The best tequila. She's the scent of flowers in human form. She's the sound of the ocean. She's music.

"Oh, shoot, I have to go!" Alessandra says. "I'm gonna be late for work."

"I'll see you on Friday night, cutie."

"It's a date! Our *fourth.*" She laughs. "Thank you again for the roses. The gorgeous *red* roses."

"*Not yellow.*"

"God, no," she says.

I smile to myself. I was hoping she'd understand the coded message I was trying to send her with those very, very red blooms. I was hoping she'd understand I want more than mere friendship with her. A lot more.

"Bye for now, Fish. *Matthew.* The Goat Called Fish Who's Hung Like a Bull."

"But not really. I'm actually quite average, to tell you the truth."

"I won't tell anyone."

"Thank you. Well, all right, cutie-pie. Get yourself to work, ya lazy bum."

"I'll see you on Friday night. Have a good writing session with the Goats."

"I will. Bye now."

"Bye."

We end the call and I lope out of Dax's game room with a huge smile on my face. I'm intending to return to Dax's home studio, but as I pass the kitchen, I discover not only Violet and Jackson sitting at the table, but Dax and Colin, too.

"You raced out of the studio like your pants were on fire," Dax says. "Everything okay?"

I plop into an empty chair next to Jackson. "Everything is fan-freaking-tastic, as a matter of fact. Just had to take a call from Alessandra. Hi there, Action Jackson."

"Hi, Unkee Fisssh."

I look at the group. "Alessandra texted me some fantastic news, so I called her back."

"Unkee Fish?"

I look down to find my nephew offering me an apple slice.

"Thanks, buddy. That's why I love you the most." I eat the apple slice and point to a baby carrot. "Can I have one of those, too? I'll be your best friend."

Not surprisingly, my nephew hands me what I've asked for. Because he's a ray of sunshine, that kid. Kind and generous by nature, just like his parents.

"Ha! Tricked ya," I say, after taking the offered carrot. "I'm *already* your best friend! Forever and ever!"

Jackson giggles, understanding the joke, and I tousle his blond hair.

"So, are you gonna tell us Alessandra's fantastic news or not?" Violet says. "I'm on pins and needles!"

"Oh. Yeah. I got distracted." I glare comically at Jackson. "By a yard gnome."

This time, when Jackson giggles, it's highly doubtful he gets the joke—seeing as how he has no idea what a yard gnome is. But I don't mind. I'll take his laughter, whether I've earned it, or not.

I tell the group Alessandra's news, and why getting that gig at the coffeehouse means so much to her—and, therefore, to *me*. And my friends totally get it. In fact, they seem as stoked for Alessandra as I am.

"You know what you should do?" Violet says. "Send her some flowers to congratulate her. Especially when a relationship is new—"

"Dude, I'm already two steps ahead of you. Three dozen red roses were waiting for Ally in her apartment when she got home from her audition."

"Look at you!" Violet coos. "I'm impressed."

I wink at Jackson. "Can you say 'Uncle Fish is a baller?'"

"Unkee Fish ith a bawah."

"Wooh! Gimme five, buddy! You nailed it!" The kid gives me five. Because, of course, he'd never leave me hanging. "Can I have another apple slice, too—to celebrate what a baller I am?"

The kid gives me an apple slice and I tap his with mine.

"As long as we're celebrating . . ." Colin says. He gets up and grabs four beers from the fridge. As he distributes them, Dax suggests ordering pizza. So we do. And then, as we've done many, many times in our lives, we sit and drink beer while waiting for our pizza to arrive.

After dinner, Violet takes Jackson away for a bath and bedtime. And we three Goats finally drag ourselves back into the studio.

As we get situated, Colin says, "It's cool seeing you this hyped about a girl, Fish Taco—and especially, seeing her return your feelings."

"Thanks, man. I'm pretty stoked about the situation myself."

"You really like her, huh?" Dax says.

I slide the strap of my bass over my head and shoulder. "I'll put it this way, brother. For the first time, ever, I *finally* understand what inspired you to write 'Fireflies.'"

FOURTEEN
FISH

Alessandra's beautiful face is glowing on my laptop screen.

It's our fourth date.

Our third on video chat.

And I'm in heaven.

I'm sitting on the bed in the guest bedroom at my mom's house in Seattle—the two-story I bought for her last year, debt free, with an awesome view of Puget Sound. Alessandra is sitting on her bed in her bedroom in Boston. As usual, our conversation has been easy and lively. Sparks have been flying nonstop. At the beginning of our chat, Alessandra sang me her song, "Blindsided," and, not surprisingly, it brought tears to my eyes. Everything about her melody and lyrics was honest and raw. And her voice on the song was alternately soaring and intimate.

After the performance, we talked—caught each other up on the past few days. Alessandra told me some of the cool stuff she's been learning in that summer class. Since then, I've been telling her about today's interview with Georgina for *Rock 'n' Roll.*

"Sounds like the interview went fantastically well," Alessandra declares.

"Didn't Georgina already tell you about this stuff?" I reply. "Don't you two talk every day?"

"Yes. But I wanted to hear the story from your perspective. I'm so excited to hear you thought the interview went as well as Georgie did. She was thrilled when I talked to her."

"I think it helped our chemistry that we all got to hang out the night before at the Morgans' for dinner. That helped break the ice, so that we were all loose and comfortable from the get-go during the official interview."

"Georgie said the same thing!"

In truth, hanging out with Georgina on Thursday night was a blessing for more than the interview itself, because it gave me the chance to ask Georgina questions about Alessandra. To find out about what Alessandra was like as a kid. To hear stories that made me like Ally, that much more, if that's possible. Before Thursday night's chat with Georgina, I already knew Alessandra is a truly sweet person. Also, that Alessandra has a goofball side. But, after talking to Georgina, I gained a new appreciation of how difficult it was for Alessandra to lose her father. I figured that, obviously. *Intellectually.* But I've never lost a parent, and Alessandra doesn't talk about it much, so I didn't fully grasp Alessandra's pain in that regard before Georgina explained it to me. Among other things, Georgina told me, "When I first met poor little Alessandra, she was like a little snail, after someone has sprinkled salt on her. Just curled into a little ball and hiding out in her shell." Man, the stuff Georgie told me made me want to drop everything and hop a flight to Boston, if only to take Alessandra into my arms and tell her I'm proud of the woman she's become.

"*Whoa.* Is that the cover of *The Violet Album* on the wall over there?" Alessandra asks.

"Yeah. My mom made this guest bedroom into a shrine of me and the Goats. All our albums are framed on the walls."

"Oooh! Gimme a tour of the shrine!"

"Careful what you wish for." Laughing, I get up and walk slowly around the room, showing Alessandra the various items of memorabilia crowding the walls, dresser, desk, and bookcases.

"Go back to the desk!" she commands.

I aim my laptop and pan across the slew of framed photos there.

"Is that a photo of you and your mom on a red carpet?"

"Yep. I took my mom to the American Music Awards a couple years ago." I show Alessandra the photo in close-up, and she "oooohs" and "aaaahs" and compliments my mother's dress. "My band was nominated in a couple categories that night," I say, "but we didn't win anything. *Fuckers.*"

Alessandra laughs. "You were sweet to take your mom as your date."

"That wasn't me being sweet. That was me having no other options."

"Are you close with your mom?"

"We're close now. But if you went back in a time machine to when I was fifteen and all I wanted to do was make music with my best friends, skateboard, and smoke weed, you'd find a mother who was *beyond* exasperated with her fuckup of a son. She constantly told me back then, 'You're never going to be able to support yourself if you don't get serious about school, Matthew!'"

"Well, damn. You showed her, didn't you?"

"Yep. As it turns out, skateboarding after school every day, smoking a blunt, and then hanging out making music in your best friend's garage until bedtime, is a perfectly valid way to set yourself up for success in life."

She laughs uproariously, and so do I.

Laughing, I say, "When I say it like that, I realize I really have won the lottery. What are the odds?"

She giggles. "You're living the dream. Hence the shrine. Continue the tour, please."

"Are you sure? It's actually kind of creepy."

"I'm sure."

I continue panning slowly. "See what I mean? This room feels like more of a mausoleum than a museum."

"Yeah, it is a little mausoleum-y. Wait, go back. Were those photo albums, Matthew?"

"You've got an eagle eye, Miss Tennison."

"Are there any childhood photos of you in any of those albums, perchance?"

"In all of them."

"*Oooh.* Any of them highly embarrassing, I hope and pray?"

"That's redundant. I could open literally *any* album to *any* page, and you'd be treated to a highly embarrassing and/or awkward photo of me."

"Let's put that hypothesis to the test!"

I aim my laptop at the photo albums stacked in the bookcase. "Pick a color. Any color."

"Red."

I grab her selected album and randomly open it on the desk. And, as expected, my theory is instantly proven. The random photo shows me at age nine or ten. As usual, I'm desperately in need of a haircut. Not to mention, I'm two years away from getting the braces I so desperately needed. I'm also skinny as fuck. I've actually been crazy skinny my whole life, other than these past couple of years, thanks to Colin making it his mission in life to "bulk me up" with protein shakes. Which, to be clear, have only resulted in me finally looking semi-normal, rather than like the doppelganger of Shaggy from *Scooby Doo*. But, anyway, from about ages nine to fourteen, I was at my all-time skinniest, as I stretched taller and taller, and my poor body simply couldn't keep up in terms of weight.

"See?" I say. "One embarrassing photo, per request."

"I don't see what's embarrassing about it," Alessandra says. "You're adorable in that photo."

"Dude, I look like a tragic mix of Gumby, Bugs Bunny, and a haystack."

She bursts out laughing. "You could say something similar about me at that age. Back then, I was a mix between an otter, a dust bunny, and a Swiffer."

"A *Swiffer*?"

"Google it."

I google it and discover a Swiffer is a puffy thing used to clean dust bunnies off wood surfaces. "I'm looking at a Swiffer now," I say. "And I can't for the life of me understand how you resembled one."

"If you saw my hair back then, before I learned to tame my waves, you'd get it."

"Okay. So, show me a Swiffer-fied photo of you."

"I don't have any with me in Boston. The only childhood photo I've got with me is one of me with my dad, but my hair is pulled back in that one."

"Show it to me."

She gets out her phone and shows me a heartbreaking photo of a beautiful little girl sitting on the shoulders of a kind-looking dude. The two of them are standing on a beach and Alessandra is glowing with pure joy.

"You're so beautiful," I say softly. "You're smiling so big."

"I always smiled when I was with him."

Sighing, she quietly puts the photo away, and my heart strains for her.

"I'm sorry, Ally."

"It's okay." She smiles thinly, but her eyes are sad. "Continue the tour. I feel like we've only scratched the surface of this mausoleum."

"I think you've pretty much seen it all."

"Then show me another page from an album. I like seeing you as a kid."

"So what you're saying is you're a sadist? Good to know." I flip to another random page. And, once again—surprise, surprise!—I look like a dork. In this particular shot, I'm about twelve years old. Wearing braces, thank God, although they make my mouth look way too big for my face. Yet again, I'm skinny as hell and in desperate need of a haircut. All of which is made more apparent by the fact that I'm standing next to three golden gods in the shot—Dax, Keane, and Kat—all of whom always foiled my extreme awkwardness growing up with their extreme lack of it. In the shot, the four of us—Dax, Keane, Kat, and me—are smiling in the sunshine in the Morgans' backyard, near their family's small swimming pool, while all of us are holding large slices of watermelon.

"Is that Dax and Kat?" Alessandra asks.

"And Keane. If I'd had any sense as a kid, I never would have let anyone take a photo of me standing next to them.

Those three never had an awkward phase. Never an awkward *day*. Actually, the whole damned Morgan family was like that. I take that back. Keane had maybe an awkward *month* as a kid. But only the way a golden retriever puppy is kind of awkward and fumbling—but still super cute, you know? Not *genuinely* awkward, like me. Like how I was a human scarecrow combined with a haystack."

She lets out a stern *tsk*. "*Stop.* If you ask me, you're the most beautiful one in that photo. Your sweet soul shines right through. You honestly melt me in that photo."

"So, you're saying you're a huge fan of the Muppets, then? Because I look like a Muppet there."

"*Stop.* I mean it. Yes, I'm a fan of the Muppets. 'Man or Muppet' is literally one of my all-time favorite songs. But that's an irrelevant fact."

"Oh my God, I *love* that song."

I burst into the chorus of the song, and she instantly joins me, making both of us laugh uproariously. And, once again, I can't believe how good she makes me feel. How *real* I am around her. Even when I'm a dork—*especially* when I'm a dork—she likes me. She gets me.

For so long, I got rejected by girls when I showed too much of my true self. So, I guess I got used to hiding that guy, after a while. Pretending to be someone cooler than I was, just to avoid the usual outcome. But, now, out of the blue, I feel safe to be me, with no filter. No faking. If I love a badass song from *The Muppets*, then I say so. It's as simple as that. And, to my shock, the more real I get with her, the more that spark between us feels like it's growing into a forest fire.

"So, have you seen enough of my childhood now?" I say. "I hope and pray."

"Yes. For now."

be of her small, braless breasts in that tank,
iffness of her nipples poking out from behind

avor, honey," I coo. "Stand in the middle of
and do a little twirl, so I can see your full

, she doesn't hesitate. She adjusts her camera
the middle of her bedroom, as requested. And
rms gracefully above her head like a ballerina.

hard. "Yep. Can I take a photo?"
can take a video, too, if you want."

press record and lick my lips as she moves
me on my screen. I say, "You're better than
to get a *lot* of use out of this video on lonely
know what I mean." Thankfully, she smiles
omment and doesn't look the least bit flustered
, just to be sure, I say, "Is it okay I said that to

okay," she replies, batting her lashes. "It
She stops her slow movement. "Honestly, I
out you . . . getting yourself off while fanta-
"
is.

en sure how to nudge our relationship to the
omething physical. At least, considering the
pect, to *talking* about something physical. But,
ssandra just made it abundantly clear she's
about that sort of thing. My cock is rock hard.
ping. "You look gorgeous," I say, my voice
Like a real ballerina."

Maybe I shouldn't say what I'm thinking. Maybe it's too
soon. Too much. But I can't resist. "Hopefully, one day, I'll be
able to give you a tour of the mausoleum in person."

She doesn't miss a beat. "I'd love that."

The full weight of what we've just agreed hits me. I think
I just said I want to take her home to meet my mother, and she
said that's groovy with her. *Whoa*. Do people normally do this
so fast? I bet they don't. And yet . . . None of this feels too
fast. It feels right on time.

Alessandra yawns. "Hey, do you mind if I brush my teeth
and get into my jammies and call you back? If I fall asleep, I
don't want to be in my clothes."

"Shoot. I always forget you're three hours ahead. Why
don't we hang up now and talk tomorrow?"

"No, no! I don't want to stop talking. I just want to be
ready to fall asleep, if my eyelids get heavy."

"Okay, cutie. Meet me back here in five."

"Roger," she says.

"Rabbit," I reply, since that's the legally required response
for anyone who's either a Morgan or has hung out with them
for any length of time.

"Hey, Matthew!" Alessandra calls out, just before I press
the button to disconnect. She smiles. "When we meet back
here, bring your guitar, cutie pie. I've played you 'Blindsided.' So now, you're finally going to play me 'Delightful
Damage.'"

FIFTEEN

FISH

Nerves unexpectedly streak through me as I position my guitar in my lap. I've never performed "Delightful Damage" for anyone other than Dax and Colin. But a deal's a deal. Alessandra finally sang me her heartrending song, "Blindsided," earlier during this video chat. So, now it's my turn to bare my musical soul to her.

I pluck out the beginning riff, trying to muster the courage to sing. Dax is the one who delivers this song on the record. And he does it beautifully. Just because I'm the one who wrote the song, doesn't mean I can deliver it even half as well as Dax.

Shit. I'm surprisingly nervous.

I play the riff again, still gathering my courage. But when I look up from my guitar, and into Alessandra's kind, waiting face, I feel emboldened. *I feel safe.* And so, for the first time in my life, I perform "Delightful Damage," the song I wrote in that lonely hotel room in Prague. The song I wrote when I wondered if I was destined to be alone forever. If I wasn't worthy of the kind of love story shared by Dax and Violet. I

sing from the depth
half as good as Dax'
tion of weight liftin
whatever's left of m

I'm showing he
her, without holding
on her beautiful face

"Take the secon
reaches its climax. A
and sings the lyrics
lilting, jazz-infused

At the end of t
"The third verse is
verse this time, Al
same ones I contribu
our voices intertwin
I feel like my very so

When our duet is
The lyrics. The mel
loved the song more
she lays her guitar o
her pajamas, since s
guitar in her lap.

"Fucking hell, w
now, I can't stand it.'

She blushes. "I d
"Oh, honey. Baby
Oh, fuckin' A. Sl
hot in that simple pi
as hell does. Even he
her purple bikini. W
Relaxed. Sensuous.

the natural sha
including the st
the soft fabric.

"Do me a
your bedroom,
body."

To my thril
and walks into
then raises her
"Like this?"

My cock is
"Sure. You
"I *want*." I
gracefully for
porn. I'm going
nights, if you
broadly at my c
or offended. Bu
you?"

"Better thai
turned me on."
like thinking ab
sizing about *me*

And there it
Finally.

I haven't be
next level—to
long distance as
thankfully, Ale
open to talking
My heart thum
turning husky. "

"I fake it pretty well. I took ballet for years as a kid."

"You don't look like you're faking it to me. You look ready to star in *The Nutcracker*."

She laughs while continuing her slow movement. "Not even close. When I was thirteen, I realized I had to choose between music and ballet classes, so I chose music." She stops dancing. "Did you get what you wanted?"

"I got a video, if that's what you mean," I reply. But what I'm thinking is, *I'm not even close to having what I want from you.*

Alessandra returns to her bed and adjusts her laptop, so that, now, only her beautiful face is filling my screen again. "You won't show that video to anyone, right? It's just for you."

"Of course. It's for my private viewing only. Like I said, on lonely nights."

She bites her lower lip. "I didn't mean to imply I don't trust you, by asking that question. I do. It's just that I've just never done anything like this before, so I don't know what's normal or not. I just want to be sure we're on the same page."

I've been assuming Alessandra is a virgin, based on various things she's said. But, now, I feel like she's given me a natural opening to find out for sure. Not that it matters to me, either way. But I think it'd be helpful for me to know exactly what she's thinking in terms of our relationship becoming physical one day.

"Hey, Ally. If this is too personal, tell me. But . . . are you a virgin?"

She nods. "That's weird, huh? I'm almost twenty."

"Not at all. I was older than you when I lost my virginity. I was twenty-one."

She looks surprised. "I thought I was the only twenty-year-old virgin in the world."

"That's how I felt, too. Especially in the crowd I grew up with. They're a horny bunch."

She laughs. "Who was your first?"

I shrug. "Just this British girl I'd met in London, right before my band kicked off our first tour, opening for Red Card Riot."

"Did she come with you on the tour?"

I try not to smile at the absurdity of her question. The innocence of it. The lack of understanding of how tours work —and who I was during that time in my life. "No, it was a one-night stand."

"Oh." She blushes, obviously realizing her question was a naïve one.

"Our album had just come out and the 'People Like Us' video was just starting to go crazy viral. We were in London for rehearsals and promo for a short bit before heading out. So, the Goats and I went out to a pub one night with C-Bomb. He's the drummer for RCR."

She nods knowingly.

"And these girls recognized C-Bomb. When he introduced us to them and said we were their opener, one of them freaked out because she'd seen our video. Dax and Colin weren't interested in her. And neither was C-Bomb. So, she eventually gravitated to me and started gushing about how much she loved the song and how great I was in the video . . . It was the first time I'd been 'recognized,' so to speak. And it was a blast for me. It made me feel like a genuine rock star for the first time." I take a deep breath. "We eventually left the pub and went back to C-Bomb's suite at the hotel. We partied in a big group for a while. And then, the girl and I headed to my room,

Maybe I shouldn't say what I'm thinking. Maybe it's too soon. Too much. But I can't resist. "Hopefully, one day, I'll be able to give you a tour of the mausoleum in person."

She doesn't miss a beat. "I'd love that."

The full weight of what we've just agreed hits me. I think I just said I want to take her home to meet my mother, and she said that's groovy with her. *Whoa.* Do people normally do this so fast? I bet they don't. And yet . . . None of this feels too fast. It feels right on time.

Alessandra yawns. "Hey, do you mind if I brush my teeth and get into my jammies and call you back? If I fall asleep, I don't want to be in my clothes."

"Shoot. I always forget you're three hours ahead. Why don't we hang up now and talk tomorrow?"

"No, no! I don't want to stop talking. I just want to be ready to fall asleep, if my eyelids get heavy."

"Okay, cutie. Meet me back here in five."

"Roger," she says.

"Rabbit," I reply, since that's the legally required response for anyone who's either a Morgan or has hung out with them for any length of time.

"Hey, Matthew!" Alessandra calls out, just before I press the button to disconnect. She smiles. "When we meet back here, bring your guitar, cutie pie. I've played you 'Blindsided.' So now, you're finally going to play me 'Delightful Damage.'"

FIFTEEN

FISH

Nerves unexpectedly streak through me as I position my guitar in my lap. I've never performed "Delightful Damage" for anyone other than Dax and Colin. But a deal's a deal. Alessandra finally sang me her heartrending song, "Blindsided," earlier during this video chat. So, now it's my turn to bare my musical soul to her.

I pluck out the beginning riff, trying to muster the courage to sing. Dax is the one who delivers this song on the record. And he does it beautifully. Just because I'm the one who wrote the song, doesn't mean I can deliver it even half as well as Dax.

Shit. I'm surprisingly nervous.

I play the riff again, still gathering my courage. But when I look up from my guitar, and into Alessandra's kind, waiting face, I feel emboldened. *I feel safe.* And so, for the first time in my life, I perform "Delightful Damage," the song I wrote in that lonely hotel room in Prague. The song I wrote when I wondered if I was destined to be alone forever. If I wasn't worthy of the kind of love story shared by Dax and Violet. I sing from the depths of my soul, even though my voice isn't half as good as Dax's. And as I sing, I feel the distinct sensation of weight lifting off my chest—off my soul—along with whatever's left of my insecurities with Alessandra.

I'm showing her everything now. Laying myself bare to her, without holding back. And I know, from the expression on her beautiful face, she knows it.

"Take the second verse," I prompt, as the first chorus reaches its climax. And to my thrill, Alessandra jumps right in and sings the lyrics to the second verse, using her gorgeous, lilting, jazz-infused voice to make the song her own.

At the end of the second chorus, Alessandra calls out, "The third verse is yours, Fish Taco!" And when I sing the verse this time, Alessandra adds backing harmonies—the same ones I contributed behind Dax on the recording. And as our voices intertwine and cleave together in perfect harmony, I feel like my very soul is making love to hers.

When our duet is done, Alessandra gushes about the song. The lyrics. The melody. My voice. And I tell her I've never loved the song more than when she sings it. Sighing happily, she lays her guitar on her bed—giving me my first glimpse of her pajamas, since she initially rejoined our chat holding her guitar in her lap.

"Fucking hell, woman," I breathe. "You look so hot right now, I can't stand it."

She blushes. "I *do*?"

"Oh, honey. Baby. Yes, yes, you do."

Oh, fuckin' A. She's a wet dream. She's not *trying* to look hot in that simple pink tank top and soft shorts. But she sure as hell does. Even hotter than she looked that very first day in her purple bikini. Why? Because, tonight, she looks *sultry*. Relaxed. Sensuous. Not to mention, I can perfectly surmise the natural shape of her small, braless breasts in that tank, including the stiffness of her nipples poking out from behind the soft fabric.

"Do me a favor, honey," I coo. "Stand in the middle of your bedroom, and do a little twirl, so I can see your full body."

To my thrill, she doesn't hesitate. She adjusts her camera and walks into the middle of her bedroom, as requested. And then raises her arms gracefully above her head like a ballerina. "Like this?"

My cock is hard. "Yep. Can I take a photo?"

"Sure. You can take a video, too, if you want."

"I *want*." I press record and lick my lips as she moves gracefully for me on my screen. I say, "You're better than porn. I'm going to get a *lot* of use out of this video on lonely nights, if you know what I mean." Thankfully, she smiles broadly at my comment and doesn't look the least bit flustered or offended. But, just to be sure, I say, "Is it okay I said that to you?"

"Better than okay," she replies, batting her lashes. "It turned me on." She stops her slow movement. "Honestly, I like thinking about you . . . getting yourself off while fantasizing about *me*."

And there it is.

Finally.

I haven't been sure how to nudge our relationship to the next level—to something physical. At least, considering the long distance aspect, to *talking* about something physical. But, thankfully, Alessandra just made it abundantly clear she's open to talking about that sort of thing. My cock is rock hard. My heart thumping. "You look gorgeous," I say, my voice turning husky. "Like a real ballerina."

"I fake it pretty well. I took ballet for years as a kid."

"You don't look like you're faking it to me. You look ready to star in *The Nutcracker*."

She laughs while continuing her slow movement. "Not even close. When I was thirteen, I realized I had to choose between music and ballet classes, so I chose music." She stops dancing. "Did you get what you wanted?"

"I got a video, if that's what you mean," I reply. But what I'm thinking is, *I'm not even close to having what I want from you.*

Alessandra returns to her bed and adjusts her laptop, so that, now, only her beautiful face is filling my screen again. "You won't show that video to anyone, right? It's just for you."

"Of course. It's for my private viewing only. Like I said, on lonely nights."

She bites her lower lip. "I didn't mean to imply I don't trust you, by asking that question. I do. It's just that I've just never done anything like this before, so I don't know what's normal or not. I just want to be sure we're on the same page."

I've been assuming Alessandra is a virgin, based on various things she's said. But, now, I feel like she's given me a natural opening to find out for sure. Not that it matters to me, either way. But I think it'd be helpful for me to know exactly what she's thinking in terms of our relationship becoming physical one day.

"Hey, Ally. If this is too personal, tell me. But . . . are you a virgin?"

She nods. "That's weird, huh? I'm almost twenty."

"Not at all. I was older than you when I lost my virginity. I was twenty-one."

She looks surprised. "I thought I was the only twenty-year-old virgin in the world."

"That's how I felt, too. Especially in the crowd I grew up with. They're a horny bunch."

She laughs. "Who was your first?"

I shrug. "Just this British girl I'd met in London, right before my band kicked off our first tour, opening for Red Card Riot."

"Did she come with you on the tour?"

I try not to smile at the absurdity of her question. The innocence of it. The lack of understanding of how tours work —and who I was during that time in my life. "No, it was a one-night stand."

"Oh." She blushes, obviously realizing her question was a naïve one.

"Our album had just come out and the 'People Like Us' video was just starting to go crazy viral. We were in London for rehearsals and promo for a short bit before heading out. So, the Goats and I went out to a pub one night with C-Bomb. He's the drummer for RCR."

She nods knowingly.

"And these girls recognized C-Bomb. When he introduced us to them and said we were their opener, one of them freaked out because she'd seen our video. Dax and Colin weren't interested in her. And neither was C-Bomb. So, she eventually gravitated to me and started gushing about how much she loved the song and how great I was in the video . . . It was the first time I'd been 'recognized,' so to speak. And it was a blast for me. It made me feel like a genuine rock star for the first time." I take a deep breath. "We eventually left the pub and went back to C-Bomb's suite at the hotel. We partied in a big group for a while. And then, the girl and I headed to my room, where she devirginized me, although I didn't mention that's what was happening."

I don't know if Alessandra wanted to hear all those details, but once I got talking, I couldn't stop. I've never told anyone that story before. And I guess I wanted her to understand the real me. I wanted her to know that, even when I finally got laid for the first time, it was with a girl who'd initially flirted with Dax and Colin, not me. Even as I had sex with that British girl, I knew I was nothing but her consolation prize. Her fourth choice. I knew she hooked up with me only to have a story to tell her girlfriends afterward. Because, hey, I was that dude in that music video! I didn't care about any of that back then, though. I just wanted to finally get lucky, especially by a cute girl with a cool accent. I guess I just want Alessandra to understand where I've been, so she understands why I want her so badly *now*.

"No regrets," I say, my heart crashing. "She was nice and had a cool accent. And I was relieved to *finally* get the monkey off my back, so I could stop lying to my friends. But I want you to understand that first time for me is basically the template of every time since. I haven't had a serious girlfriend, as I mentioned. So I've never had the experience of being physical with someone who actually cares about me, in any genuine way."

Alessandra processes that for a moment. And then, "What do you mean you were relieved not to have to lie to your friends anymore? You mean about being a virgin?"

"Yeah. I'd told my friends I'd had sex during my senior year in high school, just because I was so sick of being the last man standing, by a *long* mile."

"Who was the girl you supposedly slept with back then?"

"She didn't exist. My dad lives, like, an hour away from

where I grew up, and I used to visit him regularly. So, I told my friends I had a girlfriend in my dad's neighborhood." I roll my eyes. "It actually became a rather elaborate web of lies. I'm not proud of that, by the way."

She looks sympathetic.

"Anyhoo . . ." I exhale. "I'm only telling you this stuff because I want you to know me. The real me. Even the lame stuff. Because I want you to feel like you can tell me anything, too. Even the lame stuff."

"Thank you." She bites her lip. "I get why you lied to your friends. I hate the way everyone at school is constantly talking about their sexual exploits. No judgment on them. But I always feel like such a freak around them. Like such a Goody Two-shoes. To be honest, just holding your hand at the party was a huge thrill for me. Every time you took my hand, I thought I was going to explode from excitement. How pathetic is that?"

"Pathetic? No, Ally. Listen to me. I've had sex, many times, and holding your hand made me feel like I was going to explode from excitement, too."

"It did?"

"Swear to God. Just that simple touch made my heart rate skyrocket as much as any . . ." I stop myself. *Blowjob.* That's the word I was going to say. But, obviously, that's not the right word to use. "*Kiss.*"

She throws up her hands with sudden energy. "Speaking of which, why the *hell* didn't you kiss me that night?"

I scream in frustration, making her laugh. "I wanted to so badly!"

"I was trying to give you green-light signals all night long!"

"I'm so sorry. I was finally going to do it when Frick and

Frack showed up with Reed. The fact that I missed out on that kiss, by mere seconds, has been torturing me ever since."

She palms her forehead. "I've been tortured since then, too! You have no idea."

"I'm sure I do. I've never had a first kiss with someone like you. Someone I know for a *fact* actually likes me. I'm physically *dying* to kiss you, Ally. It *pains* me how much I want to do that."

"It pains me, too," she whispers, and my cock responds to the sultry ache in her voice. She touches her screen, like she's touching my face, and every atom in my body vibrates with arousal. "When our first kiss finally happens," she whispers, "I know it's going to be well worth the wait."

My cock throbs with yearning. "Fuck yeah, it is."

She drags her teeth over her bottom lip. "It's kind of cool we're both virgins, in a way. Even though you've had sex, physically, you've never had sex with someone you care about. So, that would be a first for you."

My heart stops at her implication. That I might, one day, be *her* first. I choke out, "Very true."

For the moment, the air between us is thick with the subtext of her words. The possibilities. She swallows hard. "Can I take a video of you now? A full-body shot, like the one you took of me? You don't have to dance for me. You can just stand there, looking hot."

"Uhhh."

"What?"

"It's just . . . Honestly, I'm *really* turned on right now. Like, *crazy* turned on."

"I don't see how that's a problem."

My heart jolts, along with my cock. "I know you can't tell this, but I'm only wearing underwear. And the fact that I'm *very* turned on is going to be extremely obvious to you in a full-body frame."

"All the more reason for you to show me your full body, then."

Whoa.

All righty, then.

My skin on fire, and my hard dick throbbing, I set up my camera and move into the frame—and when I turn around to face her, and see my own arousal reflected back at me in her face—I can barely breathe. I've been in my underwear in front of other women. Fully naked, too. Plus, I can't even count the number of times I've cannonballed into swimming pools in my underwear during tours and at parties. But this moment with Alessandra feels unique. Special. Even through our laptop cameras, I feel more intimacy with Alessandra in this moment than I've felt with anyone else.

"You're gorgeous," she says softly. "I'm recording now, okay?"

"Okay." I shift my weight and fidget, not sure what to do with my hands.

"Got it," she says after a moment. "Thank you. That ought to come in handy on lonely nights."

My heart thundering, I return to my bed and shift my laptop camera to frame my face. I didn't expect her to open the door to talking about her masturbation practices. But now that she's cracked open the door, there's no way I'm not going to kick it wide open. But before I've said a word, she asks me about the tattoo on my ribcage.

"What are those three blobby things?"

I pan the camera down to give her an up-close view. "Those are the three *goats* of 22 Goats. All three of us got the exact same ink one drunken night. On Colin's twenty-first birthday, actually."

"Those are *goats*?" she blurts incredulously.

"They look more like haystacks, don't they?"

"Or maybe piles of poop?"

I laugh. "Yeah. When we woke up the next morning and saw the atrocity on our bodies, Colin immediately wanted to get his covered with something else. But I said, 'No this shit is so bad, it's cool! It stays!' Dax agreed with me, so Colin was outvoted."

She shakes her head. "You must have been awfully drunk to put *that* on your bodies."

"Oh, we were. And very poor." I quickly tell her the whole story, which, in a nutshell, is that Colin, Dax and I got our hideous tattoos, courtesy of an aspiring tattoo artist we'd met at a party—some random guy we'd never met before who'd recently purchased a tattoo gun and promised free ink in exchange for the chance to practice. But the minute I'm done with my story, I steer our conversation back to the sexy videos we've both just captured.

"So, hey . . . How often do you think you'll use that video of me in my underwear? You know, 'on lonely nights?'"

She arches an eyebrow. "*Every. Single. Time.*"

Whoa. She looked damned hot saying that. I'll give her that. But, unfortunately, she didn't answer my question. Or at least, not the one I'd intended to ask.

"What about you?" she says flirtatiously. "How often do you think *you'll* make use of the video you shot of *me*?"

Here we go. "Every single day. Probably, twice a day. Morning and night." I chuckle at her shocked expression. "You look surprised."

"No. Well, yes. A little. I was just thinking how much time

that must take. *Twice a day*? I wouldn't get anything else accomplished!"

My eyebrows involuntarily ride up at her implication, and she cringes in response.

"I just embarrassed myself, didn't I?" she says.

"Not at all."

"It doesn't take you very long to get yourself to the finish line, does it?"

"Uh. No. It's not what I'd call a long and arduous process." I chuckle, and thank God, she laughs with me. I ask, "It takes you a while to get there?"

She's blushing like a vine-ripened tomato. But she nods.

"There's no reason to feel embarrassed," I say. "I want you to feel like you can talk to me about anything."

"I've never talked about this with anyone before."

"No one? Not even Georgina?"

She shakes her head.

"Your mom?"

She snorts. "No."

"Really? Growing up, my dad gave me a pretty detailed talk about sex and beating off. It was a little weird. But he meant well. And my best friends and I used to talk about beating off all the time as young teens."

She shrugs. "Maybe most girls talk about this stuff with their friends, growing up. But I never did." She chews on the inside of her cheek. "To be honest, I've only just started, you know, exploring myself fairly recently."

"Well, then, it makes perfect sense it takes you a while to get to the finish line."

"Sometimes, I don't even get there. It takes so long, I just give up."

"That's because you're still on the bunny slopes when it

comes to this stuff. Don't stress it. Speaking from my own experience, and everything my friends always talk about, women don't have an on-off switch like men. They're complicated. If you're having trouble figuring yourself out, then join the club, dude." When she smiles, I feel emboldened to continue. I say, "Come on. There are at least a *million* videos online teaching men how to give a woman an orgasm. And lots of it is *paid* content. You think there'd be a *paid* marketplace for that shit if it was an easy thing to do?"

She giggles and shakes her head.

"It's tough, man! But do you think there's a paid market for how to make a dude come? Nope. Because all you have to do is *this*." I move my fist up and down like I'm jerking off, and she laughs and laughs. "Plus, you've never had a partner before. So, how the hell are you supposed to know what works for you? All the Morgan dudes are always going on and on about how they took their woman to new heights and blah blah. I'm sure you'll start figuring things out way more quickly when you start experimenting with . . ." My chest tightens as I realize I was about to say "Me." That's the word I was going to use to finish that sentence. But quickly, I change course and say, "A partner."

Oh, God. Please, let that partner be me. Because the thought of Alessandra making love to anyone else is making me want to cry. Scream. Commit murder.

She smiles broadly, like she's reading my exact thoughts. And every fiber of my body heats and tingles in response.

"Thanks for saying all that," she says.

"It's all true."

I shift positions on my bed. "Can I ask you another personal question? As long as we're having an honest discussion about this stuff."

She nods. "You can ask me anything."

My heart is pounding. "Are you a virgin because you're waiting for marriage, or . . .?"

"No, not at all," she says. And I must admit, I have to force myself not to sigh with relief. "I've just been waiting to feel genuine physical chemistry with someone combined with mutual respect and trust." She flashes me a pointed look, as if she's saying, *In other words, I've been waiting for you.* She continues, "I was just talking about 'love' the other day with Georgina, in the context of her breakup with Reed. Georgie said, 'You can love someone with all your heart. But if you don't have mutual respect and *trust*, then you've got nothing.' And I think she's right. So, that's why I'm saying I want to feel respect and trust, above all else. I want to know I'm giving myself to someone who cares about me. Not just having sex with me."

I feel tongue-tied, all of a sudden. Rendered speechless. I want to say, "*I* care about you, Alessandra." But it's too presumptuous. It might make her feel like I'm jockeying to be her first. Like I'm *assuming* I'm going to get to be that guy . . . Shit. I *do* want to be that guy! Of course, I do. But I don't want to say something douchey. Or something that will pressure her. Should I say, "I respect you! You can trust me!"? No. That'd be stupid, too. Again, it'd assume too much.

Fuck.

I just realized the silence between us has become awkward.

I notice the sound of a car driving down my mom's quiet street below.

And then, the sound of Alessandra shifting positions in her bed.

And, suddenly, I realize it's most definitely on *me* to speak next. To make it clear how much I care about her. "Hey, Ally, I don't know if this is too much, too soon, for me to say. But I just want you to know I really, *really* like you. And . . ." I take a deep breath. "I'm not interested in dating anyone else. I know it's hard dating someone long distance, but—"

"I only want to date you," she blurts, like she's been holding her breath underwater. "I'll wait for you, Fish. As long as it takes. I only want you."

Euphoria flashes through me. Grinning from ear to ear, I touch her beautiful face on my computer screen. "I'd give anything to be able to kiss you right now."

"I'd give anything to be kissed."

We stare at each other longingly for a long moment. But when she yawns, and I glance at the clock, it dawns on me, with the time difference, it's closing in on *four* in Boston.

"Aw, shit. I'm such a dick for keeping you up. You've got the lunch shift at work, right?"

She yawns again and nods. "It's okay. I'll drink a ton of coffee."

"Time to get to sleep, Little Lioness."

She pouts. "I won't be able to fall asleep. I'm way too happy about what you just said."

I shoot her a stern look. "Yeah, well, those sleepy eyes of yours are telling a different story, pretty lady."

She yawns, yet again, and rubs her eyes. "Okay. I'll close my eyes and give it a try. Will you sing to me a little bit to help me drift off?"

"Sure. Close your eyes, sweetheart. I'll sing you a little lullaby."

"'Fireflies?'"

I pause. I've played that song countless times in cities all over the world, but I've never sung it before. Not the lead part, anyway. But as I look at Alessandra's beautiful face in repose, her dark lashes fanned against her smooth skin, I realize it's the perfect song for me to sing to her. Because, just like the song says, I'm feeling a whole lot of wings and lights inside me right now. In fact, I've been feeling them since the night I met her.

"A cappella?" I ask.

"Mm-hmm."

"Okay. You got it." I touch her closed eyelids on my screen. And then her cheeks and nose. I take a deep breath and begin to sing in a soft, intimate voice:

Fireflies
You got me feelin' 'em
Never before or since
All my life
Been chasing butterflies
And in just one night
One perfect night . . .
Girl, you made butterflies
Your bitch . . .

In a barely audible voice, I whisper-sing the catchy chorus, like I'm singing it with my lips pressed against her ear. And by the time I finish that portion of the song, I'm convinced she's fast asleep.

"Ally?" I whisper.

"Mm-hmm," comes her soft reply. She opens her big blue eyes and smiles beatifically at me. "You're a wonderful singer, Matthew. You have a beautiful voice to match your beautiful soul."

My heart is thundering. "Same to you."

Her eyelids flutter closed again.

"Sweet dreams, beautiful girl," I say.

"My dreams will be sweet, because I'll surely dream of you."

She blows me a little kiss and languidly disconnects the call . . .

And that's it. She's gone.

And I'm officially head over heels for this girl.

Without missing a beat, I grab my phone and tap out a text to an unlikely recipient. A dude I wouldn't call a text buddy of mine, by any stretch. But there's no doubt this is the text he needs to receive right fucking now:

Hey, Reed. I just got off a video chat with Alessandra. She played me an amazing song she wrote called "Blind-sided." If you listen to one thing I say in this lifetime, then let it be this: As soon as you can, get your ass to Boston and watch Alessandra perform her new song. You're welcome.

SIXTEEN

FISH

I t's Sunday afternoon in Seattle. I'm at Claire Morgan's
first birthday party. And, damn, I wish Alessandra were
here with me in this backyard.

At present, the forty or so people in attendance at the party
are gathered around the birthday girl in her highchair,
watching her mow through a small chocolate cake like she's
that T-Rex in *Jurassic Park*. You know, the one that mowed
through a full-grown cow in one loud gulp.

"Okay, Claire-Bear," Ryan Morgan, the birthday girl's
father, says. He leans over his baby, clearly intending to
extract her from the chair, and she throws up her chocolate-
smeared hands in protest.

Of course, the crowd loves her reaction. If there's one
thing the Morgan family adores, it's a high-spirited kid.

"*Yes*, baby girl," Ryan's wife, Tessa, says to her daughter.
"Cake time is over."

"No!" Claire shouts, splaying her messy fingers. And,
again, the crowd hoots and eggs her on.

Out of nowhere, Keane and Maddy emerge from the

crowd and stand next to Claire's chair. Keane says, "Hey, before you take her away, can Maddy and I ask the birthday girl to help us, real quick?" Without waiting for a reply, Keane hands his chocolate-smeared niece a slender white stick. "Hey, Claire-Bear. Will you hold this up for us?"

I'm not sure what the stick is, but whatever it is, Claire wants to eat it. As she brings the thing to her mouth, Tessa leaps forward to grab it. And when she holds it up, and everyone surmises it's a positive pregnancy test, an explosion of joy bursts from the crowd.

"Please tell me you washed that thing before handing it to my child," Ryan says, whacking his little brother across the top of his blond head.

"That's not a real test!" Keane says, laughing and covering his head. "I got it off a gag website!"

The crowd converges on Keane and Maddy to congratulate them and pepper them with questions. We learn Maddy's at the end of her first trimester and feeling well. And that the baby is due at the end of the year. But that's all the information I can absorb for now, even though I'm thrilled for Maddy and Keane.

The truth is, these days, I can't focus on any topic for long before my thoughts drift to Alessandra. We video chatted again last night, after I got back from taking my mom out to dinner for her birthday. And, once again, our conversation was magical. So much so, by the time we hung up, I felt like our relationship had progressed, yet *again*.

The crowd laughs at something Keane says, jerking me from my thoughts, and I realize Dax and Colin have walked away. That, in fact, they're now sitting in a corner with Zander and Dax's oldest brother, Colby.

I motion to Kat's husband, Josh, on the other side of the

crowd, and then to the corner where the guys are now sitting, and that's all Josh needs to follow me.

When Josh and I arrive in the corner, we pull up chairs and join the conversation in progress. They're talking about Colby's latest addition—his newborn daughter, Hayley, who's presently swaddled in Colby's arms.

I listen for a bit. Again, I'm happy for my friend. But, soon, once again, my mind wanders to Alessandra. When the hell can I get to Boston to see her?

"What about you, Fish Taco?" Ryan, the second-oldest Morgan sibling and our host for today, says. When I look at him, Ryan says, "I asked how your love life is going these days."

"Oh. It's going well. I've actually got a girlfriend. Alessandra." I feel my cheeks turning warm. I *think* Alessandra's my "girlfriend," based on the stuff we said to each other on Friday night. I said I only want her and she returned the sentiment. So, that makes her my "girlfriend," right?

"That's great, Fish," Ryan says.

"Unfortunately, she lives in Boston," I reply. "So, we're doing a long-distance thing at the moment."

Ryan asks me how I met Alessandra, so I tell him, and his older brother, Colby, too, neither of whom were at Reed's party, the entire story. And when it becomes clear Reed's party was a mere nine days ago, I can tell both dudes are thinking I'm putting the cart before the horse. Getting too attached, too quickly. Assuming too much. But I don't think they're right about that, if that's indeed what they're thinking.

"Well, now I understand why you haven't said a word about our mother's hotness today," Colby says. He gestures across the backyard. "Momma Lou's been standing over there doing happy dances about Maddy's pregnancy for the past twenty minutes, and you haven't said a word about her."

I glance across the backyard at Louise and discover she is, indeed, doing a lovely happy dance at this very moment. I force myself not to smile. "I don't know what you're talking about. Momma Lou is like a second mother to me."

Ryan snorts. "Well, then, I guess we should add *Oedipus* to your list of nicknames, eh?"

Everyone laughs, including me.

Keane says, "We all know you've been thirsting after our momma for ten years, brah. Maybe even longer."

I shrug. "*If* that's true—not saying it is—then I think the days of me thirsting after her are now officially over."

"*No*," Colin says.

"Yup. I'm a one-woman man. Thirsting after anyone, even Momma Lou—and even in jest—feels like I'm betraying my girlfriend."

Keane snorts. "Even in jest, my ass."

I roll my eyes.

"So, when are you going to see this girlfriend in Boston?" Ryan asks.

"Not for a couple months, unfortunately. Our schedule is packed."

Dax says, "Violet and Reed are putting together a huge charity concert in New York next month. If you guys are down, let's do it. You could see Alessandra then."

Colin and I confirm we're game. And, suddenly, out of nowhere, I've got a date when I'll get to see my woman—assuming she's available to come to New York on the night of the concert.

Dax says. "Why don't we plan to play that concert and then take a full week off afterward? It'll put us behind the eight ball a bit on finishing the album in time, but I'm willing to put in extra-long days after that, if you guys are. This way, Fish can spend time with his woman. I can take the fam on a little tropical vacay. And Colin can . . . whatever."

"I can't believe I'm gonna get to see her," I say, more to myself than anyone else. "God, I hope she can make it."

Dax says to Colin, "Will your billboard be up in Times Square by then?"

"It should be."

Keane asks, "What billboard?" And just like that, the conversation shifts to Colin's underwear campaign, which, of course, elicits raucous conversation and commentary. But, quickly, my mind drifts again. Alessandra. I'm going to see her again!

Out of nowhere, a weird cocktail of excitement and anxiety floods me. Obviously, I'm dying to get physical with Alessandra when/if I get to see her in New York. I don't know, for sure, if Alessandra will want to have sex with me there, or at some future time, but what if she does? *And what if she wants to do it in New York?* I've never been with a virgin before. I wonder if there's something specific I should know to make it extra special for her?

My gaze drifts across the faces in the group, and I suddenly realize, in aggregate, these men have ten lifetimes' more sexual experience than me. So, I decide not to miss out on a golden opportunity.

"Hey, guys, can I ask you for some confidential advice?" I glance toward the women on the far side of the party, making sure they can't overhear me. "If I get to see Alessandra in New York, I don't know how physical our relationship will become. We haven't even kissed yet—it's a long story. So,

I'm not sure exactly what might happen. I mean, we're going to kiss. Obviously. But beyond that—"

"She's a virgin and you're asking for advice?" Keane says.

"Shhh! Peenie. *Jesus.*"

"Just trying to help. Isn't that what you're so artfully getting at?"

I exhale. "Yes. I'm not assuming anything, mind you. I just . . . don't want to blow it for her if it turns out things go that direction."

Colby, our calm and quiet Master Yoda, says, "How old is she, Fish?"

"Nineteen. Turning twenty in two months. She said she's been waiting for the right guy. Someone she really trusts. She didn't say that guy was going to be me, mind you, but she kind of implied I *might* be on her short list. So . . ."

Colby looks down at his sleeping daughter in his arms. "My best advice? Don't pressure her. Ever."

"Oh, yeah. That's a given. I'd never do that. But, I mean, I think it's fair to say she's thinking about doing this with me, without me pressuring her. And, you know, that'd be great with me. But, like I said, I'd want to give her the best possible experience . . ."

"Just watch all my early 'Ball Peen Hammer' videos," Keane says. "Those will tell you everything you need to know about ringing the bell."

He's talking about the YouTube series he stars in, that's shot by his wife, Maddy. In recent years, their show has become about their relationship and adventures as a couple. But in the beginning, Keane—as his alter ego, "Ball Peen Hammer"—talked about women and sex and the best techniques for making women reach orgasm on command.

"I've got some advice," Zander says. "Whatever you do,

don't turn into the Flash on her in The Big Moment. My very first time, she was a virgin, too, and I was so damned excited, I lost it within seconds of going in. I'll never forget that poor girl furrowing her brow and saying, 'Is that *it*? *Did we do it*?'"

Everyone grimaces and laughs, including me.

"Just to be sure you last, you should beat off a few hours beforehand," Keane declares.

"Man, I wish I'd done that," Zander says.

"I've got some advice," Ryan says. "*Foreplay.* Engage in *lots* of it with her. Like, a ridiculous amount."

"Well, obviously."

"No. Way, *way* beyond what you think is obvious," Ryan replies. "With anyone, but especially a virgin."

"Maybe try hitting her with The Sure Thing, as foreplay?" Keane says.

Everyone in the group, other than me, tells Keane that's the stupidest idea they've ever heard and he needs to shut the fuck up.

"She needs to get her sea legs first, before you hit her with that, Fish," Ryan says. "You know that, right?"

I feel myself blushing. "Oh, of course. I wasn't planning to do that . . . any time soon."

"Oh, shit," Keane says, scrutinizing me. "You've never gotten The Sure Thing working for you, have you?"

Damn.

I'm a terrible liar.

Always have been.

It practically killed me when I lied to these guys about my supposed sexual exploits with my fake girlfriend in high school. And I really don't want to go through that again. I'm a grown man now. Done with lying about anything. Plus, if it turns out Alessandra picks me as her first, then I'd kick myself if I didn't use this amazing think tank to get the best possible advice. "Um. That's correct. I've never figured out The Sure Thing."

"Dude!" Keane says. "I've got an entire video on it!"

Ryan puts up his hand. "Stop, Peenie. The Sure Thing isn't what he should be focusing on right now." He looks at me. "All you need to worry about is making sure you know how to ring her bell, the good old-fashioned way, no matter what. You can do that, right?"

"*No matter what?*"

"Right. Every time. Without fail. *No matter what.*"

I open my mouth, like I'm going to speak, and then close it. And I guess that's enough to answer Ryan's question in the negative.

Everyone around me sighs like a whole bunch of disappointed dads.

"Aw, come on," I say. "You guys are *honestly* able to get your women to reach the finish line every *single* time you have sex or fool around?"

They all say some version of "yes" and "every fucking time."

"But couldn't they be faking it sometimes?" I ask innocently. And I swear, by their reactions, I might as well have asked if their women sneak off in the middle of the night to suck other guys' cocks.

"Sorry," I say. "Calm down." I rake my hand through my hair. "What do I know? I've never had a girlfriend! I've never had the pleasure of getting to know *one* woman and what works best for her. I've never had the chance to practice my skills! It's hard to figure women out! They're complicated, especially when, to be perfectly honest, it's often abundantly clear I wasn't their first choice. Sometimes, it's like they're going through the motions with me—closing their eyes and pretending I'm someone else. So, it's no wonder I don't feel some kind of white-hot electricity, and neither do they."

There's a long silence.

I suddenly feel vulnerable.

Like I've admitted too much.

Colin says, "What about that girlfriend you had in high school—the one who lived near your dad?"

I rub my face and exhale. "She didn't exist. I was a virgin until we went to London, right before the RCR tour."

Colin and Dax look at each other . . . and smile.

"We already knew that, Fish," Dax says. "Sorry you felt like you had to lie to us. That sucks."

"But thanks for *finally* unburdening your conscience and coming clean," Colin adds with a snort.

I'm aghast. "You *knew*? How?"

Colin scoffs. "Well, first off, you can't lie to save your life, Fish Filet. It's one of the best things about you. You always wear your heart on your sleeve."

"And, second off," Dax interjects. "When you burst out of that hotel room in London the following morning, you were singin' a happy tune, son. Like nothing I'd heard ya sing before."

Colin laughs. "You were fucking *yodeling,* dude."

Everyone laughs.

"Why didn't you tell me you knew?" I ask.

Dax shrugs. "We knew why you lied. There was no reason to rub salt in the wound."

I shake my head. "That girl in London wasn't even that amazing an experience, looking back. I knew she was settling for me. But I was so relieved to finally get that monkey off my back, I didn't even care. But now, I do. I want to be with someone who genuinely wants to be with me. And that's Alessandra. She's amazing, guys. She's everything I've ever wanted. So, if it turns out I get to be her first, I want to make it perfect for her. Magical."

"You know what you should do?" Josh says, out of nowhere. "Talk to Kat about this."

"To *Kat*?" I echo. This dude wants me to talk to his *wife* about sex?

Josh nods. "Sex is *literally* her favorite topic. Look, you want to know how we get our women off? We'll send you links to some books to read and some videos to watch. Chief among them, those early 'Ball Peen Hammer' videos. Some of them are damned good."

"Thank you," Keane says proudly.

"But if you want to know what would make a woman's first time special and *magical*, then you're going to have to ask a woman. And, trust me, there's no better woman in the world to ask than my wife."

I look across the patio at Kat. "Do you think she'd be willing to talk to me about this?"

"I think she'd be elated."

He pulls out his phone and taps on it, and, ten seconds later, his gorgeous wife is standing before me, her blue eyes sparkling.

"What's up, Fishy Wishy?" she says, cradling her baby bump. "My hubster tells me you want to talk about sex."

SEVENTEEN

FISH

"**Y**ou've come to the right place," Kat says.

She and I are sitting together in Ryan and Tessa's living room. I've just finished stumbling and stammering through my explanation of why I wanted to speak with her in private. "If it turns out I'm Alessandra's first at some point," I say, "I don't want to blow it. I'll want to make sure it's really special and perfect for her."

"That's so sweet."

"So, do you have some advice or tips for me?"

"I do." She points at my phone. "Take notes, honey. I've got some pearls for ya."

I pull out my phone and swipe into the notepad. "Okay. Lay those pearls on me, dudette."

"Foreplay," Kat says reverently. "Everything you do with Alessandra will be a first for her. Every touch, every sensation. So, you need to give her time to adjust and settle in, each step of the way. Make like *molasses*, honey. At least, at first, while she's still learning. You understand?"

I nod.

"I'll send you some links about foreplay. Some videos. I promise, you'll thank me." She points at my phone. "Write down 'molasses.'"

"Already did."

"Good boy. Don't forget 'foreplay' is *both* physical and *mental*. Every conversation is *foreplay*. Every smile. *Compliment her frequently*."

"It'd be impossible *not* to compliment her constantly. She's amazing."

"Good boy. Now, listen. Don't say anything about her turning you on because she's 'so pure' and 'chaste' and 'innocent.'" Kat rolls her eyes. "That's fetishizing her virginity, Fish. And it will ultimately backfire on you. It might lead to her feeling insecure about her sexuality, or maybe even ashamed of it. She might not feel comfortable exploring her wild side with you. And you don't want to miss out on her wild side." Her eyes gleam. "Trust me, that's the best part of any woman."

"Damn, Kat," I murmur, and she laughs. "Don't worry. I'd never think Alessandra's only sexy because she's a virgin. She's just sexy. Period."

"Good boy. Always reinforce that messaging—that's she's hot to you, not because she's a virgin, but because she's *Alessandra*."

I nod. "Got it. Thank you."

Kat leans back into the couch. "Last but not least, when it comes to sex or fooling around, *always* make sure she gets *hers*. Whether it's her first time, or her millionth. Never, *ever* get yours and leave your woman hanging. You hear me? *Never.* If you leave your woman hanging, then you're a hideous monster, and not the good kind."

I feel myself blushing crimson. "Um . . ."

"What? I'm here and I'm an expert. Ask me anything."

"The thing is . . . I'm totally down for that rule . . ." I scratch my chin. "In theory. But I'm not some kind of sex god, to be honest. I can't *guarantee* to get a woman there, every time. No matter what. Also, Alessandra has told me— and this is confidential, Kat—that she's not always successful with *herself.* So, if *Alessandra* can't reliably make it happen for her, then—"

"I get it. Oh man, I'm so glad you're telling me this." She points at my phone. "O-M-G yes dot com." When I look at her blankly, she repeats the comment before explaining, "It's a website *by* women *for* women about the female orgasm. You're right to wonder how you're going to get Alessandra there, reliably, if she can't do it for herself. What Alessandra needs to do is watch videos on that website and figure out which techniques get her off, pretty much without fail. Once she knows what works for her, she can communicate that to *you.*"

I'm incredulous. "You're suggesting I tell Alessandra about a website that teaches her how to masturbate effectively?"

She nods. "And then tell her to send *you* links to whichever videos—"

"Are you high?" I whisper-shout, so nobody in the nearby birthday party will overhear us. "Kat, I can't talk to Alessandra about any of that! Yes, she's told me she's a virgin, but it's not like we've *expressly* agreed I'm going to be The Guy!"

"I thought it was a done deal."

"No! She's *hinted.* Implied. I'm *hoping.* But I can't make that kind of presumption and tell her to send me links to her favorite masturbation techniques so I can use them on her! Do you have any idea how presumptuous and douchey that would be of me?"

"Well, shit. Don't get your little Fish-panties in a twist. I misunderstood." She taps the indentation in her chin. "Okay, new plan. *I'll* tell *Georgina* to tell *Alessandra* about that website. When Georgie spent the night at my house the other day, we talked about *everything*, including how much Alessandra adores *you*. So, I can confidently tell you—*in confidence*—you're not the only one in your relationship who's thinking about these things."

My heart stops. "Georgina told you Alessandra wants to have sex with *me*?"

Kat presses her lips together. "I've already said too much. All you need to know is I'll sprinkle a little fairy dust on my end of things and help Alessandra along—which, in turn, will help you both down the line." She winks. "But the missing link is that, one day, *if* the opportunity presents itself, then you need to be ready to encourage Alessandra to communicate with you about what works for her."

I rub my forehead. "Thank God I talked to you about this, Kat. *Thank you.*"

"My pleasure." Her features soften. "At the end of the day, the most important thing is for you to be your darling self with her and, I promise, she'll be putty in your cute little Fish fins."

I scoff. "Says the woman who greeted me with 'Fuck off' for a solid year in middle school."

"I did not."

"You did and you know it."

Kat grimaces. "I'm sorry. I don't know why I was so mean to you."

"I do. You knew I had a huge crush on you, and you were trying to find out the outer limits of my loyalty."

"I'm a horrible person."

"You are. But you're also the best."

"You didn't deserve that. You've always been a sweetheart. Although, if you don't mind me saying, these days you're a sweetheart *and* a hunk. What the heck have you been doing to yourself lately, Matthew? You've turned into a fox."

I scoff.

"It's true. Even my mother noticed during your last tour. She said, 'Matthew's looking so handsome these days!'"

I blush. "She did not."

"She did!"

I can't help smiling broadly. "It's nothing. The last couple tours, Colin's been forcing protein shakes down my throat, and I've been surfing a ton since I've been home."

"No, it's more than that. You've got confidence now."

I shrug. "I dunno. I'm a late bloomer, I guess. I finally stopped growing and my body was able to catch up."

"No, you've got swagger now."

I snort.

"You do! Well, whatever it is, you're a freaking smoke show now, honey." She winks. "That Alessandra is one lucky girl."

Before I've figured out what to say to Kat in response to that, my phone buzzes on the coffee table.

"It's her!" I blurt. "It's Ally."

Kat pops up from the couch. "Don't forget: *every* conversation is foreplay!" With that, she glides out of the living room, her baby bump leading the way.

I connect the call. "Hey, beautiful!"

"I just got the most incredible news!" Alessandra shouts

happily. "Georgie and Reed are coming to Boston this week to watch me perform at the coffeehouse!" She tells me the whole story without taking a breath, and I express excitement.

"Georgie is coming with Reed?" I say. "Are they back together?"

"They are! Apparently, Reed did some epic groveling." She giggles. "So, will you help me decide on my set list? I *really* want to impress Reed."

"You bet. We'll go over it tonight. But, of course, you'll want to kick things off with 'Blindsided.'"

"Okay!"

"I actually have some great news to tell you, too. I'm coming to the East Coast, much earlier than expected!" I tell her about the charity concert next month and invite her to join me in New York, and she flat-out freaks out.

We make plans, deciding to spend a few days sightseeing in New York after the concert and then fly to Boston together to hang out there for a full week after that.

"Oh, I have to go," she says. "My mom is calling on the other line."

"I'm sure she's excited about Reed coming to your show."

"I haven't told her yet. You were my first call. Bye, babe!" And she's gone, leaving that electrifying "babe" swirling in the air, like the finest perfume.

Babe.

I've been called all sorts of endearments by women. Baby. Sweetie. Honey. Cutie. Every twist on the nickname Fish. Surely, I've been called babe, too.

But never has an endearment hardened my dick the way Alessandra's "babe" just did.

Man, these next several weeks awaiting my reunion with Alessandra in New York will be torture. I'll literally be counting the minutes. But that's okay. Because I know what I'm waiting for now. And I know it's going to be well worth the wait. In truth, I'd rather date Alessandra via phone calls, texts, and video chats for the next however many weeks, than date literally anyone else, in person.

"Holy shit," I whisper to myself, my heart clanging in my chest. But, after a few deep breaths, my hard-on has subsided a bit. My heart rate slowed to a manageable level. And so, I get up, shift my package in my pants, and saunter back into the party, feeling like I'm on top of the fucking world.

EIGHTEEN
ALESSANDRA

I jeté like a goofball into my small apartment, leaving Georgina and Reed chuckling behind me at my exuberance. I'm a tipsy girl tonight, thanks to the fancy champagne Mr. Fancy Pants ordered at Georgina's birthday dinner earlier—the fabulous meal Reed, Georgie, and I enjoyed . . . *right after Reed Rivers made all my dreams come true*! Oh my God! At the end of my set at the coffee house, Reed hugged me and said, "That was *exactly* the kind of performance I wanted you to give me at my party, Ally! Let's make 'Blindsided' a worldwide hit!"

My roommate, McKenna, bursts into the living room from her bedroom, apparently lured by the sound of Reed, Georgina, and me entering the apartment. Almost certainly, McKenna is intending to ask me how my performance at the coffeehouse went earlier, and the minute she finds the head of River Records standing in the middle of our apartment, she gasps like she's seeing a ghost.

I bound over to McKenna and pull her over to Reed and Georgina. "McKenna, this is my beloved sister, Georgina, and her *boyfriend*, Reed Rivers—the founder and CEO of River Records—which, as of tonight . . . *is my new* record *label!*"

McKenna's jaw practically clanks to the floor.

"Yep," Reed says. "Ally is now officially a River Records artist. Well, we've come to a verbal agreement, anyway. Paperwork will be signed this week."

McKenna looks shocked. She chokes out, "Are you messing with me?"

And when I swear I'm not, when I swear Reed signed me to a one-song deal, she throws her arms around me and squeals.

"It's only for one song," I murmur into McKenna's hair, not wanting to make this sound like a bigger deal than it is. I mean, it *is* a big deal. The biggest deal of my life, besides getting into Berklee. But I'm not a fool. I know Reed only signed me because he's trying to win favor with Georgina. At dinner, Reed denied that was the case. He said, "I'd never compromise my business judgment for anyone or anything, even Georgie. My name and reputation are far too valuable for that." And, of course, I appreciated his assurances. But I'm young, not stupid. So much so, halfway through dinner, I actually contemplated turning Reed down.

But then, I thought, *Are you crazy, Alessandra?* I realized, while I probably got this chance through nepotism, what matters *now* is what I do with that chance. It's not the same thing, but I thought about Fish saying he didn't have to audition for 22 Goats because he's known Dax since second grade. And I thought to myself, "Regardless of how Fish got into his band, look how much he's learned and blossomed through the years! Well, Alessandra, you can learn and blossom, too, just like Fish, under Reed's expert guidance!"

And it won't only be *Reed's* guidance, either. At dinner,

Reed said he wants to hire freaking Zeke Emmanuel, the hottest producer in the music biz—the architect of Laila's blockbuster sophomore album—to produce my single! And how could I say no to that, even if Reed is only signing me as a gift to Georgina? Plus, it's not like I totally sucked tonight. On the contrary, I sang all my songs better than ever. Especially "Blindsided." When I sang that one, I felt like I'd cracked open my very soul for the audience!

"Should we open this up, ladies?" Reed says, holding up the bottle of fancy champagne he brought with him from the restaurant.

"Does a bear poop in the woods, Reed Rivers?" I shout, and both Reed and Georgie look at each other and guffaw.

"She's hilarious when she drinks," Reed says.

Georgina giggles. "She does it so rarely, I always feel like I'm watching a shooting star streaking across the sky, when she does."

"I'll get cups!" I sing out happily, and then jeté joyfully across the room into my small kitchen.

Flowers.

I stop short when I see them on the kitchen counter—a spectacular bouquet of stargazer lilies and purple lilacs. I rush over to the vase and inhale deeply, and then snatch up the small envelope on the counter with my name on it.

"Break a leg tonight, Little Lioness. I know you're gonna SLAY. Sending lots and lots of kisses. TGCFWHLB.BNR."

I laugh out loud when I decode the sender's initials: *The Goat Called Fish Who's Hung Like a Bull. But Not Really.*

Obviously, my darling Fish intended me to get this gift *before* my gig tonight, but I wasn't here all day to receive them. "Oh, Matthew," I whisper to myself, holding the card to my breasts. I lean down and smell the fragrant flowers again, and feel my skin erupt with goose bumps at the coded messages embedded in these special blooms.

Almost certainly, Fish didn't *personally* choose the flowers in this bouquet. Surely, the florist did, after consultation with Fish. I'm sure Fish told the florist his recipient was hoping to impress a big record label guy, so the florist smartly suggested *stargazers* as the perfect bloom.

As for the purple lilacs . . . Yes, they're making my heart burst with excitement. But that's because *I'm* a weirdo who knows exactly what they meant in Victorian times. Surely, though, Fish has no idea what purple lilacs mean! The florist probably asked Fish my favorite color, and he correctly guessed purple, thanks to the bikini I was wearing when he met me.

But, damn.

It's no use.

Even though my brain knows this bouquet couldn't possibly mean what the flowers are screaming at me, my heart desperately wants to believe Fish knew *exactly* what he was telling me—but only because the coded messages in these flowers are all the same things I'd tell Fish, if only I had the courage.

Take the stargazer lilies, for example. In the language of flowers, lilies connote romantic love, but in a much different way than red roses. Whereas red roses are all about burning, carnal passion, lilies connote a more heartfelt, poetic kind of romance. When a lady in Victorian times was sent lilies by her suitor, she knew he wanted to make her his lover. But not only physically. That, too, yes. But lilies meant he wanted her to become his lover in every sense of the word. In his bed, and in his life.

I admit I could be overanalyzing the lilies. Indeed, if they were standing alone, then they could mean, simply, joy. Or purity and innocence. Maybe even prosperity.

But the purple lilacs.

They're the flowers that *always* mean the same thing.

The first pangs of love.

Which means, no matter what, this bouquet would be a declaration of the first pangs of love from Fish, *if* he were obsessed with the language of flowers, like me. Which he's not. And I know it. So, they're not. But, hey, regardless, the bouquet is stunning and thoughtful and smells divine.

Sighing happily, I grab four cups from a cupboard and return to the living room.

Reed pours the bubbly, Georgina makes a sweet toast that makes me tear up, and we sit with our glasses and tell a flabbergasted McKenna the story of the night. After a while, though, I get thirsty and offer to refill everyone's empty glasses with water.

"I'll help you," Georgina says. And off we go into the kitchen.

When Georgina sees the bouquet on the kitchen counter from Fish, she stops and gasps the same way I did. "They're gorgeous!" she says. "How romantic!"

And what do I reply? "I want to lose my virginity to Fish when I see him in New York!"

Georgina laughs at my bluntness. "Had you decided that *before* drinking those three glasses of champagne tonight—or *after*?"

I blush. "*Before.* You know I've been thinking about this.

The champagne is just truth serum."

"I know, honey. I'm so happy for you. I can't imagine a more perfect guy for you. He's as sweet as you are."

We walk to the sink and begin washing and drying the four glasses together.

I hand Georgina a glass to dry. "I'm dying to get naked with him. If he were here right now, I'd kick you and Reed out, drag him into my bedroom, and lose my V-card *tonight*."

Georgina chuckles and takes the next glass from me. "This seems like a good time to ask if you checked out that website I told you about?"

"I sure did. It's a gold mine."

"Isn't it?"

"It made me realize I'm not weird or defective. I just didn't understand my body. But now, I'm ready and rarin' to go, baby!"

Georgie laughs again. "Good for you."

The sound of a violin wafts into the small kitchen and Georgina pulls a face I'd caption as, *What the hell?*

"McKenna," I say, by way of explanation. My roommate is a brilliant violinist who's hoping to play for a renowned symphony one day.

"She's amazing," Georgie says.

"She is. I'm shocked she's playing for Reed, though. She's usually even shier than me."

We quickly fill the four glasses with water and head into the living room, where we discover Reed on the couch, watching intently as McKenna stands above him and plays for him.

Georgie and I quietly take seats on either side of Reed, and when McKenna is done, all three of us clap and compliment her.

"*Very* impressive," Reed says. "When you graduate, drop me a line. I don't know anyone at any symphonies, but if I know of anyone looking to add violin to a track, or to a tour, I'll hook you up." With that, Reed gulps his water, rises from the couch, and extends his hand to Georgina. "Ready to go, Birthday Girl? I know parting is such sweet sorrow when it comes to you and Ally, but I've got one more birthday present waiting for you, back at the hotel."

He smirks and Georgina flashes him a scorching smile in return. And it doesn't take a genius to know they're both itching to head back to their hotel to bang the ever-loving hell out of each other.

Georgina hugs me. "Bye, sweetie. We've got an early flight to LA tomorrow. We'd better hit the hay."

"Mm-hmm," I say, trying to control my snark. "Happy birthday, love."

When Georgie and I disengage, Reed hugs me goodbye. And to my surprise, his embrace feels warm and enthusiastic. Lovely and sincere. Not the least bit performative or polite. Clearly, this hug isn't a show for Georgie's benefit. He's expressing genuine affection. And it touches me.

"Goodbye, kiddo," Reed says into my hair. "Welcome to River Records."

Tears prick my eyes at his warmth. "Thank you, Reed. This is the best day of my life."

"God, I hope not." He smiles at me, his dark eyes sparkling. "Owen will send the paperwork this week. He'll be your main point of contact, regarding initial logistics. I'll be in touch, as necessary, regarding substantive matters."

"Okay." I salute him. "Yes, sir."

Georgina squeezes me again, and holds me for a very long

moment, like she's memorizing how I feel in her arms. "I love you," she says simply.

"I love you, too."

We say our final goodbyes, and off Reed and Georgie go into the night, presumably to screw like rabbits.

The moment our front door closes, McKenna flops onto our couch, throws her head back in abject surrender, and screams mournfully. "Oh my God! I thought I was gonna puke!"

Giggling, I flop down next to my friend and pat her leg. "You've got balls, Ken. I'm impressed you played for him when you had him to yourself."

"Are you crazy? I'd never do that! Reed *insisted* I play for him! He asked what I study, and I told him. He asked my favorite piece to play, and I told him. And the next thing you know, fuck my life, I was standing there playing Shostakovich for Reed freaking Rivers!" Shaking her head, she grabs the champagne bottle off the coffee table and takes a long gulp. "No wonder you melted down at his party. Dude, you said he was intimidating. But I had *no* idea."

"Yeah, but, unlike me, you didn't collapse under pressure."

"Only because I didn't have anywhere to run!"

We both giggle again.

I take the bottle from her and finish it off. "He's actually so much nicer than he initially seemed to me. He has this way of talking that seems so . . . stern. But once you understand that's just the way he looks, you realize he's actually a sweetheart. Really sincere and generous."

"If you say so."

"He just offered to try to get you jobs after graduation!"

"He wasn't serious."

"But he *was*. That's what I'm saying. He's actually very nice. And he's so good to Georgina. It's so lovely to see how much he respects and likes her. They're friends, not just lovers."

McKenna cocks her eyebrow. "Speaking of *lovers* . . . I'm assuming you saw the flowers from *your* loverrrrr in the kitchen?"

"I did. They're gorgeous."

"What do they mean?"

I feel my cheeks warming. "Oh, just, you know . . . good luck, basically. He knew Reed was coming to my show and I was shooting for the stars. So, he sent stargazers."

"Clever."

I look at my watch. "It's actually perfect timing for me to give my *loverrr* a call to thank him."

I rise, and so does McKenna.

"Congratulations on getting signed, Ally. I'm so happy for you."

"It's just one song, and Reed only did it as a birthday gift to Georgina."

McKenna startles me by putting her palms on my cheeks. "*No.* Don't say that. Reed did it because he knows a rising star when he sees one."

I press my lips together, to keep my emotions at bay. "Thank you."

She squeals and takes my hands. "You're a River Records artist, bitch! The same as Aloha, Laila, and Red Card Riot!"

"Don't forget 22 Goats!"

McKenna palms her forehead. "Can you believe this is your life, Ally?"

I laugh, shaking my head. "No, I can't. Not even a little bit."

NINETEEN
FISH

I'm in bed in LA. Alessandra's in bed in Boston. And for the past half hour she's been telling me about her amazing day, including the part where Reed offered her a one-song recording and publishing deal for "Blindsided."

Alessandra twirls a lock of her dark hair around her finger. "You know what *other* cool thing happened tonight?"

I smile. "I think I know. But tell me, anyway."

She leans forward, so that her big blue eyes fill my entire laptop screen. "I found out I *really* like champagne!"

I laugh. That's got to be the seventh time she's said that during this conversation. "Wait. What?" I tease. "Alessandra Tennison likes *champagne*? Huh. I hadn't heard that."

Giggling, she drags her fingertip across her laptop camera, like she's touching my face. "Oh, Matthew. You're so beautiful." She arches an eyebrow. "And *hot*." She drags her fingertip across her plush lower lip. "Hey, Matthew?"

"Yes, beautiful?"

She cocks her head. "Have you been putting that video you took of me to good use . . . *loverrrr?*"

Whoa.

Since that amazing night when we recorded videos of each other, we haven't talked about them. In fact, we haven't talked about anything sexual again. But I've got to say, I like where this conversation is headed.

I smile. "As a matter of fact, yes, I've been putting that video of you to *very, very* good and frequent use. What about you? Have you been putting that video of *me* to good use?"

Alessandra sinks into her pillow, taking her laptop with her. "Yes, sir. Very, *very* good and frequent and highly *effective* use. Do you remember how I said I sometimes have trouble reaching orgasm?" She winks. "Scratch that. I'm a pro now, baby."

Jesus. "Is that because of that video of me, or has something else helped you figure things out?"

"That video of you, plus other visual aids. Photos of you on the internet. Interviews of you. Music videos featuring you. Thoughts and fantasies I have about you, while I'm in bed and in the shower. All of it, used along with a few techniques I've recently learned, thanks to a really cool website."

Eureka. I feel like I'm a gold digger who's just hit the mother lode. "Tell me more about this website."

"It has videos that help women figure themselves out. So, I watched a few things and realized what I'd been doing wrong. What I could do *right*. And, *boom*, practice makes perfect."

Thank you, Kat.

Thank you, Georgina.

Thank you, Baby Jesus.

I take a deep breath, not wanting to let on how excited I am. How aroused and enthralled and hard. "What's the website called? I'll check it out."

"Oh, no. It's not porn. It's for women to learn."

"Yeah, but . . ." I trail off, not sure how to proceed. Obviously, I want to explain the big picture to her . . . The fact that, if this stuff works for her, then I should know about it, too. Duh. But we still haven't gone there explicitly, and I don't think *I* should be the one to kick open that door.

"What are you thinking, Matthew?" she says, sounding very much like a woman who's been drinking some happy juice.

I pause. Weigh the pros and cons. And decide, fuck it, I'll inch this conversation forward a bit. "I'm thinking I wish I could be a fly on the wall when you masturbate."

There.

I said it.

That wasn't pressuring her, right? She asked me what I was thinking and I told her one of my honest thoughts.

Thankfully, Alessandra doesn't look the least bit upset with me. Only turned on. So I forge ahead. "I like imagining what your face looks like when you have an orgasm. I think about that *a lot*."

Her nostrils flare. "I like imagining that very same thing about you."

"Is that so?" I begin stroking myself slowly underneath my covers, well out of frame. "Good. Because now I'm imagining *you* imagining *me*. And that's a turn-on."

She smiles. "What do you picture when you fantasize about me masturbating?"

At her question, my cock jolts in my hand. I begin beating off a little faster. Breathing a little bit harder. "Um. Well, I . . . imagine you lying naked in your bed. I imagine your legs spread and your hand touching your . . . pussy."

"Mm-hmm?"

"I imagine your bare breasts and hard nipples. Your eyes are closed. Your lips parted. I imagine your hair splayed on your pillow." I swallow hard. "I imagine you moaning. And then, when you finally come, you scrunch up your face and kind of whimper and groan."

"Oh, wow. This is a detailed fantasy. Are you there with me? Or just a fly on the wall?"

"I'm there with you now."

"What are you doing?"

I can barely breathe. "Lying next to you."

"Are you naked?"

"Is it okay for me to be naked?"

"Yes."

"Then, I'm naked. Can I touch you?"

"Yes. Would you touch my breasts if you were here with me now, Fish?"

I literally convulse at the thought. "If you'd let me."

Her breathing hitches. "I'd not only let you touch me, Matthew. *I'd beg you.*"

I let out a little moan and let go of my dick so I won't jizz, right here and now.

"Alessandra," I choke out. "You turn me on so much. I'm obsessed with you. Only you. I don't think of anyone else."

She moans, ever so softly, and it suddenly occurs to me . . . Holy fucking shit! I'm not the only one touching myself off-screen! Alessandra is doing it, too!

I decide to nudge her to confess it to me. "Can I make a confession to you?" I slide my hand to my hard cock again. "I'm touching myself right now."

She flushes crimson. "Me, too."

Bingo.

Arousal floods me in an overwhelming torrent. Pre-cum

drips onto my hand. I can barely breathe. "Alessandra, will you make yourself come for me, off-screen, while I watch your face?"

She looks like she's considering it. She whispers, "I don't think I could get myself there, with you watching me."

"No harm in trying."

She licks her lips. Her breathing is heavy. "Maybe if you do it first? I'd love to see your face when you come." She pauses. "But just your face, okay? For now."

For now.

Hot damn.

This is an awesome conversation.

"Whatever you want. Are you sure about this? You've been drinking."

She scoffs. "I've been wanting this since long before I took my first sip of champagne tonight. The champagne is only giving me the courage to tell you what I want."

"You never need champagne or anything else to do that, okay? You can always tell me what you want."

She nods, her big blue eyes wide. "Will you do it for me while I watch your face?"

"That's what you want?"

She nods. "But before you get going . . . Are you in your underwear right now?"

"No. I'm naked in bed."

"Good. Will you pan your camera down and let me see you?"

"You want to see my . . .?"

"Hard dick."

I laugh, simply because that wasn't the word choice I was expecting.

"Is that okay?" she says.

"It's fantastic."

"If you pan down and let me see *you*, then, in exchange, I'll flash you a little nipple afterward."

"You've got yourself a bargained-for exchange, pretty lady. Are you ready now?"

She's breathing hard. "I'm ready."

"Okay. One hard dick coming up!" I remove the blanket from my torso. "Dicks ahoy, baby! Well, *dick* ahoy. I only have one." Without further ado, I pan my camera down . . . past my chest . . . down my abs . . . following my treasure trail . . . "You're still at yes?" I call out.

"Yes!"

I aim my camera at my straining cock—eliciting a soft "Oooh" from Alessandra—before returning the camera to my face. "And there you have it. Objective proof I'm not *actually* hung like a bull. Like I told you, I'm just an average dude with an average-size dick."

"I dunno, dude. You look hung like a bull to me."

I snort. "Based on your vast experience."

"I've seen dicks on the internet. Granted, I'm no dick *connoisseur*, but . . ." She giggles. "I guess 'hung like a bull' is a relative term, depending on who's saying it. A dick probably looks a whole lot bigger to the girl who's planning to get impaled by it, than the boy who's going to be the impaler."

And there it is.

She actually said it.

Out loud and explicitly.

"Hello?" Alessandra says, even though she's staring right at me. "Did you have a stroke?"

"You've been thinking about having sex with me?"

She rolls her eyes. "Only every day of my life."

I exhale. "Same."

Alessandra looks a bit shy, all of a sudden. "We'll have to take it slow when we see each other, though. One baby step at a time."

"Of course."

"But, yes, eventually, I want to do every freaking thing there is to do with you, when we see each other in New York."

I open my mouth to speak, but nothing comes out. In fact, I think I might have died and gone to heaven.

"Matthew? Are you okay?"

I close my eyes and make a blissful face. "*I'm so happy.*"

She giggles. "You wanna see my nipple now, loverrrr?"

I nod effusively. "Nipples, ahoy!"

"Only *one* for now."

"Nipple ahoy!" I slide my hand underneath the covers again, straight to my hard cock, readying myself for the singular beauty I'm about to behold. "I'm ready."

Her nostrils flaring, she leans into her camera and gives me a little kiss. And then, she pans her camera down, showing me the pink fabric of her tank, before, suddenly, without warning, pulling the fabric down and exposing her perky breast and hard nipple. And, just like that, I'm on the bitter cusp of coming.

Her face returns to the screen. "You're the first boy to see that, ever."

"You're gorgeous. That almost got me there."

"You're close?"

"Very close." My balls tighten. Tingles shoot through my dick in my hand. "I'm so fucking close."

She leans into her camera and speaks in a sultry voice. "God, I wish I could lie down in that bed with you, naked, and touch your hard dick the way you're touching it right now."

Well, that does it. With a strained grunt, I come onto my stomach, while doing God knows what with my face.

"And there it is," Alessandra whispers, apparently reading my facial expression to a T.

I take a few deep breaths and smile at her. "That was a damned good one. Hearing your voice was really hot for me. Thank you."

"You're very, very welcome." She flashes me a naughty smile. "I touched myself toward the end there. I didn't finish, though. I'll do that after we hang up."

"We don't have to hang up for you to do that."

"No, we do. I'm not as brave as you yet."

Yet.

"Okay, baby. Whatever is comfortable for you. Like you said. Baby steps. We'll do everything at your pace."

"Thank you." She smiles beautifully. "Good night, Matthew. My loverrrrrr."

"Good night, Little Lioness. Sweet dreams."

"They're always sweet, because I always dream of you."

She leans into her camera with puckered lips, and I do the same.

"Huge congrats on your record deal, you little badass."

"I couldn't have done it without you."

"Yes, you could. Send me whatever paperwork Reed sends you. I'll ask our lawyer to take a look."

"Oh. Thank you. That didn't occur to me."

"Reed would never try to screw you over, given the dynamics. But let's take a look, anyway."

"What would I do without you?" She flashes me a beaming smile that lights my soul. "Oh, Fish. *Matthew.* I'm counting down the days until I see you again."

"Me, too, sweetheart. Honestly, I'm counting the minutes. The seconds."

She flashes me a lovely smile. "Me, too. Good night now, my darling."

"Good night, beautiful. Talk soon."

TWENTY
ALESSANDRA

I rush into my small kitchen, throw my keys onto the counter, and immediately start making myself a peanut butter and jelly sandwich. I've got just enough time to stuff some food down my throat and change into my work clothes before racing to the café for my shift. But midway through making my sandwich, my phone rings—and when I look at the screen, I drop the knife in my hand like a hot potato.

Reed.

The big boss hardly ever calls me personally. It's always Owen, his right-hand man, or Zeke, the hotshot who produced my single. In the end, Zeke Emmanuel turned out to be every bit as talented and brilliant as his reputation suggested. After recording all the musicians for my song in LA, including Fish on bass, Zeke came to Boston to personally coach me through recording my vocals.

"Hello?" I say.

"Hello, Alessandra. It's Reed. How are you?"

"Good. You?"

"Great. Listen, a bunch of my A-listers are playing at a charity concert in New York at the end of next week. Georgie and I will be there, and I'd like you to come, too."

"I'm already coming to that show as Fish's guest!"

"Perfect. I should have known. Now, listen. There's going to be an army of prestigious music journalists there, backstage before the show, and I've arranged for a couple of them to briefly interview *you*."

"*Me?*"

"Don't freak out on me, kid. Georgie will be there, so she can be your emotional support animal, as needed. And the interviews will be extremely brief."

"Okay," I squeak out. "Sounds great."

"Oh for the love of fuck, Ally. Aren't we past this shit now?"

"What shit?"

"The shit where you clam up when you're stressed out?"

"Uh, no. We're not past that shit. I don't think we'll ever be past that shit. Sorry."

Reed sighs. "There's nothing to worry about. With all the big names performing that night, nobody's going to give a rat's ass about little Alessandra Tennison and her debut single, no matter how much I try to talk you up. The journalists who've agreed to interview you aren't doing it because they give a shit about you. They're doing it because they owe me a favor."

"Does *everyone* in this industry owe you a favor?"

"Pretty much." He begins speaking to someone offline. So, I wait patiently for him to return to me. Finally, he says, "Hey, kid. I need you to defend me. Georgina walked in while I was saying nobody gives a shit about you, and her Momma Bear got all riled up. Would you please tell my feisty woman I was actually being nice to you—cruel to be kind?"

"Put her on."

"You're gonna defend me, right?"

"I'm going to tell the truth."

"Well, don't do that. *Defend me.*"

I laugh. "Reed Rivers. You're *scared* of Georgina Ricci, aren't you?"

"*No*," he says righteously. "I'm *terrified* of her."

We laugh together.

"Put Miss Ricci on," I say. "The truth shall set you free."

"I'm trusting you, Ally."

"Put her on."

"I'm putting you on speaker. Okay, tell her what a great guy I am."

"Hi, Georgie," I say.

"Hi, love. Was Reed being mean to you?"

"No. He was helping me. It's a relief to hear that nobody gives a shit about me. It takes the pressure off. And that's exactly what I need."

"*See?*" Reed says indignantly. "Ally might be your sister, but she's *my* artist. And if there's one thing I know how to do in life, it's how to handle *my* artists. So tell your Momma Bear to calm the fuck down."

"*Fine.*" Georgie laughs. "Alessandra, aren't you *so* excited about everything Reed's lined up for you?"

"*So* excited."

"When he told me about your music video—"

"Georgie!" Reed chastises. "I haven't mentioned that yet. I was just getting to that."

"Whoops."

"*Video?*" I eke out.

Reed exhales. "Here we go again. Yes, I've decided to shoot a music video for your single, while you're in New York. We'll shoot the day after the charity concert, so you'll need to adjust whatever plans you've got with Fish. Now, calm down, if you're freaking out. It'll be a simple one-day shoot—a quaint little performance video. Nothing fancy. We've rented out a coffeehouse in Brooklyn for the shoot and I've already lined up Maddy Morgan to direct."

"Oh my God! Maddy is amazing!"

"I've been meaning to give her a shot for years. Now, don't worry. All you have to do is look into the camera while singing along to your track. Just pretend to be at your regular gig in Boston. You can do *that*, right?"

"I can do that."

"Good girl."

"Although I should warn you I'm not all that great on camera."

"That's not true. You're very photogenic."

"With my friends and Georgie. But when there's lots of people staring at me, I tend to get weirdly stiff and awkward on camera."

"Oh, for the love of—"

"You've got this," Georgie interjects. "I'll stand next to the camera the whole time, so you can look into my eyes while singing."

"Thank you. That's a great idea."

"Here's the bottom line," Reed says. "I'm not going to let you fail. Because when you fail, I fail. *And I don't fail.*"

My heart skips a beat. Damn, he's good. And, wow, Reed is really going all in on my little song! When Reed signed me, I didn't think he'd do anything but record the song and post about it on River Records' social media channels. "Thank you for everything, Reed," I say, my voice cracking with emotion. "I can't believe you're doing all this."

"Aw, don't cry. *Please.* This is business." But his tone sounds anything but businesslike.

I sniffle. "I'm not crying. I'm totally emotionless right now."

Georgina laughs. "Oh, Ally."

"Has Fish already booked your accommodations in New York?" Reed asks.

"Yes. He's taken care of everything. After New York, he's coming to Boston with me for a whole week!"

"Sounds fun. I'll have Owen reimburse Fish for the New York portion of your trip, now that you're coming for official business."

"Oooh. It sounds so exciting when you say it like that. *Official business.* I'll tell Fish."

"Great. I have to go now. Busy day. See you in New York."

"Bye! See you soon."

"Don't hang up yet, Ally!" Georgie calls out. "I have something *huge* to tell you!"

I lean my butt against my kitchen counter. "About what?"

"Fish. Reed and I went to Dax and Violet's place for dinner last night. And during dinner, Dax said Fish has been racing out of the studio every day, rather than hanging out afterward, like he always used to do, because he's always so excited to get home to video chat with *you.*"

"Aw. He's so sweet."

"Dax said every time Fish races out the door to talk to you, he says, 'Gotta dip, dudes. I've got another hot date with my hot girlfriend.'"

"He does not say that!"

"That's what Dax said!"

"Fish has never called me his girlfriend!"

"But wait, there's more! When I said I was so happy for you and Fish, because you're perfect together, Violet chimed in and said, and I quote, 'I've never seen Fish *head over heels in love* before.' Violet said, 'It's so wonderful to see Fish in love like this, especially with someone as sweet as Ally.'"

I clutch my heart. "Violet used the words 'head over heels *in love*?'"

"She did. And Dax was sitting right there and didn't correct her, so it must be true!"

I fan myself. "I wonder if Fish actually used those words himself, or if Violet was *deducing* that Fish is in love."

"I don't know. All I know is it seemed like a fact to both Dax and Violet that Fish is in love with you."

My heart feels like it's exploding in my chest. "Holy hell, Georgie. If Fish doesn't say 'I love you' when we see each other in New York, I'm going to say it first. I can't stand it anymore."

"I'm sure he's waiting to say it in person, the same as you. Oh, honey, by the way. I don't know if Reed mentioned this to you, but, apparently, Reed and all the artists playing at the charity concert are going to be busy that whole day with sound check and promo, so do you want to hang out with Violet, Jackson, and me that day, before we head over to the arena around six?"

"That sounds great."

"I'll pick you up from the airport that morning. Send me your flight info."

"I'll have to change my flight to the morning. I was supposed to arrive in the late afternoon."

"Yeah, definitely change it. Oh, I've got to run. I just got an important text from my boss. I can't wait to see you next week!"

"I can't wait!" As I hang up with Georgie, my phone buzzes with an incoming call. And when I look down, it's my boss at the café.

"Oh, crap," I say, suddenly remembering I was supposed to be at work fifteen minutes ago. I press the button to answer my boss' call. "Patti, I'm *so* sorry!"

"Are you okay?" my boss says. "You're *never* late."

"I'm fine. I'm still at my apartment. Just as I was getting ready for work, I got a call from the head of my record label with some fantastic news. I'll change my clothes now and—"

"No, no. We're fine. Kendall hasn't even left yet. What was the fantastic news?"

I tell Patti everything. Not just about the music video, but the interviews Reed arranged in New York, as well. I tell her about how Reed said, "When you fail, I fail. *And I don't fail.*" I gush about what a whirlwind this entire process has been. How Reed is unexpectedly using the full muscle of his renowned label to make my song a worldwide hit. And when I'm done talking, Patti congratulates me and expresses joy for me. But she also says something that shocks me.

"Honey," Patti says, "I think the time has come for us to have an honest conversation about your employment."

"Huh?"

"I've loved having you as my employee. Everyone loves you. But ever since you told me you got signed, you've been distracted. I've been wondering when you're going to give me your notice."

I place my palms on the kitchen counter, feeling the need to steady myself. "I wasn't planning to give my notice. It's just one song, Patti."

"You just told me the label has hired an *Oscar-nominated* director to shoot the music video for that *one* song."

"But that's only because Maddy is a friend of Reed's. Reed's got all these friends who—"

"Alessandra, you're already taking time off for your trip with your boyfriend next week—which I think is wonderful, by the way. Good for you. But I've got a business to run. I think the time has come for you to focus all your time and attention on your budding music career. Surely, the record label paid you some up-front money? You're not going to go hungry while you wait for the song to be released?"

She's right. River Records did, indeed, pay me a small sum when I signed the contract—an amount Fish's lawyer said was double the market rate, in fact. But, still, I wasn't planning to live off that money. I was planning to save it and use it for my tuition in the fall, in case my single tanks spectacularly, and that money turns out to be the only income I ever see from my so-called "music career."

"I did get paid some money," I admit. "But it's not a lot. And I'm almost certainly going to need it for tuition in the fall."

"*Tuition in the fall?*" Patti makes a little *tsk* noise. "Oh, sweetie. After everything you just told me, it's clear you're not coming back to school in the fall!"

"The contract is for only one song, and the music industry is a brutal one, even when River Records is backing you. I'm not expecting anything life changing to happen here, based on *one* song. I can't let myself expect anything too big to happen —if only to keep myself from feeling crushed when nothing does."

"If I'm wrong about this, I'll figure out how to rehire you in the fall. But for now, I'm going to give your hours to

Kendall and release you to focus all your attention on this incredible opportunity. Have fun, Ally. Give it your all, without holding back or trying to juggle your old and new lives."

I say nothing. Did I just get fired from a job I love?

"You'll thank me one day," Patti says, breaking the silence between us. "One day very soon."

I take a deep breath to keep myself from crying. "Okay. Well, tell Kendall thank you for covering my shift today."

"I will. She loves that band your boyfriend is in, by the way. She was going on and on about them to me the other day."

"Yeah, they're amazing."

"Honey, everyone here is rooting for you. We can't wait to say 'We knew her when.'"

"Thank you. I hope I don't disappoint you."

"You won't. No matter what, we love you."

We say our goodbyes and end the call, and I collapse onto my elbows over my kitchen counter. With the end of my job at the café, I'm now officially a full-time River Records artist. Or, I guess, I will be, technically, in a month, when my single is out and my summer class is officially over. But, quickly, I'm not thinking about any of that. I'm too busy remembering I've just received objective confirmation that Fish is 'head over heels in love' with me, his 'hot girlfriend,' every bit as much as I'm head over heels in love with him.

TWENTY-ONE
ALESSANDRA

I plop onto my bed and place a call to Fish, eager to tell him about my conversation with Reed. But, unfortunately, my call goes straight to voicemail.

"Tell me something good," Fish's outgoing message says. *Beep.*

"It's me!" I chirp. "Call me whenever you can. I just got some amazing news from Reed!"

I hang up and sigh.

I can't believe how quickly Fish has become my rock. My best friend and lover, even though we haven't even kissed yet. But so what if we've never actually touched? We've had some good, hot times, remotely! Since Fish first let me watch his face as he jerked himself off out of frame, we've been exploring the physical side of our relationship more and more, over the past several weeks. I've now seen him standing before me totally naked, with an erection. And he's seen me, standing before him, in nothing but cotton undies. No tank top or bra. And, man, does it turn me on to see how much that boy loves my boobs.

A few days ago, Fish let me watch him masturbate to completion—this time, with the camera framing his head *and* torso, so I could see every detail as it unfolded. *And, holy hell, did I get turned on!* Right after that, during the same call, I let Fish watch me touch myself. Granted, I only let him see me reaching into my undies. And I wasn't able to reach the finish line in front of him. I did that after we hung up. But, still, it was massive progress in terms of me letting go of my inhibitions. Indeed, the intimacy I've been feeling with Fish these past weeks—the bond I feel with him—is incredible. So amazing, I don't have a doubt in my mind I'm ready to give him every inch of me in New York. In fact, I can't wait.

My phone rings, yanking me from staring at my bedroom ceiling fan—and when I look at my phone, it's "Channing Tate-Yum" returning my call on FaceTime.

"Hey, you!" I say, breaking into a wide smile.

"Hey, beautiful," Fish replies, his sweet face lighting up my screen. "I thought you were working right now."

I shift onto my side on my pillow. "I got fired."

"*What?*"

I tell him the story. And then, all the amazing news from Reed. "So, listen," I say flirtatiously. "When I talked to Reed, he mentioned he'd reimburse you for my hotel room in New York. He said my trip is now 'official business.'"

"Nah," Fish says. "I don't want Reed's money. This trip is my treat."

"That's so sweet of you. You've booked two rooms in New York, right? You said we have adjoining rooms?"

"Yep. We can open an interior door and make it like one huge suite."

I bite my lip. I've been thinking about saying this next thing to Fish for a few weeks now. But now I'm sure. "I think you should cancel one of the rooms. As far as I'm concerned, we're only going to need one room." I smile. "And one bed."

His breathing halts.

I add, "I mean, if that's okay with you."

"Yes, that's very, very okay with me."

"Good. Because I've been thinking . . . I can't wait to sleep naked next to you every night . . . *and make love to you.*"

Fish yelps. "Hang on. I'm at Daxy's house. Someone could walk by and see the gigantic stiffy you just gave me." Like a bat out of hell, he sprints through Dax's house and winds up in some room, where he closes the door behind him and throws himself into an armchair. "Baby, listen to me." His breathing is labored. "Remember that website you told me about, a while ago? The one that helped you figure out how to get yourself off?"

I nod, feeling myself blush.

"That website is gonna become my new best friend. Send me your log-in information, okay? Tell me which videos— which techniques—have been working for you. And between now and New York, I'm going to watch those videos on repeat and make them part of my DNA."

I shudder with excitement. "I'll text you the info right after we hang up."

Fish runs a shaky hand through his hair. He's panting. "Oh, Alessandra, I . . ." He pauses, causing the hair on my arms to stand up. *Love you.* That's what's hanging in the air between us. *I love you.*

But, no, Fish sighs and changes course, probably deciding, the way I have, to say those once-in-a-lifetime, magical words to me in person—when he can look into my eyes and seal them with our very first kiss.

"I can't wait to see you, sweetheart," he finally says. "To *kiss* you."

"I can't wait, either." I smile. "Once I finally get to touch you, I don't see how I'm ever going to force myself to stop."

TWENTY-TWO

FISH

NEW YORK

I stare across the bustling greenroom, willing Alessandra to appear in the doorframe. Or, more accurately, *praying* with every fiber of my being for her to appear.

The minute our sound check was over about two hours ago, I texted my hot girlfriend to say, "I'm done earlier than I thought! Come noooow!" But, unfortunately, she was still at the Central Park Zoo with Georgie, Violet, and Jackson. She texted back: "We're leaving soon, then dropping Jackson off with his nanny at the hotel, then getting a quick bite. I'm DYING to see youuuu!" She attached a GIF of that old lady from *Titanic* to her message with the tagline "It's been 84 years . . ." And, man, was that deadly accurate.

Someone says my name, so I peel my eyes off the doorway to look at my friends. I'm sitting with Dax, Colin, Aloha, Zander, and our business manager, Clive, in a corner of the greenroom. Dax's personal bodyguard, Brett, is nearby, along with the PA assigned to us. And, of course, a whole bunch of other artists and their various entourages are scattered around the room, too, all of them awaiting the start of the press junket, the same as us.

"Fish, look at this," Colin says. He's holding up his phone to me, showing me a photo.

I lean in and see Keane and Maddy, mugging in front of a distant billboard of Colin in his Calvin Kleins. "Ha! That's awesome!"

Owen Boucher, Reed's right-hand man, appears, wearing a headset. "Dax," he says. "Security just notified me your wife and her group are in the building. A PA's bringing them here now."

"Thanks."

I leap out of my chair, too amped to sit still. Alessandra is with Violet! If Violet's somewhere in this arena, that means Alessandra is, too!

Reed strides up. "You okay, Fish? You look like a kid who needs to use the toilet."

I exhale loudly. "Alessandra will be here any minute."

"If you need some privacy when she gets here, feel free to use Greenroom Five. It's mine for the night."

"Thanks, man. Hey, uh, Reed? I've been meaning to say something to you for a while now." I exhale. "I'm sorry for what happened at your party."

He looks at me blankly.

"When I ripped you a new asshole after you'd talked to Alessandra about her music. In retrospect, it's obvious you were trying to help her grow and develop as an artist. I was out of line when I said you're 'always' a prick. I'm sorry."

Reed shrugs. "I don't even know what you're talking about." He winks. "Although, now that you mention it, I do recall that I was happy to see you get onto your white horse to defend Alessandra's honor." He smiles. "Georgie's kept me in the loop. I'm happy to see how everything's worked out for you two."

"Thanks. I'm happy for you and Georgina, too. Alessandra's kept me in the loop."

Reed says something in reply, but I don't catch it. Because . . . over his shoulder . . . I finally see her . . . *Alessandra!*

Without another word to Reed or anyone else, I take off running toward my woman like a dog chasing a car. "Alessandra!"

When she sees my sprinting, flailing frame, she takes off running toward me, until we meet in the middle and crash into each other. I grab her and clutch her to me, like a soldier returning to my woman after war. And, in response, Alessandra throws her arms around my neck and presses the length of her body against mine with full force.

Euphoria.

That's what's ripping through me like lightning.

Joy.

Elation.

Love.

Love.

Love.

In this moment, I feel happier than I've ever felt in my life. I feel whole. Alive. Relieved to finally be where I'm meant to be. I'm *home*.

She tilts her face up to me, her lips parted slightly, and I finally do the thing I've been dying to do for so long. I lean in and press my lips to hers, and give her the most passionate, heartfelt kiss of my life.

And it's *everything*.

Electrifying.

Healing.

Perfect.

Alessandra's lips are sweet, like I knew they'd be. Only better. Her scent is intoxicating. Her body warm in my arms. As her tongue dances with mine, it feels like we were born to kiss each other—and *only* each other. Like we were designed for this, by a higher being. We're two parts of a whole, Ally and me. Meant to be.

As I kiss my love, my cock hardens to its full length and strains against her, aching to burrow inside. An explosion of fireworks is ricocheting inside me as our lips devour and our tongues dance. So much so, I begin grinding and jolting against her, too aroused and overwhelmed with excitement and lust and love to stand still.

I've had some amazing moments in my life, especially these past few years. Getting signed to River Records. Opening for Red Card Riot. Song after song miraculously hitting number *one*. Getting to witness tens of thousands of people singing along to songs I've helped create. I've been to awards shows. Experienced all my childhood dreams coming true. But this moment beats them all. *I'm in love with this girl.* And the best part is I've got no doubt she's in love with me, too.

Slowly, the world around us begins to infiltrate our bubble. I begin hearing titters and applause. And then, outright hoots and whoops. All of a sudden, I realize Alessandra and I have an audience. And they're obviously deeply amused.

Shit.

It's a common thing to see people making out in green-rooms, of course. That's rock 'n' roll for ya, baby. *But never like this.* Not when so many of the people here are my friends —and so many of them have heard about my long-distance love. Not when it's so obvious the two people kissing in a greenroom are doing so much more than making out. They're two souls becoming one.

Grudgingly, I disengage from Alessandra and nuzzle her nose. "Looks like we've given everyone a show."

"Who?" she says innocently. "We're not alone?"

Smiling, I grab her hand. "Come on, baby. Let's talk in private." I pull her toward the greenroom door, getting back-slapped here and there along the way.

"You've got *five* minutes!" Owen calls out to me, just before we've reached the doorframe. "Reed wants to *personally* introduce Alessandra to a few journalists before they get distracted!"

"Got it!" I call back. "We'll be in Greenroom Five!" I look at Alessandra and say the next thing for her benefit, not Owen's. "I just need a few minutes alone with my hot *girlfriend*."

We walk down a hallway and stop in front of Greenroom Five, where a large bald man with a beard is positioned.

"Hey, man. I'm Fish from 22 Goats. Reed said—"

"Owen told me." The dude opens the door and motions. "It's all yours, Fish."

"Thanks."

He calls out to my back, "Reed said the bottle of Cristal on ice is all yours!"

I pull Alessandra through the door and to the couch. And that's where we attack each other again, even more passionately than in the other greenroom. I hold her face as I kiss her, my cock throbbing with desire. Suddenly, I'm on top of Alessandra, kissing the living hell out of her, grinding my hard-on into her sweet spot while she jerks her pelvis up and grinds herself into me. As we make out, white-hot pleasure and desire like nothing I've felt before is racking my nerve endings. I've made out with other women before. But nothing, *nothing* I've done with anyone else has prepared me for this nuclear explosion of excitement going off inside me. This incredible *connection,* both physical and emotional. Just like Alessandra said to me weeks ago, I feel like I might as well be a virgin, too.

Groaning with desire, I guide Alessandra's thigh to rest over my hip, opening her sweet spot to me completely. And when I press myself into her again, this time, with her legs opened and her pelvis angled to receive my urgent, grinding thrusts, she gasps and writhes underneath me like I've flipped a switch inside her.

"Oh, God," she chokes out. "This is even better than I thought it'd be."

I kiss her again, deeply, grinding myself into that same bull's-eye. And the guttural growl that escapes Alessandra's mouth makes pleasure rocket through my cock as surely as if she'd licked my tip.

Unfortunately, though, all good things must come to an end. A knock at the door interrupts our makeout session, followed by a low voice calling out, "Reed is on his way."

"Fuck," I whisper. "You want a glass of champagne real quick?"

"I think I should," she says. "You know, to loosen me up for my little interviews."

I get up and open the bottle with a loud pop, making her clap and squeal. I hand her a glass of bubbly and raise my glass to her, intending to finally tell her I love her. But a knock at the door stops me.

Owen pops his head into the room. "Sorry, guys. Reed is

ready for Ally now. Fish, get your ass into the other green-room with the other Goats."

I look at Ally, not wanting to leave her. Never wanting to leave her again, as long as I live.

"Go on," Ally says, reading my mind. "I'll be fine. Reed and Georgie will be with me. Go be a rock star now, honey."

Still, I don't move. I literally can't command my limbs to walk away from her. I need to be in her presence like I need air to breathe.

"Come on, Fish," Owen says. He grabs my arm and physically drags me away, making Ally laugh.

"You're gonna be great in your interviews, baby!" I shout as Owen pushes me toward the door. But in the doorway, I stand my ground and grip the frame. "Will you be sitting in the front row with Violet?"

"Yes! With Reed and Georgie, too!"

I smile broadly, my heart leaping. "I can't wait to look down at you when I play."

"Go!" Owen says, pointing sternly. "You'll see your lovely and talented girlfriend *after* the show."

I wink. "See you later, my lovely and talented girlfriend. Give those reporters hell."

She bites her lip, her blue eyes sparkling. "See you later, my lovely and talented *boyfriend*. Break a leg. I'll be waiting for you after the show—ready to give you a whole bunch more kisses."

TWENTY-THREE

ALESSANDRA

"How'd your interviews go?" Violet asks, as Georgina, Reed, and I take our seats next to her in the front row of the arena.

"Alessandra was a star!" Georgie gushes. "She *nailed* both interviews!"

Not quite. I look at Reed for a reality check. Because, God bless her, my stepsister would say I was amazing, no matter how badly I might have flailed. Which I'm pretty sure I did. But Reed? No. I've come to realize that man is incapable of blowing smoke up anyone's ass, including mine—even if it would make Georgie deliriously happy. Frankly, it's the thing I like best about him.

"You were perfect," Reed confirms with a wink. "Just the right balance of adorable and awkward and totally out of your element. It was a home run, kid."

I'm shocked. "Really?"

"Really. You done good."

I sigh with relief.

It's not that I've got low self-esteem, generally speaking.

I'm shy, yes, but that doesn't mean I think I'm worthless or unlikeable or totally lacking in talent. I know my worth. Hell yeah. Mostly. Usually. But, in Reed's world, I feel like a sore thumb, especially here, when I'm surrounded by such heavy hitters. Plus, those two journalists were bigwigs. Celebrities in their own rights. Of course, I did my mighty best during those short interviews, but, still, I could feel myself stammering and fidgeting my way through them.

Maddy and Keane appear before us and we all rise to greet them effusively.

While bro-hugging Keane, Reed addresses him as "Frick." So, I'm assuming that means Zander is "Frack." Reed says, "I didn't realize you were coming along with your wife on this trip!"

Keane replies, "My shooting schedule got changed at the last minute, so Maddy Behind the Camera hired me as part of the crew for the music video."

As the pair gets settled, small talk ensues. Violet asks Maddy how she's feeling, her words implying Maddy's got a bun in the oven—and when Maddy's response confirms her happy condition, the rest of us erupt with congratulations.

But, suddenly, a booming voice interrupts our conversation, saying, "Ladies and gentlemen, welcome our first band of this special night for an amazing cause . . . It's *Watch Partyyyy!*"

The crowd erupts as blinding lights illuminate the stage, and there they are: the scrappy, energetic members of Watch Party, led by Davey the Magnificent himself. In a matter of seconds, the band kicks off their first boisterous song—their biggest hit—and away we go for the night.

After Watch Party performs their short three-song set, a string of heavy hitters performs, one after the other, each artist's set getting progressively longer, as each performer's clout gets noticeably bigger. Laila Fitzgerald, Fugitive Summer, Aloha, 2Real. *Bam, bam, bam,* they come, fast and furious and sparkling, with each act bringing down the house.

Finally, though, it's time for the headliner to take the stage. The announcer says the magic words: 22 Goats! And Dax, Colin, and Fish, along with a couple supporting musicians, appear under blinding lights to an explosion of cheering and applause.

All of a sudden, I feel like I'm having a bit of a mini-stroke. Like my brain is feverishly trying to reconcile the *intimacy* I feel with my beloved *Matthew* with the pure celebrity-fangirling I feel for *Fish* from 22 Goats. Fish is the cute boy I used to have a crush on from afar, based solely on interviews and music videos and some of the best damned bass playing and backup singing I've ever heard. *And there he is*! Being his rock star self on that stage. Looking uber cool and quietly confident. Holding down the fort.

But my sweet and gentle Matthew is there, too. The boyfriend who just gave me my first real kiss that wasn't a quick peck behind a shed. The man who's my first love, and who'll soon become my first in every way, when I finally get him alone later tonight at the hotel. I love Matthew Fishberger so much. But looking at him playing his bass on that stage for tens of thousands, I can't help feeling like a fangirl, too. Frankly, it's a great problem to have. A wonderful one, to feel this blown away by the man I adore.

In rapid-fire succession, the Goats rip through hit after hit. "Judas," "Sweet Craving," "Ultra Violet Radiation," "Hit-woman Elvis Disco Momma," "Don't Count Me Out," "You Caught Me Violet-Handed," "Can't Stand to Wait." And, as the band performs, as Dax keeps finding his wife in the front row, Fish keeps finding *me*. It's the same thing Fish did at Reed's party, way back when, when he jammed with his friends. Only this time, it feels even more electrifying to be singled out, given that Fish is focusing on me as tens of thousands of people, instead of only hundreds, scream and sing along.

When the latest song comes to an end, Dax leans into his microphone and says, "Will you help us out with this next one? Take out your phones and light this place up!"

Well, of course, the crowd goes wild. We all know 22 Goats asks their audiences to create the illusion of swirling fireflies during their famous hit. I've never been to a 22 Goats concert, but, thanks to YouTube, even *I* know that's what Dax always says before launching into "Fireflies."

As everyone in the audience, including me, raises their lit-up phones into the air, the Goats kick off the song. At the end of the instrumental introduction, Dax leans into his mic, like he's about to sing, right on cue . . . but then, abruptly, backs off.

"On second thought," Dax says, letting the instrumental portion continue. "Would you guys be cool with *Fish* singing lead vocals on the first verse this time?"

The crowd cheers their approval, even as Fish looks shell-shocked. Clearly, this idea of Dax's wasn't discussed in advance.

Dax continues, "Fish's 'hot girlfriend' is here tonight. And from what my buddy's told me, she's made him feel quite the swarm of fireflies in his belly since the first night he met her."

My jaw hanging open, I look at Fish and find him staring at Dax, his expression matching mine. I look at Georgie next to me to find her expression adding to our slack-jawed collection.

"Take it away, Fish Tacoooo!" Dax shouts.

I return to Fish to find his eyes already on me.

I nod, letting him know he's got this. As I'm well aware, Fish has never performed lead vocals in his band before. I don't even think he's sung privately to anyone, really, other than Dax, Colin, and me. Maybe his mom?

But when the cue for the first verse rolls around again, Fish goes for it. His eyes on me, he leans into his microphone and opens his mouth—and then gifts the world with his sweet, pure, honest singing voice:

Fireflies
You got me feelin' 'em
Never before or since
All my life
Been chasing butterflies
And in just one night
One perfect night . . .
Girl, you made butterflies
Your bitch
Oh, Fireflies
Oh, In your eyes . . .

Of course, the audience sing-shouts that last line of the verse—"You made butterflies your bitch!"—in unison with Fish. Because, duh. It's one of the most famous lyrics in the world. Instantly recognizable by anyone who's heard a lick of popular music in the past few years. Of course, Fish's voice is nothing like Dax's, but it's every bit as lovely and compelling, in its own way. And this crowd is definitely sending Fish their love and appreciation for his unique talents.

As the crowd explodes, Fish points jubilantly at me in the front row, his face ablaze, like he's telling the arena *I'm* the 'hot girlfriend' Dax mentioned. *I'm* the girl who gave Fish fireflies the night he met me. *I'm* the girl who made butterflies her bitch.

Georgie grips my arm and points at the jumbotron. And when I look to where she's indicating, I see my face on the screen, broadcast to the arena as big as a school bus.

"Holy fuck!" I shout at the top of my lungs, and the arena instantly explodes even more, apparently fully capable of reading lips. I cover my blushing face with my hands, feeling dizzy, which only provokes the crowd to react even more enthusiastically. I guess a girl who shouts "Holy fuck!" after being serenaded, and then covers her blushing face, is entertaining? Because, damn, this crowd is going absolutely bonkers.

Thankfully, when I come out from behind my hands, the screen is once again filled with the image of our fearless heartthrob, Dax, as he launches into singing the melodic, sing-along chorus of "Fireflies." The melody that's now ingrained into the world's collective consciousness.

But even after the song has moved on from that once-in-a-lifetime, magical moment for me—I can't believe my boyfriend just sang one of my favorite songs to me, in front of tens of thousands of people!—I know the moment will live on inside my heart and soul for the rest of my life.

After "Fireflies," the guys perform two additional hits. Until, finally, Dax says, "This will be our last song tonight, guys."

"Booo!" the crowd yells, making all three Goats, and their couple of supporting musicians in the back, laugh uproariously.

Dax says, "Thank you for supporting such a great cause. Big shout-out to my wife, Violet Morgan, for her hard work on this event. Also, Reed Rivers, the head of our label, and his team. Let's hear it for all of them, guys."

The crowd applauds uproariously.

Dax smiles at his wife in the front row and blows her a kiss, before returning to the crowd and saying, "Let's finish this party right! Let's go back to the beginning!"

Well, we all know what that means, so, of course, we in the audience lose our collective minds. The band begins playing their debut smash. "People Like Us." The song that started it all, with a music video that went batshit viral across the world. And, of course, the entire arena sings along enthusiastically with every word. Because, at this point, the words to this smash hit song are part of the world's gray matter.

But while everyone around me is almost certainly glued to Dax during this epic song, I can't take my eyes off Matthew Fishberger. That man is a smoke show every time he plays any musical instrument—but especially on a big stage under a canopy of colored lights and strobes, while being cheered by the masses. I love watching Fish's lips moving as he sings his harmonies. I love watching his hips moving, especially now that I've felt them grinding into me, as we made out in that greenroom. And I love, love, love watching his tattooed forearms flexing as he expertly fingers his strings . . . and imagining those very same fingers expertly touching *me*.

The first chorus of "People Like Us" comes to an end, and the band plays the short instrumental riff that segues into the second verse. And that's when Fish leans into his microphone and says something I never saw coming, despite what happened earlier with "Fireflies."

"Hey, Daxy!" Fish shouts brightly. "Would you mind terribly if I take the second verse, just this once, brother?"

The audience cheers, fully realizing they're once again going to witness something no other 22 Goats audience has ever seen.

Dax doesn't hesitate. "Hell yeah!"

Fish says, "It is a charity show, after all." He looks at the crowd. "Okay with you, guys? My hot girlfriend once told me this song was her favorite off our first album. She said, '*There's nothing like your first love.*'" His eyes shift to me. "And now I can tell you, for a fact, that's absolutely true."

My heart stops. Without even thinking about it, or worrying that I'm saying it first, I mouth, *I love you.* And, without missing a beat, Fish smiles broadly upon receipt of my message and mouths the words right back to me.

"Go, Fish Tacoooo!" Dax shouts as the vocal cue approaches.

And Fish doesn't hesitate. Right on cue, he leans into his mic, this time with full rock star swagger, his eyes glued to mine, and belts out the famous words, with accompaniment from the entire arena:

All my life
Been looking low and high
Aching to find
The ones to call my tribe
But now I know
People like us, baby
There's no group
People like us
There's only two

We're a tribe of two, baby
It's just me and you
Starting now
It's you and me
Against the world
'Cause 'people like us'
There's only me and you

I clutch my heart as my boyfriend, my beloved, my best friend, my lover-to-be, sings to me. I've heard this song probably twenty billion times by now. *But never like this.* Never when the man I adore with all my heart, the man I love and trust and respect, sings it to me in front of tens of thousands of singing, screaming, adoring fans. From what Fish has told me, Dax wrote this song, all on his own, without any input from Fish or Colin, other than their instrumental parts. But in this moment, Matthew Fishberger wrote this song to Alessandra Tennison.

As Fish finishes singing, the jumbotron once again finds my face. But this time, when my image lights up the arena, I don't cover my face. I don't hide. I don't flinch. I don't even blush. Nope, I stare at my beloved, hoping my eyes are conveying my unwavering, unconditional adoration and love for him. We belong together, Matthew and me. We're a tribe of two. Just like this amazing song says. People like us? There's only Matthew and me.

TWENTY-FOUR

FISH

A burst of laughter rises up from the other side of our long dinner table, a surefire sign that Davey from Watch Party just told everyone around him a dirty joke. He does that quite frequently. And, somehow, he *never* misses, unlike me. But this restaurant is too noisy, and our table too long, for me to know for certain if Davey caused that burst of laughter.

We're at a pricey restaurant in Midtown, enjoying a loud, booze-filled, post-concert dinner party that's hosted by Reed. I'm sitting next to my hot girlfriend, of course. Holding her hand. Lightly stroking her thigh underneath the table. Occasionally, looking into her big blue eyes. Feeling the need to touch and look at her beautiful face constantly, despite the people and distractions around us.

Georgina and Reed are seated next to Ally, on her right. From there, it's Maddy, Keane, Aloha, Zander, Dax, and Violet. Colin and his longtime girlfriend, Kiera, are bringing up the rear of this train, so to speak, but neither of them looks happy tonight, so we're all sort of ignoring them.

"Hey, Ally," Reed says, turning away from the intense conversation he's been having with Maddy. "Change of plans for your video tomorrow. I didn't know Maddy was bringing Keane to the shoot to help her. But now that I know he'll be there, I think we'd be missing a golden opportunity not to give him a starring role in the video. Keane says he's up for anything—"

"Yup."

"So Maddy and I just now put our heads together and came up with an entire storyline for him."

"Oh, wow, that's exciting," Alessandra says, squeezing my hand fiercely. "Thank you, Keane."

"Happy to do it. It sounds like a blast."

Alessandra looks at Georgina, and then at me, her face bursting with unadulterated excitement. And I don't blame her. Keane's a star on the rise these days, thanks to his popular Netflix show. And he's definitely easy on the eyes, too. To put it mildly. So having him featured in Alessandra's debut music video will almost certainly give the song huge buzz.

"Now, don't feel any stress about tomorrow," Reed says soothingly. Apparently, he's well aware of his young starlet's penchant for flailing or wanting to barf when she feels stressed or anxious. "From your end of things, Ally, you'll still *mostly* be doing what we talked about, okay? You'll still *mostly* be performing onstage at the coffeehouse."

Alessandra's body stiffens. "*Mostly?*"

But Reed is a pro. He calmly says, "Yes. Maddy and I have come up with two storylines. A love triangle involving Keane. Also, a cute little love story involving you and Fish." Reed looks at me. "If you're game, that is, Fish Taco."

I'm shocked at the suggestion. Especially considering it's coming from a dude who once told me to drop out of my band because, among other things, I wasn't "charismatic" enough for the big leagues. But, as shocked as I am, I'm also thrilled to join Alessandra's coming out party, to support her in any way I can, with whatever clout or buzz I can bring. "Sure," I say. "Count me in."

Alessandra fidgets next to me. "What will Fish and I have to do for this 'cute little love story?'"

"Don't worry, Ally," Maddy interjects, leaning across Reed to be heard over the din of the crowded restaurant. "You'll be the performer onstage at the coffeehouse, as we discussed, and Fish will play the shaggy barista across the room. All you two will have to do is make googly eyes at each other, from afar, like you're totally smitten with each other."

Smitten. The word strikes me like a thunderbolt. It's the perfect word for how I feel when I'm with Alessandra. Yeah, I'm in love with her. Obviously. Yes, I'm in lust with her, shamelessly. But I'm also feeling a certain kind of giddiness that's like a kid on Christmas. A feeling of total infatuation that feels like the best possible drug. I look at Alessandra, even though I'm replying to Maddy's comment and say, "Well, speaking for myself, that shouldn't be hard to do."

Alessandra winks at me. "Yeah. I think I could manage that."

Reed addresses Georgina next to him, his countenance becoming businesslike and determined. "Georgie, you're going to star in this thing, too."

"*Me?*"

"Yes. You and Laila are going to be in a campy love triangle with Keane."

He explains the two storylines cooked up by him and Maddy—and everyone on our end of the table expresses resounding enthusiasm. "Wait till you hear this next thing," Reed says, looking at Alessandra. He motions to the dizzying array of top-tier artists seated at the far end of our table. "See all those rock stars down there?" He juts his chin. "They've all agreed to stop by the coffeehouse tomorrow to shoot quick cameos for the video."

"*Whaaaat?*" Alessandra blurts, making everyone on our end of the table guffaw.

"You've hit the jackpot, Alessandra Tennison," Reed says, laughing. "Having all these superstars in your debut video—plus, having Laila, Keane, and Fish in starring roles alongside you—is going to give you so much street cred, it's ridiculous. Without a doubt, all this star power is going to make this video go viral. Which, in turn, my dear, is going to rocket your song to the top of the charts."

Alessandra is quite obviously flabbergasted. She looks at me, her blue eyes wide, and I nod, letting her know I wholeheartedly agree with Reed's assessment. Indeed, with a launch like this for her little song, I can't imagine it *not* becoming a monster hit. Top 20, at the very least, by the time it peaks.

The group on our end of the table peppers Reed and Maddy with questions about the video concept, and they describe their ideas in further detail, the gist of which is that Alessandra and I will be unrequited lovers at the coffeehouse. Alessandra, the shy performer onstage. And me, the shy barista behind a counter who watches his crush from across the room while writing secret love notes to her. Notes, by the way, the barista never gives to her, but, instead, always throws into the bin.

Keane, for his part, will play a douchebag customer who finds my discarded love notes and uses them to seduce and two-time the waitresses of the coffeehouse—Laila and

Georgina. Neither of whom knows the other is being romanced by Keane.

"All those famous faces down there will make cameos as customers of the coffeehouse," Maddy explains. "They've all agreed to drop by tomorrow, whenever they can, to shoot their cameos."

Alessandra looks a bit overwhelmed. "Can I ask a question?" she asks timidly. "I'm not trying to look a gift horse in the mouth here. I can't believe how lucky I am. But why are all these famous artists willing to make cameos in some *nobody's* video?"

Reed shrugs. "Every last one of them owes me a favor. But also, and this is the truth, Alessandra, none of them would do this if they didn't *genuinely* like you and believe in your song."

"Oh my gosh," Alessandra whispers, squeezing my hand. "Thank you so much, Reed. I'm going to hop up and thank each artist around the table, individually!"

"No, no," Reed says, laughing. "Thank them tomorrow if they actually show up. Also, there's no need to thank me. I wouldn't be doing any of this if I didn't think I'd make my money back, and then some."

Alessandra looks at me, her eyebrow cocked at Reed's last comment. She's told me before she thinks Reed wouldn't have signed her, if not for his love for Georgina. And I've told her in reply, "It doesn't matter how you got there, sweetheart—it's what you do with the opportunity." But even as I've said those words to her, I've understood her self-doubt, since I've experienced similar doubts over the years about myself, and how I came to be where I am in life.

But now, I know, for a fact, Reed is being sincere. Yes, he loves Georgina. That much is clear and would be obvious to anyone who spends more than two minutes in their presence. The man is absolutely head over heels in love. But I also believe now, with all my heart, that Reed wouldn't throw *this* much weight and clout and resources behind Alessandra and her little song if he didn't sincerely think he was holding a tiger by its tail.

"Reed is telling the truth," I whisper to Alessandra, squeezing her hand. "He's a businessman, through and through. His reputation is too important to throw this much firepower at a 'present' for his girlfriend, no matter how much he loves her."

Alessandra's shoulders soften, and I know, for the first time, ever, she genuinely believes me this time. "Thank you, love."

Love.

We said it to each other during the show, from afar. But we haven't said it intimately yet.

"I love you, Alessandra," I say simply.

"I love you, too, Matthew. With all my heart."

And that's it. We're in love and we both know it. And it feels so good.

"Open a case of your finest champagne!" Reed shouts to the waiter. "We're celebrating an amazing charity concert and the imminent birth of a superstar!" He indicates Alessandra with his whiskey glass at those last words, and then shouts, "Mark my words, this girl here is about to make every person at this table look like a fucking amateur!"

TWENTY-FIVE

ALESSANDRA

Wrapping up his story, Fish says to the group, "So, if any of you want Dax and me to grant your lifelong wish like two genies in a bottle, just say the word, and we'll cast a magic warlock spell for you on German TV."

The entire group laughs. The same way everyone laughs whenever Fish makes any sort of joke. Although, to be fair, this crowd would probably laugh at pretty much anything even slightly amusing right now, thanks to the booze and amazing food we all consumed at dinner earlier. To put it mildly, this isn't a tough crowd for a comic.

Our group is entering Times Square now, after floating here from the restaurant a few blocks away. The usual crew surrounds us—all Fish's closest friends, plus, Reed and Georgina, of course, and Georgina's boss and her husband, and a smattering of bodyguards and personal assistants and significant others.

"Where is this damned billboard?" Dax says, looking around.

"Just around this corner, I think," Keane says.

"No," Maddy says. "This way, guys."

"What the hell, Peen," Colin says to Keane. "Weren't you here mere *hours* ago?"

"Yeah, but I was sober then," Keane replies, chuckling.

We turn a corner behind Maddy, our fearless leader, and, suddenly, there he is. *Colin.* Twenty feet tall. With ripped abs and a smolder like the cartoon hero in *Tangled.* Wearin' nothin' but his Calvins.

"Ka-*bam*, son!" Keane shouts, flinging his arm toward the billboard. "Told ya!"

"That's not where you said, honey," Maddy murmurs.

"Dude!" Fish exclaims, gawking at Colin's towering, smoldering, ripped image. "*Look at the size of your wang!*"

Everyone bursts out laughing, because it's exactly what we were all thinking. Damn. That's one massive wang.

"It's a sock," Colin admits. "I'm a big boy, but I'm not *that* big."

We reach the perfect spot for photos, and everyone pulls out their phones and starts taking selfies, most of them including perfect imitations of Colin's posing and smolder in the billboard.

When it's Fish's turn to stand in front of the billboard and imitate Colin's body positioning and facial expression, he nails it. In fact, he's doing the best imitation of Colin *by far*, even better than Keane's. So, naturally, everyone standing around Fish begins screaming with laughter and cheering him on.

Which attracts attention . . .

And then causes a group of passersby to recognize some of the famous faces in our group. A frenzy of excitement ensues as fans ask for selfies, which then provokes the body-guards in our group to step forward to manage things.

Fish and I step back from the fray, our hands clasped, and watch the mayhem for a long moment. There are several famous people here, of varying degrees. But, clearly, the two biggest draws are Dax and Aloha. There's no doubt about it.

"Do people react like this to Dax, often?" I ask, as a young woman literally bursts into tears as she hugs him.

"Every day," Fish confirms.

"I'd have a nervous breakdown."

"He's often right on the cusp. If it weren't for Violet and Jackson, I'm sure he'd have had one by now."

"And you and Colin," I say.

"We do our best."

"Fish!" a voice shouts. And when we look toward the sound, a young woman is excitedly jumping up and down and asking for a selfie. "You're my favorite Goat!" she squeals. "I was at the show tonight! I cried so hard when Dax *finally* let you sing!" She shoots a withering glare across the crowd at Dax. "He should let you do it more! I've always said you have an *amazing* voice!"

Fish chuckles. "Thank you. But I'm quite happy letting Dax sing our songs. Trust me, he's not holding me back."

The girl notices me and shrieks. "You're his girlfriend! The one from the jumbotron!"

"Hi."

"Can I take a selfie with you, too? You're so cute!"

"Uh." But she's flinging herself between us, so I huddle up and smile for the camera.

Her photo taken, she says to me, "You're so lucky. I hope one day someone will look at me the way Fish looked at *you* tonight." She swoons. "The way he sang to you . . . Gah!"

I smile at Fish. "I hope that for you, too. It's pretty awesome."

A bodyguard arrives and escorts the young woman away, gently. And as she leaves, Fish suggests we take our first-ever photo of the two of us. We take several selfies, one of which features Fish kissing my cheek, and Fish asks if he can upload that one to not only his personal Instagram account, but the official 22 Goats account, too.

"The whole world is probably uploading videos of me singing to you tonight," he explains. "I kind of want to make us 'Instagram official' myself."

"Awesome."

He uploads the shot of him kissing my cheek with a caption that reads, "My beautiful, talented, hot girlfriend. #OneLuckyGoat."

And that's it. Suddenly, I can't stand sharing my hot boyfriend with the world any longer. I want to be alone with him. Naked in his bed. I want to give myself to Matthew, in every possible way.

He smiles lasciviously, like he's reading my mind, and puts out his hand. "I'd better get the rising star back to our room, eh? She needs her beauty sleep for the cameras tomorrow."

"Well, she needs to get to *bed*. That part is true."

Reed appears. "Get our girl to the hotel, Fish. She's got a long day of shooting tomorrow, now that we've added so much to the storyboard."

"I was just saying the same thing," Fish replies.

Reed turns his head and calls to Maddy. "Hey, Director! What time is Alessandra's call time in the morning?"

Maddy strides over. "Seven." She grimaces. "Sorry. With all the new scenes we've added, we need to get all your performance scenes into the can before we start shooting with everyone else. A car will pick you and Fish up at your hotel at six thirty. Just roll out of bed and flop into the back seat. We'll have hair and makeup there for you. Bagels and coffee and several different wardrobe options."

"Such a production," I say.

"Of course," Maddy replies. "We're going to hit this out of the park for you, girlie. This is going to be an amazing video."

"Owen!" Reed calls out. "Would you make sure there's a shit-ton of coffee on set in the morning?"

"Already done, boss. I've got everything under control."

"Of course you do."

I say goodnight to everyone, give Georgina an extra-tight squeeze, and then hop into the back seat of a yellow cab with Fish to head back to our hotel . . . where, to be perfectly honest, I don't intend to get my "beauty sleep" any time soon. Because, hey, that's what coffee is for. As far as I'm concerned, a girl only gets one chance to lose her virginity on the night her sweet rock-star boyfriend sang "Fireflies" and "People Like Us" to her in front of tens of thousands.

TWENTY-SIX

ALESSANDRA

"After you," Fish says, motioning to the opened door of our hotel room. And when I walk past him into the room, I discover it's absolutely crammed with roses. Mostly red bouquets. But one yellow, too. *And they're everywhere.* Spraying out gloriously from vases on the dresser, nightstand, a side table, desk, and coffee table.

"Aw, Matthew," I whisper, whirling around to face him. "Thank you."

We kiss passionately, until he pauses and looks at the clock on the nightstand.

"I'll be fine tomorrow," I say, reading his facial expression. "Adrenaline and caffeine will keep me going all day tomorrow, I promise."

He's breathing hard. "I want you to know there's no pressure tonight. No rush. No expectations . . ."

I launch myself at him without replying. And our conversation is abruptly over.

Panting, he pulls off his shirt and pants and briefs, as I do the same—stopping, however, when I'm standing in my bra and undies. I want to get naked, of course. But I've never stripped down completely naked during any of our video chats, and I've been fantasizing for quite some time about Fish removing these last literal and symbolic swaths of cloth.

I look him up and down, my breathing labored and my body on fire. His penis is hard and straining. His eyes ablaze. And I'm struck at how aroused I feel at the sight of him. Before tonight, I've seen Fish's naked body on my computer screen. But there's no comparison for the full effect of his nakedness, combined with his body heat and proximity. Especially when I'm gazing at his nakedness while the scent of roses swirls in the air.

Visibly trembling with excitement, Fish leads me to the bed, where I sit on the edge, barely able to breathe through my excitement.

Fish murmurs something about taking off my bra, so I lean forward, thinking I'm helping him reach the clasp on my back. Unfortunately, though, I've moved sharply forward at the exact moment he's bent sharply down and forward. Which means we knock foreheads, rather forcefully.

"I'm sorry!" I blurt, touching the point of impact. "Are you okay?"

"I'm fine." He's rubbing his forehead, too. "You?"

"I'm fine." I gasp, remembering the video shoot tomorrow. "Is there a bump? A mark?"

Fish scrutinizes me carefully. "No. Nothing."

I sigh with relief, and he kisses my forehead gently.

"I'm sorry. I was going to take off your bra."

My chest heaves. "Please do."

He puts up his palm. "Stay perfectly still for a minute, okay?" When I nod and sit still like a statue, Fish slowly sits next to me on the bed and begins kissing me again. As our kiss ramps up, and my body ignites again, he reaches behind me and fingers the clasp on my back. And fingers it. And fiddles with it. Until, soon, it's obvious the damn bra isn't coming off any time soon.

Fish pulls out of our kiss. "How the fuck do you open this thing?"

I laugh. "Sorry. There's a trick to it. You have to kind of *twist* it. I'll do it." I reach behind my back and easily release the snap, which causes my bra to fall forward slightly at my breasts. "I shouldn't have worn this bra. It's like a freaking boob chastity belt."

He laughs. "No, I'm just stupid." He looks down at my loosened bra. "Can I . . . pull it off?"

"Yes. My underwear, too."

He takes a shallow breath and trembles again. And then, slowly, pulls off my bra completely, baring my small breasts to him.

He looks into my eyes. "I love you."

"I love you, too."

He guides me to lie down and pulls off my undies, making me whimper with excitement and anticipation. With a loud and quavering exhale, he crawls on top of me, the same way he did in that greenroom, presses his body against mine, and begins making out with me. We kiss passionately. Grind our naked bodies together. We caress and explore each other. Our hands alternately grabbing and brushing lightly. Until I realize Fish has touched every inch of me, other than the pulsing, throbbing swollen bundle of nerves that's aching to be touched the most.

"Can I touch between your legs?" he whispers, his fingertips skating across my inner thigh.

I tell him yes in a strained, desperate voice. I beg him to

please touch me there. And, in response, he slides his fingers inside me, gently, and slowly begins moving them in and out.

At the sensation of being penetrated for the first time in my life, I moan at the fireworks going off inside me—and then flat-out growl when Fish's fingers unexpectedly move from my wetness to my aching, throbbing clit and begin moving it around with masterful precision.

Oh my fucking God.

I've recently gotten pretty good at touching myself exactly like this, so I thought I knew what it'd feel like for Fish to do it the same way. But, no. There's absolutely no comparison between my own touch and Fish's. Fish's touch is exponentially more exciting, pleasurable, and *intense* than anything I've ever managed to feel on my own. In fact, I literally can't lie still as Fish works me with expert fingers. I'm not only groaning and shaking and moaning with plea-sure, I'm writhing uncontrollably. Gyrating into his confident hand.

"I've been fantasizing about doing this for so long," he whispers into my ear as I moan. *"This is so hot for me, Ally."*

His breathing is heavy. His skin against mine warm. And his fingers! Oh, God. Every single touch is taking me closer and closer to the brink of pure ecstasy.

"I'm . . . *Ooooh*, Matthew." For a split second, I feel like I've looked straight at the sun and am now awaiting the inevitable sneeze. My body feels suspended, momentarily. I feel a sharp retraction inside my womb, ever so briefly. And then, nirvana, as the most explosive, pleasurable orgasm of my life throttles me.

I cry out with my release, bucking and jolting against Fish's hand. And as I do, Fish growls about how hot I am. How wet he is. How much he loves touching me.

When I come down from my pleasure, I blurt, "Make love to me, Fish."

He doesn't hesitate. He scrambles to his nearby suitcase, grabs a foil packet, and covers himself. When he returns to me, his face is a portrait of unbridled lust. I know he loves me. But in this moment, clearly, this man wants to *fuck* me. And that's perfectly fine with me.

Without hesitation, he crawls on top of me, and I open my legs wide, inviting him inside me. Certain it's what I want, without a shadow of a doubt.

"You're sure?" he whispers.

"I've never been surer of anything in my life."

Fish touches my wet entrance, briefly, and then presses his covered tip against it. But he pauses. I feel the sensation of him entering me, but only the slightest bit.

"Ready?"

I nod, barely able to breathe.

With an exhale, he slowly pushes himself inside me. And I tremble and pant through the initial discomfort.

"Are you okay?" he chokes, his body trembling against mine.

I nod. "Keep going." But it's all I can manage. I'm too thrilled and overwhelmed and relieved to say more.

He thrusts, slowly, his green eyes locked with mine. But just when I feel my body beginning to fully relax to receive him, just when I think, "Hey, I think I could really like this!", Fish stiffens sharply, growls, and shoves his hips forward, all the way. I feel a rippling sensation against my innermost walls inside me, and then, Fish's body goes slack.

Apparently, that's it.

The deed is now officially done.

"Shit," Fish whispers. He's still inside me, though he's

perfectly still now. "I'm sorry. I wanted to last a really long time for you, but you felt *so* damned good, I—"

"No, it was perfect. I loved it."

"Next time, I'll last way—"

"No, no, it was amazing. Don't apologize. I'm excited you were so excited. Plus, this way, we've gotten the 'big moment' out of the way, so that, next time, I'll be totally relaxed and rarin' to go, right out of the gate."

Fish lies alongside me and pulls off his condom. "I wanted to make tonight perfect for you."

"It *was* perfect. In every way." I roll onto my side. "Matthew, this has literally been the best night of my life."

He smiles. "Mine too."

He takes me into his arms and we cuddle for a few minutes before hitting the shower together. From there, we brush our teeth and get ready for bed, before crawling into bed and turning out all the lights.

"I'm nervous about tomorrow," I say. "Or, rather, later today."

He kisses the top of my head. "You're going to do great."

We lie together, quietly, for a long moment. Long enough that I think maybe Fish might have fallen asleep.

"Matthew?"

"Mm-hmm."

He's got his left forearm draped over his forehead, so I can see his iconic fish tattoo. I trace it with my fingertips. "I'm so glad you were my first." *And last.*

Fish removes his arm from his face and looks at me. "I'm glad you were mine. I wouldn't have it any other way."

We share a smile.

I touch his stubble. Stroke his shaggy hair. Run my fingertips across the three tattooed haystack-poop-pile-goats on his ribcage. "I love you so much," I whisper. "Thank you for making me feel so special tonight."

"That's because you *are*." He pulls me to him, to rest my cheek on his chest, and kisses the top of my head. "I love you, too, Alessandra the Lioness. Now, get some sleep. You've got a big day ahead of you."

TWENTY-SEVEN

FISH

"I hope that's a quadruple shot," Keane says, flopping down on a chair at my table. He's referring to the coffee cup on the table in front of me. "You look like shit."

"It's only a triple," I reply. "Although, granted, it's my *second* triple of the past thirty minutes."

We're sitting in the coffeehouse in Brooklyn that's been rented for Alessandra's music video shoot today. Our rising star is sitting in one far corner with Georgina and a makeup artist. In another far corner, our fearless director, Maddy, and the big boss who hired her are huddled with Owen and a small film crew, presumably figuring out how the heck they're going to cram all planned scenes into one day of furious shooting.

"Is Maddy stressed out?" I ask, looking at her gesticulating form across the room.

Keane nods. "She knows this is a huge opportunity for her. But also for Alessandra. She wants to hit it out of the park for her, even more than she wants to impress Reed for herself. When we got back to our room last night and she started plotting out the schedule for today, in detail, she said she realized the storyboard she and Reed had concocted at dinner over several drinks was hella ambitious. She said, in a perfect world, she'd have *two* full days to shoot this thing and get it right, especially with all the drop-in cameos planned throughout the day."

"Why not expand the shoot to two days?"

"The coffeehouse isn't available tomorrow. But, regardless, Reed said everything has to be captured today because he's taking Georgina on some elaborate vacation tomorrow and doesn't want to change any of his plans."

I roll my eyes. "God forbid the emperor ever has to change his plans."

Keane looks over at Maddy. "This is a huge opportunity for her."

I bat his forearm. "She'll be great. If anyone can pull a rabbit out of a hat, it's Maddy Behind the Camera. That woman is amazing at what she does."

"Yes, she is. She never ceases to amaze me." Keane leans back into his chair and sips his coffee. "So, why the two triples in rapid succession this morning, brah? Did you and the little missus stay up until sunrise, by any chance?"

I glance furtively across the coffeehouse, making sure nobody could possibly overhear our conversation. "We had a special night. I'll leave it at that."

Keane smiles. "Did any of the advice you got from Kat, or any of us dudes, turn out to be useful to you, I hope?"

In a flash, I see Alessandra's face last night, at the exact moment she had that amazing orgasm against my fingers, and I can't help smiling like a Cheshire cat. I'd watched the videos Alessandra tagged for me, at least a hundred times each, determined to do it exactly right for her. And by the way she came—so hard I felt the tiniest amount of fluid release inside her, against my fingers—I knew I'd hit a grand slam home run for her.

"Attaboy," Keane says, apparently reacting to my smile.

"I've confirmed nothing," I say flatly. "A gentleman doesn't kiss and tell."

"When he asked for advice from his friends on making his woman's first time 'special and magical,' he sure as shit does," Keane retorts.

But I ignore him and drink my coffee.

For a while, we sit quietly together, watching the highly entertaining swirl of activity around us. We watch the crew setting up cameras and lights. And Maddy and Reed conferring with one of the camera operators and Owen, while plotting things out on a whiteboard.

Suddenly, out of nowhere, Keane says, "So, I take it from that smile you didn't turn into the Flash on her?"

I don't know what I'm doing with my face. Indeed, I'm trying my damnedest to look neutral. Impassive. Totally blank. But whatever Keane the Peen sees on my face provokes him to throw up his hands and whisper-shout, "Noooo!" He leans forward. "I told you to beat off beforehand, ya dumbshit!"

I glance across the coffeehouse and lean forward. "When was I supposed to do that, ya dumbshit? Ally and I came straight from the concert to the restaurant to Times Square to the hotel!"

"Where there's a will, there's a way, my son. You could have done it in the restaurant."

I roll my eyes.

"Don't roll your eyes at me. Whatever you do tonight, you have to last for her. Round Two is when you take her off the bunny slopes and show the girl how fun skiing can really be. Don't let her down, dude. Tonight's where the *real* memories get made."

My stomach clenches. "Stop talking. You're giving me performance anxiety."

"No need for that. Just make sure you beat off a few hours beforehand this time and study up on some of my earliest BPH videos. And, *voila*, you'll be a sex god tonight. I promise."

I glance across the room. "I can't beat off beforehand tonight, dumbass, any more than I could have done it last night. We're gonna be here all day long, and then at the late-night dinner Reed is hosting as a wrap party."

Keane brings his coffee to his lips, like he's the Queen of England sipping tea. "Where there's a will, there's a way, my handsome and happy lad."

I sigh and lean back.

And for a long moment we're quiet again. Watching the swirl of activity around us.

I look at him. "Tell me the God's truth, Peenie. Does The Sure Thing *really* work the way you guys always say it does?"

"Like clockwork."

"You can get *any* woman off, multiple times a sesh that way?"

"Any woman. Best orgasms of her life. One after another, until she's speaking in tongues. Usually, you'll get some tears out of her, too. Maybe even make her squirt. But I guarantee, no matter who she is, you'll get at least two out of her, and they'll be full-bodied *O*s like nothing she's *ever* experienced before with a clitoral *O*."

Well, that shuts me up.

I finish off my coffee, my mind reeling.

I haven't tried the technique too many times. But when I have, it's seemed completely useless to me. Like a whole lotta bullshit.

"The thing is," Keane says, "you have to do it *exactly* like I explain it in the video. Don't do a single thing differently than I say. Not one single modification."

I pull a face of disdain. "The dirty talk isn't really me."

"I knew it!" he booms, slamming his palms on the table.

"Shhh! Peenie. Jesus."

He leans forward, his blue eyes blazing. "The dirty talk is *critical*. It's how you keep her mind in the moment, so she doesn't start thinking about her grocery list, or whatever shit she's got to do tomorrow at work . . . It's the only way to keep her focused. Without the dirty talk to go along with the fingering technique, most women can't get there. Maybe one in ten will get there without the dirty talk."

"Shit. Why didn't you say that in the video?"

"I did, dumbass. Repeatedly."

"Well, you didn't make it clear enough."

He scoffs. "Trust me, do The Sure Thing on her tonight, exactly as instructed, and you'll take her places she didn't even know existed."

"Don't be stupid. I'm not going to even *attempt* The Sure Thing on her tonight! You heard Ryan. He said she has to get her sea legs first, and we're not even close to that milestone yet. Last night was her first time, Peenie. Jumping straight to The Sure Thing on Night Two would be like dragging a woman who's never ridden any kind of roller coaster straight onto the Takashiba."

"The *Takashiba*?"

"It's this megatron roller coaster in Tokyo. I ride it every time we play a show there and nearly crap my pants, every time. Put it on your bucket list. It's life changing."

"Thanks for the tip."

I glance at Alessandra again. She's still engaged in conversation with Georgina and the makeup artist. I say, "There's still plenty of stuff I need to do with Ally to help her get her 'sea legs' before we even attempt any of the more advanced stuff. Baby steps, man."

"Ah. I see. Give me your phone."

"Why?"

"Just do it."

I give him my phone and tell him the code when he asks. And he returns it with a "Ball Peen Hammer" video cued up —a video entitled, "Give Your Woman Oral Sex That Will Make Her Scream!"

Keane winks. "Do your woman a favor, and watch that video at least ten times before tonight, Fish Filet. *You're welcome.*"

TWENTY-EIGHT

FISH

"That was great, Alessandra," Maddy says soothingly, when Alessandra finishes her second run-through of lip-synching her song for the cameras.

But even from here, I can tell it wasn't great. Not at all.

Alessandra has looked stunning over there on that small stage, as she's sung and played her guitar along with the track. In fact, when Alessandra first walked over to me earlier to show me what the makeup artist had done to her, my jaw practically dropped to the floor at how stunning she looked. But the minute Maddy asked her to begin lip-synching with the cameras rolling—and every crew member staring intensely at her—her sparkling ease when she showed me her makeup vanished, instantly replaced by self-consciousness.

It's perfectly understandable for Alessandra to need some time to settle in and get comfortable in front of the myriad cameras and crew. She's a complete newbie, after all, and this is quite a production. Far more so than she was likely expecting when Reed first told her about his planned music video. Surely, any newbie, other than a total extrovert like

Keane, would react to this situation the same way Alessandra has been doing. Like she's made of wood. Unfortunately, though, even if Alessandra's stiffness is understandable, we simply don't have enough time in today's crammed shooting schedule for her to slowly figure her shit out and find her sparkle. Somehow, she needs to do those things on a bullet train.

"Are you sure that was okay?" Alessandra says to Maddy.

"It was great!" Maddy chirps. "How about we try it one more time, just for fun, even though we already have every-thing we need. Only this time . . ." She gives Alessandra some gentle direction. A little nudge. While, somehow, keeping any hint of panic out of her voice.

Alessandra takes a deep breath. And it's suddenly clear to me the next time through is going to be as big a shitshow as the prior two times, if I don't step in. I have no desire to usurp Maddy's authority or hijack this situation. On the other hand, I know what's at stake and how little time we've got to get this performance footage, and get it done right. All the rest of the storyboard is fun and cute, but if Alessandra can't play and sing her song with confidence and charisma, everything else is going to fall flat.

I stand. "Hey, Maddy?"

Maddy pauses and turns around to face me.

"Sorry to interrupt. I was just wondering if you'd mind me standing behind the barista counter during this next time through?" I point toward the counter, which is immediately across from where Ally's seated on a stool. "Seems like you've got a lot of footage of Ally looking at Camera A already. Would it screw things up in terms of your camera setup if Alessandra sometimes sings to me over there?"

Maddy visibly exhales with gratitude. "That's a great idea,

Fish. Yeah, we've got enough footage of Ally looking into Camera A. Thanks, Georgina."

"No problem," Georgina replies. She's been standing next to Camera A, as a focal point for Alessandra, this whole time.

Maddy continues. "Give us five minutes, Fish. We'll put a camera and light setup on you, too. Might as well have the option of using whatever footage of you we might capture during Alessandra's next run-through."

"Perfect."

As the crew sets up their cameras, I head over to Alessandra sitting on the stage.

"I'm sucking," she says. It's a statement, not a question.

"Not at all. You're perfect," I lie. "This is what always happens on music video shoots. They get everything they need, and then move on to trying some different stuff, jut for the fun of it. This is par for the course."

"Really?"

"Really."

Her shoulders soften. "Okay. Good. I was worried I was sucking."

"Not at all."

"Okay, we're ready!" Maddy calls out. She comes to a stand next to me and addresses Alessandra. "We've already got everything we need from you. So, this next time through is just for fun."

"See?" I say, and Alessandra beams a relieved smile at me. I look at Maddy. "That's what I was just saying. You've got everything you need. This is just belts and suspenders."

"Exactly."

I turn away from Alessandra to walk to my mark behind the barista counter, and as I turn, I catch Maddy's eye and flash her a secret "we're in deep shit" look that makes her turn her face away from Alessandra and chuckle.

"All right," Maddy says with authority, once everyone is ready and in position. "Cue music, please!"

The song begins blaring, and, once again, Alessandra begins strumming along. But this time, with her eyes on *me*, rather than Georgina.

Instantly, it's clear this was a brilliant idea. Because when I smile at Alessandra to encourage her, she lights up in a way she wasn't doing when she was performing to Georgie.

On a whim, just to see if I can get those blue eyes sparkling like crazy, I mouth the words, "*I love you.*" And the effect is unmistakable. Alessandra's face lights up like a Christmas tree, even as she doesn't miss a beat in performing her song.

"Yes!" Maddy says excitedly, her back to me. "Keep flirting with Fish as you sing, Ally! This is pure gold."

I know Maddy will be overdubbing the track in the final product, which means I can say or do anything to elicit a reaction from Alessandra, and my end of things won't make it into the video. And so, I decide to jump right in, without holding back.

I begin catcalling to her. And, again, the effect is remarkable. Solid gold.

"Yes!" Maddy yells enthusiastically. "Fish, whatever you're doing back there, keep doing it, only turn up the heat!" She addresses Alessandra. "Ally, while he's doing that, your job is to keep singing and playing, without ever actually smiling. Got it?"

"Got it," Ally says.

"Cue music from the top!" Maddy calls out. And there's

no missing the genuine excitement in her voice. She's on the cusp of capturing magic, and she knows it.

When the song starts again, I'm a man on a mission, determined to make my woman smile, even though that's exactly what the director just told her not to do.

For a while, I'm a mime stuck in a box. Then, I'm a mime descending and ascending stairs behind the bar. I'm a flapping fish caught on a hook, being reeled into a boat. I'm a tragedy-comedy mask playing peekaboo with Alessandra, as I appear and reappear from behind the counter.

And through it all, the effect on Alessandra is un-fucking-believable. She's glorious. Charismatic. Mesmerizing. *Adorable.* Indeed, there's no doubt now Maddy's got everything she needs to make Alessandra a star, and then some.

"Okay, one last time through the song!" Maddy yells. "We've got what we need. So this time really is a free pass. Just have fun with it, guys. Leave it all out there."

I'm at a loss. I feel like I've already shot my wad by now, in terms of figuring out ways to amuse and entice Alessandra to smile.

"Take it off, baby doll," Keane says from a corner. When I look at him, he winks. "Show her what the good lord gave ya, Fish Boy. Shake that skinny ass."

I can't help chuckling. Of course, that's what Ball Peen Hammer would suggest, given his past life as a highly successful male stripper in Seattle. But, hey, just because the idea came from a guy everyone calls *Peen* doesn't make it a bad one. But if I'm going to do this, then I'm going to do it right—from where Alessandra can see the entirety of my man meat.

As the song begins again, I step out from behind the bar,

where Alessandra—and everyone else, unfortunately—can see every inch of me. And that's where I launch into a no-holds-barred dance/striptease. Off comes my shirt, which I twirl above my head like a cowboy with a lasso, before chucking it across the room. Next, I peel off my pants, shaking my ass with fervor as I do. My dance moves in my underwear are herky jerky and awkward, and I know it. Probably highly embarrassing. But, still, I'm giving it all I've got. And, no regrets, baby, because Alessandra is absolutely loving it.

But when I begin tugging at the waistband of my Calvin Kleins with a brazenly lascivious look on my face, Alessandra finally breaks. "No!" she shouts, standing up. "*Fish, no!*"

I burst into laughter, which sends Alessandra laughing in relief, and in short order, the entire room—every single person in this coffeehouse—is laughing uproariously, like they'd been holding it in throughout my entire performance.

Maddy calls "Cut!" and flashes me a grateful smile. At which point, Alessandra barrels to me, her face aglow.

When my love reaches me, I open my arms to her and she crashes into me.

"Thank you!" Alessandra breathes. "Thank you so much."

I kiss the top of her head. "You didn't need me. You were already a star."

"You saved me from total and complete disaster," she says, squeezing me. "I can't believe you did a striptease for me."

I smell her hair. "Baby, I'd do *anything* for you. Just name it, and it's yours. *Always.*"

She looks up, her eyebrow cocked. "Anything?"

"*Anything*," I reply. And I don't feel the slightest bit of anxiety when I say it. It's the truth. This girl can take it all. Anything and everything, it's all hers.

Alessandra smiles devilishly. "That's good news. Because later tonight, I want you to show me the rest of that striptease."

TWENTY-NINE

ALESSANDRA

"Best day *ever*," I say to Fish as we stroll, hand in hand, toward the door of our hotel room—and it's the truth. Thanks to Fish, we snatched victory out of the jaws of defeat today at the music video shoot. Or, at least, I was able to give Maddy enough to be able to stitch together something that won't be too embarrassing.

Thankfully, everyone else in the video gave *stupendous* performances today, so maybe nobody will notice me in the final product too much. Fish was adorable! And Keane, Georgina, and Laila were amazing! Plus, the rock stars who promised to show up for cameos actually did it! And all of them oozed star quality during their brief stints on camera. And to top off this incredible day, Fish and I got to enjoy a wonderful meal in Brooklyn after the shoot—a boisterous "wrap party" at a trendy eatery hosted by Reed and attended by everyone involved in the video. And now, the cherry on top? Fish and I are heading back to our room to finally be alone, and naked, again.

We reach the door to our room and release our hands so

that Fish can unlock the door. When he opens the door for me, I leap through the opening with aplomb, like a ballerina entering from stage left in a tutu, and Fish makes me laugh by leaping into the room after me like he's Prince Siegfried in *Swan Lake*.

When the door shuts behind our loping frames, I spin around, laughing, to face my prince—my Prince Charming—and, without hesitation, barrel into him and begin attacking him.

In no time at all, we're both down to our underwear. And, to my surprise, this time Fish unsnaps my bra with ease, before flinging it across the room.

"Impressive!" I exclaim.

Fish winks. "I practiced last night after you fell asleep. Shame on you if you fool me *once*. Shame on *me* if you fool me twice." As I giggle, Fish leans down and voraciously kisses my bare breasts, causing my knees to buckle underneath me.

"I have to lie down," I choke out, too aroused to rely on my legs another moment.

I tumble happily onto the nearby bed with a squeal, and clap as Fish reaches for his underwear, clearly intending to rip them off.

"Wait!" I command. "You promised me the grand finale of today's striptease."

"Ah, yes."

"A deal's a deal."

Chuckling, Fish lets go of his waistband and pulls his phone out of his jeans on the floor. He fiddles with his device for a moment, his rock-hard bulge straining behind his undies and his chest heaving with excitement, until, finally, a song begins blaring from his phone. It's a rock song that's either really, really old or really, really new and intending to sound super cool and retro. I'm truly not sure which.

After placing his blaring phone on the nightstand, Fish gives me a show, to the thumping beat of the song. And as he dances and shakes his ass in his underwear, I can't help noticing the lyrics of the song. Clearly, my hot boyfriend chose this song purposefully—as a love letter to me. The words of the song are simple ones that get straight to the point. There's no poetry here. No metaphors. The singer wants to be with his girl all the time. "Day and night." Indeed, he says, quite passionately, he never wants to leave her side, *ever*, because he only ever feels "all right" when he's with her. By her side.

"What is this?" I ask, indicating the phone.

"The Kinks!" Fish says. He stops dancing. "'All Day and All of the Night.' It's a classic."

I shrug, confirming I've never heard this one before. And he faux scowls at me, like I've somehow offended him.

I laugh. "Is it from the seventies?"

"The sixties! For the love of fuck, woman. It's one of the greatest love songs ever written. Listen carefully. They're saying everything I feel, to a T." He smiles. "I've actually had this song stuck in my head for weeks."

How is it possible for a man to be this sweet and loving? He's like a puppy. There's literally not a single mean or hurtful bone in his body. But lucky for me, he's also sexy as hell. And, currently, hard as a rock behind those tighty-whities.

My smile turns sexual and heated. "Can I snap a photo, before you take off those undies? You look incredible right now. I never want to forget this moment."

He shrugs. "Knock yourself out."

I grab my phone off the nightstand. And to my surprise, Fish poses for me with enthusiasm this time, looking far more comfortable in his skin than the time he posed for me in his underwear during one of our earliest video chats. Wow. Fish isn't self-conscious or shy this time. He's not wondering what to do with his hands. No, this time, my hunky boyfriend is smoldering at me, every bit as much as Colin did on that billboard in Times Square.

"Well, that shot ought to come in handy on lonely nights," I say, plopping my phone onto the nightstand.

"Let's not talk about lonely nights this week," Fish says. "I don't even want to think about being away from you, ever again."

Oh, my heart. "Same."

We share a look of pure longing at our predicament—at that fact that, in about a week, Fish will hop onto a flight back to LA, while I stay in Boston.

"I shouldn't have mentioned that," I say. "Come on. Continue your striptease—but fast-forward to the part where you whip it out, if you don't mind."

Without hesitation, and no finesse whatsoever, Fish rips off his undies and flings them across the room, making me laugh. And then he stands before me, his dick straining, his green eyes blazing, and his hands on his hips. "Come to Papa," he murmurs.

Giggling, I lie back onto the bed and spread my legs slightly, letting him know I'm his for the taking. That I'm not nervous tonight. *At all.* Only excited and wet and ready.

Fish crawls onto the bed next to me, pulls off my underwear, and begins kissing every inch of my body. My breasts. Rib cage. Belly button. He licks and sucks my stiff nipples, making me groan and clutch his hair. He kisses my inner thighs, making me shudder violently with arousal and anticipation.

After a while, when I'm moaning and shaking, he begins brushing his fingers up and down my folds, making me quiver and yearn like nothing I've felt before.

Breathing hard, he begins tracing the recent pathway of his fingers with his mouth. But he's teasing me. Kissing my delicate folds with precision, while seemingly taking care never to make contact with my throbbing, aching clit.

He spreads my thighs wide and inhales me before hovering his lips over the hard, swollen tip that's aching for him. I feel his warm breath tickling me. *Teasing* me. I've never felt the sensation of a warm, wet mouth on my most intimate places, but I've imagined it, many times. And now that it's about to happen, I can honestly say I feel physically *desperate* for it. So wet and needy, I begin whimpering softly.

Finally, Fish brushes his fingertip against my clit, ever so gently, and I literally scream in response, making him jolt.

"Sorry," I choke out. "I couldn't help it."

"Don't apologize. I loved it. Scream. Moan. Don't hold back."

When I nod, and gasp for air, Fish flashes a smile, the likes of which I've never seen from him before—like he's a mob boss, ordering a hit—and then, he spreads my thighs, yet again, opening me wider than before, and finally, thank God, the man leans in and gets to work.

Holy Mother of Pearl.

I knew this was going to feel good, but I had no idea it would feel *this* good.

As Fish's tongue and mouth devour me, he slides his fingers inside me and strokes a spot just on the inside of my entrance. And the combination of the two types of stimulation

—his mouth on my clit and his fingers stroking that spot—is making my eyes roll back into my head in ecstasy.

He's relentless.

Steadfast.

Merciless.

Masterful.

As my body ramps up and up and up, Fish doesn't slow down or speed up. He just stays the course, deftly guiding me closer and closer to the brink—to a place where I feel like I'm going to lose complete control of myself.

All of a sudden, my body tightens sharply.

And, then . . . *heaven.*

As pleasure unleashes inside me, I *scream.* I mean, I freaking *shriek* at full volume in response to the tidal wave of pleasure, bliss, nirvana slamming into me.

As I come down from my very loud orgasm, Fish lifts his head, looking drunk. Tousled. And visibly proud of himself.

He says, "That scream was the hottest thing I've ever heard in my life."

I feel ravenous to be penetrated. Greedy. Hungry. *Desperate.* "Make love to me, Matthew," I say in a breathy voice. "I want you inside me. I want you deep inside me."

"Oh, Jesus."

Practically hyperventilating, he gets himself covered and crawls over my writhing frame. He pushes his tip against my wet entrance, and pauses briefly, causing every atom of my body to seize with yearning and need. I grab his bare ass, egging him on, and he pushes inside me, slowly.

He's panting. "Good?"

"Good," I whisper. "Don't hold back."

He rests his forearms on either side of my head and begins thrusting, this time, with a lot more enthusiasm than last night, and I grip his ass and move my pelvis back and forth to maximize his movements.

As our synchronized bodies gain momentum, he pulls my hands above my head and kisses me deeply, sending an electric current coursing through me. Is that Fish's heart beating against my sternum, from the *outside*, or is it mine, beating from the *inside*? I honestly can't tell. As cliché as it sounds, I feel in this moment like our hearts are beating as one.

Fish picks up the pace and intensity of his movements, yet again, and I let him know I'm loving it. And soon, we're kissing and moving with abandon. Like animals. Both of us lost in each other and the pleasure.

"Still good?" he gasps out, our pleasure making us sweat and grunt and kiss with abandon.

"So good," I choke out, digging my nails into his back.

"I wanna try another position," Fish grits out. "I want to make you come again."

No argument from me.

He guides me onto my hands and knees and enters me again—this time, fondling my clit as he thrusts. And, holy shit, it's an incredible sensation. Totally different than when he moves on top of me. Quickly, my pleasure feels like it's reaching another boiling point.

He comes first. *Hard.* But when I move, thinking we're done, he tells me to stay put and begins eating me out from behind while fingering me. Quickly, the result of this new kind of stimulation is another screaming orgasm that makes me collapse onto the bed in a sweaty, panting heap.

Fish lies next to me, on his side, also breathing hard and sweating.

"Damn," I say. "Now I understand why the entire world is obsessed with sex."

"The entire world is obsessed with *trying* to have sex like that," he replies. "Before you, I thought people were exaggerating when they said they had sex that made them 'see God.'"

"You saw God?"

"I did. He needs to trim his beard a little bit."

I laugh.

"Seriously, Ally, that was exponentially better than anything I've ever experienced. So, so, so, soooo good. It's amazing how different it is when there's a genuine connection."

I smile. "It was amazing for me, too."

He snorts. "That was best of *two* for you? That's quite a compliment."

I laugh and run my fingertip across his tattooed forearm. "Honey, I have a feeling we're going to get really, *really* good at sex this week."

THIRTY

ALESSANDRA

F ish opens the door to our new hotel room, this one in Boston, and I'm once again blasted with the glorious smell of roses. Just like in New York, Fish has arranged for dozens of roses to greet me in our hotel room . . . All of them a deep crimson, except for one symbolic and lovely bouquet of yellows.

"Matthew!" I shout, leaping into the room. "You can't keep doing this for me!"

"Don't tell me what to do, woman. I'll do what I want. I'm a rock star. A rebel."

I twirl through the room, squealing, my arms bowed above my head in fifth position, while Fish follows me into the room, chuckling at my exuberance.

We unpack and stow our suitcases and guitars, seeing as how we're going to be staying here for a full week this time. And then, we drink champagne from crystal flutes while checking out the view from our lovely balcony.

I point out a few buildings in the skyline, since Fish has never played tourist in Boston. He's performed here with his band, apparently. But he's never stayed long enough to wander around and check out the usual sights.

"I'll show you everything," I say. "All the usual tourist stuff, and also the most important places from my life."

"I can't wait to see all of it. Especially the stuff from your life."

My old life, I think. But I don't say it out loud, simply because I don't want to jinx it. "Hey, I was thinking, for dinner, we could go to the café where I used to work. I'd love to introduce you to my boss and a couple friends there."

"Cool."

"They have the best damned vegan enchiladas in the world."

"Well, since I've never had vegan enchiladas, I'll take your word for it."

"You should. They're amazing." I take a sip of my champagne and sigh happily against his shoulder as we lean against the railing of the balcony together. "Tomorrow, how about I give you a tour of campus?"

"I'd love to see campus. If I'd gone to college, it would have been Berklee."

"Oh! My summer professor would love to meet you. She's a huge fan."

"No way."

I nod effusively. "If you're up for it, maybe you could come with me to class on Tuesday! I was planning to play hooky from class all week, in order to hang out with you, but if you're willing—"

"I'd *love* to sit in on a class. I'm honestly dying to do that."

"Not just sit in. Maybe you can do a Q and A for the class.

Everyone is going to shit a brick when I walk in with you." I snort. "Prepare to be *mobbed*, dude."

"I'll wear my suit of armor."

"You squeezed a suit of armor into that little suitcase?"

"I'm an excellent packer." He smiles. "Honestly, I'll probably have as many questions for your professor and the class as they have for me. I wish I could have gone here. It seems so cool."

I grin at him, feeling overwhelmed with love for this humble, sweet boy. "Oh! I'll take you for cupcakes at my favorite bakery! They make the best cupcakes *ever*."

"Okay. I've got to stop you right there, babe. Your bakery might be good. Maybe even great. But the best cupcakes *ever* are made at *my* favorite bakery in Seattle—which, by the way, I'm taking you to at my first opportunity."

I gasp excitedly. "You're going to take me home to Seattle?"

He nods. "I've already told my mom about you. She's dying to meet you."

"What'd you tell her about me?"

He turns to face me, placing his palms on my shoulders. "Well, let's see. I told her I have a girlfriend who's the most beautiful, sweetest, most talented woman in the world. I told her I'm in love for the first time in my life, and it's the best feeling in the world. And I think I told her you like it doggie style."

I swat at him as he guffaws.

He leans his side into the balcony railing. "Have you told your mom about *me*?"

"I did. But only because she was getting mobbed with messages about us, after you serenading me in New York was all over the news."

"Did you want to keep me a secret?"

"Of course not. I just wanted to tell my mother about you after we'd said, 'I love you.' Which, as you know, was that same night." I sigh. "The truth is, my mom is really sweet. But she's kind of an opinionated person about certain things. Like, she doesn't believe in premarital sex, for instance. That sort of thing."

"Ah."

"So, I just figured I'd tell her about you, and how much I love you, when I could say, 'Yes, Mom, he's my *boyfriend* and we're hopelessly in love. Yes, Mom. We've said, 'I love you' to each other. Yes, Mom. He's really, really good to me.'"

"I get it."

"When I called her, she'd already seen footage of you serenading me all over the news, so she was already duly impressed."

"Who knew that story would blow up like that, huh?"

With today's rapid-fire news cycles, our moment to shine didn't last long. But for a hot minute, clips of Fish singing to me, and me freaking out on the jumbotron, were *everywhere* on social media. The feel-good story of the moment.

"The good news," I say, "thanks to those clips, is that you've already won my mom over. After seeing those clips, she told me, and I quote, 'He's a keeper.'"

"Ha! That was easy."

"Will I have as easy a time with your mom? Is she the kind of mom who thinks nobody is good enough for her darling baby boy?"

"Well, I've never brought anyone home before, as you know. So I don't know about that. But even if Mom were the toughest nut to crack in the world, I know, without a doubt, she'd still instantly love you." He takes my hand and kisses the top of it. "If someone doesn't love Alessandra Tennison, then they also don't love puppies and kittens and fields of flowers and the ocean and music."

"Oh, Fish." I slide my arms around his neck. "I love you."

"I love you, too." He kisses me gently. "Today is the happiest day of my life, Ally."

I'm shocked. Fish doesn't say that constantly, the way I do. And he didn't say it like he was kidding. But how could *this* day possibly surpass all the amazing days he must have had with his band? All the fabulous milestones and accomplishments and adventures he's experienced? All we did today was wake up and have sex, have some brunch, and then head to the airport for our flight to Boston.

He puts his finger underneath my chin. "I'm serious," he says, reading my mind. "Maybe it sounds crazy, but just knowing you love me back the way I love you, just being so comfortable with you . . . It's like, each day is better than the last."

"It is." I brush my fingertip over his cheek. "I wish my dad could have met you. He would have loved you."

"Aw, sweetheart. I'd give anything to meet him."

"Have I told you my dad played in a garage band in college?"

"No."

"He did. When I take you to meet my mom, I'll show you photos."

"I'd like that. What instrument did he play?"

I smile. "Guitar and bass. Mostly, bass."

He flashes me a radiant smile. And I know he understands. As far as I'm concerned, Fish was heaven sent to me by my father.

But before we've said anything further, my phone rings in my purse. I pull away from our embrace to grab it, thinking it might be Georgina. She left a voicemail during our flight, and when I called her back upon landing, I reached her voicemail.

When I see Georgina's name on my screen, I instantly connect the call. "Hey, you!"

"*I'm engaged!*" Georgina shrieks. "Reed asked me to marry him and I said *yes!*"

I'm shocked. From everything I've seen and read about Reed Rivers—not from Georgina, but from the world at large —I thought Reed wasn't the marrying kind. Plus, Georgina has said many times she has no desire to marry before the age of thirty—and that's an age that's still several years off for her.

"Congratulations!" I shriek, and then quickly tell Fish the news. I ask Georgina how Reed popped the question and she tells me the story in a long ramble that makes me swoon and squeal along with her.

"Reed wants to talk to you," Georgina declares.

And two seconds later, Reed's voice says, "Hello, lil sis."

I giggle. "Hey there, big bro! Congratulations!"

"Thank you. We're both over the moon."

"As you should be. You two are perfect together. A match made in heaven."

"We are, aren't we?" Reed sighs happily, while Georgina says something incomprehensible, making Reed laugh. Reed says, "Listen, sis, before Georgie and I board our flight, I wanted to quickly tell you some exciting news. I saw a rough cut of your music video earlier today and it *far* exceeded my highest expectations."

"No way! Can I see it?"

"Nope. Not yet."

"Aw. Come on, big *bro!*"

Reed laughs. "Patience, lil sis. I've sent Maddy a few requested revisions, and she's already hard at work. When the video is *precisely* the way I want it, I'll have her send it to you in final for approval and/or requested revisions."

"But I'm *dying* to see it *now*, big bro."

"I never let my artists see their videos in draft. Too many cooks in the kitchen."

"But I'm not merely your *artist* now," I say, using my most persuasive tone. "I'm your lil sis."

"Nope."

I flap my lips together. "Well, you can't blame a lil sis for trying. Hey, can I put you on speakerphone, big bro? Fish is standing here, staring at me, wondering what the hell is going on."

"Put him on."

I push the button for speaker mode and Reed graciously repeats himself about the amazingness of the music video— only this time, he heaps all sorts of praise on me and Fish for our "adorable" and "sparkling" and "relatable" performances. "You two are *gold* in this video," he declares. "Maddy wanted 'smitten' glances and smiles, and, man, did you two deliver in spades." He chuckles. "And it sure doesn't hurt that the footage of Fish singing to you at the Garden has gone viral. Even before this video, you two have given the world a cute little love story."

"It's all a master marketing strategy, Reed," Fish deadpans.

"Oh, I know. Of course." He laughs. "This music video is gonna go viral, sis. I'd bet the farm on it. Which means 'Blindsided' will rocket up the charts on the back of the video. And *that* means, my darling little sister . . . Hold on.

Georgie wants me to put you on speaker for this next thing."

Georgie's voice suddenly shrieks, "Hello!"

"Hello!"

Reed continues, "And *that* means, once the single is released, we're going to want to capitalize on its momentum . . . with the release of . . . a *full album*, as soon as possible!"

I'm too shocked to react. I must have misheard that. Imagined it.

"Alessandra?" Reed says. "Honey, I'm hereby offering you a full-album deal with River Records! Do you accept? I promise the terms will be favorable."

I look at Fish with my mouth in the shape of an *O*, before shrieking, "Yes! Yes! Oh my God!"

Laughing, Reed says, "You'll get full promo treatment. The best production money can buy. I'm going to make my lil sis a fucking star. And not because I adore you. *Which I do*. But because you're going to make me a mint, kid."

I lose it. Babble. Shriek. Thank him profusely. And hug Fish like he's just pulled me out of a stormy sea.

Reed says, "As soon as Georgie and I are back from our vacation, we'll gear up to release the single. I'm thinking we'll release it three weeks after we get the final video. Right around the time of the release, I'll fly you to LA for some promo and a meeting with my team and Zeke, so we can figure out the schedule and next steps for the album. Sound good?"

"Yes! Perfect!"

"I'll have Owen contact Zeke to find out his availability while I'm out of the country with my fiancée. Zeke is in demand and hard to pin down, but we'll get him."

"I don't know how I'm going to sleep or eat until that meeting in LA!"

"No, no," Reed says. "Put it out of your mind for now, if you can. It won't be for several weeks. In the meantime, relax and enjoy the calm before the storm. Because once the single releases, it's going to be a whirlwind for you. Judging by the way the world devoured Fish singing to you, everyone is going to lose their minds over that video."

"I can't believe this."

"To be clear, though, even as you're relaxing, if any new songs or melodies come to you, jot them down. Don't feel like you *have* to start writing the album yet. After our meeting, I'll assign a couple co-writers to the project, as necessary, if we're in a time crunch."

"Co-writers?"

"As *necessary*. Nothing wrong with that, as long as we always keep in mind the most important thing is preserving *your* authentic voice. *Your* personality."

"Okay." My gaze meets Fish's blazing green eyes. "So, do you think I should maybe drop my summer class and move to LA *now*, or . . .?"

"No, no. Finish your class. I know how much you love it. Frankly, I think that particular class will serve you very well in your future career. Relax and enjoy your vacation with Fish. We'll talk about next steps during our meeting in LA in three weeks to a month."

"Okay," I say, trying not to sound a bit disappointed. But I can't deny I'm secretly bummed about this one tiny thing. Reed is right. I *love* my summer class. It's the most enthralling class I've *ever* taken—and that's saying a lot. But I'd be lying if I didn't admit I was hoping this turn of events would be my excuse to drop everything and follow Fish to LA in a week.

"Time to board our flight," Reed says. "Have a great time this week, you two."

Fish and I thank him. We wish Reed and Georgie safe travels and congratulations on their engagement. And when we hang up, I collapse into Fish's waiting arms and break down into sobs against his chest.

Fish strokes my hair. "Are you laughing or crying?"

I nuzzle into him, trying to understand my strange reaction. "A bit of both, I think. I'm beyond elated—absolutely *euphoric*—but also overwhelmed. This is life changing. My body doesn't know how to react."

Fish lifts my tear-streaked face and smiles down at me. "Well, lucky for you, *I* know how to react." He kisses me. "Come to bed, superstar. Let me make you feel good. And after that, we'll get washed up, and celebrate this amazing news with 'the world's best vegan enchiladas.'"

THIRTY-ONE

ALESSANDRA

"Hmmm," Fish says, twisting his mouth in concentration. He strums his acoustic guitar and looks up at the ceiling of our hotel room like he's hoping to find some inspiration there. "Should we try an A-minor in the pre-chorus?" He plays his idea, and I express enthusiasm, before he launches into singing, "I'm so smitten with you. I'm in love, babe, delirious. Thanks to your sexy boobies, feet, and oh so sweet . . . *clitoris*."

I burst out laughing. "Give that boy a Grammy!"

We've been writing this song all night. Half of the time contributing serious lyrics. The other half gems like that. Actually, we've been writing songs all week here in Boston. After getting back from whatever fun thing we did by day, we've come back to our hotel room in the evenings and had a blast, just Fish and me. A tribe of two.

Besides having plenty of sex in our room during our evenings together, we've also enjoyed jamming and writing, watching movies, and ordering tons of room service, too. As it turns out, we're both total homebodies, even when we're supposedly "on vacation" together—far happier hanging out in our little room, as a simple party of two, than going out on the town.

"I couldn't possibly top an internal rhyme of 'delirious' and 'clitoris,'" I say. "You win."

"Aw, come on. Quitting is for losers."

"I'm not *quitting*. Just saying you win."

He scoffs. "Come on. Dig deep."

I strum and think. "I've got it!" I strum with gusto and sing, "*I'm so smitten with you. I'm in love, babe, delirious. Once a lioness, now a sex kitten—thanks to your talented fingers, tongue 'n' dick 'n' have I mentioned how much I love youuuu? Your wit 'n' charm and forearms, too? It's true, I love you, babe, and, oh, how I love to blow youuuuu.*"

He laughs. "That's literally my favorite song lyric in the history of time."

I lay my guitar down. "I told you I had nothing."

"No, that was damned good." He moves his guitar and motions to his sweatpants, where a prominent bulge is now poking from behind the fabric. "The proof is in the sweatpants."

There's a knock at the door and a voice announces our room service has arrived.

"Saved by the bell," Fish says, hopping up and winking at me.

"Not *saved*," I say coyly. "*Interrupted.*"

He shoots finger guns at me. "Baby, I like your style."

Fish answers the door and gets our food and we sit at a table and start our meal.

"You know, in all seriousness," I say, eating a french fry, "I think we should write a duet for my album."

"A duet about your clitoris?" he says.

I laugh. "No. A duet about being smitten. I love that word. Don't you?"

"I do. It's the perfect word for how I feel about you."

"Same."

"Of course, I love you. With all my heart. But 'smitten' captures that giddy feeling I always have when I'm with you or think of you."

I beam a huge smile at him. "When I think of how I feel for you, I picture myself twirling through a field of poppies."

He laughs. "You're so cute."

"Seriously, though, if we write a duet, would you be willing to record it for my album?"

"If that's what you want."

"It is."

"Then, yes."

I squeal happily, making him laugh. But when my phone buzzes on the table, I glance down and discover Maddy's name is *finally* gracing my screen!

With a gasp, I quickly connect the call. "Hi, Maddy! Fish is here and you're on speaker."

"Hey, guys! Reed just gave me the green light to send you the *final* cut of your music video! I'm sending the link as we speak!"

I shriek with excitement.

"After you and Fish watch it," Maddy continues, "let me know if you have *any* changes, and I'll relay them to Reed for approval. He said he wants this finalized ASAP, so he can release the single in about three weeks."

"Oh my gosh!"

We quickly say our goodbyes, grab my laptop, and hurl ourselves onto our bed. And a moment later, we're watching the video in stunned silence.

"It's incredible," Fish says, midway through. And I couldn't agree more. It's perfect. Funny. Heartwarming. Touching. Dazzling. Campy, at times. All of it beyond anything I could have hoped.

When the video ends, we watch it again, to see if there's a single frame we'd change. But there's nothing. We call Maddy and gush. And then call Georgina's phone. Not surprisingly, though, given that she and Reed are still traveling internationally, her voicemail picks up.

I leave Georgina a message, asking her to call me back, and then lose it the minute I hang up.

"Happy tears?" Fish asks.

I nod. "Mostly."

He looks concerned. "What's up, cutie?"

I pause to gather my thoughts. "What if this song is a huge hit like Reed says it will be?"

"It will be. You don't want it to be?"

"No, I do. With all my heart. But what happens then . . . to us?"

"What do you mean? I'll be cheering you on, louder than anyone."

I probably shouldn't say it. But I can't help myself. "But would I go on tour if the song is a hit? Or would I wait to tour until after the full album has come out?"

"Reed would make that call."

"And if I go on a tour, would my schedule overlap with yours? Would we be on opposite ends of the globe? Is that the future that awaits us, Fish? Constantly being on different ends of the globe and in a relationship that's mostly on video chat?"

Fish flushes. He opens and closes his mouth. And that's how I know my question isn't a stupid one.

"I'm sorry," I say quickly. "I don't know why this is hitting me, all of a sudden, when I should be nothing but happy. Maybe it's because you're going back to LA tomorrow and I'm freaking out at the thought of being away from you again. I survived being away from you before because I didn't know any better. But now that I know . . ."

Fish's face softens. "Sweetheart, you're getting ahead of yourself. These next few weeks will be hard on us. But after that, everything is going to work out." He sighs at whatever he's seeing on my face. "Come here, love." Fish pats the bed in front of him and I crawl to him. "We'll make it work."

"We will?"

He nods. "We will. We're meant to be, Ally. We're fate. *Destiny.* And that means everything's going to work out fine."

I decide to believe him. I surrender to his kiss, his touch, his certainty. And, in short order, we've got our clothes off and we're making out, passionately, in the bed.

After he makes me come with his fingers, as he's done many times before, I grip his hard penis and beg him to make love to me—which is also something that's happened before. That's the way it goes with us. I have an orgasm, and then we make love.

But this time, Fish puts his hand on mine and says, "Not yet, baby. I've been wanting to try something new with you." When my eyebrows lift, Fish's usual smile turns into a smolder that stiffens my nipples. He guides me back onto the bed. "Relax," he coos, his green eyes flickering with heat. "I'm going to do something new to you, baby—something that's going to rock your fucking world."

THIRTY-TWO

ALESSANDRA

Right out of the gate, Fish performs enthusiastic oral sex on me, which leads to me enjoying an intense, screaming orgasm. But that's nothing "new." Not that I'm complaining.

"That was just a primer," Fish says, coming out from between my legs. "I'm just getting you loose and relaxed for the new thing that's coming next."

"Which is . . .?"

"I'm going to make you come in a whole new way with my fingers."

That doesn't sound "new" to me, either. But, again, I'm not complaining. "Is there something I should do?"

His green eyes are on fire. "Nope. Just lie back and relax and listen to my voice. I'll take care of the rest."

I have no idea what the hell he's planning, but I trust him. So, I close my eyes and await whatever. And a moment later, Fish slides his fingers deep inside me and begins stroking a spot he's never touched before. At first, I'm not all that impressed, to be honest, simply because that spot doesn't feel

262

all *that* exciting or sensitive. At least, not compared to the usual places Fish usually touches to bring me to orgasm.

But when Fish leans into my ear and starts dirty-talking to me as he strokes that unexpected spot, something kind of crazy starts happening inside me. Deep inside me. I feel like my insides are twisting and stretching to near breaking, as if my very womb is getting ready to have a seizure.

I gasp out, "What are you doing to me?"

"It's a *technique*," Fish whispers, his voice husky. "I'll tell you about it later. For now, focus on my voice. Don't think about anything but my voice and how wet you are. Can you feel how wet you're getting? Wetter than you've ever been."

He's right. I'm so wet, the movement of his fingers is making crazy sounds, the likes of which I've never heard before.

"It feels like my insides are . . . *twisting*."

"They are. They're tightening before releasing. This is gonna make you come so hard, you're not gonna believe it. It's probably going to take you longer to get there than when I eat you out or massage your clit, so don't worry about that. Because once you come the first time, I'll be able to do it again, over and over."

I groan with extreme arousal and writhe against his fingers.

"Oh, fuck, Ally. You should see your face right now. This is the hottest you've ever looked."

I whimper, incapable of speaking.

"Imagine me fucking you," Fish whispers into my ear, his voice a low growl. "Imagine the head of my cock pounding you on this same spot, over and over again. Imagine I'm pounding into you so hard, you feel like you're going to pass out."

Well, that does it. My eyes roll back into my head. My deepest muscles clench sharply. Twist almost painfully, like they're retracting after touching a flame. And then . . .

Bliss.

White-hot pleasure seizes me as my innermost muscles release in forceful, pleasurable, waves that make me babble, and then keen like an animal.

"Holy fuck," Fish whispers. "I thought my friends were exaggerating about this!" He kisses my cheeks, tracking my salty tears with his soft lips. "That was the hottest thing I've ever seen in my life."

I throw my arms around his neck, gasping. I tell him I love him. I thank him for giving me the most pleasurable experience of my life, by far, and then beg him to "fuck me"—using that phrase for the first time in my life.

"Not yet," he says excitedly. "Supposedly, if we try this again, you'll have another orgasm, only even *better* and more quickly."

"*Supposedly?*"

Fish smiles. "I've never done this before. I've always thought it was bullshit. But I'm a big believer now."

"I'm game to be your guinea pig."

With a heated smile, he begins the whole thing again. And I'll be damned, in half the time it took the first time, I have another powerful orgasm—this one even more delicious than the first.

When I come down from my release, I'm a wreck. Incapable of speaking. Absolutely wiped out. And so freaking horny, I think I'm going to die if I don't get this man's dick inside me. I tell Fish I'm done for now. And I want him inside me.

"Fuck me, Fish," I command. And the effect on him is not difficult to surmise.

Quickly, Fish covers himself, rests both my thighs against his shoulders, and plunges himself inside me . . . and to my thrill, thanks to how wet I've become, my body receives his, molds to his, cradles his, like never before. Fish and I have had some damned good, animalistic sex this past week, as we've grown more and more comfortable with each other, but this time, by far, feels like something supernatural.

When we're done, we lie silently in each other's arms for a long while. But, finally I can't keep myself from saying the thing I've been thinking, on a running loop, for the past few days.

"Will you produce my album?"

Fish pauses. "What about Zeke?"

"Zeke is great. But I'd rather have *you*." When Fish says nothing, I sit up in the bed and look down at his shell-shocked expression. "Reed said the most important thing is that my album should reflect *my* voice. Well, who better to coax that out of me than *you*?"

Fish looks pained. His Adam's apple bobs. "Honey, I've never produced an album for another artist. Only for 22 Goats —and as Dax's *co*-producer, at that."

"You were basically my 'producer' at the music video shoot! And you've already had a thousand brilliant ideas for my album. I've loved coming up with ideas this week with you. It's been magical. *And so easy*!"

Fish looks floored. "I was assuming I'd pass those ideas along to Reed and Zeke. Love, you're in great hands with them."

Shit. I hate that I'm coming off like an ingrate. But the truth is, as successful and talented as Zeke is, I just don't think he's a perfect fit for me. To be honest, something about the production of my single has felt off to me for a while now. I didn't trust my inner voice about it, at first. I told myself I was crazy not to *love* Zeke's approach to my song. But now that I've spent the week with Fish, writing and brainstorming, I can clearly see what's missing from "Blindsided." *My authentic voice.* Now that I've been working with Fish, I'm positive Zeke's touch on my song was too heavy handed. Too slick. The song sounds like a surefire hit, that's for sure. But it's not quirky enough for me. It's not warm enough.

Breathing hard, I choke out, "Zeke doesn't understand me like you do. I went with the flow, and let him and Reed do their thing on my single, because . . . Who the hell am I? They know this business. They know how to make a hit! But this week with you, I've gotten clarity that I don't want success at the expense of my authentic voice. I'd rather the song doesn't do quite as well, but I'm thrilled with it. Fish, there's no doubt in my mind *you*, as my producer, would know *exactly* how to make hits for me, without also sacrificing the weird and quirky stuff that makes me *me*!"

Fish drags his hand over his face. "Fuck, Ally! I *totally* agree with you about the production on that song! I didn't say anything because I thought you loved it and I wanted you to be happy. But I think Zeke was *way* too heavy handed."

"Exactly!" I suddenly feel hot. Like I'm about to have a panic attack. "So, what do I do? Should I say something? It's still an amazing song and the production is totally top notch, right? Should I just go with the flow?"

Fish shakes his head fiercely, looking as intense as I've ever seen him. "We need to speak up so they can redo the mix before release. There's still time. It'll be easy for Maddy to slip the new version of the song into the video. We'll tell Zeke to take out some layers and let your voice take center stage. Maybe add some weird sounds in the bass register and some distortion to the guitar."

"See? I knew you'd know exactly what to do! I need you, Fish. *Matthew.*"

He takes my hand. "You don't *need* me. You just need to have faith in yourself and speak up. This is *your* music. *You're* the artist. It's a great production of a great song. And as it stands now, it'll be a smash *pop* hit. But you don't want to be a pop star, do you?"

I shake my head.

"You belong on the alternative charts, love. That's where your *true* heart will take you."

I look out the window of our hotel room at the Boston skyline. I'm trembling. I'm scared, but not confused. He's right, and I know it. I return to Fish and nod. "I'll tell Reed I want some changes."

"I can talk to him, if you want."

"No. It should be me. I'm also going to tell him I want the single to remain a standalone that's not part of the album. I love 'Blindsided,' and I'm proud I wrote it. But it's not right for the album. This album is going to be a love letter. To you. To myself. Reed said the album needs to be honest. Well, if I'm being honest, I'm happy now. In love. And I want the album to be about that." I grab his hand. "The reason I want *you* to produce my album is because it will be a labor of love. And you're the one who *loves* and knows me like nobody else."

Fish looks touched . . . but, also, distraught. And, suddenly, I realize I've asked too much of him. For God's sake, Alessandra, he's Fish from 22 Goats! Not simply Matthew, your sweet and adoring boyfriend! He's taken a week off from his crazy schedule to hang out, like he's got nothing else to do. But the truth is he's one-third of one of the world's most successful bands. He's got hundreds of people counting on him to stick to the schedule! Fish has told me how much pressure he feels about the army of people depending on his band. The crew who've become like family to him, after four long world tours in a short space of time. Plus, Reed said my album will be fast-tracked to capitalize on the single. And Fish simply can't do both things at once. Given Fish's schedule, it was flat-out selfish of me to even *think* of asking Fish to produce my album.

"I shouldn't have asked that," I declare, cutting through the awkward silence between us. "I said all of that without thinking of the realities of your life and schedule."

Fish looks positively heartbroken. "You know I'd love nothing more than to produce your debut. In a perfect world, I'd spend every waking minute with you, from this day forward. All day and night, every day. But right now I've got some intense obligations already lined up and I can't just—"

"Of course you can't. For a minute there, I forgot about the real world outside our bubble. I got swept up in the magic of this week, when it's just been you and me. A tribe of two." I smile sheepishly. "Please, pretend I never said a word about you producing me. Zeke will be great. I just need to be more assertive, that's all. I can't expect him to know me, the way you do. With you, I don't even have to explain. You just *know*. So, with him, I'll learn to speak up and push back when my gut tells me we're going in the wrong direction."

"He won Producer of the Year at the Grammys last year for Laila's album."

"I know. He's amazing! I'm lucky to get to work with him."

Fish looks decimated. "I'm so sorry, baby."

"Don't apologize. You've been my prince on a white horse! I'm the one who should be apologizing to you for my total selfishness. I'm a narcissistic sociopath for even bringing it up." I force a smile. "Honestly, I think I'm just freaking out that we have to say goodbye tomorrow. The thought of not being with you every single day is making me think and say crazy shit."

"Oh, honey." He pulls me to him and hugs me close. "I love you so much. And I *love* your music."

"I know you do. Please, let's forget I said it. I'm sorry."

"Don't apologize. I'm the one who owes you an apology."

"For what? You're in a world-famous band! You can't drop everything on a whim to produce your girlfriend's debut album! I was a jerk for asking." I snuggle into him. "Let's not think about it anymore. It's our last night together for a long while—the last time we'll be able to sleep together for three or four weeks." I squeeze him and nuzzle into his chest. "All I want to do for the rest of the night is snuggle you and kiss you and memorize exactly what it feels like to fall asleep in your arms."

THIRTY-THREE

FISH

"Cheers, boys," Dax says, raising his tequila to the group. After three long weeks of nonstop recording on our fifth album, Dax, Colin, and I are having a much-needed boys' night "in" with Keane and Zander at the beautiful home Zander shares with his pop star wife.

Z's lovely bride isn't home this fine evening. Aloha is off with Maddy and Violet and a few others for a girls' weekend before Maddy hits her third trimester. And even though I'm sitting in a perfectly decorated room with an expansive view of the canyon and my four best friends—not to mention enjoying some fine weed and tequila—and even though we three Goats have finally finished recording the main "bones" of our album, and will now get to focus on adding layers and riffs and harmonies to our songs—all of which is cause for celebration—I'm nonetheless feeling like shit tonight. Fucking miserable. A wreck. Which is the same way I've felt for the past three weeks.

Oh, God, how I miss Alessandra! Her touch. Kiss. Skin. That flowery *scent*. The twinkle in her bright blue eyes that doesn't fully translate on a computer screen. We've talked quite a bit these past three weeks, but it's not enough. Not nearly enough. Especially when I feel so guilty about saying no to her when she asked me to produce her album. At the music video shoot, I said to her, "Baby, I'd do anything for you. Just name it, and it's yours. Always." And I meant it! I really did. So it pains me beyond words to discover my words were fucking hollow.

Since Boston, Ally hasn't mentioned that conversation we had in Boston—the one where she asked me to produce her album. And she's been as sweet as ever to me during our video chats and phone calls. So I don't think she's holding anything against me. But *I* am. In fact, my feelings of guilt and shame and regret have been tearing me the fuck apart.

Also, I can't deny I've been freaking out about the future. I played it cool when Alessandra said she was worried about it —about our careers eventually pulling us apart. But now that I've had some time to reflect, I think maybe Ally had a point about that. When her single comes out next week and inevitably blasts up the charts, will Alessandra start getting offers from big hitters in the indie pop space to open for them? I'm guessing she will. Or at least, she'll get those kinds of offers after her album drops, and everyone finds out what a quirky little genius she is. At any rate, whenever those opportunities start pouring in, which they will, I know in my heart she should run with them. She should absolutely tour the world and spread her music near and far, without a thought about my schedule or obligations.

I've thought about trying to get Alessandra slotted as the opener for 22 Goats on our next tour, obviously. That's the "obvious" answer to this logistical pickle. But I don't think that plan is a great one. First off, we Goats don't call the shots on slotting our tours. Reed has final say on that, and he's got a notoriously Machiavellian mind when it comes to business matters.

But even assuming Reed would say yes, out of the goodness of his heart, I'm not sure that plan would be the best one to launch Alessandra's budding career. It wouldn't be a *total* miss, if she opened for us. Any new artist opening for my band would get tons of exposure. But in my heart, I know Alessandra shouldn't be playing in arenas for fans like ours. She should be opening for someone like Laila, who plays far more intimate venues and also has an audience that would fully appreciate Ally's quirky appeal.

"Fish. Yo."

I turn my head. It's Dax offering me the latest joint we've been passing around. I crawl a few paces across the hardwood floor and take the thing from Dax, who's sitting on Zander's couch. "Thanks." I sit over my bent knees, with my back against the bottom of the couch, take a long hit, and try to pass the thing to Colin. But he looks deep in thought and miserable on the other end of the couch and isn't paying attention.

"You okay, Underwear Model?" I ask.

He looks down at me, his eyes glazed over. "No."

"What's up?"

Colin takes the joint, sucks on it, and exhales a long plume of smoke before saying, "Kiera and I broke up for good."

"When?"

"Two days ago."

Keane and Zander stop talking. Those two have been sitting in side-by-side armchairs bantering. But something in Colin's tone apparently caused them to stop talking and listen in.

"What's going on?" Zander asks.

I fill them in.

Dax says to Colin, "No wonder you were such a dick in the studio yesterday."

Colin scowls, making it clear he's in no mood to be teased right now.

Dax softens. "Sorry, man. You really think it's for good this time?"

Colin leans back into the couch, his body language defeated. "Yep."

"Why didn't you tell us yesterday?" I ask.

Colin looks out one of the floor-to-ceiling windows of Zander's gorgeous living room again. "I guess I just wanted to get lost in the music and not think about it. Kiera got offered a world tour that's going to last eighteen months and she took it." Colin provides some details. He names the pop star Kiera will be dancing behind on tour—Kiera's a professional dancer —and adds, "In the past, whenever she's been offered extra-long tours like that, she's always turned them down, so we wouldn't be apart too long. But this time, she wants to go. And not only that, she flat-out told me she plans to fuck other people while she's gone. *Lots* of other people."

The rest of us grimace and say some version of "That sucks" and "Sorry, man."

Colin exhales loudly and runs his tattooed hand through his dark hair. "It's probably for the best. The spark in the beginning with Kiera was off the charts. Like nothing I'd felt before. I would have sworn back then we'd be together forever. But with both of us having careers that put us on the road for long stretches . . . being forced apart so much just snuffed out our flame, I guess. It was inevitable."

Fuuuuuck. This is literally the last thing I need to be

hearing right now.

Or, hell, maybe it's exactly the thing I need to be hearing.

"Well, look on the bright side," Keane says, taking the joint from Zander. "At least, you'll get to enjoy all the attention you've been getting from that underwear ad. You're a hot commodity with the ladies these days, son. Enjoy it."

Colin nods, still looking miserable. "Yup. That's exactly what I'm going to do. I'm done having a girlfriend for a long while. I've realized if I'm ever going to have one again, she has to be someone like Violet. Someone who can drop everything and follow me ingloriously around the world while I—"

Dax interrupts, "What does that mean? Violet has never 'dropped everything' to *ingloriously* follow me around, motherfucker."

"Oh, Jesus," Colin says, rolling his eyes.

But Dax isn't finished. He says, "Besides taking care of Jackson and me, my wife works her ass off heading up a global cancer charity that—"

"Dax, I know."

"Helps so many people! And while she's doing that—"

"You misunderstood me."

"She's *also* designing incredible wedding dresses for women who are willing to pay top dollar for her designs. So don't you dare—"

"Calm down, Daxy Pants. You misunderstood me."

"Say there's anything 'inglorious' about a goddamned fucking thing my wife is doing with her life. Violet Morgan does more *glorious* shit in one day than Colin Beretta, Drummer and Underwear Model, manages to do in a single fucking *year*."

Colin rubs his face and chuckles to himself. "This is *way* too much passion for my stoned brain to process right now."

He comes out from behind his hands and points energetically at me on the floor, the same way he pointed at me when we were thirteen in Daxy's garage, when Mrs. Morgan caught him with that can of Mountain Dew. He shouts, "It was Fish!" And, of course, everyone in the room laughs at our lifelong joke, even Dax. Because, come on, no matter what tension might precede that particular joke, it *always* vanishes immediately the minute it's told.

Dax takes a long swig of his tequila. "Just think before you speak, once in a while, fucker."

Colin replies, "Dude, I'm stoned out of my mind precisely because I don't want to think before speaking. I don't want to think at all. I know Violet's a unicorn, Daxy. That was my point. What I was *trying* to say is I don't have high hopes I'm going to be able find myself a unicorn like Violet. Someone who's got the kind of *lifestyle* and *career* and *temperament* where she can be a badass in her own right while still following my sorry ass around. I just meant I don't want a woman who's got absolutely nothing going on that doesn't revolve around *me*, and *yet*, she can still ingloriously follow me around—"

Zander interrupts, "So, by that logic, do *I* 'ingloriously' follow Aloha around, since I've got absolutely nothing going on in my life that doesn't revolve around *her*?"

"Oh, for the love of fuck!" Colin shouts, throwing up his arms. "Of course not, Z. You're Aloha's personal *bodyguard*! Your actual *job* is following her around the world. There's nothing inglorious about that. My point is I want someone to follow me around the world *and* be interesting enough for me not to get totally bored with her!" He shakes his head with exasperation. "What's in this weed tonight? Anabolic steroids? Jesus."

"Hey, Col," Keane says, a mischievous twinkle in his blue eyes. "I'm planning to take a bunch of time off work after my baby arrives. Will *that* count as *ingloriously* dropping everything for my wife and kid?"

Colin screams in frustration, and Keane bursts out laughing.

"I was kidding," Keane says. "I wasn't even listening to whatever bullshit you said. I just heard the word 'inglorious' and thought it was *kewl*."

"It's a good word," Zander agrees. "Use it in a sentence, Peenie Weenie. That's the best way to remember a new word."

Keane purses his lips in contemplation. And then, "Despite his rock-hard abs and smolder to die for, the drummer slash underwear model *ingloriously* went down in flames with his rock star best friend, thanks to whatever stupid shit he was babbling about that I didn't hear."

Zander laughs.

"Lemme get you up to speed," I call out to Keane from my spot on the floor. "Colin didn't say this outright, but reading between the lines, he *basically* said he thinks I should be rooting for Alessandra's album to tank, so she can 'ingloriously' follow *me* around the world, whenever she wants."

Colin scoffs. "Sure, Fish Fuck. That's what I said."

I sprawl onto my back on the floor and moan loudly, suddenly feeling incapable of containing the misery I've been hiding from my friends for the past three weeks. "I need help, fellas," I groan. "I'm freaking out. I've suddenly realized the more success Ally has, the harder it's going to be for us to line up our schedules. If *she's* always touring, and *I'm* always touring, and our schedules are never the same, then when the hell will we ever see each other again?"

"That's an easy one," Dax says. "Let's make her the opener on our next tour."

"I'm not sure Reed would say yes to that," I say. "And even if he would, the timing of our tour is almost certainly going to be different from hers, considering the release date of her album versus ours. Plus, would that really be the best fit for Alessandra's career? I don't want to fuck her over, just because I want my girlfriend with me at all times."

"It'd hardly be fucking her over, Fish," Colin says.

Keane agrees. "Sorry if this is a stupid question, but wouldn't it be an amazing thing for *any* new artist to open for a powerhouse like 22 Goats?"

"I shouldn't have said it'd 'fuck her over,'" I concede. "That was an overstatement. But I want the best for Ally. And my gut tells me she'd do better opening with someone like Laila or Aloha. Or even Fugitive Summer. They've got that weird, quirky vibe, just like Ally. And their venues are smaller than ours, which would fit her music best. Not to mention, she gets stage fright, guys. I don't know if an arena tour is the best fit for her at this point. Not yet."

"What do you mean she's got a quirky vibe?" Dax says. "Not trying to be a dick, but when I heard her single at the music video shoot, there was nothing 'quirky' about it. It sounded like a straight down the middle pop song to me. A surefire hit. Don't get me wrong. But not 'quirky.'"

I sigh. "The song is being re-mixed, as we speak. Zeke's gonna strip it down. Add some flavor and distortions."

"Glad to hear it," Dax says. "I didn't want to say anything, because I thought Alessandra was happy with it, but I thought Zeke overproduced the hell out of that song. Alessandra isn't fucking Britney Spears."

I sigh loudly. "I know. I didn't speak up, either, for the

same reason. And Alessandra was too green to realize she needs to be the captain of the ship, not a fucking oarsman."

"Lesson learned," Dax says. "Good thing she learned it on a single, rather than an entire album."

Guilt ripples through me as I think about Alessandra's album again. She'll be able to communicate her artistic vision to Zeke going forward, right? Now that she's learned her lesson on the single? That's what I keep telling myself, anyway. But the more I think about it, the more I know I'm the one who should produce that album. I'm the one who understands her, without needing to be told. I look at Keane. "Hey, Peenie, how do you and Maddy make it work, when you've both got careers that take you all over?"

Keane shrugs. "It's a give and take. Luckily, my show shoots here in LA on a predictable schedule, so we work around that. And when I'm not shooting, I go on location with Maddy, wherever her next job takes her. Once the baby comes, I'm sure we'll both have to forego some cool jobs for a while. But that's okay. Whatever we have to do, we'll make it work. The important thing is we both want the other to be happy, even more than we want happiness for ourselves. When you've got a relationship like that, it's easy to make decisions as things come up."

That's it.

I sit up on the floor, feeling like I've been hit by a lightning bolt.

I want Alessandra's happiness more than I want my own.
That's the truth.
That's why I'm miserable.
Because I've picked my own shit above hers!
Suddenly, I can't deny it: *Alessandra means everything to me now.* Even more than my own band. The same way Violet

and Jackson rightly mean *everything* to Dax. If Dax were forced to choose, for some hideous reason, between his wife and kid and his band, there's no doubt he'd choose Violet and Jackson. And we'd all understand.

"I just realized something," I blurt, my heart thumping in my ears. "I want to produce Alessandra's album. Which means we're going to need to carve out some time in our schedule for me to do that."

"What about Zeke?" Dax says.

"I'm going to tell Reed to cut him loose."

"Is the album already written?" Colin asks.

"No. I'd have to help her write it, too. So, that would take a bit of time, as well."

Colin looks incredulously at Dax, like he can't believe his ears. And Dax purses his lips, but says nothing. Colin returns to me. "I don't think either of us has an issue with you co-writing and producing her album, man. Godspeed. I think you'd do an amazing job for her. It's just the timing. We've already got all the dominoes lined up. You know the drill. There's no time in the middle of the schedule for you to take a couple months off—probably more, if we're being realistic—to create an entire debut album with your *girlfriend.*"

I look down at my hands, so I won't tell Colin to fuck off. So I won't say something I might regret and storm out of the room. Coming here tonight, I never in a million years thought I'd contemplate flat-out quitting my band over this. Or over anything. But I suddenly feel the urge to say those unthinkable words in this moment. *Fuck it. Fuck you. Fuck this. I quit.*

"I think you should do it," Dax says, breaking the thick silence. And when I look up at him, I see nothing but sincerity in his eyes. "Like Keane said, we'll make it work because, at the end of the day, we care more about *your* happiness than our own."

"*Dax*," Colin spits out. "You know damned well how many people are counting on—"

"They can wait!" Dax booms, going from zero to sixty in a heartbeat—which is so unlike him, it's shocking. Dax stands and throws up his hands, his eyes blazing. He's towering over Colin on the couch now, shouting at him. "Why the fuck are we doing any of this, Colin? Why have this band at all if it keeps us from doing the things we want to do the most—especially for the people we love the most? I know you're jaded right now because Kiera dumped you . . ." He points at me on the floor. "But our boy is in love for the first time in his life— and probably the *last* time, too, I'm guessing—and he wants to do this amazing thing for his woman. For the woman he *loves*. Well, fuck the world! Fuck the schedule. And fuck our band if any of it means our boy can't do this for the love of his life! The world can wait a little longer for the *fifth* fucking album from 22 Goats. Our music isn't a goddamned cure for cancer! Our fans will survive. But *Fish* won't survive saying no to his woman about this! Haven't you noticed he's been slowly disintegrating before our eyes these past weeks? Well, obviously, *this* is why!"

I could cry. In fact, I'm swallowing hard to keep tears from forming and rolling down my cheeks.

"Preach!" Keane bellows, his arms raised like Dax is a Baptist preacher.

Dax sits next to me on the floor. He tousles my hair, the way I always tousle Jackson's. "Do it, Matty-boy. Nobody but you should produce that album, just like nobody but Zander should guard Aloha. You're going to make her shine. The same way you've always made *me* shine. Because when you love someone, that's what you do. You make it all about *them —and you make them shine.*"

Well, fuck. Tears well up in my eyes, despite my best efforts. If I speak, they'll drip down my face. So, I don't speak. I just pat Dax's arm in gratitude and then place my forehead against his shoulder.

There's a very long moment of silence.

Until, finally, Zander says, "So . . . does this mean Peenie and I are witnessing the breakup of 22 Goats?"

Keane blurts, "*Whoa.* Is Ally 'Yoko-ing' the band?"

"Shut up, Peen," Dax says softly. "Ally isn't Yoko." He pats my head. "We're simply agreeing we're just going to slow things down a bit. Delay our album and tour to carve out three or four months for Fish to focus on this project. Right, Colin? That's what we're agreeing to here, right?"

I look up to peek at Colin's face. And he looks like he's having a thousand thoughts, all at once.

"Hand me that, Peenie." Dax points at his tequila. His big brother dutifully complies and brings him the glass, and Dax takes a long, measured sip before saying, "I have a confession to make." He takes a deep breath and places his glass on the floor next to him. "It's something I've been wanting to say to you guys for a while now. Even if Fish hadn't brought this up . . . when this upcoming album and tour cycle were over, I was going to tell you I need to slow down quite a bit, or quit all together. The current pace isn't good for Jackson. And it's not good for me. I need our tours to be shorter. I need more time between albums. I need to be able to recharge my batteries with my family for much longer stretches. And if that's not doable for everyone, then . . ." He shrugs, making it clear these requests aren't negotiable.

"That all sounds great to me," I confess. "Obviously, I

don't have a wife and kid. But even I've been feeling like I'm barreling toward burnout lately, too."

I glance at Colin again. He looks stunned. Vaguely panicked.

"I'm sorry, Colin," Dax says. "I know this isn't what you want. You, more than either of us, thrive on the thrill of it all."

Colin furrows his brow. "Umm, actually . . . I think you're misreading me. I'm not freaking out about what you're saying. I'm panicking because I turned down an offer yesterday—something really exciting Clive called me about—and I'm suddenly hoping to God it's not too late to call them back and tell them *yes*."

We all say some variation of "What's the offer?"

Colin says, "The Calvin Klein thing opened the floodgates for me, guys. I've never been inundated with side offers like this before. Modeling, acting. It's been crazy. The offer I'm talking about is a small role in a war movie. I'd be a dumb jock soldier who gets blown up by a grenade midway through. It's not a huge role, but it'd be awesome to do it. I didn't think I could because our touring schedule conflicts with the filming schedule. But if we're going to change things up . . ."

The room explodes with excitement for him. Encouragement. Questions. All of which results in Colin picking up the phone and calling Clive to tell him he wants the job.

When Colin gets off his call with Clive, he's lit up. He says, "Clive didn't even answer them yet! He said he'll call them right now and tell them *yes*." Colin runs his hand through his dark hair, looking elated. "This is gonna be so fucking cool."

"Goat hug," I say. And, without hesitation, Dax, Colin, and I get up from our various seats and perform a three-way huddle, the same one we always do backstage before every show. To my surprise, though, it's Colin who makes the first little goat sound. He's *never* the first. In fact, he's made it clear he thinks the way Daxy and I make goat sounds in our pre-show huddles is a bit stupid, even though he always goes along with it. It's a small gesture for him to start the ritual, but a meaningful one. One that doesn't need to be explained. Of course, Dax and I echo his little "Maaa!" with similar ones of our own, until we all wind up laughing and wiping our eyes.

"Aw, look at our herd of little baby goats," Keane says to his best friend. "They've grown into such fine young men, right before our eyes."

Zander chuckles. "They sure have. I feel like a proud poppa."

We three Goats break apart, all of us still wiping our eyes.

"Onward," Dax says, his gaze bouncing between mine and Colin's.

"Onward," we echo.

It's what Dax always says whenever something doesn't go according to plan, or there's a sense that we're turning some kind of momentous page in our lives. But this time, when Dax says the word, it feels particularly poignant.

Onward.

Yes.

The future is *ours* to design. *And nobody else's.*

And speaking for myself, my future will *always* include me doing *anything* for Alessandra. Making her happiness my top priority—even above my own. No matter what happens, I now understand my love for Alessandra is *everything* to me. Literally. And I'll never pick anything or anyone above her, again.

THIRTY-FOUR

FISH

"Hello, gentlemen," Reed says to Dax, Colin, and me as we file into his spacious office.

We take seats in a corner and make small talk about Reed's engagement, his recent luxury vacation, the progress on our album. But soon, it's clear Reed is a busy dude and we should get to the point.

Dax takes the lead, as agreed in advance among the three of us. "So, Reed. We asked for this meeting today because we've decided we want to slow down a bit. We need some additional time to complete our album. Which means we also need to reschedule the tour. Push it back by at least four months."

Reed is clearly floored. But since he's a pro at crisis management, he calmly says, "Why? From the rough mixes I've heard so far, it sounds like you're right on target with the album."

"The issue isn't whether we *can* meet current deadlines," Dax explains. "It's that we want to slow down to make room for other things. Speaking for myself, I want to have more time to chill with my family. I've talked about all of this with Violet, of course, and she wholeheartedly agrees slowing down would be the best thing for Jackson and our family."

Reed presses his lips together. His sister's opinion has always meant the world to him.

Colin interjects, "Fish and I also have side projects we want to jump into for a bit, too. So, slowing down is in everyone's interest. Not just Daxy's."

"Side projects?" Reed says.

Colin looks at me, asking if he should speak first. And I motion like I'm giving him the floor, simply because what I have to say will take this conversation into an entirely new direction.

Colin says, "I've had quite a few modeling and acting offers recently. In particular, there's a small movie role I'm excited to take. Originally, I didn't think I could do it because of our current tour schedule. But I've now told the director I can do it."

Reed's eyebrows shoot up. But that's the only "tell" that his mind is racing. He looks calmly at me. "And you, Fish Taco? What 'side project' are you excited about?"

My heart is thumping. "Alessandra's album. I'm going to co-write and produce it."

I'd caption the tilt of Reed's head and arch of his eyebrow as, *Is that so?*

Suddenly, I realize I probably should have at least given lip service to the fact that River Records "owns" Alessandra, as an artist, every bit as much as it "owns" 22 Goats. Which therefore means I *probably* should have said, "I'd very much *like* to produce Alessandra's album. *Please.*" But I don't have the time or energy to bullshit this man. The truth is I'm not walking out of this room today without that producer job in my pocket.

Reed sinks into his armchair and steeples his fingers. "Zeke is already locked and loaded to produce Alessandra's album."

"Yes, I know. And I think Zeke is an incredibly talented guy, obviously."

"He's one of the best."

"He is. But he's not the right man for *this* job. Alessandra needs a producer who understands her and will bring out the absolute best in her. And that someone is *me*. Not Zeke."

The slightest hint of amusement flickers in Reed's dark eyes, but he says nothing.

"Alessandra feels safe with me in a way she doesn't feel with Zeke," I continue. "Or anyone else, for that matter. Not even Georgie. You saw what I did for Ally at the coffeehouse during the music video shoot. That wasn't a fluke. What I did for her then, I'll do it again while co-writing and producing every song. This album will be our joint labor of love. Ally and I will work on it, day and night. Round the clock. We'll eat, sleep, and breathe this album. And the result will be something amazing. I guarantee it."

Reed takes a long moment to process before exhaling a long, steady stream of air. "Look, Fish, in a vacuum, it'd be a no-brainer to say yes. The problem is *timing*. As you boys know, we've already set the wheels in motion on your album and tour—"

Dax interrupts, "You'll just have to *un*-set the wheels, then. The question is this, Reed. Would you rather 22 Goats keep making music, on the timeline we've suggested, or for us to burn out, sooner rather than later, and quit the whole fucking thing because the band has started to feel like a gilded cage?"

Well, damn. Dax has Reed's attention now. Not to mention *mine*. I think this boy just laid down an ultimatum. A threat to quit the band, if Reed doesn't make this work, exactly as requested. Which, of course, would be a tragedy for all of us. As much as I'm dying to produce Alessandra's album, I certainly don't want my own band to break up. I love being in 22 Goats. The truth is, I want it all.

"You're feeling like you're burning out, Daxy?" Reed asks. And it's impossible to miss the genuine concern in his voice. In this moment, he doesn't sound like Reed Rivers, founder and CEO of River Records, anymore. He sounds like Dax's brother-in-law. Violet's big brother. Jackson's uncle.

"Honestly, yes," Dax says. "But not when it comes to the music itself. It's just the rest of the shit that sucks me dry, man. I need to slow down now, so I can keep doing this until I'm old and gray. That's what I want. To be a part of 22 Goats *forever*, until we're three old geezers doing a 'reunion tour' for an audience of old geezers and their kids and grandkids."

We all chuckle at the imagery.

"But I'm at a fork in the road," Dax admits. "And I can't ignore that any longer. I'm tired, man. I'm so tired."

Reed looks surprisingly emotional. "Thank you for your honesty, Daxy," he says. He pauses to collect himself. "As long as we're honest with each other, we can find a solution that suits everyone." He takes a deep breath. "We'll make this work, okay? I can do whatever the fuck I want. That's the best part of being me." He addresses me. "Produce your girl's album, Fish. Make her shine."

My heart lurches in my chest. "I will."

"I know you will. What you did for her in New York, at

the shoot, that was nothing short of brilliant." He looks at Colin. "Congrats on that movie. If you need any introductions in the entertainment industry—maybe a good talent agent—I know a lot of people."

"Thanks. I'd love some introductions."

"Clive is a good man," Reed says. "He genuinely cares about you boys. But his specialty isn't fielding offers for acting and modeling. It's giving investment advice. You'll want someone in your corner who's in the mix in Hollywood. I'd suggest asking Keane for an intro to his people. If that doesn't work out, for any reason, ask me. I'll set you up."

"Thanks. I appreciate that."

Reed looks at the three of us, and when nobody says anything, he rises, obviously assuming we're done here. But we're *so* not done.

"Hold on," I say. "There's one more thing."

Reed settles back into his chair and waits, his face impassive.

I swallow hard, mustering my courage. "When you look at rescheduling our tour, I don't want our new dates to conflict with any tour you might put together for Alessandra in the future."

Reed rolls his eyes. "That's not something I can promise, Fish."

"It's nonnegotiable."

Reed scoffs. "There are too many moving parts for me to promise that. Is this a backhanded way of demanding I put Ally on your next tour, as the opener? Because the problem with that is twofold. One, I'm not sure Alessandra's music and audience are a perfect fit with 22 Goats. And, two, part of the reason I've been wanting to put a rush on Ally's album is so she can open for *Laila* later this year."

I'm floored. Shit. Touring with Laila would be an A-plus result for Alessandra! Both professionally and personally. If Alessandra didn't love me, there's no doubt she'd pick touring with Laila—her personal idol!—as her top pick.

I run my hand through my hair, feeling like my heart is crashing violently against my sternum. "Ally should tour with Laila," I concede on an exhale. "That's the best possible tour for her."

Reed looks like the weight of the world is pressing on his broad shoulders. For a long moment, he doesn't speak, but, rather, looks silently out his office window at the traffic on Sunset Boulevard below. Finally, he returns to the three of us and says, "Would you boys be willing to add a song to your next album for purely marketing purposes—to allow me to cross-promote you in another market?"

We look at each other, and shrug.

Dax says, "Depends on the song. What do you have in mind?"

"What if we added a '22 Goats featuring Laila Fitzgerald' song to your next album? Something with a touch more of a dance vibe than you're known for—sort of like how Coldplay did that song with Rihanna?"

Coldplay.

The man is smart. He knows the bands and artists we idolize.

"I'd be down to do that," Dax says. "Assuming the song isn't trash."

Colin and I agree with that statement.

Reed's gears are plainly turning now. "If we do this right," he says, "this collaboration will be a mega-blockbuster—something we could use to sell a whole lot of tickets to a joint 22 Goats/Laila tour." He smiles at me. "A tour that would feature the cute and quirky opener, little Miss Alessandra Tennison."

"That sounds amazing, Reed," I choke out, barely able to contain my excitement.

"You know," Reed says. "As long as we're thinking about cross-marketing . . . Maybe we should double- and triple-down on this idea." He looks at me. "Do you think Ally would be willing to include a duet with you on her album?"

I'm shocked he's thinking this way. I'm not an artist in my own right. I'm the bass player and backup singer in 22 Goats. A sidekick. Not to mention, way back when in Maui, Reed said I should consider dropping out of my own fucking band to allow Dax to become a solo artist! While it's true Ally and I have talked about writing a duet, Reed doesn't know that! And now, suddenly, he thinks I'm good enough to sing *co-lead* vocals on a song on his new artist's debut?

"You slayed it when you sang lead vocals in New York," Reed says, reacting to whatever he's seeing on my face. "You made 'Fireflies' and 'People Like Us' your own. And the crowd absolutely loved it. Plus, you and Ally on a duet would be insanely easy to market. The world already loved you sere-nading her in New York. When they see the music video, I promise you two are going to become the world's favorite love story. So, let's give them an actual duet!"

I can barely breathe through my exhilaration. "As a matter of fact, Ally's already asked me to record a duet on her album."

"Perfect! I'll talk to Laila about maybe doing one with her, too—in addition to the song with 22 Goats."

My heart leaps and bounds in my chest. If Laila says yes to a duet with Alessandra, I think it's highly likely my baby will literally pass out at the news.

Reed gets up and strides to his large desk. He slides into his leather chair and starts clacking energetically on his keyboard for a moment, before saying, "I think we could line everything up with Fugitive Summer's next release, too, so we could include them on this joint tour we're putting together. Maybe 2Real, as well. Hell, we could expand the entire concept and make this more of a traveling music festival than a conventional tour. The type of thing where people would travel *to* the show, in select cities, rather than the show traveling to *them*. That would mean far less time on the road for you guys, more time to relax and recharge. Less overhead expense for me. Plus, we'd have so many avenues for 'festival merch,' in addition to merch for each artist, we'd probably make as much, or more, in profit than if we'd arranged a bunch of individual tours."

"I love it," Dax says. "See if you can add Aloha to this lineup. We had a blast touring with her that last time. If we're going to be hanging out for long stretches with a bunch of artists, we'll want Zander and Aloha there."

Reed nods and looks at his watch. "I've got to get the team going on this, boys. There's a lot to do."

Dax, Colin, and I rise and thank Reed.

"Hey, Fish," Reed says, making me stop and turn around just short of the doorway to his office. He says, "I've been assuming this whole time Ally wants you, and not Zeke, as her producer. That's an accurate statement?"

"It is. She begged me to produce."

Reed winks. "She's a smart girl. Do you want to be the one to tell her the good news, or do you want her label to do it?"

"I want to do it. She's arriving in LA tomorrow. I'll tell her in person."

"Also tell her we've got everything lined up for the release of the single next week. I'm calling it now. She's going to hit Top 20 by week three. Top 10 by week four."

"God, I hope you're right."

He winks. "I'm always right."

I roll my eyes, as memories of Reed telling me to drop out of my own band flash through my brain. "Sure, Reed. You're *never* wrong." I turn to leave again. But, again, Reed stops me.

"Hey, you should plan to stay for dinner tomorrow after you pick Ally up from the airport."

I look at Reed for a long beat, trying to decipher his confusing words. I should *stay* for dinner? What does that mean?

Reed clarifies, "When you drop Ally off at my house from the airport, you should plan to stay for dinner. I know Georgie would love that. So would I."

I open and close my mouth, still confused. Why does Reed think I'm going to drop Ally off at *his* house from the airport tomorrow? Alessandra and I have never discussed where she's planning to stay in LA. But that's only because I've been *assuming* she'll stay with me. At my bungalow in Venice Beach. Of course.

Reed says, "You didn't know Alessandra is going to live in my guest house for the foreseeable future?"

I pause. "*No.* Ally didn't mention that to me."

Reed leans back against the edge of his large desk. "I offered my casita to her because Zeke lives about a mile from me. I figured it'd be good for her to live, rent free, near Zeke, while they were working on her album, and she agreed. Plus, obviously, Ally and Georgina were thrilled at the chance to get to see each other every day."

Shit. Now that I think about it, it makes perfect sense Ally didn't *assume* she'd be living at my place! I never explicitly invited her, so she probably figured she'd better make other arrangements. Damn. Why am I such a dumbshit?

"I'll talk to Ally about her living arrangements," I say. "See what she wants to do. But I can tell you one thing, for sure, I won't be dropping her off at your house tomorrow night. Dinner sounds great. But not tomorrow night. Tomorrow, I'm bringing Ally to my place at the beach."

Reed bites back a huge smile. "Of course. Let me know."

"One more thing," I say. "I think this is obvious, but I'm going to play bass on Ally's album. Probably some other instruments, too."

"Of course, you will," Reed says. "I wouldn't have it any other way. It's important to me that my little sister-to-be has only the best musicians supporting her debut album."

Okay, that's it. I can't keep my mouth shut anymore. "Is that so?" I say, unable to keep the snark out of my voice. "That's not what you said about me in Maui."

Reed looks confused.

"At Josh and Kat's destination wedding, you said I should quit my band because my musicianship was 'tepid' and my charisma was 'lacking.'"

Reed laughs. "I said that?"

"You did."

"Well, in my defense, those statements were true back then." He laughs. "Aw, come on, Fish. Who gives a shit what I said back then? I was half-drunk on mai tais most of that week. Maybe I was testing you to see what you were made of. Maybe I was putting a fire under your ass to step up your game." He shrugs. "Either way, I'm not sorry because, maybe, just maybe, those comments played a part, however small, in turning you into the brilliant musician you are today—one of the very best in the business. I think it's pretty obvious at this point 22 Goats wouldn't be what it is today without all three of you contributing."

Dax, Colin, and I share a look of complete astonishment.

"If I was a prick to you in Maui, then I apologize," Reed says. And damned if he doesn't sound sincere. "If I was trying to put a fire under your ass, there were probably better words I could have chosen. God knows what I was thinking. Maybe I was simply getting off on being a prick."

Again, Dax, Colin, and I exchange looks of complete shock.

"Damn, Reed," Dax says. "What kind of spell has Georgina cast on you? I don't think I've heard you apologize to anyone but Violet."

Reed shrugs. "It's the new me." He winks. "Good thing I'm hardly ever wrong, eh? So I don't need to make a habit of this."

We all chuckle.

"Now get the fuck out," Reed says. "I have work to do."

We say our goodbyes and head through the lobby of River Records toward the elevators.

"Well, that went well," I say.

"Yeah, that was . . . crazy," Colin says.

The elevator doors open.

We step inside.

Dax scrutinizes me. "You okay, Fish Taco?"

"Huh?"

"You look deep in thought."

I smile. "I was just thinking about tomorrow. What I'm going to say when I pick Alessandra up from the airport."

"She's not going to be staying in Reed's casita, ever, I take it?" Dax says, returning my broad smile.

"Correct. If I get my way, my woman's gonna be staying with me while we write and record her album. And then, as long as we both shall live."

THIRTY-FIVE

ALESSANDRA

A s I enter the baggage claim area at LAX, I scan the milling crowd around the carousels until my eyes lock onto the most handsome face in the world. My hot boyfriend. My loverrr. He's scanning the crowd while holding a lovely bouquet of red roses. And, of course, he looks like a tasty fish filet in his T-shirt and jeans.

I take off toward him, shouting his name. And when he spots me, Fish takes off running, too.

We meet in the middle and crash into each other.

After kissing me passionately, he presses his forehead against mine and coos, "God, I missed you."

"I missed you, too."

He jolts and looks down at the roses crushed between us. "Oh. Crap. These are for you." He steps back and hands me the bouquet. "Welcome home. I love you. I've missed you. Happy birthday."

I giggle. "I'll take three out of four, but my birthday isn't for five days."

"It's your birthday month. That's good enough for me to

start celebrating."

A baggage carousel a few yards away whirs to life and we drift over to it, holding hands and smiling giddily at each other.

"I have lots and lots of stuff to tell you," he says. His smile widens. "I'm going to produce your album, baby. I've already cleared it with Reed."

"*What?*" I shout.

"Assuming that's still what you want?"

"*Yes!*" I throw my arms around him and kiss him enthusiastically, unwittingly sending a few rose petals fluttering to the ground. I jerk back. "But what about *your* album? Your schedule? Fish, no. As much as I'd love to have you as my producer, I can't let you—"

"Yes, you can. We've worked it all out. I'll tell you everything in the car. But, long story short, Dax and Colin and I are going to slow things down to make room for side projects and family time. We're all on board with this. *I promise.*"

A group of people squeeze next to us at the baggage carousel, forcing us to take a step to the side.

Fish continues, "And that's only the beginning of the stuff I'm excited to tell you about." He pauses for dramatic effect. "Reed wants me to sing a duet with you on the album, if you're still down for that."

"Yes!"

"It was totally Reed's idea, by the way. I didn't say a thing."

"Did you tell him yes?"

"Of course. So I guess we'd better get to work on that little ditty we started in Boston, huh?"

"Yes!" I clutch my heart, overjoyed, sending more petals fluttering to the ground. "This is the best day of my life!"

Fish laughs. "But, wait, there's more! Actually, hold onto me for this next bit, sweetheart. I think you might fall over after hearing this one."

"I already feel like I'm going to fall over."

"All the more reason to hang onto me now." When I grip him, as instructed, Fish smiles and says, "Reed asked Laila to record a duet with you . . . *and she already said yes.*"

I drop the flowers, grip Fish's arm with both hands, and scream. But when I remember we're standing in an airport, I clamp one palm over my mouth, making Fish guffaw at my over-the-top reaction.

When I'm sure I can refrain from screaming, I remove my hand from my mouth and babble incoherently for a long moment, jumping up and down with excitement as I talk. And Fish laughs and laughs at my exuberance.

"But, wait, there's more!" Fish calls out, his green eyes twinkling.

"No. No more. I can't take any more."

"Oh okay," he says calmly. He bends down to pick up the bouquet on the ground. "I won't tell you the rest, then." He turns and faces the baggage carousel. Looks down at the flowers in his hand. Pretends to yawn. "What color is your bag?"

I grip his arm and shake him. "*Tell me!*"

"No, no. Wouldn't want you to freak out at an airport."

"Matthew!" I shake him again. "Tell me!"

Fish laughs and turns to me, his face aglow. "Reed is putting together a joint tour, Ally. I'll tell you everything in the car. But he's already confirmed 22 Goats, 2Real, Laila, Aloha, and Fugitive Summer on the bill . . . along with our opener, *Alessandra Tennison*."

I crumple into Fish's chest and literally weep with joy and

he wraps his arms around me and coos into my hair.

"Aw, baby," he says, holding me tight. He kisses the side of my head. "Please tell me those are happy tears."

I nod into his chest, sniffling and whimpering. "The happiest tears *ever*." I heave out a whimpering sob. "This is the best day of my life."

He pulls back, puts his fingertip underneath my chin, and lifts my face to his. "From now on, it's us against the world, baby. I'd do *anything* for you. This time, I mean it."

I wipe my eyes. "I'd never let you do 'anything' for me that isn't the best thing for *you*."

"That's exactly why I can promise you that."

We kiss again. And then hug fiercely, like we're hanging onto each other in a hurricane.

He kisses my cheek. "These past weeks without you, I've realized I literally can't be happy without you by my side."

"Me, too." Someone behind me jostles me slightly, apparently reaching for their suitcase, so I guide Fish a few feet away. I think I saw my suitcase zip by a moment ago, but I don't care. It'll come around again. I look into Fish's green eyes and say, "I've felt physically sick without you these past weeks. Video chat isn't enough."

"Not even close," he agrees.

"I thought it would be okay," I say. "Just like before. But everything is different now. I can't live without you."

Fish's chest heaves. "Please, don't stay in Reed's guest house. Stay with me at my place."

My lips part in surprise. I didn't know Fish knew about Reed's offer for me to stay at his casita. I was planning to talk to Fish about that in person. Of course, I've been fantasizing about staying with Fish, but he's never invited me. And I've convinced myself these past weeks that's probably for the best. I've told myself living with my boyfriend would be a huge step. Too much, too fast. Not to mention, my mother has always had harsh words about people "shacking up" before marriage. Or at least, an engagement.

When I say nothing, simply because my mind is racing, Fish exhales like he's been holding his breath underwater. He says, "At least, stay with me while we work on the album. I've got a small studio in my spare bedroom, and I'll buff it out. We'll record the entire album there. We can work at any crazy hour we want. If we get writer's block, we'll sit on the beach, right outside my door, and have ourselves a picnic. We'll watch the sunset every evening together." He sighs and touches my cheek. "Regardless of the album, I just want you to be with me, Ally. I want your face to be the first thing I see every morning and the last thing I see at night."

Aw, screw it. I don't care if this is a huge step. I don't care what my mother thinks about "shacking up." Her marriage to Georgina's father, Marco, only lasted a year—and he's *literally* the sweetest man alive. So I don't think she can claim to be an expert in relationships.

"Yes," I blurt, nodding enthusiastically. "I'll stay with you. Thank you for asking me."

Fish looks as euphoric as I feel as he leans in for a kiss.

We kiss and kiss, until we're both laughing from joy.

When our lips finally disengage, I lay my cheek on his chest and squeeze him tight. "This really is the best day of my life."

"I feel like I've heard that a time or two before."

"And it's been the truth, every time." I look up. "But this time is the granddaddy of best days *ever*. Honestly, honey, this really, truly is the very, very best day of my entire freaking life."

THIRTY-SIX

FISH

lessandra "oohs" and "aahs" her way through my small beach bungalow, like she's touring Reed's sprawling, hilltop mansion.

"And this is my bedroom," I say, opening the door.

"Oooh," she breathes.

For a split second, I'm not sure if she's reacting to the flowers or the sparkling ocean view outside my window. But when she beelines to one of the many bouquets in the room, rather than the large windows, and then bends down and pointedly inhales, I know what's gotten her attention. It's not the literal sea. It's the sea of white roses filling every spare surface of the room. I googled and found out white roses mean "new beginnings," "eternal love," and "eternal loyalty." So, I got as many white roses as my room could possibly contain.

According to the internet, white roses can also mean "innocence and purity." But I don't give a shit about that. Yes, I'm Alessandra's first—and, hopefully, her last. And, yes, being her first was insanely special. But that's not why I love her. I love this girl because she's Alessandra. Because she's perfect. Because she's mine and I'm hers, no matter who or what came before, or didn't, for either of us.

When Alessandra turns to me, her eyes are wide and as blue as the ocean. She puts a palm on her heart. "Did you look up the meaning of white roses?"

I nod. "The same way I've looked up the meanings of every flower I've ever sent you."

"Aw, Matthew. I thought a florist had to be making those selections for you."

"How dare you." Smiling, I take her hands. "I know exactly what these white roses mean. *Forever.* That's why I chose them. Because 'forever' is how long I'm going to love you. I love you like the sky is blue, baby. Forever and ever."

"I love you forever, too," she chokes out. "I'll be smitten, always."

Arousal floods me. And by the look on Ally's face, it's clear she's having the same reaction. We kiss each other passionately, and begin making out on my bed. And, soon, glory be, we're peeling off our clothes.

"Holy Hot Girlfriend," I say when I behold her undies and bra. For the first time, ever, Alessandra is wearing classically "sexy" pieces—a blue G-string and lacy bra. And, damn, she looks fine as fuck.

Alessandra strikes a classic 'pin-up girl' pose on the bed. "You like my present, *loverrr*?"

"'Like' isn't a strong enough word to convey my feelings on this particular topic."

She giggles. "Well, then, you're *really* going to like my next present." She straddles me on the bed and grinds herself into my hard-on. "Guess what, Matthew? I started taking the pill right before New York." She winks. *"Condoms no longer needed, baby."*

My chest heaves with excitement. "I've never had sex without a condom."

She grinds herself against my bulge. "Well, here's to yet another first."

With an excited growl, I remove her sexy bra with only a small amount of trouble and lay her down on the bed. After kissing her torso and the outside of her gorgeous undies, I remove them with my teeth, making her shriek. When she's fully naked, I spread her out and lick and lap at the sweet flesh between her legs, including that magical cherry on top— until, in no time at all, Alessandra is gripping the sheet underneath her and coming palpably against my mouth and fingers.

As she comes down from her orgasm, I crawl on top of her, my balls tightening with anticipation, and sink myself inside her . . . and literally convulse at the pleasure streaking through me as my body slides inside hers.

"You feel amazing," I gasp out. But it's an understatement. I haven't even started thrusting yet, and I'm already feeling like I'm glimpsing God. She's perfect. A tight, warm, wet glove designed precisely for my body.

"It feels amazing for me, too," she says. "I love there being nothing between us."

We begin making love. And it's the best sex of my life. But, after a bit, I'm desperate to look at her as I fuck her. Dying to make her come while I'm inside her.

"Get on top, baby," I whisper. "I want to touch you where it counts and look at you as I fuck you."

We rearrange ourselves, with her riding me, and I proceed

to grip her slender hips with one hand, while massaging her clit with the other.

Well, damn. I'm a genius. In no time at all, Alessandra is going completely crazy on me. She throws her head back, showing me the curve of her slender neck, while I move my hand from her hip to her breast, losing my mind along with her.

As she moans, she slides her fingertip into my mouth, making me groan in reply.

The sound of waves crashing beyond my window is our soundtrack. The scent of roses our mutual perfume. And I'm quite certain, in this moment, I've literally never been happier in my life.

Somehow, through sheer force of will, I last long enough to make it through Alessandra's eventual orgasm. But the moment she comes, I lose it, too.

When our bodies have quieted down, we tumble onto the mattress together, onto our backs, side by side, and exhale with satisfaction.

"That felt so good," I say. "I never want to use a condom again."

"You'll never have to," she replies. And her meaning is clear. She wants to be the last woman I sleep with, ever.

"Absolutely," I reply, taking her hand.

We stare at the ceiling for a moment, both of us lost in our thoughts. But, after a bit, I lie on my side and prop my cheek onto my palm.

"I wrote a song about you," I say, running my fingertip across her belly.

"Really?"

"It's not a masterpiece or anything. Just a silly little ditty. But I like it."

"Sing it!"

"I was just fooling around."

"Sing it!"

"Okay. Don't judge it too harshly. I was just—"

"*Sing. It!*"

"Okay, okay." I get up excitedly and grab an acoustic guitar from the other room, and then settle into a chair in the corner of my bedroom. As I tune the guitar, I say, "This song will never see the light of day on an album or at a public performance. It's just for you. My Little Lioness."

She sits up onto her forearms, getting into prime listening position.

"In a shocking twist," I say. "The song is called 'Alessandra the Lioness.'"

She giggles.

"Like I said, don't judge it too harshly."

"*Stop.* I'll love it."

I take a deep breath, strum for a moment to collect myself, and begin to sing:

I'm a Goat called Fish
Would love to say
I'm hung like a bull
But I'd be lyin'
I'm just an ordinary guy

You're a Leo in purple
With the voice of an angel
Would love to say
You're mine

'Cuz, baby, I'd do anything for ya

Roar, baby
Aless-andra the Lion-ess
Roar, baby
Hold your mane up high
Aless-andra the Lion-ess
I'm so lucky to be your guy

I'm a Goat Called Fish
And I love you like the ocean is blue
Roar, baby
Aless-andra the Lion-ess
I promise, baby
I'll always love you

When I finish the song, Alessandra walks over to me in the chair, removes my guitar from my lap, and takes its place. "I loved it." She kisses me gently. "Best. Little ditty. *Ever.* On the best *day* ever. Sung by the best boyfriend *ever.*"

"It's silly, I know."

"It's adorable." She kisses my cheek. "One small note?" She grimaces. "Honey, female lions don't have manes."

I laugh and throw my head back. "Oh, fuck. I'm such a dumbass." I straighten up and beam a huge smile at her. "See? That's why I need you as a co-writer. I can't do this alone."

She strokes my stubble. "This is gonna be so much fun."

"It is. We're gonna write the best songs."

"No, I meant *this.*" She gestures to the bedroom. To the

place we're hopefully going to wake up every morning to the sight of each other's faces for the rest of our lives. "Me and you. A tribe of two. Forever."

I kiss her cheek. "That's for damned sure, Alessandra the Lioness. *Forever*."

THIRTY-SEVEN

ALESSANDRA

"I want a rematch!" I shout dramatically across the ping-pong table, where Zander and Aloha—*Zaloha* to our friend group—has just soundly trounced Fish and me. *Alfi*. That's what our friends and fans call Fish and me these days. Although, at the present moment, I'm living up to my *other* nickname among my friends. *Diva.*

We're at Reed and Georgie's house for a late-afternoon birthday party for Violet and me. Violet's birthday is in four days, while today is mine. My twenty-second. And, lucky us, everyone we love the most is here to celebrate. Apparently, though, just because it's my birthday today, doesn't mean *Zaloha* is willing to let me win in a game of ping-pong.

In dramatic, diva-like fashion, I toss my paddle onto the table and scrunch up my face into a scowl, the same way Keane and Maddy's high-spirited toddler, Billie, always does when she's pissed off. Which happens a lot. And everyone laughs in response to my shenanigans.

"You're heartless!" Fish yells across the table, after wrapping me in a protective hug. "You can't even let this girl win a game on her frickin' *birthday*?"

"No mercy," Zander deadpans in his low baritone. But, of course, he flashes me one of his megawatt smiles after saying it.

Aloha lays down her paddle next to her husband's with a sniff. "I think Diva knows by now it's my cosmic destiny to beat her, in every game we play."

Fucking hell. She's right. Aloha's winning streak against me is nothing short of supernatural at this point. It started last year during our tour and has continued ever since. Whether we're playing ping-pong or cornhole or HORSE at Reed and Georgie's, like today, or Cards Against Humanity or drinking games during one of our regular game nights at our friends' houses, Aloha *always* beats me. *And I can't figure out why.* All I can think is that, despite the close friendship Aloha and I have formed at this point, I've still got some sort of residual mental block about her being my childhood idol.

I wag my finger at Aloha. "Watch yourself, Disney. You're pissing me off now. I'm coming for you."

Aloha laughs uproariously, and so do Zander and Fish. It's the same way they always react when I try to act menacing. During our tour, I was able to bring my friends to *literal* tears, on occasion, with my "diva" act. And it was a source of pride every time I did it.

"Cake time!" Georgina's amplified voice sings out from a distant area of the party. "Violet and Ally! Come to the patio to blow out your caaaaandles!"

"Saved by the Georgina, *again*," Aloha tosses out jokingly, as our foursome converges to head to the patio.

We reach the main area of the party and discover everyone crowded around the small stage that's been set up near the pool. Georgina is standing onstage with a microphone, and when she sees our foursome, her face lights up.

"There you are, co-birthday girl! Come join Violet over here by the cake!"

I join Violet by the cake to find it inscribed in bright pink icing with the words "Happy Birthday, Flower Girl and Diva!"

It's a funny thing, nicknames. Despite me being a florist's daughter and notoriously loving flowers, it's Violet, not me, who's called "Flower Girl" by this crowd, thanks to her floral name, while I'm stuck with a nickname that couldn't be further from the truth.

I acquired the "Diva" nickname last year on tour, when Keane and Maddy visited everyone with their new baby, Billie. After my set, Fish and I and the Goats and several others were hanging out with Keane and Maddy—*Kaddy*, to our friend group—and, somehow, everyone started telling stories about my ridiculous niceness. "I thought it had to be an act, at first," Savage from Fugitive Summer said. "I thought, for sure, at some point, her inner diva would finally show itself. But, nope. It turns out Alessandra really is the female version of Fish."

Well, that was that. When Keane heard that comment, he immediately started calling me "Diva." And once Keane Morgan christens you with a nickname, that's your name, dude. You're stuck with it. "Diva" caught on like wildfire with everyone on tour—other artists, crew, visiting friends— and, quickly, it became a nonnegotiable fact of my life.

Diva isn't my only nickname, of course. My friends also call me Ally Cat and Bowling Ally. The latter of which led to them calling me "Gutter Ball" for a while. Which was a little weird. But whenever we all get together for parties, the minute anyone starts drinking, they always revert to calling me "Diva" more than anything else. It's okay, though. Fish once told me having a nickname in his extended family is "a sign of acceptance and love—*especially* when the nickname is just a tiny bit mean."

The crowd standing around the cake begins singing "Happy Birthday" to Violet and me. And as they do, I take Fish's offered hand. I still can't believe the journey we've been on these past two years, both personally and professionally—although those two things are really one and the same when it comes to us, simply because making music together is like another form of making love.

Thank God for my boyfriend. Thanks to Fish, "Blindsided" ultimately sounded like *me* when it was released two years ago. And even without its prior pop slickness, the song still managed to peak at number *eight* on the charts. Would it have reached number one if we'd left it alone, as originally produced by Zeke? Maybe. Especially with that music video, which, as Reed predicted, went totally viral. But I don't care about what might have been. I'm proud of what *was*. Because what I've realized is this: I'd rather hit number eight, or eighty, or eighty-thousand, sounding like *me*, than number one, sounding like someone else.

Luckily, I didn't have to choose between my artistic vision and commercial success with my beloved album. Thanks to Fish's masterful producing and co-writing, the album wound up sounding authentically like me, to the extreme, and *also* spun out *three* top twenty hits, including our number *one* smash duet, "Smitten." In the end, much to my shock, that sweet and simple love song with Fish about the pure joy of being in love and smitten, did even better than my duet with Laila. Although, of course, my song with Laila was a success, too. It peaked at ten on Billboard's Hot 100 chart and fifteen on the alternative chart, and was featured in a whole lot of movies and commercials. So, that song was nothing to sneeze at, either, even though "Smitten" was far and away the biggest hit on the album.

As the crowd continues singing, I let my gaze drift from my beloved Matthew to the faces around me. To the people I love the most. My mother isn't here today. Not because she doesn't love me or is staging some sort of protest. Mom never attends gatherings hosted or attended by Georgina or Georgina's father, Marco, thanks to the bitterness of her divorce from the latter. In light of that, Fish and I are going to my mom's place for dinner tomorrow night, which will be wonderful.

When I eventually introduced Mom to Fish, early on, she already adored him, thanks to those viral videos of him singing to me at Madison Square Garden. And when she got to know him as a person, she adored him even more. Even after I dropped the bomb that I was already living with Fish at his cute little bungalow on the beach, Mom didn't bat an eyelash, despite her *often*-stated aversion to "young people shacking up these days."

I said to my mother back then, "I know you don't approve of me living with my boyfriend, but—" And Mom cut me off to say, "Oh, honey. You've got an album to create together, on a short timeline! And it's obvious you two are a match made in heaven. Of course, you're living together. It makes perfect sense!"

I couldn't believe it. Ya think you know someone . . .

Speaking of mothers, even though my biological one isn't here to celebrate today, I'm not motherless at this party. I've got my two adopted moms in attendance: Fish's sweet mother,

Lorna, who's treated me like a daughter since the day I met her. And, of course, my beloved Momma Lou. Louise Morgan. From the moment I met that delightful woman in Seattle, I absolutely loved her. From minute one, she made me feel every bit as much like a daughter-in-law to her as Violet and Maddy and the others.

From Mrs. Morgan, I let my gaze drift to my adopted big sister, Kat. She's singing next to her husband, Josh, who's holding their baby, Arabella, while Kat wrangles their two older kids.

From there, Keane and Maddy are standing next in line. And then there's Colin, who's holding the hand of Keane and Maddy's firecracker, Billie. For some reason, Billie is *obsessed* with her Uncle Colin, every bit as much as her Uncle Zander, which is saying a lot. Billie follows Colin around, batting her eyelashes at him. And constantly, as she's doing right now, demands to hold his hand. I'm not sure if Colin being here as Billie's "date" means he's single and ready to mingle again. I can't keep track of Colin's love life these days. Nobody ever seems to last very long.

Finally, when the crowd reaches the last notes of their song, I return my gaze to the man standing next to me. My hot boyfriend of two years. My songwriting partner and producer. My best friend and lover. The Goat Called Fish Who's Hung Like A Bull. But Not Really.

Fish isn't looking at me because he's presently gazing down at his nephew, Jackson, who's holding his hand and singing his little heart out. And I think, as I often do when looking at Fish, *You're my first, my last, my best, my only . . . love.*

When the birthday song ends, Violet and I blow out our candles, eliciting cheers and applause. I wrap Violet in a hug and wish her a happy birthday, and she whispers the same to me.

Violet flashes me her most charming smile. "Would 'Alfi' be willing to give me a little birthday present?"

I know exactly what she means. During our tour, Violet never once missed a performance of "Smitten." No matter what, she *always* figured out a way to be standing there, front and center, or in the wings, to watch the performance of at least that particular song.

"You want it now?" I ask. And when Violet nods effusively, I reply, "I'll tell Georgie to announce us!"

I reach Georgie on the far side of the patio, where she's presently enjoying a champagne-infused giggle with Mrs. Morgan. When I reach the pair, Mrs. Morgan hugs me tightly and wishes me a happy birthday. We chat for a bit. Mrs. Morgan gives me an update on her life and the "Seattle Branch" of the family who couldn't make it today. I tell Momma Lou that Fish and I are in the middle of writing our second album and that it's going to be even better than the first one.

"I can't wait!" Mrs. Morgan gushes. "I *love* your first album. Especially 'Smitten.' I listen to that one all the time."

"Thank you. Speaking of which, Violet just requested Fish and I perform that song as her birthday present."

Mrs. Morgan expresses extreme excitement, as does Georgie. I ask my stepsister to announce the performance, since she's been playing emcee all afternoon, and Georgina promptly beelines onstage and grabs a mic.

"Hey, everyone!" Georgina says. "We've got another performance for you!" The milling crowd quiets down. "Our birthday girl, Violet, has requested a performance from our other birthday girl." Georgina's hazel eyes twinkle. "Ladies and gentlemen, I give you *Alfiiiii!*"

Fish and I take the stage to applause. Fish grabs one of the acoustic guitars from its stand and briefly tunes it, while I grab the ukulele—the treasured one Fish gave me as a gift two years ago for my twentieth birthday. We approach our microphones. Say hello to the crowd. I wish Violet a happy birthday and then look at Fish. He winks at me—his way of asking if I'm ready to start—and I wink back, letting him know, yep, I'm good to go, baby. And away we go, singing our familiar, happy song about being in love and smitten—a song that never gets old to sing.

As always, I sing the top of the first verse: "Oooh I . . . I love you ever so much, much. I'm living for your every touch, touch. And your every kiss . . . is . . . bliss!"

Fish takes the next half of the verse, as always, inverting my melody slightly: "Oooh I . . . I love your big blue eyes, love. I'm living for your every smile, love. And your every kiss, kiss, kiss!"

We launch into the pre-chorus in unison, our voices meshing in harmony:

Every day with you I'm smitten
Every day I have a crush
Feelin' infatuated.
Every day I'm so in love!

As we've been singing, the small children at the party have started dancing and twirling at the foot of the stage, making everyone, including Fish and me, smile with delight. And now, Fish and I launch into our euphoric chorus, each note sung in perfect harmony:

> *It's loooove!*
> *I'm so in love with youuuu!*
> *Just like the sky is bluuuuue!*
> *You're my first. My last. My best. My only.*
> *Looooooove!*
> *Don't want no one but youuuuuu!*
> *Because this love is true!*

Fish wraps up the chorus melody with the line, "Can't get enough of youuuuuu-ooooo!" while, underneath him, I sing, in harmony, "You're my first, my last, I'll be smitten, always."

As the cuties continue dancing at the front of the stage, Fish and I return to the verse melody. Only this time, it's Fish who sings the top half of the verse:

"Oh, you," he sings. "How'd you get so lovely? You're like the sun above me. Every smile a ray of light."

I sing, "Oh, you. How'd you get so funny? You make the gray skies sunny. And your every kiss is bliss."

We sing the pre-chorus and chorus again, play a little instrumental part, and then harmonize in duet on the staccato bridge: "You're my home. My port in the storm. The first one I call. The face I'm searching the crowd for!"

Fish calls out to the crowd to join us in singing our last chorus, and they do, loudly, as the children at the front of the stage continue bopping and twirling to the music.

When our happy little song is over, the crowd cheers

enthusiastically and demands another. So, Fish and I launch into a cover tune—our mid-tempo, duet arrangement of The Kinks' banger, "All Day and All of the Night." After that one, we perform "Buddy Holly" by Weezer in duet, just to keep the dance party going. And then another two upbeat songs from my album.

After that, we invite Colin and Dax onstage, and, to the thrill of the crowd, 22 Goats performs stripped-down versions of a few hits, including "Fireflies" and "People Like Us," with me singing giddy backups for them, along with Fish.

When the four of us finally leave the stage, it's to high-fives and hugs.

Reed squeezes me and says, "Happy birthday, lil sis. You looked like you were having a blast up there."

"I was." I sigh happily. "This is the best day of my life."

Reed chuckles, having heard me say that before. He says, "I bet that performance felt like a nice moment of redemption, huh?"

I tilt my head. "Redemption?"

Reed nods. "It wasn't all that long ago I suggested you hop onstage at a party at my house and perform *exactly* the way you just did—and you sprinted away, with your tail between your legs. And look at you now! You got up there like a little badass and *owned* that stage."

I make a face that says, *I do believe you've got a point.*

Reed continues, "If you'd have sauntered onto that stage back then and performed with half the confidence you just displayed, I'd have signed you to a full album deal that very night."

"Well, then, I guess it's a good thing I *didn't* saunter onto that stage back then, huh? If a single thing had happened differently that night, maybe Fish and I wouldn't be together now. Maybe Fish wouldn't have been the one to produce my album."

"Probably not."

"Well, there you go. If some kind of butterfly effect would have taken away the very best parts of my present life, then I'd never want to risk going back and changing a single thing."

"Fair enough."

"Hey, birthday girl," Georgina says, sashaying toward me with two glasses of champagne. When she comes to a stop, she hands me one of the flutes, and calls Fish over, telling him she wants to propose a toast. When Fish arrives, a beer bottle in hand, Georgina raises her flute and says, "Happy birthday, Ally. You're the light of my life. I'm so proud of everything you've accomplished and, even more so, the beautiful person you are."

Reed and Fish agree and everyone clinks and drinks to me.

Reed says, "I was just telling our little Diva that her performance just now felt like a nice moment of redemption, given what happened two years ago when I tried to get her to perform at a party."

We all reminisce about that party for a bit—at how it feels like a lifetime ago. We talk about how far I've come since then, as a person and performer, and how excited we are for the new crop of songs Fish and I have been working on.

But, finally, Fish says, "If you two will excuse us . . . Ally got her 'redemption' tonight. It's time for the Goat called Fish to get *his*."

THIRTY-EIGHT
ALESSANDRA

Fish takes my hand, the same way he did the first night we met, like it's the most natural thing in the world, and leads me away from the crowded party, toward the farthest, darkest reaches of Reed's expansive backyard. And, quickly, I realize my beloved is taking me to the very spot where Reed, Keane, and Zander interrupted what should have been our first kiss two years ago.

"Redemption, huh?" I ask playfully, squeezing his hand.

Fish smiles playfully. "I want a do-over on that kiss I didn't have the balls to get that very first night."

After turning a corner, and stepping over a low retaining wall, we reach our destination and sit on the ground, shoulder to shoulder, our hands clasped.

The sounds of the party are a distant din now. The last remnants of the sunset are sprawled before us in the sky.

"Such a pretty view," I whisper. But when Fish doesn't reply, I turn my head . . . and receive his passionate kiss.

"Wow," I whisper when our kiss ends.

Fish presses his forehead to mine. "That's the exact kiss I was about to give you that night, when we got interrupted."

I return his grin. "You couldn't possibly have given me a kiss like *that* back then. That smooch told me you love me, forever and ever."

"I do." He strokes my hair and looks deeply into my eyes. "Did you know, before I met you, I used to say 'Fuck it, shit happens,' like, three times a *week*? Maybe even more. But now, how often do I say that?" He shrugs. "And if I do say it, it's only for stupid stuff, like when I can't find my keys."

I laugh. He's right.

But, to my surprise, Fish doesn't join me in laughing. In fact, he looks a bit nervous. Like his mind is racing.

In a flash, the hair on the back of my neck stands up. I suddenly feel like Fish is gearing up to say something important.

And then it hits me . . .

Today is my birthday . . .

And Fish brought me to *this* nostalgic, romantic spot . . .

At sunset . . .

Holy crap.

Is Fish going to . . .?

His breathing shallow, Fish grabs my hands. "Alessandra, I'm only happy when I'm with you. I want to be with you, and love you, *forever*. But not as your *boyfriend*." He reaches into his pocket. "I want to go through life with you as your—"

"Yes!" I shout, overcome with emotion and excitement.

"*Husband.*"

"Yes!" I shout again, just in case my interruption somehow negated my first *yes*.

Exhaling with relief, Fish kisses me gleefully as I throw

my arms around his neck. But suddenly, he pulls back sharply from my lips and says, "You heard that last word, right? Just to be clear, I just asked you to *marry* me."

"Yes! My answer is *yes!*"

We kiss again.

But, again, Fish pulls back sharply. "Oh. I should probably give you the ring." His entire body quaking, he opens the little box in his hand, revealing a stunning diamond solitaire inside.

"It's beautiful! I love it!"

He slips the ring onto my finger, at which point, I burst into soggy tears. Crying, I pull his face to mine and kiss the hell out of him, feeling like I'm soaring on a wave of euphoria.

We kiss and kiss. Until, soon, we're flat-out mauling each other—making out with abandon, the same way we do when we're naked at home. Although, actually, this moment is even hotter than being at home in our bed, because we're both well aware our closest family and friends are nearby and could, in theory, stumble upon us.

I mean, not really. The sun has set by now, so we're completely hidden in this dark corner behind a freaking wall. For anyone to see us, they'd have to be standing right over us. Either way, though, I'll only be proposed to once in my life. I might as well make this moment extra memorable with a little high-risk nookie.

Panting, I unbutton Fish's jeans, telegraphing my intent, and Fish yelps in surprise and excitement. These days, I initiate sex all the time. I'm the first to admit I'm a horny little thing. But I've never initiated *risky* sex like this before. *Public* sex where we could, in theory, get caught. But, as Fish knows, I'm all about racking up "firsts" with him, whenever I can.

His cock freed from his buttons, I straddle him, pull my undies to the side to bare myself to him, and growl at him to fuck me. Without hesitation, Fish fingers me, moaning when he feels how wet I am—and, a moment later, I'm riding him furiously while kissing him voraciously.

As our pleasure mounts to near boiling, nearby voices suddenly invade our consciousness. Male voices. Laughing ones. It's Keane and Zander! Maybe some others, too. But definitely them!

I freeze on top of Fish, my eyes wide, panting, trying to decipher the trajectory of the voices. But Fish isn't taking any chances. While gripping my hips, firmly keeping me in place, he shouts, "Go away! Whoever you are, turn around and go away!"

"Shit," Keane's voice says. He laughs. "Sorry, Fish."

The footfalls recede. The low din of the faraway party becomes our subtle soundtrack again, along with the small sounds emanating from the canyon below. Once again, we're alone in our dark bubble. *A tribe of two.*

"Now, where were we?" Fish whispers.

We resume our prior activity, giggling at our close call. Reveling in our naughtiness. And in no time at all, Fish comes underneath me, growling with pleasure. He quickly finishes me off with his fingers, calling me his "hot fiancée" as he does.

When I come down from my orgasm, I slide off his lap. After putting ourselves back together, I sit next to my fiancé, my back against the wall, and lean my cheek against his shoulder.

"When do you want to get married?" I ask.

Fish takes my hand. "I don't care. We're already married, as far as I'm concerned."

"Well, would you like to do it before or after the next tour?"

He shrugs. "Before, I guess. That way, everyone on tour can call you Mrs. Fish." He chuckles. "We'll be a Goat *and* a Lioness called Fish."

"That's it!" I say. And he laughs. It's been our running joke for a while now. Any time either of us says something weird, we pretend we've found the perfect name for our next album.

I look down at my sparkling ring. "It's so perfect. So *me*."

"I can't take credit for that, to be honest. Mrs. Morgan, Georgie, and Kat helped me pick it out. I mean, I was there with them. But they all said, '*This is the one!*' And I said, 'Kewl.'"

I giggle. "When was that?"

"A year and a half ago. Right before we left on tour."

I sit up from his shoulder, in shock. "You waited all that time to propose to me *here*—on this exact spot?"

Fish grimaces. "No. I waited all that time because I was trying to find the perfect moment. I've had that ring in my pocket for a year."

"Fish!"

He laughs. "I wanted to propose on our first Christmas together. That was my original plan." He's talking about the Christmas we spent in Seattle with his mother and the Morgans. And now that I think about it, he *did* seem kind of out of sorts that entire trip.

"Why didn't you do it then?"

"Because I convinced myself it was too soon, and you'd turn me down. Maybe say you were too young. So, then, I decided to wait until you could legally drink champagne on the day of your engagement."

"And here we are a year later," I say.

"Well, then we were on tour, and . . ."

"I would have said yes whenever you asked me, you know."

"I just wanted it to be right. I was going to do it a hundred different times during our tour. Every time we performed 'Smitten,' I had the urge to do it after the song. But, then, I figured the reason I hadn't done it yet was because my gut was telling me not to do it with anyone else around. Especially not a whole bunch of strangers in an audience. I know that's the way lots of people propose—with a huge, public audience. But I'd already done the 'public declaration of love' thing at the Garden that time. So, I decided to pop the question when nobody else was around. Just to do something different."

"This was perfect. Romantic and sweet and intimate." I wink. "And *hawt*."

"Whew, hot momma. You were on *fire*."

"Something came over me when you slipped this ring on my finger. I just had to have you." I look down at my splayed hand. "Seriously, the way you did it is the best of all worlds. It was just you and me when you asked me—which means we got to celebrate in the most intimate way possible. And, now, we get to float back into the birthday party and celebrate with everyone we love the most."

"I love you the most of the most. You know that, right?"

"I sure do. Back at you."

Fish stands and pulls me up. "Come on, my hot *fiancée*. Let's go tell everyone I asked the girl of my dreams to marry me—to become my hot wife and grow old and gray with me —and, thank God, she . . . said . . . *yes*."

He slips his hand in mine and guides me over the retaining wall.

"Damn, I'm a lucky little lioness," I say softly, more to myself than Fish.

But, of course, Fish heard me. He returns my huge, beaming smile and whispers, "And I'm one lucky Goat."

EPILOGUE

ALESSANDRA

"**P**erfect!" I say to my grandson, Alfie, after he fingers a perfect C-chord on his brand-new ukulele.

I'm sitting on a blanket on the sand with Alfie in front of my house—the beach house I've shared with my family for the past thirty years. When our son, Winston, was born twenty-three years ago, Fish and I considered moving to a larger house. A place more like Dax and Violet's sprawling compound on the cliffs of Malibu. In the end, though, we decided we liked our little home in Venice Beach too much to leave it. So, we added a second story—a spacious master suite with a massive bathroom and balcony—and that was that.

Granted, things got a bit cramped during Winston's teenage years, after he became as obsessed with music and musical instruments as his mom and dad. Even more so, actually. Beginning around age thirteen, Winston started bringing home one musical instrument after another. The "usual" ones, like guitars and bass guitars and harmonicas. But also a dulcimer and Wurlitzer and accordion, too.

Even when Winston had no idea how to play a particular

instrument, he'd nonetheless bring it home, and thereafter become obsessed with learning it. Winston would barter with kids at his school, promising them signed 22 Goats memorabilia to sell or give to their parents as a gift, in exchange for this or that instrument. Or Winston would run across some weird thing at a yard sale and simply *have* to have it. One time, my crazy son brought home a freaking didgeridoo! And, damned if he didn't learn to play that one, too. Sort of.

But, anyway, putting aside Winston's teenage obsession with collecting musical instruments—not to mention, his penchant for sneaking girls into his downstairs bedroom, when he *incorrectly* thought his father and I were asleep—I think it's fair to say our beach house has *almost* always been spacious enough to accommodate the three of us, all our various musical instruments, and our son's raging teenage hormones. Our home isn't massive, like Violet and Dax's or Reed and Georgie's, but it works for our family and always will.

"Like dis?" Alfie says, strumming the C-chord again.

"Just like that!"

We practice the simple chord again and again. After which, I ask, "You want to try a new one, honey?" I move my grandson's fingers into position. "This is *G*."

"G," my darling boy says solemnly, like I've just told him the secrets of the universe.

"That's right, my love. Now, strum."

Alfie strums and scowls at the tinny sound.

"You moved your fingers." I reposition his tiny fingers. "Try again."

Alfie strums and, this time, delivers a lovely, crisp G that rings out over the sound of the nearby ocean.

"Now see how much easier it is to play this than that big

guitar you wanted to play? You can learn on this ukulele and play your daddy's big guitar when your hands get bigger."

"I want to play Daddy's guitar. I want to be like Daddy and Unkee Jackson."

"I know you do, my love. And one day, you will be. But before then, while you're still so little—"

"I'm not *little*." Alfie scrunches up his darling face. "I'm *big*. I'm *three*."

I bite back my laughter. "You're right. You're big. In fact, what are you doing here? Why aren't you working on Wall Street?"

"Huh?"

I snort, thoroughly amused with myself. "Just a little Grandma humor. Would you like me to show you how to play a song with those two chords you've learned?"

My grandson nods excitedly, reminding me so much of Winston, his father, at the same age, my heart bursts.

I position my own treasured ukulele in my lap. "This song is called 'Skip to My Lou.' You're gonna love it. It's a banger."

Alfie looks confused.

"More Grandma humor. That means it's a good song. Okay, cutie, watch my fingers as I play the song. Watch how I move my fingers from C to G." I play the simple song for him, much to his delight. And, quickly, it's obvious I've got a fish on my line—yet another Fishberger who's absolutely hooked on music.

When I'm done playing, Alfie demands we swap ukuleles. Apparently, the kid thinks those pretty sounds I just made are attributable to the *instrument* in my lap, rather than the musician playing it.

I give Alfie my prized ukulele, but warn him he can't take

it home with him. "This one was a birthday present from Grandpa when I turned twenty. That's even younger than your daddy."

Alfie nods knowingly. "You played it for 'Smitten.'"

"That's right! I did!" I don't know why I'm surprised my grandson knows that. He's obsessed with that song and always has been. He's probably seen the music video a million times in his young life. Not to mention several performance videos, too. And in every single one, I'm playing this very ukulele.

It's not only my grandson who adores "Smitten," by the way. Even thirty years after its release, Fish and I can still easily sell out any medium-size club in the world, if we're so inclined, thanks to that song's enduring popularity. Since "Smitten" first hit number one a full three decades ago, it's been covered by lots of artists, featured in countless movies and commercials, and slowly wormed its way into being regarded as a "classic" love song. So much so, *Here Comes the Bride* Magazine recently included it on their list of "The Top Twenty 'First Dance' Wedding Songs of All Time."

Being named on that list was a particular thrill for me, considering Fish and I sang "Smitten" to each other on our own wedding day, exactly twenty-eight years ago *today*. Finding out other couples choose to make our little duet a part of *their* special memories, especially after all this time, warms my heart.

To this day, if I happen to hear "Smitten" on the radio or in a grocery store, I get physical goose bumps. Not only from hearing the recording itself, but from the memories the song evokes inside me. I love hearing my young, giddy voice mingling with Fish's, and remembering the giddiness we both felt to have found each other. I love remembering those enthralling months we spent writing that first, magical album together. And remembering all the times we had to stop writing or recording to make love, simply because creating music together always got both of us so hot and bothered, we simply couldn't continue working.

We were so damned smitten back then! So infatuated and horny and in love, we *literally* couldn't stand being apart for a single night! Actually, we're pretty much the same way now. We still can't stand being apart.

I remember, so clearly, that first time I met my husband at Reed's party. I told Matthew there's nothing like a girl's first love. I let him think I was talking about a song when I said that. But I think I knew, even then, somewhere deep in my heart, I was talking about *him*.

"Daddy!" Alfie shouts, leaping up from our blanket, and I'm barely able to grab my beloved ukulele from him to prevent it from plopping into the sand.

I glance to where Alfie is running and discover my son, Winston, walking across the beach toward us, alongside my nephew, Jackson. I quickly lay the two ukuleles down onto our blanket, and then get up to greet the men.

Oh, how I love my son, Winston. And the fact that his name is a tribute to my late father. Winston was my father's middle name—*his* mother's maiden name. Nobody but me ever calls my son by his given name, actually. To the rest of the world, Winston Fishberger is and always has been "Wi-Fi." But, regardless, it's a source of joy for me to know my son's name honors my beloved father.

"Hey, boys," I say. I hug my nephew, Jackson, first, since Winston is picking up his son.

Winston never meant to become a father three years ago, at age twenty. But, sometimes, life doesn't go according to plan—especially when your horny, dumbass son doesn't use a condom. But, that's okay. Now that Alfie is here, none of us would have it any other way, including Winston or Alfie's mommy, Emma.

Speaking of Winston's ex-girlfriend, Emma, she's a lovely young woman. And a wonderful mother to Alfie, too. She's simply not in love with my son, unfortunately. And that's okay. If you ask me, it's far better to be honest about that sort of thing, from the start, than to make promises to someone, for the sake of a baby, that simply can't be kept down the line.

It was certainly generous of Emma to agree to Alfie's name. Apparently, when Winston first suggested the idea to her—unbeknownst to Fish and me, of course—Emma said, "Your parents have brought so much joy to the world through their music and also as an example of what love can be. I can't think of a better name for our baby." And that was that, apparently. As the story goes, Emma and Winston settled on our grandson's cute little name in two minutes flat. If only every decision by those two could be settled that easily.

I hug Jackson and he kisses my cheek.

"Hey, Aunt Ally," Jackson says. "How are you?"

"I'm wonderful. How'd your recording session go?"

"Great," Jackson replies. "Wi-Fi was *incredible*. Everyone was impressed."

Winston looks thrilled at Jackson's compliment. And I don't blame him. My nephew is a big fucking deal these days, every bit as much as Dax, his father, always was and still is. The fact that Jackson Morgan invited Winston, seven years his junior, to record with him and his famous friends for the past three days was a *big* deal. But, still, I know when to play it cool. I've been around musicians my whole life, after all.

"Glad it went well," I say calmly. But I can't resist shooting my son a little wink.

"Is Uncle Fish home?" Jackson asks. And I'm not surprised. Whether that kid is thirty or three, he'll always have a special bond with his Uncle Fish.

"Yeah, he's inside the house," I say. "He wanted to take a nap, since we're going out to dinner tonight, so I took Mr. Ants in His Pants outside for a bit." I smile at my grandson in his father's arms. "Alfie and I looked for shells, had a picnic, and then played our ukuleles. Didn't we have fun, bubba?"

Alfie agrees we had a blast, and starts excitedly babbling to his father and uncle about our adventures. As he talks, I gather the blanket and remnants of our picnic, hand the ukuleles to my nephew, since Winston is holding Alfie, and then walk with the group across the sand toward the house.

"We were at my parents' place earlier," Jackson announces. "Mom said everyone's coming over on Friday night for dinner and a jam session."

"Yep. We're going to talk about the reunion tour. You and your band should come jam with us." I look at my son. "You too, honey. Everyone would love to see you."

Jackson says, "Yeah, my dad already invited both of us. My friends are coming, too. They're amped about it. My drummer in particular is excited to meet you."

"*Me*? You mean Fish."

"No, you. Both of you. My drummer is a huge 'Alfi' fan."

I snort. "Please, honey. Don't blow smoke up your auntie's bum. Your friends have never heard of Ally and Fish."

"Sure they have," Jackson says. "My drummer grew up listening to you. He said his mom used to play your stuff all the time. He knows every word."

"That's so cool! I can't believe someone your age knows *my* songs."

"Mom, don't be lame," Winston says. "Everyone knows 'Smitten,' at the very least. Even if they don't know who sings it, they've *all* heard that one."

"That's so cool! Isn't that *cool?*" I grab my son's free arm as we walk across the sand. "Promise you'll bring Alfie to one of the shows on the reunion tour. You know, with protective earphones. I want Alfie to see his grandpa rocking out like the rock star he is."

Winston chuckles. "And his grandma, too." He kisses the side of my head. "Of course, I'll bring him, Mom. To the opening show. After that, I was thinking of leaving Alfie with Emma and her parents for a couple weeks and tagging along on the tour, if that'd be okay with everyone."

"*Okay?* It'd be a dream come true!"

"I was too young during the last reunion tour to fully appreciate it. I wanna hang out with everyone this time. You know, backstage. Have drinks and hear all the old stories, so I can remember them all."

"I'm so excited!" I shriek. "You could sit in with my band a few shows, if you'd like! Play any instrument you want!"

"Oh my God, Mom. Seriously? I'd love that."

"Just not bass."

Winston rolls his eyes. "Well, *obviously.*"

I can barely breathe, I'm so excited. But, somehow, as we reach our back patio, I still remember to call out, "Rinse your feet before going inside!" It's what I've been calling out for the past thirty years. First, to Fish, who never remembers. Then, to Fish *and* Winston. Then, to Winston and all his crazy friends. I swear, if I didn't say that, *nobody* would ever do it—

which means, by now, there'd be as much sand inside our house as on the beach itself.

I follow the group through the back door, and the minute I step foot inside my house, I'm hit with the glorious scent of *flowers*. I turn a corner, and there they are. White blooms. *Everywhere*. Roses, lilies, hydrangeas, and peonies. All of them symbolizing eternal love and loyalty, in slightly different ways.

"Matthew Fishberger!" I shout.

Like magic, my husband appears from the kitchen, looking showered and gorgeous. "Happy anniversary," he says, an excited smile on his face.

Fish opens his arms and I barrel into them.

"I can't believe you did this! Twenty-eight isn't even a biggie!"

"Every anniversary is a biggie," he says. "Plus, it's really our thirty-year anniversary to me. I was married to you the day I met you."

I release my sweet husband and twirl through the room. "It smells like heaven!" I stop when I see our dining table has been set up meticulously for a lavish meal. I whirl around. "I thought we were going out to eat."

Fish shrugs. "I thought I'd make you a nice dinner here, if that sounds okay."

Oh, my heart. "Of course." I hug him again, swooning at his sweetness. This man is so damned thoughtful. And so damned sexy, too. Suddenly, all I want to do is make love to my hot husband. *Right now.* I turn to the boys, all of whom have settled onto the couch like they plan to stay a while. "Time to go, boys."

"We're gonna have a late lunch, Mom."

"Sorry, no. It's our anniversary. Time to go."

Jackson laughs and gets up, but Winston stares at me, dumbfounded. Like he thinks I'm kidding.

"You heard your mother," Fish says. "The kitchen is closed, son. It's our anniversary. You've gotta get the hell out."

Jackson and Winston exchange a chuckle before leading Alfie toward the door.

"I'll see you boys on Friday night!" I chirp. I grab Alfie's new ukulele and hand it to him. "Practice the song Grandma taught you, love. And, next time, I'll teach you two more chords." I address Winston. "I taught him C and G and played him 'Skip to My Lou.'"

"Got it."

Fish bends down to our beloved grandson. "Bye, little dude."

"Bye, Grampa. I'm not little."

"Sorry."

"Hey, Uncle Fish," Jackson says. "You want to surf this week?"

"Any time."

"As long as it's not *right now*, apparently," Winston murmurs sarcastically.

Bye, bye, bye. Kiss, kiss, kiss. We say all necessary good-byes, and, finally, Fish closes our front door and turns around, a wicked smile on his handsome face.

"Liar," I say playfully as he strides toward me. "You didn't take a nap, did you, Old Man?"

Fish scoffs. "Hell no. I'm strong as a bull, woman. I just needed time to get everything set up for our little anniversary party."

I kiss him deeply, feeling physically intoxicated by the glorious fragrances floating around me, not to mention his cologne. "You clever man. You know flowers always make me extra horny."

Fish waggles his eyebrows. "I was counting on it."

I grab my husband's hand and pull him upstairs toward our "new" bedroom. The one we built twenty-odd years ago after our son was born. When we get upstairs, I discover it's also filled with white blooms—various ways to promise forever.

"Oh, Matthew. Thank you."

We tumble into our large, comfy bed and peel off our clothes. As we've done many times before, we kiss and caress, worship and whisper. As my husband licks me into a frenzy, I run my fingers through his hair that's nowadays streaked with a bit of sexy silver.

I've never made love to anyone but my beautiful husband. My eternal love. As crazy as it sounds, I've never even kissed anyone else. And I wouldn't have it any other way. In fact, I'm quite certain if I'd slept with a hundred men before Fish, searching for the perfect man, the perfect lover and best friend, I would have immediately stopped searching the moment I met Fish. *Matthew*. The same way I actually did. Whether Matthew Fishberger was my first or my hundred-and-first, there's no doubt I would have known, instantly, he was The One. My one and only. It just so happens I found him first. Lucky me.

When we're done making love, we lie in each other's arms, listening to the sounds of the ocean through our bedroom window.

"Are you hungry?" he asks.

"Not really. You?"

"Not really. There's a bottle of champagne chilling on the

balcony. I thought we'd open that bad boy up and watch the sunset."

"*Ooh.*"

"After that, whenever you get hungry, I'll make you the best anniversary meal you've ever had."

"What are you making me?"

"Vegan enchiladas."

"Patti's recipe?"

"Of course."

"Oooh, honey. You spoil me."

"Oreo pie for dessert."

"Gah! Best anniversary *ever.* I got you a present, too. Hang on." I run to the closet, grab the box, and launch myself onto the bed. "Here you go. It's not much, but . . ."

Fish unwraps the gift and discovers a little photo album I've created commemorating our thirty years together, beginning with the first photo I ever sent him—a picture of me holding the very first bouquet of flowers he'd sent to me in Boston—a stunning spray of red roses.

"*Red* roses. *Not* yellow," he whispers, making me smile. He touches my young face in the album, and then looks up at me. "I already knew I loved you by the time I sent those flowers to you."

"I already knew I loved you when I got them."

We share a huge smile, before Fish flips the page. And there I am, so very young again, wearing a pink tank top and shorts. It's the photo Fish snapped remotely while I danced for him that very first time in my bedroom in Boston. Fish and I talk about the image for a moment—the memories—before he flips another page.

This time, we're looking at our first-ever selfie, taken in

Times Square. As we both know, that selfie was snapped on a magical night of firsts. We had our first kiss that night. We exchanged our first "I love you's." After Fish serenaded me at Madison Square Garden, he uploaded that selfie to make us "Instagram Official," as we kids used to say. And, of course, my husband and I made love for the first time that night, too. Fish and I reminisce about all of it, before Fish turns the page again.

And now, we're looking at Fish in his underwear, smoldering at the camera like an underwear model, in a photo snapped by me in our hotel room in New York, the night *after* our night of big firsts.

"Why the hell did you include this one?" Fish says, laughing.

"Because that's one of my all-time favorite photos of you," I reply. "Because you were gorgeous in that moment. Sexy. Confident. Charismatic. Romantic. *Perfect*. And you're still all of those things today, all these years later."

Fish flips another page. And another one. And each page reflects yet another special memory from our thirty years together. Until, finally, by the time Fish reaches the last image —a snapshot taken last month at Alfie's third birthday party— he's got tears in his green eyes.

"Thank you, sweetheart." He closes the book. "I love you so much."

I wipe my eyes. "I love you, too. I've loved every minute of this life with you."

Fish wipes at my cheek with his thumb, but he doesn't speak. By now, my husband knows I often cry when I'm happy—when I'm too overwhelmed with happiness to contain it.

He kisses my salty cheek and asks me if I'm okay. When I say I am, that I'm wonderful, he says, "Good. It's almost time for the sunset. You want to open that champagne now?"

"Absolutely."

We throw on soft clothes and head onto our balcony. Fish opens the bottle and pours and we sit on our love seat with our bubbly, cuddled up, and watch the sky turning spectacular shades of orange and pink above the glittering ocean.

"Happy anniversary, love," my husband says to me, tapping my glass. "I wouldn't change a thing about our life. Not a single minute."

"Neither would I. Not a single minute." I snuggle closer, and whisper-sing, "You're my first, my last, my best, my only . . ."

And, of course, my husband, my best friend, my lover doesn't leave me hanging. Right on cue, he whisper-sings the final word of the refrain we wrote together so many years ago. The word that's every bit as powerful and true today, as it was back then. Even more so.

"*Love.*"

Check out Ally and Fish's song, "SMITTEN," as well as the musical world of River Records and 22 Goats, here: http://www.laurenrowebooks.com/river-records!

If you want to find out how feisty Georgina Ricci brings stubborn Reed Rivers to his knees, start with BAD LIAR, the first book of The Reed Rivers Trilogy.

If you want to read the soaring, sexy, romantic love story of Dax Morgan and Violet Rhodes, read the standalone ROCKSTAR, and be sure to check out 22 Goats' original music, including "Fireflies," under the "MUSIC FROM ROCKSTAR" tab of Lauren's website.

To read about Keane and Maddy or Aloha and Zander, check out the related standalones: BALL PEEN HAMMER and MISTER BODYGUARD, respectively. Or, read about the two eldest Morgan brothers in HERO, about firefighter Colby, or CAPTAIN, about alpha hottie, Ryan.

Be sure to sign up for Lauren's newsletter (http://eepurl.com/ba_ODX) to find out about upcoming releases!

Find Lauren on social media by clicking the links below!
FACEBOOK - https://www.facebook.com/laurenrowebooks/
INSTAGRAM - https://www.instagram.com/laurenrowebooks/
TWITTER - http://www.twitter.com/laurenrowebooks
FACEBOOK GROUP - Lauren Rowe Books
BOOKBUB - https://www.bookbub.com/authors/lauren-rowe

ACKNOWLEDGMENTS

A huge thank you to Sophie Broughton for all you do!

Thank you, Melissa Saneholtz. You're incredible.

Thank you, Letitia Hasser of RBA Designs.

Thank you to Madonna Blackburn for your eagle eyes and big heart.

And thank you so much to my beta readers: Sarah Kirk, Lizette Baez, and Selina Washington. I love you ladies! I'm so grateful and honored!

BOOKS BY LAUREN ROWE

Standalone Novels

When aspiring singer-songwriter, Alessandra, meets Fish, the funny, adorable bass player of 22 Goats, sparks fly between the awkward pair. Fish tells Alessandra he's a "Goat called Fish who's hung like a bull. But not really. I'm actually really average." And Alessandra tells Fish, "There's nothing like a girl's first love." Alessandra thinks she's talking about a song when she makes her comment to Fish—the first song she'd ever heard by 22 Goats, in fact. As she'll later find out, though, her "first love" was actually Fish. The Goat called Fish who, after that night, vowed to do anything to win her heart.

SMITTEN is a **true standalone** romance that will make you swoon.

Smitten

The Reed Rivers Trilogy

Reed Rivers has met his match in the most unlikely of women—aspiring journalist and spitfire, Georgina Ricci. She's much younger than the women Reed normally pursues, but he can't resist her fiery personality and drop-dead gorgeous looks. But in this game of cat and mouse, who's chasing whom? With each passing day of this wild ride, Reed's not so sure. The books of this trilogy are to be read in order:

Bad Liar

Beautiful Liar

Beloved Liar

The Club Trilogy

Romantic. Scorching hot. Suspenseful. Witty. The Club is your new addiction—a sexy and suspenseful thriller about two wealthy brothers and the sassy women who bring them to their knees . . . all while the foursome bands together to protect one of their own. *The Club Trilogy* is to be read in order, as follows:

The Club: Obsession

The Club: Reclamation

The Club: Redemption

The Club: Culmination

The fourth book for Jonas and Sarah is a full-length epilogue with incredible heart-stopping twists and turns and feels. Read *The Club: Culmination (A Full-Length Epilogue Novel)* after finishing *The Club Trilogy* or, if you prefer, after reading *The Josh and Kat Trilogy*.

The Josh and Kat Trilogy

It's a war of wills between stubborn and sexy Josh Faraday and Kat Morgan. A fight to the bed. Arrogant, wealthy playboy Josh is used to getting what he wants. *And what he wants is Kat Morgan.* The books are to be read in order.

Infatuation

Revelation

Consummation

The Morgan Brothers

Read these **standalones** in any order about the brothers of Kat Morgan. Chronological reading order is below, but they are all complete stories. Note: you do *not* need to read any other books or series before jumping straight into reading about the Morgan boys.

Hero.

The story of heroic firefighter, **Colby Morgan**. When catastrophe strikes Colby Morgan, will physical therapist Lydia save him . . . or will he save her?

Captain.

The insta-love-to-enemies-to-lovers story of tattooed sex god, **Ryan Morgan**, and the woman he'd move heaven and earth to claim.

Ball Peen Hammer.

A steamy, hilarious, friends-to-lovers romantic comedy about cocky-as-hell male stripper, **Keane Morgan**, and the sassy, smart young woman who brings him to his knees during a road trip.

Mister Bodyguard.

The Morgans' beloved honorary brother, **Zander Shaw**, meets his match in the feisty pop star he's assigned to protect on tour.

ROCKSTAR.

When the youngest Morgan brother, **Dax Morgan,** meets a mysterious woman who rocks his world, he must decide if pursuing her is worth risking it all. Be sure to check out four of Dax's original songs from *ROCKSTAR*, written and produced by Lauren, along with full music videos for the songs, on her website (www.laurenrowebooks.com) under the tab MUSIC FROM ROCKSTAR.

Misadventures

Lauren's *Misadventures* titles are page-turning, steamy, swoony standalones, to be read in any order.

- *Misadventures on the Night Shift* –A hotel night shift clerk encounters her teenage fantasy: rock star Lucas Ford. And combustion ensues.

- *Misadventures of a College Girl*—A spunky, virginal theater major meets a cocky football player at her first college party . . . and absolutely nothing goes according to plan for either of them.

- *Misadventures on the Rebound*—A spunky woman on the rebound meets a hot, mysterious stranger in a bar on her way to her five-year high school reunion in Las Vegas and what follows is a misadventure neither of them ever imagined.

Standalone Psychological Thriller/Dark Comedy

Countdown to Killing Kurtis

A young woman with big dreams and skeletons in her closet decides her porno-king husband must die in exactly a year. This is *not* a traditional romance, but it *will* most definitely keep you turning the pages and saying "WTF?"

Free Short Stories

The Secret Note

Looking for a quickie? Try this scorching-hot short story from Lauren Rowe in ebook FOR FREE or in audiobook: He's a hot Aussie. I'm a girl who isn't shy about getting what she wants. The problem? Ben is my little brother's best friend. An exchange student who's heading back Down Under any day now. But I can't help myself. He's too hot to resist.

All books by Lauren Rowe are available in ebook, paperback, and audiobook formats.

Be sure to sign up for Lauren's newsletter to find out about upcoming releases!

AUTHOR BIOGRAPHY

Lauren Rowe is the USA Today and international #1 best-selling author of newly released Reed Rivers Trilogy, as well as The Club Trilogy, The Josh & Kat Trilogy, The Morgan Brothers Series, Countdown to Killing Kurtis, and select standalone Misadventures.

Lauren's books are full of feels, humor, heat, and heart. Besides writing novels, Lauren is the singer in a party/wedding band in her hometown of San Diego, an audio book narrator, and award-winning songwriter. She is thrilled to connect with readers all over the world.
To find out about Lauren's upcoming releases and giveaways, sign up for Lauren's emails here!

Lauren loves to hear from readers! Send Lauren an email from her website, say hi on Twitter, Instagram, or Facebook.

Find out more and check out lots of free bonus material at www.LaurenRoweBooks.com.